Kirkwood

By

John Alvah Barnes, Jr.

&

Naomi Lynn Barnes

This book is a retelling of the story from my original first novel that I copyrighted in
1994. I always believed it was a good story, and now that Lynn is my co-writer and not
just the editor, I think it's even better. We've learned a lot in thirty years.

We dedicate Kirkwood, in loving memory, to Lynn's father, Edwin F. Schoppet, who
provided the story of Papa Joe's first date so many years ago. The story is a true account
of his first date with Lynn's mother.

Also by John Alvah Barnes Jr

Jay Barlow Collection
Kirkwood
Kirkwood
Esbenshade
Esbenshade
Rollover
Rollover

Standalone
Roadwork
Roadwork

Also by Naomi Lynn Barnes

Jay Barlow Collection
Kirkwood
Kirkwood
Esbenshade
Esbenshade

Standalone
Roadwork
Roadwork

There was blackness all around me and voices, many voices, murmuring softly and blending together—one steady buzzing sound as you might hear in a crowded theater while waiting for a show to begin.

A steady beeping sound, actually several steady beeping sounds, penetrated the murmuring, some nearby and some farther away. Occasionally there was a clatter of metal, like tin plates being hit against one another. Something went by on wheels in dire need of lubrication. Squeak...squeak...squeak.

The air was cool, almost chilly. It wasn't cold or particularly uncomfortable, yet I felt that the air should be clearing my head enough for my sight to return. I felt something cool and wet dab at my forehead.

There was an odor of rubber and plastic and... something antiseptic. The odor was familiar; I knew that I had been here before. I began to get vaguely angry with myself. I knew where I was, dammit, why couldn't I supply a name to go with this strange, dark place?

What was wrong with my eyes? Why couldn't I see? I felt as if they should work. I felt that I knew the picture that explained the incessant din that seemed to be coming from within my head. Though I was sure that it was not inside my head, or was I? What twist of fate had caused me to arrive in this fuzzy, confused, unexplained state?

I began to take stock of what I could discern. I was lying on something fairly hard and cold and I wasn't sure why, but I felt that I was elevated above the ground. How far above it I didn't know.

1

Was I floating in midair? Or was I on some kind of petrified magic carpet on some other planet? I didn't know and I was starting to feel agitated because of it. I felt the cool dampness touch my forehead once again. It felt good and I clung to the feeling, reaching out with my mind as best I could, hoping that the answers would follow.

"Jay, Jay are you with us?" The soft, feminine voice was familiar. I had heard it before, but where?

"Come back to us, Jay, come on." The voice had taken on a mild urgency, and it made me more desperate to know what was happening. I felt the coolness on my forehead again as the voice continued to plead with me. I tried to speak to the voice, tried to open some kind of communication, but my mouth didn't seem to work any better than my eyes. I continued to float in this void, this nonexistence that flowed through and around me in a sort of continuous circle.

The voice was now joined by a second voice. The second voice was male but carried the same sense of barely suppressed concern. "Any reaction yet?"

"No, he's still unresponsive."

"That was quite a hit he took. Do you know what the machine was set on?"

"Three hundred, sixty joules."

"Three sixty! He's lucky to be alive."

Well at least I was alive. That was good news. But what had happened to me? The female voice had said three hundred, sixty joules... and then from the depths of my brain, burned into my memory, I saw the spark. Spark really wasn't accurate; it was more like a fireball. Brilliant orange, completely unexpected, and then... dark. Suddenly I knew where I was! The emergency room! The female voice belonged to a pretty young nurse named Debbie Farrell, and the male voice belonged to a tall, thirty-something ER doctor name Craig Scott.

The ER! How many hours had I spent here putting the machines through their paces, hooking them up to my various pieces of test equipment and making them beep their little electronic hearts out? I felt like a drowning man that had been thrown a life preserver. My slow, groggy brain began to piece together the events that had brought me here.

I had been in one of the medical-surgical units inspecting a defibrillator that must have had a bad paddle cable. So that was what it was like being 'defibbed'. One of my worst nightmares had suddenly been realized. While in electronics school I had gotten accidently zapped quite a few times, but a defibrillator was supposed to be used intentionally.

I heard Dr. Scott's voice again. "How does his ECG look?"

"Stable now."

"Any sign of V-tach?" Oh God, I thought. V-tach was short for ventricular tachycardia, a state the heart can enter just before ventricular fibrillation when it stops pumping effectively, and the only way to deal with fibrillation was with a defibrillator. There was no way that I was going to get defibbed again if I could help it.

I decided that it was time to try harder to respond. I tried to open my eyes to no avail. They felt as if they had been taped shut. I tried to move my arms, but they felt as if they'd been weighted down with lead. I tried to speak, but my mouth felt as if it were filled with cement.

Jay, I said to myself, if you don't do something soon, they may use a defib on you. I had worked on enough of these machines to know how they functioned. I knew them inside and out, and I also knew that I wanted no more close encounters with them from this perspective. After all, once was enough. With Herculean effort I attempted to scream. All that managed to escape my parched lips was a moan, but it was enough, because I heard Debbie's voice again.

"Dr. Scott, he's coming around!"

I felt fingers gently prying my eyelid open, and then a beam of brilliant light assaulted my blurred vision. It seemed to burn through my brain to the back of my skull. That eyelid was released and then the other one was opened, and the light came again.

Oh, please leave me alone and let me just lie here, I thought. Then I remembered my motivation—the avoidance of the white-cased machine with its coil-corded paddles and gleaming metal contacts. I thought that maybe I might try opening my eyes again. Little by little I managed to open my lids until I was looking up at white ceiling tiles with fluorescent lights embedded in them.

I've done it! I thought with triumph. Suddenly, the tiles started to melt into each other and then started to turn around and around. I was hit by a wave of nausea that raised me up from the gurney on which I had been lying.

A plastic emesis basin appeared as Debbie put a hand on my back, and I retched again and again until there wasn't anything left, and my insides ached from the strain. I lay back down, exhausted, and then once more I floated into unconsciousness.

A rushing sound awoke me. I opened my eyes and felt disorientation. How much time had passed?

When my sight cleared enough to see beyond my ER bay, I saw that the sound was a medical team pushing a patient along on a gurney as they ran beside it. It seemed like they were far away, though rationally I knew that they were really only a few feet in front of me.

I realized, on at least some level, that recent events had skewed my perception. I could see the paramedics and the nurses busily working on the patient as they headed for the first trauma room. I knew their actions were frantic at this point, but it seemed as if they moved in slow motion and were borne on some strange cushion of air that both supported and propelled them in the direction they were going. They didn't even need to move their feet. I lay watching, fascinated. How could they float like that? And then the darkness came again...

I became aware that someone was being wheeled into the bay next to mine. Something told me that it was a woman, at least it looked like a woman.

She seemed to be thrashing around a lot. Her body was thrashing around anyway; her arms were strapped to the rails of the gurney on which she lay. She was moaning and whimpering as they wheeled her into place. They pulled the curtain around the bed, and soon she quieted down.

As I lay there, I realized that I was wearing a hospital gown. When did that happen and what happened to my clothes, I thought groggily? And again, darkness came...

After what seemed like days of this on again off again consciousness, I came to a reasonably stable state of mind. I became aware of Debbie standing over me, again mopping my brow with a wet cloth. The coolness felt good on my forehead, which was beginning to ache with a dull throb.

Her face held a look of concentrated concern, and headache or no, I was beginning to relish the attention. I lay mesmerized by the swell of her breasts against the pink fabric of her scrubs. They were not particularly large; they fit her frame very well. If she was aware of my attention, she gave no indication of it.

"If you want my opinion, electrocution is a lousy way to try and kill yourself," she said softly as she continued her ministrations.

My voice still didn't seem to be connected to my brain yet, so I tried to smile as I looked up at her face. This girl wasn't just pretty, she was *very* pretty. Why hadn't I noticed before? Her hair was dark brown and cut in a pixie style that I was particularly fond of. Her face was round with high cheekbones, and her eyes were large and blue. Her hands felt soft as she caressed my forehead. She had abandoned the damp cloth, and I lay clinging to the touch of her hand.

After several tries, I was finally able to speak. "Tylenol!" I croaked.

"Headache?" she asked, and I nodded. "I'm not surprised." She brought me two tablets and a cup of water, and then helped me sit up enough to swallow them. I lay back down, and she stroked my forehead a little longer until sleep overcame me once more.

I awoke to the sound of a crash and commotion in the next bed. I looked over to see an IV pump lying sideways on the floor. It was still attached to its pole and still had plastic tubing attached to it. The IV bag had broken open, and there was solution everywhere. From the grunts and groans that could be heard on the other side of the curtain, I surmised that there was quite a wrestling match going on.

Debbie appeared at my side once again. "Hi, how are you feeling," she said, ignoring the events transpiring next door.

I tried my voice again and was relieved to find that it still worked, though my throat hurt and the sound that emanated from it was raspy. "Better, thanks. What's going on over there?" I indicated the next bed, where there could still be heard the sounds of a struggle.

She looked at me reassuringly, as if everything were perfectly normal. "Let's just say that you have a very lively next-door neighbor."

"It certainly sounds like it."

She looked at me curiously. "How in the world did you manage to shock yourself?"

I tried to recollect the events that had transpired before I had arrived here in the ER. "I remember I was checking a defib on one of the units. I guess the connection between the cables and one of the paddles was bad; I've never seen anything like it. I remember charging the defib, pressing the paddle buttons, and... that's about all I remember."

"I heard that it was spectacular."

"That all depends on your point of view."

There was a loud grunt, and the curtain billowed out as someone next door was pushed against it. Debbie seemed not to notice, as if it was a normal occurrence like the mail being delivered. My head was beginning to ache rather badly again.

"You're lucky you weren't more seriously hurt. As it is, you're going to have to stay here for a while under observation."

"I can't stay here. It's a heavy inspection month, and I already have several machines waiting for my attention on the bench."

"Well, the hospital is just going to have to do without one of its mechanical marvels for a little while." She smiled at me, a smile that I felt all the way down to my toes.

"Electronic marvels, thank you very much."

There was another crash from next door, and I looked down in time to see a suction regulator hit the floor where it bounced once and then rolled away. Debbie again seemed not to notice.

"Honestly, Debbie, I have a lot to do."

Dr. Scott's face appeared around the curtain. "Is he complaining already? They're usually awake in here for at least an hour before that starts."

"He says he has too much work to do to stay here," explained Debbie.

"Let's not forget that your work is what put you here. We want to make sure you're okay before we send you back to the front lines," Dr. Scott said.

There was a muffled growl from next door, and the white pant legs of an orderly suddenly poked straight through the curtain, directly between Debbie and Dr. Scott, as he tackled someone on the gurney. Dr. Scott ignored the interruption. "How do you feel?"

"I've felt better... not to mention more dignified." Debbie chuckled softly and I smiled at her.

Dr. Scott shined his light in my eyes again. "Any more nausea?"

"Not since I finished puking my guts out."

"Dizziness?"

"No, not now."

"Well, I'll tell you what," he said, sounding as if he knew that I wasn't going to like what he said next. "You got quite a shock from that defibrillator, and I want to keep an eye on you for a while."

"Meaning?"

"Meaning I want to check you into a room overnight."

Scott had been right; I definitely didn't want to spend the night no matter how bad I felt.

"Doc, please, the guys in my department are never going to let me live this down as it is. Couldn't I just go home and go to bed?" I pleaded.

"You live alone?" he asked with one raised eyebrow.

"Yes."

"Then I'm sorry; I just don't want to take the chance. I want you under a nurse's watchful eye for the night. Just think of it as checking into a fancy hotel as our guest."

I felt dejected. I knew that the hospital offered first class care, but I definitely didn't want to be a patient in it. After all, I thought, who would want to spend the night at work? Dr. Scott left my bay to get back to *his* work. I must have looked as dejected as I felt, because Debbie didn't follow him.

"Is there anything I can do?" There was genuine concern in her voice and her eyes.

"I'm getting kind of tired of looking at the ceiling," I said.

"Well, that's no problem," she said, as she readjusted the gurney so that my head was raised. As she came nearer to me, I caught the lightest scent of soap and fresh shampoo from her skin and hair. My stomach picked that moment to rumble with a deep growl. She looked at me and there was that lovely smile again. "Can I assume that you'd like something to eat?"

"I do feel kind of empty."

"I'm not surprised after the events of the afternoon."

"That's a polite way of saying I lost my lunch and probably my breakfast as well."

She put a hand lightly on my arm. "I'll take care of it. I'm on 'til eleven. We'll get you something to eat, though I'm sorry it'll just be broth; you're on a liquid diet for the time being until we see how your stomach handles that. Then we'll get you a room and I'll stop up later to see how you're doing."

"You're too good to me."

"It's all part of the friendly service." She gave my hand a little squeeze and then was off to tend to other patients, leaving the curtain open.

I lay there looking around the ER. There was always something going on. I was in one of the central bays, as they were called. I supposed that it was because they were reminiscent of the service bays that you might see in a large auto repair shop.

Each bay held a gurney and an ECG monitor mounted on the wall behind it. All the monitors were wired to a central monitor behind a large circular counter or station in the center of the room, which also held a large desk area where the doctors and nurses read reports and dealt with paperwork. At the central monitor, one person, usually an EMT/clerk, could monitor all the bedside machines.

There were thirty-four bays arranged around a huge octagon, each one separated by a curtain from the next. Three trauma rooms were located off the back wall behind the central station. Serious accident and heart attack victims were initially taken to these rooms for primary treatment. In addition to ECG monitors, each trauma room had its own defibrillator and other resuscitation equipment.

Kirkwood Medical Center had the largest ER and trauma facility in the region, as well as two large EVAC helicopters. Most of the emergency calls in the area were brought here. On a busy day or night, it was not uncommon to see all the bays and trauma rooms full and gurneys with patients lining the corridors.

As I tried to relax, I could hear the woman in the next bay. The curtains were still drawn around her, and she was softly moaning, "Sam... oh, Sam." She kept quietly calling the name over and over again. Sam must be her boyfriend or husband or son, I thought. I couldn't help but feel sorry for her. She sounded like she was in great pain and needed someone.

I couldn't stand the moaning any longer. I flagged down a passing nurse and indicated the next bay. "Isn't there anything you can do for her?" I asked.

The nurse was a mostly gray-haired woman named Betty who, despite the fact that she was on the downhill side of middle age, was of sufficient size and stature to make a person think twice about giving her an argument. She had been around emergency rooms for years, and I had always enjoyed listening to her endless war stories about the ER. She had an air of seasoned authority about her.

Betty gave me a sad sort of half smile as she shook her head and pantomimed putting a needle in her arm. "Honey, the only thing that's going to help her is coming down." With that short but complete explanation she was off to attend to other business.

I lay there listening to "Sam... oh, Sam" for what was beginning to seem like forever, when suddenly the moaning stopped. I looked toward the next bay and saw a pair of bare feet touch the floor beneath the curtain.

The curtain was pulled back and there stood my neighbor. She was a big woman, rather overweight, with stringy black hair that hung limply around her shoulders. She had tattoos on both of her breasts, which I had no trouble seeing because she was stark naked.

She looked at me with dark, pleading eyes that seemed out of focus. "Have you seen Sam?" she asked mournfully.

I gulped involuntarily. "Uh, not lately." I managed to catch Betty's eye at the central station and hoped she could see the building panic on my face.

"Uh, Betty?" I called, trying to suppress the urgency in my voice.

Betty saw the woman and nearly ran, grabbing helpers as she went. They descended on the naked woman like a swarm of locusts on a field of cotton, and I could hear a great struggle once again as they replaced the curtain and set about resecuring the woman to the gurney on which she had been lying. The curtain billowed out, and there was much shuffling of feet and grunting until, after a while, things calmed down again.

Betty came around the corner with her hair askew, trying to smooth out her rumpled blue scrubs. "I don't know how she got loose from those straps; they're strong enough to hold down The Hulk."

"Maybe she works out a lot," I offered.

"Are you okay?" she asked as she eyed me appraisingly.

"I've had better days. Any word about a room for me upstairs?"

"I'll take care of it." And with that she was gone again.

Less than five minutes later, an elderly male volunteer appeared at my bedside with a wheelchair. The volunteers were, for the most part, elderly people who wanted to feel useful while getting some exercise. They showed up regularly to help out with whatever they could, not because they had to, but because they wanted to. They were an integral part of the hospital, and their eagerness and energy never ceased to amaze me.

"Hi, I'm Jim," the volunteer said cheerfully. "They have a room ready for you upstairs."

"Hi, Jim, I'm Jay." I sighed and, with Jim's help, I climbed somewhat awkwardly into the wheelchair.

I found it ironic that I wound up on the same med-surg unit where my little accident had occurred. I had been working at the hospital for nearly three years now as a biomedical electronic technician, but this was the first time I'd ever been a patient here.

I was given the full treatment. I had electrodes stuck to my chest, with wires that ran to a telemetry transmitter, which was a little box about the size of a pack of cigarettes. The transmitter was in a bag being held in place by straps that went around my neck and waist. This picked up and broadcast my ECG waveform by radio to a receiver located in a storeroom down the hall. From the receiver, the signal went by wire to the nurses' station in the center of the unit, where it was displayed on a monitor and recorded, if necessary.

So far there had been no cardiac irregularities, but Dr. Scott wasn't taking any chances. He had assured me that if my ECG remained normal overnight, I'd be able to get back to work in the morning. I figured that would be the case unless I farted, in which case there would probably be a medical team with a crash cart bursting into my room at any moment.

As I lay there in the bed looking around the room, I was struck by how different it seemed from this perspective. It was cooler than it usually felt. Of course, I was normally working and moving around when I was here, and I wasn't normally wearing a light cotton gown that offered, to anyone who cared to look, a free peepshow from the back. I speculated briefly on why this particular design was necessary and came to the conclusion that it must have been instituted by an administrator with an ass fetish.

I was in a semi-private room, but at the time I was the only occupant. The curtains that would normally divide the two semi-private patients were pulled back to the wall, which made the room seem bigger than it would have under semi-private conditions. I couldn't help but wonder if my insurance company would receive a semi-complete bill when all was said and done, but I doubted it.

It wasn't a bad room over all. Even with the standard neutral beige walls and the floral watercolor prints that were surely required by federal statute, it had a brightness that had been designed to promote a more positive mental attitude in the patients. At least that's what it said in the brochure that someone had left in the drawer of my rolling bed table. I wondered how long it would be before I began to develop a more positive mental attitude.

I was more aware of the antiseptic smell of the place; I supposed that most of the time I was simply too busy to notice. I also finally understood why patients were always complaining about the beds—the damn thing was hard as a rock!

I looked up and saw Dan Harris' head poking around the door jamb. Dan was my boss, the Director of the Biomedical Engineering Department. He was a big, burly Irishman who had worked at the medical center for most of his adult life, starting as an apprentice technician and working his way up the ladder. Dan had done his level best to raise joking and teasing to an art form. He had a rough honesty about him that caused people to trust him immediately, and he made friends wherever he went.

He had a gruff manner of speaking, and when I first met him I had made the mistake of assuming that this signified a lack of intelligence. I could not have been more wrong, for as I got to know

Dan, I realized that his speech was a facade behind which lay a sharp wit and a very analytical mind. Dan had more political savvy and more natural insight into human nature than anyone I had ever met.

I had first met Dan four years before. At the time I was a struggling musician and sound engineer for a rock band. Actually, floundering musician would be a more apt description. I had started with dreams of stardom and wealth, but suddenly I realized that I was twenty-seven years old and basically going nowhere. I had played in bands all up and down the East coast, one club after another, one cheap motel room that looked the same as the one before. After nearly ten years on the road I was tired of the whole thing. Stardom had become less of a golden dream and more of a tarnished nightmare.

I was back at home staying with my mother between gigs when I got a call from an old friend, a part-time bass player who I had worked with occasionally. He had been working at Kirkwood Medical Center in the biomedical electronics department for almost two years and loved it. The department had an opening for an equipment inspector, and they needed someone with a background in electronics. I had years of experience in audio electronics and was definitely ready to try something new, so I had applied, not really expecting anything to come of it. Surely there must be plenty of people more qualified for the job than I was, I thought. I was surprised when Dan called me for an interview.

I had arrived at the hospital with plenty of time to spare, and then spent nearly twenty minutes trying to find the shop; the place was huge! After asking directions at least four times from as many different people, and after many wrong turns, I finally found the shop and realized that I was ten minutes late. Great first impression I was making, I had thought.

I walked into the shop and was met by Dan. He ushered me into his office and sat behind a huge oak desk indicating the chair in front for me.

"You're late," he stated simply.

"I'm sorry, Mr. Harris..."

"Call me Dan."

"I'm sorry, Dan. I underestimated the size of this place. I knew that it was big, but not this big!"

"How many times did you ask directions?"

"Four, I think."

"That's real good," He said with a nod of his head. "The last guy asked six, the guy before that gave up and went home. You know what dykes are?" There was something in his open, straightforward manner that made me feel at ease with him immediately.

"I assume you mean wire cutters and not lesbians?" Dan didn't bat an eye, and I wondered if I had gone too far.

"You know how to use them?"

"Wire cutters or lesbians?"

The hint of a smile came to his face, and he reached across the desk and handed me a pair of dykes (wire cutters) and a piece of electrical wire. "Strip me a good end."

This was child's play, literally. I had been doing this kind of thing since I was a kid and first developed an interest in electricity. I didn't realize until later that was exactly what Dan wanted to know. I stripped a short piece of wire on one end, and then I turned the wire around and stripped a longer piece on that end. When I had finished, I handed it back to him.

"Why did you strip both ends?" he asked.

"I didn't know if it was for a solder terminal connection or a screw terminal connection."

"What's the difference?"

"For a solder terminal you only need a short end; for a screw terminal the wire has to be long enough to go around the screw."

He was still wearing a vague little smile. "Okay, you've got the job. Can you start tomorrow?"

I was stunned. "I... ah...sure, tomorrow."

Later I realized that Dan already knew my background in electronics from my friend who had told him that I had graduated from a trade school with honors. What Dan had wanted to know was if my interest was practical, had I actually worked with my hands. By picking up the dykes and easily, familiarly stripping the wires, I had shown him that I had been doing it for a long time. My lack of prior biomedical experience didn't matter to Dan; he was going to train me his way, and with me he was starting with a clean slate.

It was fitting that Dan was the first one to come and see how I was doing. He was more sedate than usual as he inquired about my well-being, and I knew him well enough to know that he had been worried about me. Once he saw that I was really okay, he became more like himself.

"I suppose I could chain you to a bench in the shop to keep you out of trouble. Naw, that wouldn't work. You'd just stick your screwdriver—or something more vital—into an outlet and light up like Times Square on New Year's Eve anyway!"

"Gee, thanks Dan. You always know just the right thing to say to make a guy feel better."

Dan's face assumed a rare serious look. "Jay, what happened?"

"I've been doing a lot of thinking about it in the few hours I've been lying here. I don't have your experience, Dan, but I've never seen a defibrillator cable malfunction like that and there was no prior warning."

"You didn't notice anything odd about it?"

"No. The inspection stickers were up to date."

We inspected and performed preventive maintenance on all the equipment in the hospital every six months, placing a sticker with the current date and the initials of the inspector on them.

"The unit looked clean." I told him. "I would have expected to see burn marks on the cable, or possibly fraying around the connection with the paddle itself. I feel a little embarrassed about it. I have to accept that it was my own stupid fault, that I should have done a continuity check or something. The thing is, Dan, I swear the unit looked perfectly fine."

"It still does."

Something in the way he made the comment caused me mild alarm. "What do you mean?"

He took a breath and let it out. "I mean, Alan took the machine down to the shop and he can't find anything wrong with it."

Alan was one of our senior techs. "What do you mean he can't find anything wrong with it? I'm not stuck spending the night in the hospital because of my imagination."

"Jay, there are no burn marks, no compromise of cable integrity, and he test fired it a dozen times. There's nothing wrong with it."

"But, that's impossible! I had the thing set for three hundred, sixty joules; at that power the cable should have melted!" I was starting to feel dizzy again.

Dan held a look of concentration. "Jay, are you sure you didn't ground yourself and contact one of the paddles?"

"How? You know that defibs are designed to prevent that. That's why you have to hit both discharge buttons simultaneously to make it fire. There's no way I contacted a paddle. I have too much respect for the capabilities of the machine to be careless, regardless of the safety features."

Dan's expression changed again. "Well don't worry about it now; we'll figure it out later. You just get yourself together and come back to work, we need you." In another moment his impish demeanor was back. "The next time you get the urge to be electrocuted, let me know and I'll plug you in myself."

"You'd enjoy that, wouldn't you?" I was trying to shrug it off, but I was mystified. I couldn't imagine what I could have done wrong, but I also knew that I wasn't going to figure it out from a hospital bed.

A white-haired woman volunteer came into the room carrying a tray. "Dinner," she said cheerily.

Dan didn't miss a beat. "Hot damn! Chef's special, served in bed yet. I'll have to check myself inta this hotel." He looked at the woman and winked, and she smiled, blushing slightly, and left the room.

"Let's see what gastronomic delights we have in store tonight," he said as he lifted the beige plastic plate cover. There was a plastic cup of what I assumed to be chicken broth, a plastic container of juice, and a plastic container of orange jello. "Mm, mm, just like mother used to make," Dan observed.

"How do they make jello that color? It looks like chemotherapy solution," I said.

"What do you mean? There's always room for jello."

"I forgot, I'm on a liquid diet. No wonder people lose weight when they stay in the hospital." I had heard patients complain about the food, but I had never really taken them seriously. I was used to getting food in the employees' cafeteria where the fare was excellent.

"Don't worry none, kid," Dan said conspiratorially, "I'll have somebody smuggle you up something decent from downstairs."

"For that I would be forever in your debt, sir."

"I'll remember that." Dan made his excuses and left.

True to his word, about a half-hour later an orderly came in bearing a cheeseburger and fries, which he set on my tray table. The aroma instantly made my mouth water and my stomach rumble. Unfortunately, he was closely followed by a nurse.

"This patient is on a liquid diet. Doctor's orders. He can't eat this." she said.

To say that I was disheartened would be an understatement as my burger and fries were whisked away as quickly as they had appeared.

Debbie came to visit shortly after dinner. I could tell by the way she stood and the way that her shoulders were beginning to sag slightly that she was tired.

"Busy day?" I asked.

"They usually are. That's okay, I'm used to it."

"You look tired," I commented.

She looked at me for a beat. "Well, you don't exactly look ready to pose for the cover of Esquire."

I held my hands up defensively. "Whoa, I didn't mean that you weren't well worth looking at."

In an instant that beautiful, warm smile came to her face again, and I could have sworn that she blushed a little. "Sorry, I tend to get a little testy this time of day. So, how are you doing?"

"Better now," I said.

She was still smiling. "Are you flirting with me?"

"Would you mind if I was?"

She looked briefly around my room. "I try to avoid flirting with men in hospital beds."

I looked around my room with its institutional beige walls, landscape prints and white board telling me the day of the week, the date and who was on duty. "Yeah, I guess I can understand your policy."

She moved a little closer to my bed as her demeanor changed slightly. "Seriously, Jay, how are you doing?"

"Okay, considering my surroundings. Dan was up to see me."

"How was he? He wasn't hard on you, was he?"

"No, he was pretty low key compared to his usual self. I think I scared him."

"You scared us all. Didn't the cable or anything else on that defib look bad or something before you tried testing it?"

"I've been over it at least a hundred times in my mind; everything looked perfectly normal. I've inspected thousands of defibs; I've never seen one do anything even remotely like what that one did."

I didn't tell her what Dan had told me about the machine checking out normally. Something was definitely wrong, and I got the feeling that I was probably going to have to figure it out for myself.

"Until that moment, I wouldn't have even thought that it was possible to get shocked that way," I told her.

"Well, don't do it again."

"Believe me, I'm not planning on it."

Debbie looked at her watch. I knew that her time was limited.

"What time is it?" I asked her.

"It's after eight. I have to get back; my break's over."

"I know. Thanks for coming to check on me." I was looking up into those big, clear blue eyes, and I had the strongest urge to just reach up and wrap my arms around her neck. But after all, I still hardly knew this woman. I knew in my heart, however, that was going to change.

She hesitated like she was expecting me to say something more. I didn't know what I was supposed to say or do, and the moment began to feel awkward.

"You try and get some sleep and I'll see you tomorrow," she said as she pulled the sheet up to my neck, sounding disappointed.

"I haven't been tucked in in a long time. It's kind of nice," I said softly.

She smiled, then was gone.

I became aware that I was floating in a void again, unstuck in time and space, somewhere between reality and fantasy. I was vaguely aware that I was dreaming, though it wasn't unpleasant so much as mildly disorienting.

Suddenly I was standing in a long, dimly lit hallway. Defibrillators lined the walls on both sides. I was making my way slowly, pushing my rubber-wheeled, aluminum inspection cart before me. I test fired each one in turn waiting for the one that I knew would erupt into spark and flame with a push of the paddle buttons.

Finally, I stood looking at the very last one—the one that I knew would be 'it'. The white plastic surface glowed ominously in the low light; the control dials seeming to gaze at me like an absurd pair of animal eyes in the dark just before an attack.

I pushed the charge button and heard the high-pitched whine as the machine built to full power. I slowly lowered the paddles onto the metal contact pads of my power analyzer and positioned my fingers on the fire buttons. The full charge tone sounded, and just as I was about to push the buttons, I heard Debbie's voice. "No!" she yelled as she reached across from my right side and switched the machine off.

From behind me I heard another female voice, this one seemingly old and cracked. "Jimmy... Jimmy is that you?" I turned and saw an old woman, white haired and stooped over. She shuffled slowly across my room toward my bed, all the time calling, "Jimmy... Jimmy is that you?" She was right before me now; I could feel her hot breath, slightly sour, upon my face. "Jimmy?"

I opened my eyes. Now I was wide awake, and there was the face of my neighbor from the ER no more than six inches from my own. "Jimmy... Jimmy is that you?" I nearly fell out of bed on the opposite side, but I managed to catch myself at the last moment.

Suddenly Michael, the night nurse on duty, appeared in the doorway. "Janice, please. You've got to stop wandering and stay in bed."

"But I've got to find Jimmy!"

Michael looked at me apologetically as he took the woman by the arms. "Sorry, Jay, she managed to slip past the nurses' station. She moves faster than she looks."

"I know, I've seen her in action before."

"I was hoping that I wouldn't have to restrain her... she won't bother you again," Michael said as he began ushering the woman from my room. "I'll come back and check on you in a few minutes."

I'd met Michael at the hospital fair two years before when we'd wound up together in the three-legged race. We'd each had a leg fastened together in a burlap sack, and we'd managed to find a rhythm, pulling ahead of the other contestants. We were inches away from winning when one of us had tripped, we were still debating who, and we'd tumbled off to the side of the course, laughing our heads off. We'd been friends ever since.

He'd told me his name was Michael Evans, and when I'd told him the name sounded vaguely familiar, he'd told me that it was the name of the actor that played Jimmy J.J. Walker's little brother on the 70's sitcom 'Good Times'.

True to his word, Michael came back to check on me in a few minutes.

"How did things go with Janice?" I asked him.

"She's a handful, but we've got things under control," he told me. "So, how are you doing?"

"To tell you the truth, Michael, I'm starving. You don't have any crackers, or anything do you? Dinner was pretty sparse."

"That's because they've got you on a liquid diet."

"Tell me something I don't know. Did you ever try to eat iridescent orange jello?"

He laughed. "I know, it's pretty gross. I saw a can of Campbell's chicken noodle soup in the other room. How about if I dump the noodles and heat that for you?"

"That would be great, Michael. And if you forget to dump the noodles, I really wouldn't mind."

He left and returned in a few minutes with a steaming cup of broth, which I accepted gratefully.

I looked in the cup. "No noodles, huh?"

"Sorry, Jay, orders are orders. You should do better in the morning," he told me and left.

I carefully sipped my broth, glad to have something going into my stomach. When I got to the bottom of the cup, I found that he'd left me three noodles. I almost laughed, and then I gulped my noodles down and tried to get back to sleep.

I couldn't relax. I couldn't get Debbie out of my mind. I kept picturing the way she'd looked as she tucked the covers around me, so soft, so lovely, so caring. I'd wanted to wrap my arms around her and hold her, to whisper in her ear how good and kind she was, and so sexy it took my breath away.

I tossed and turned for some time, no easy feat in the confines of my hospital bed. I lay on my back and stared at the ceiling, telling myself that I really needed to sleep. Eventually Michael came back to check on me again.

"I thought you'd be asleep by now," he said quietly.

"I've got things on my mind."

"I'm not surprised after you tried to kill yourself with a defibrillator."

"You heard about that?"

"The whole hospital has heard about it, Jay," he said as he put a blood pressure cuff on my arm and pressed the button on the machine.

"I guess I'm famous, huh?" I said as the cuff tightened on my bicep.

"I don't know about famous, infamous maybe. Is that why you can't sleep?"

"Not really."

"What's the problem? Do you need something to help you nod off?" He asked as he wrote the pressure down on his chart.

"No, I don't want a pill."

"Who said anything about a pill? I was going to get a mallet and bonk you on the head," he said as he took my pulse.

"That's why you're such a good nurse, Michael. You have such a great bedside manner."

"Uh huh." He stood for a few moments writing something else on my chart.

"Do you know Debbie Farrell?" I asked.

"From the ER? Sure." he stopped writing and held the chart at his side. "She and I had a couple of classes together. Why?"

"Do you think she's cute?"

"For a white woman."

"What?!"

"I'm just messing with you, Jay," he said, grinning at me. "She seems like a nice person, and yes I think she's cute. Is she why you can't sleep?"

"That and somebody keeps disturbing me to take my vital signs."

"You know it's part of my job."

"I know, I'm just messing with *you*." I paused for a beat. "I can't stop thinking about her, Michael. She came to see me before you started your shift. She tucked me in before she left."

"She tucked you in?"

"Is that so odd?"

"It's not exactly in the nurses' manual."

"There's a nurses' manual?"

"Not really. I don't guess tucking you in is so out of the ordinary, of course it would make more sense if you were a kid."

"I really think I'm falling for her, Michael."

"Have you asked her out?"

"Not yet, but I'm planning to. What do you think?"

He treated me to another grin. "It's not about what I think, Jay."

"You know what I mean."

"I think you should go for it. I think the two of you would be good together."

"I'm glad to hear you say it."

"There's just one thing you have to remember, Jay."

"What?"

"The hospital rumor mill. If you don't want the news heard far and wide, you'd better keep things on the down-low."

"Good point."

The rest of the night passed without incident, and to my own amazement I actually managed to doze off again. Though when the sun finally did shine through my window, I didn't feel particularly well rested. After they discharged me, I drove back to my apartment to shave, shower, change and make myself a sandwich and a small pot of coffee, which helped to revive me somewhat before making my way back to work.

As I drove up the front drive, I marveled as I always did, at the impressive facade of Kirkwood Medical Center. Building of the hospital had been completed in 1984, some four years before I came to work here, and had taken nearly three years.

The main part of the building was comprised of four massive towers of brick that reminded me of some huge, neo-medieval fortress. Had it not been for the hundreds of smoked glass windows that fronted the place, I would have expected to see men in armor on the roof, ready to pour vats of molten lead onto the hapless enemy below.

The most impressive time to see the place was at night. There were thousands of red anti-collision lights embedded all over the immense building, because there were helicopters taking off and landing frequently. The first time I had driven up the front drive at night, it was near Christmas. I remember thinking, 'Wow, they really go all out with the decorations here, but I wonder why there aren't any green ones'.

The front drive was nearly a quarter-mile in length and was lined with evergreen trees on both sides. Also, on either side were two lakes that covered several acres each. They had been dug for fill dirt to level the ground for the myriad parking lots that surrounded most of the building. I had heard that prior to construction, a model of the hospital and surrounding grounds had been built to a scale of one inch equaling ten feet, and it took up a space of approximately forty by fifty feet.

There were many interesting stories about the construction of Kirkwood that had become local legend. The original architect had died under mysterious circumstances. His car had been found at the bottom of a gully off a back road not far away, in the middle of the former farmland on which the hospital now stood.

The ensuing investigation had determined the car had rolled downhill for some distance before catching fire. The only way they had determined the identity of the body found in the car was through dental records. The rumor was that he was a man with a gambling addiction who had gotten in way over his head, and his debtors had gotten overzealous in their quest for reimbursement.

I found it an interesting coincidence that it wasn't until the entire hospital had been built that it was realized that the architect had neglected to include the instillation of a morgue. It occurred to me that to build an enormous hospital without a morgue was either an act of sheer stupidity or the greatest demonstration of confidence ever expressed in our medical capabilities.

Once the oversight had been realized, extra space had to be found on the lower level for the installation of the morgue. The space that was utilized consisted of several storerooms that happened to be located right across the main hall from the smaller hall leading to the biomedical electronics shop.

The door to the morgue was extra-large to accommodate the gurneys that frequently went in and out. It was completely unmarked, which is odd for a hospital where every door has a plaque with a legend, including the housekeeping and maintenance closets. That in itself seemed to be a sign: if you wanted to find the morgue, you just looked for the door with no plaque beside it.

During the hospital's construction, there had been one worker killed in a fall from an I-beam six stories above the ground. Evidently, he hadn't heard about the lack of a morgue.

His ghost had been said to haunt the medical intensive care unit on the sixth floor. I had heard stories from the nurses about electronic blood pressure machines and ECG monitors that turned on all by themselves late at night. They were adamant about the truth of these stories, and we hadn't been able to come up with a logical explanation for the phenomena.

One late shift nurse had been so unnerved by these occurrences that she had walked out of the hospital never to be heard from again. Of course, I had also heard she had been on medication for a manic-depressive disorder before she had left. Whatever the true explanation was, the whole thing was decidedly strange.

The rest of the night nurses had taken to calling the 'ghost' Fred. It seemed every time I visited the sixth floor MICU to investigate an equipment problem, I heard about how Fred had done this, or Fred had done that. It also seemed the best thing for me to do was play along, besides, I truly believed there were many aspects to this life that we didn't really understand.

I made a left onto the access road that wound around to the rear of the hospital. As I neared the emergency room wing, I drove past the twin helicopter pads for the EVAC helicopters. One helicopter was sitting on its pad with its rotors turning slowly, as if it were contemplating flight. They always struck me as looking anxious for the next call, so they could swoop off in search of adventure like some mechanical bird of prey on the prowl.

I passed the four enormous emergency diesel generators, each the size of a railroad boxcar. I had once asked Orville, one of the maintenance electricians, about the power these generators produced, and he told me they could easily power a medium-sized city. That's more or less what I thought of the hospital—a self-contained city. It was a living, breathing thing that ran by its own rhythm and never slept. Its pace slowed down after dark, and it was always eerie walking through its corridors at night, for though it seemed to be asleep, you knew it was always partially awake.

I turned into the employee parking lot. I was late coming in and, as I expected, I had to park all the way in the back of the lot. No matter, I thought, it was shaping up to be a pretty day and a hike in the fresh air would be just the thing to refresh me. I walked through the lot, passed the laundry building, and entered through the employee's entrance.

As I walked up the long hall, I fell in with the crowd of employees making their way to wherever their jobs required them to be. I heard a familiar BEEEEP behind me and everyone in the hall stepped closer to the wall simultaneously, as if moved there by an invisible hand. A long laundry train went by with its attendant standing in the electric tractor with its amber warning dome light flashing while he steered, and the procession of large carts trailed behind.

These trains always reminded me of the trams at Disney World that were used to transport large numbers of people quickly, but these trains carried laundry and trash throughout the many access corridors on the lower ground level. They ran twenty-four hours a day, often at a speed that was faster than I would have thought prudent. I imagined that their operators considered it a badge of personal honor to be the first down the hall and back with a load.

The first time that I had come through the back door, I had nearly been run over. I had just stepped through the door, when to my immediate right came the screaming BEEEEP! It scared me so badly that I nearly jumped into the arms of the person walking behind me.

I traversed the rest of the main hall and turned left down the secondary hallway across from the morgue that led to the biomedical electronics shop. The door to the shop awaited me at the end of the hall, and as I got closer to it my apprehension grew. I didn't know what awaited me, but I knew this crew, and I knew that there would be something other than a traditional warm welcome.

As I opened the door to the shop, I saw that the interior lights were off. Oh, oh, I thought, here it comes. As I closed the door and turned, a pin spotlight came on illuminating a white defibrillator on some sort of raised platform. I then heard a chorus of voices, led by Dan of course. "All hail to the master!" A pair of hands came out of the darkness and lifted the defib paddles from their holders on either side of the machine. I then heard the familiar whine as the charge button was pushed, then the paddles came together and there was a loud POP! Followed by a flash and a shower of sparks as the machine discharged. There was laughter all around, and as the lights were switched on, I saw all the other techs sitting in various places around the shop, some on stools, some leaning against work benches covered with various medical equipment in various stages of repair.

Their mood was infectious, and I realized that I was laughing too. They had welcomed me back in their own way, and I was suddenly very glad to be back with them, feeling like one of the gang again. I knew they had all worried about me, and this was their way of making light of what could have been a tragic situation.

Dan came up beside me and put a hand on my shoulder. "Well, the afternoon shift is here. Glad you could join us. Did you have a nice vacation?"

"You do realize that playing around with those," I said indicating the defib, "can be dangerous?"

"Not in the hands of seasoned professionals," he said.

"Gee, thanks."

Dan had a large office with his desk on one side and a large conference table on the other. It was our custom for the senior techs to eat lunch at the conference table instead of in the cafeteria. Dan's office had privacy. We could say what we wanted or be loud if we felt like it, and there was no one around to be offended.

Dan held court at the head of the table, and an old friend of his, Teeny, who worked in one of the storerooms, always sat to his right. Teeny weighed three hundred, fifty pounds if he weighed an ounce, and his head was unusually large. He was a kind and good-hearted soul with whom Dan had shared a thousand adventures. The two of them would tell stories of their exploits until the rest of us nearly choked with laughter. Lunch was usually the highlight of the day.

Will Stanski sat to Dan's left. He was the most senior tech in the shop. He had been with the medical center for almost as long as Dan, having started in the old county hospital that pre-dated Kirkwood. He was in his fifties, lean and lanky, and one of the best electronic technicians I have ever known. I worked with him whenever I could, hoping to learn as much as possible. I had seen Will take a malfunctioning machine, remove its cover, and literally sniff out the problem, determining by smell which component was not working properly. He was amazing to watch.

He was also one of the most laid-back people I had ever met and for a very good reason that Dan had explained to me one day. He took antidepressants regularly. Dan explained to me this was because of Mrs. Stanski, a woman that I only knew from Dan's nickname for her, 'Hemorrhoid'. And although the Stanskis' and Harris' frequently did things together, that was the only name I had ever heard Dan call her. "Will's upset today because Hemorrhoid is on his back again for something," he would say, as Will seemed to me to be as laid-back as ever.

I had been feeling a little self-conscious since my return, because Dan had seemed to be going out of his way to take it easy on me until he was sure I was back on my feet. I appreciated the concern, but it felt like everyone was taking on more work than I was. Nobody complained or seemed to mind though, except for Alan.

Alan Labinowitz sat next to Will and was the runt of our crew. He was short and slight, with a nervous disposition. Unfortunately, the more nervous or upset he became, the more gas seemed to build up in his system. Once, shortly after he had started with the medical center, as the story went, he had arrived straight from temple. In his haste to get to work, he had forgotten to remove his yarmulke.

Dan had taken one look at him and asked what had happened to the propeller that went on top of his beanie. I was told that it happened almost immediately. He had ripped the yarmulke from his head and made a beeline for the bathroom, and as he moved towards the door everyone was serenaded with what could only be described as earth-shaking flatulence. At the top of his voice, looking astonished, Dan had said, "Who was that masked man?!"

At times I felt sorry for Alan, but more often than not, he invited the wrath of the other techs upon himself. He was very intelligent and had more education than anyone in the shop, but he had never learned much about dealing with other people. He often came off as arrogant and superior to his coworkers, an attitude that did not lend itself to group acceptance, especially this group. Still, I tried to maintain a working relationship with him even though it was mostly one-sided.

We were eating and talking as usual, and I was getting a lot of light-hearted ribbing, when Alan said to no one in particular, "I guess it pays to be stupid enough to zap yourself silly, you get to hang back and let everyone else do the work!" It wasn't what he said so much as the fact that he sounded like he really meant it.

The conversation around the table dropped to a dead, uncomfortable silence, for though it was unspoken, lunch was a sacred event that was not to be spoiled by pettiness or bickering. Dan presided over the table like a proverbial father, and it was understood that any problems or disputes among the techs were to be left outside of his door until later.

I could see Dan beginning to seethe, but Teeny jumped in before Dan had the chance to speak. He lowered his massive head in my direction, giving me a wink and looking conspiratorial. "Have you checked yet, Jay?"

I was mystified. "Have I checked what, Teeny?"

"Since you lit yourself up, have you checked to see if your pecker glows in the dark?"

The sudden relief was evident in the laughter that seemed to gush from around the table. Dan didn't miss a beat. "At least that way she'll be able to see it coming!"

Alan sat stone-faced while everyone around him was doubled over. Once again, I found myself feeling sorry for him; he just didn't get it. Will, the tech sitting next to him, clapped him on the back as if to say, 'It's a joke, lighten up!' Alan got up and left. Will turned to me and just shrugged his shoulders.

Seated next to Alan was Bobby Gilford who was the Romeo of the group. Bobby was in his early thirties, thin and ginger complected, with a face that had been scarred by adolescent acne. He always had a story about his latest conquest, frequently a nurse from the hospital. With Bobby, age was not a consideration. Young, old, innocent, or matronly, if she was endowed with female attributes, Bobby was interested. Dan often referred to Bobby as 'the human tripod'. "Bobby thought he had three legs until one of them pissed on him," was one of his favorite sayings. Regardless of Bobby's proclivities, he was a regular member of our little group, and everyone, including me, got along well with him.

Joe Travello, the oldest tech in the shop, sat between Teeny and me. Joe was in his mid-sixties and spent a lot of time pouring over literature pertinent to retirement, trying to decide where he wanted to retire. He had told me that he wanted to move South where the weather was warmer, but he didn't want to move to Florida, as it was too full of old people, and he didn't want to move West, as it was too full of weirdos. He had narrowed it down to one of the Carolinas. When I pointed out that weirdos could be found everywhere, he smiled and said, "That's true, Jay, but I think that they're easier to identify when they're speaking with a Southern drawl."

Joe wasn't much bigger than Alan, but there was something in his demeanor that made it a moot point. He had let it slip in conversation that he had seen action in WWII, but it wasn't something he talked about. He had a quiet, understated, dry sense of humor, and could be very funny if you listened closely. He was usually addressed as 'Papa Joe', and he didn't seem to mind the title.

Finally, there was Trevor Bodenstab who always sat on my right. He was the friend, the bass player, who had helped me get the job, so consequently he had given me most of my initial training. He had obtained his biomedical electronic training in the army and assured me that he had been considerably easier on me than they had been on him. Trevor was taller than me, six-foot two to my six feet, and at twenty-six, a year younger . He had become one of my best friends, a confidant that I had shared more than a few adventures with.

Trevor was undeniably the best looking among us. He had an easy-going nature and an innocence that seemed to draw the attention of the female hospital staff like a magnet. Women were constantly fawning over him, but most of the time he seemed not to notice. He once explained his thoughts on the subject to me. "I don't want to start anything with anyone from the hospital, because as soon as I did everyone else would know about it." I understood what he meant; rumors traveled through the hospital like fire through dry underbrush.

As I grew to know Trevor better, I realized that he was an intensely private person who simply didn't care to have aspects of his private life known to everyone. It was a part of him that I respected, and I always felt somewhat honored when he opened up to me. It was his way of saying that he trusted me and valued my opinion enough to tell me what he wouldn't tell anyone else.

As Trevor theatrically clapped me on the back after I had become choked with laughter, I realized for the first time that coming so close to death had an effect on me. The daily routine and the pressures of the job sometimes got on my nerves, but it was good to be back after all. I felt that I had purpose, that I was a part of an important team.

After lunch, Trevor and I were working at a bench trying to determine why the fetal monitor before us was not working as it should. The machine had me stumped, so I asked Trevor to take a look.

"You know what the problem is, Jay," he said as he joined me at the bench.

"I do?"

"Of course, you do."

"So, what's the problem?"

"It's either a short or an open."

I looked at him sideways. "Oh, you're hilarious!"

I must explain that a standard joke among electronic technicians is that when a device malfunctions, the problem is always either a 'short' or an 'open'. All electrical devices work on the same basic principal: electricity must travel from point A, through the device on an electrical pathway, and end up at point B. If the electrical pathway becomes bridged at some point and doesn't travel all the way through the circuit before arriving at point B, then you have a 'short'. If the electrical pathway becomes broken and never arrives at point B, then you have an 'open'.

Understand that this is a gross oversimplification, since there seemingly can be miles of electrical pathway between points A and B, but essentially the only thing that can go wrong is that the pathway becomes bridged or broken entirely. In its simplest form the problem is always a short or an open; the solution lies in figuring out which component/components among possibly hundreds is/are not doing what it/they is/are supposed to do.

Dan came up between us and clapped a hand on each of our shoulders. "I have a mission for you two. Dr. Linville has a problem."

"We know that," Trevor said, dryly. "What's the mission?"

"Dr. Linville had a problem with an ESU during a procedure this morning, and he wants to talk to someone from this department about it."

Trevor and I both groaned simultaneously. "Couldn't you send Papa Joe?" I asked. "It sounds like this mission calls for a sage-like presence." I figured it was worth a shot.

"Joe handled him last time. Besides, you two need to start gathering a little wisdom of your own. Papa's not going to be here to take care of you forever."

We knew there was no sense in attempting further argument. Dan's mind was made up, and that was that. I decided to get all the information I could before we jumped into the fray. "What problem did the good doctor have?" I asked.

"He was doing a ligament repair and insisted on using the old ESU that I tried to get rid of three years ago."

An ESU is an electrosurgical unit, which is a machine that uses radiofrequency electricity for cutting, instead of a scalpel, and simultaneously coagulates blood vessels to stop bleeding. It works on a simple electrical principal. A contact pad is applied to a patient's back which acts as a ground, and an electrical circuit is completed when an electrosurgical 'pencil' comes into contact with the patient's body tissue.

The newer ESUs had a built-in safety feature that shut the machine down if the ground pad lost contact with the patient's body. The older machine that Dr. Linville had insisted on using, however, did not have such a safety feature.

Dan continued. "It sounds like he was in the middle of the procedure when the ground pad came loose. He must have grounded himself to metal because Donna says he shocked himself good." Donna was the head OR nurse.

I looked at Trevor. "He grounded himself instead of the patient."

"Do we know what he grounded himself to?" Trevor asked Dan.

"Donna said he was using a microscope, and when he put his eyes against the eyepieces he jumped and yelled."

Trevor and I both grimaced. "Was the patient hurt?" I asked.

"No. Luckily the pencil tip wasn't near the patient at the time. Anyway, you two know how this goes. Go up and listen to pain-in-the-ass for a few minutes, tell him you'll take the machine to the shop for repair, and maybe I'll be able to get rid of the damn thing this time." Neither Trevor nor I made any abrupt move for the door. "Go on, get moving...today!"

Besides nurses, our work brought us in contact with a lot of doctors. Most of them were very interesting to work with. They were serious about their jobs, sometimes downright intense, but they could often be very funny, often with a dry sort of humor that I have always related to. Collectively, I think they have the greatest egos of any group of people I have known. I don't mean to be derogatory in this statement; I have always considered that a large ego is essential to what they do. I don't see how it would be possible to make decisions that could potentially have an enormous impact on another person's well-being without a lot of self-confidence.

Most of them see this inflated sense of 'self' for what it is and keep it in check, but a few do not. Every once in a while, we'd run across one of these healers whose control mechanism was either out of whack or nonexistent.

Dr. Linville was a classic case in point. To say his ego was overblown would be like saying that Hitler was slightly power hungry. I imagined that by his own account, he was an arthroscopic surgeon who had invented the concept of skeletal surgery. There was nothing more for him to learn, since he had already learned and mastered everything there was to know about human locomotion.

Biomedical electronics is a constantly evolving field; there are new inventions and improvements coming along seemingly every week. A lot of our time and energy was spent on just trying to keep up with current changes. This included keeping the medical staff informed of and trained on new equipment. We were constantly attending new device seminars and giving in-house demonstrations and training. Dr. Linville was always a notable absentee at these sessions.

Whenever Dr. Linville experienced an equipment problem, the machine was 'broken'. There was no doubt that the failure was due to an oversight on our part, or that we weren't doing our job, or that we didn't know what we were doing. It was irrelevant that he hadn't bothered to attend the training session or even read the instruction manual. If the machine didn't perform to his expectations, it 'had a short in it'.

Trevor and I walked up the hall and took one of the elevators up to the OR on the fourth floor. OR was a misnomer; it was actually a complex consisting of thirty-nine operating rooms radiating off four huge, glistening, interconnecting hallways. The rooms themselves were numbered one through forty, there being no OR thirteen. The administration had been worried that no doctor would want to be scheduled for surgery in an OR numbered thirteen. Personally, I hoped most doctors would be thinking of things other than triskaidekaphobia.

We got off the elevator, turned right, walked a couple of yards, and turned right into one of the OR entrance hallways. I pushed the button on the wall, and a large set of double steel doors automatically swung open, revealing a nurses' station on the left and the doctor's lounge through a doorway on the right.

Donna Fielding was standing behind the nurses' station counter. Donna was the RN in charge of the OR. She had a reputation for plain speaking, calling things as she saw them, which I admired, but

I knew it didn't always endear her to the hospital administration. She was an old friend of Dan's, and I liked her immensely. I also had a healthy respect for her; she ran a very tight ship and was known for putting people in their place when they didn't meet her expectations.

Donna was what I would describe as a handsome woman. She was about fifty, fairly short, with a body that was leaning toward the chunky side, though still quite attractive. Her mid-length hair was a striking silver, though now it was bundled up in a surgical cap. Even dressed in scrubs she carried an air of authority.

I walked up to her and spoke in a low, quiet voice. "So, how're things going?"

She flashed me a wry smile. "About as good as can be expected. I see the great Harris didn't have the balls to come here himself."

"Well, that's what us peons are for, ma'am," Trevor said.

Donna grinned slightly and addressed us both seriously. "Look, we all know what the score is, and I know what happened is in no way your fault. That machine should have been out of here years ago, but I've got to keep the old dimwit happy. Just do me a favor. Bow and scrape a little bit, and then take the thing down stairs and check it out." She lowered her voice, and said conspiratorially, "If you can find something terminally wrong with it, maybe we can finally get rid of it for good."

"Just leave it to us, Donna." I said quietly.

Donna leaned a little closer to us. "Look, before you talk to Linville there's something that I should tell you. When he had his little incident this morning... it left a mark." She put a hand to her forehead. "How can I put this, it..."

At that moment we heard Dr. Linville behind us coming out of the doctor's lounge. "Ah ha! There you are! What did you do to my machine?!"

Trevor and I spun around simultaneously and took in the good doctor. He was of medium height, about five foot, seven or eight inches, but the girth of his belly and the stockiness of his arms and legs made him seem shorter. He was mostly bald but grew his peppery hair long in the back and combed it forward in a futile attempt to hide his pate. At this moment however, the hair was forgotten and hung limply down the back of his neck. His dome glistened with the sweat of rage, and his nose was bright red underneath his small angry eyes.

"Dr. Linville I..." I stammered and nearly lost my composure, for there, covering the rim of his right eye, was a wide, black circle. It looked as if someone had punched him, hard. I could see several of the OR nurses that had to deal with this tyrant of a man behind him. They were covering their mouths with their hands trying desperately not to laugh out loud.

Here I stood facing the terrible, indignant Dr. Linville, and all I could think of was the dog Petey, from the old black and white films of the Little Rascals. That cute, angle-headed mutt with the black ring around one eye. I could see Trevor out of the corner of *my* eye. He was trying to turn away as nonchalantly as he could so Linville wouldn't see his smile.

I bit both cheeks and tried with great concentration to continue. "I don't know how it could have happened," I managed.

"That doesn't surprise me at all!" Linville continued. "I don't know where you morons get your so-called training. This is what I have to contend with!" With that he shoved an ESU pencil under my nose. "This pencil has a short!"

I will never know where I found the strength to keep from laughing. I suppose it has something to do with knowing how much worse the situation might get if I did. I simply took the pencil from him. "Dr. Linville, I assure you that we'll take the equipment to our shop and thoroughly investigate until we get to the bottom of the problem."

"Well, see that you do! I will not be made a fool of over the incompetence of the maintenance staff!"

The way he said maintenance staff made it sound like he was referring to something he'd scraped off the bottom of his shoe. He spun on his heel and retreated back into the lounge.

I turned back to see Donna shaking her head.

"What did I do?" I asked her.

"Nothing, Jay, you were just there." She wheeled the ESU in question out from behind the counter. "Why don't you two just get this thing out of here?"

"Sure, Donna."

Trevor and I took the machine and wheeled it down to the shop. As we walked in, we could see Dan in his office, hanging up the phone. He got up and walked into the shop. "That sounds like some little episode you guys had."

I didn't know what he had heard. "Dan, let me explain," I said.

He held up his hand. "There's nothing to explain. Donna just told me all about it."

"We didn't do anything wrong, Dan."

"I know you didn't do anything wrong, that's what Donna told me." Trevor had gotten the ESU analyzer out and begun hooking things up. "What are you doing?" Dan asked him.

"I'm going to check the machine out," Trevor said.

"No, you're not," Dan said. "You're going to take that piece of shit down to the trash masher and see that it falls in."

"But what are we going to tell Dr. Linville when he asks where his machine is?" I asked.

"You let me worry about that. The old windbag is writing up an incident report, but Donna and I are going to call him on it. Tell me somethin', will you?"

"What's that?" I asked him.

"Was his eye really that black?"

"Remember Petey, the dog from the Little Rascals?"

It was several days later when Dan walked into the shop from his office and eyed Bobby and me, who were sitting at a bench repairing equipment. "I just got a call from Shay Ingram. MICU 6 has got a problem with their IV pumps. You two go check it out." I looked at Bobby, and he just shrugged.

"Okay," I said. "What's the problem?"

"She says that all of their pumps are running too fast."

"All of them?" Bobby asked. "That's impossible."

"Sounds like Fred's at it again," I said.

"Then go exorcise the ghost." Dan walked back into his office without another word, and Bobby and I grabbed an equipment cart and headed out the door to set about our task.

Medical Intensive Care Unit 6 was on the top floor of the northernmost tower. We had made our way to one of the lower level north elevators and were on our way up, when the elevator stopped on the first floor, the doors opened, and an elderly couple got on.

They looked to be in their eighties at least. They held hands, and in his other hand the man carried a cane that he leaned heavily upon as they boarded the elevator. They nodded and smiled at us and we silently replied in turn. As they turned to face the front, Bobby nudged me and gave me a knowing wink, though I wasn't sure what I was supposed to know.

They hadn't pushed any of the buttons, so Bobby leaned forward and tapped the man on the shoulder. "Excuse me, what floor would you like?"

The old man half turned and raised his hand to his ear. "What?"

"What floor would you like," Bobby asked, a little more loudly.

"What?"

The woman turned to her husband and, raising her voice to the level of a bullhorn in the confined elevator, repeated the question. "He asked what floor you would like, Dear?" I resisted the urge to cover my ears with my hands.

"What floor are we on?" he asked.

Neither of the couple saw Bobby roll his eyes slightly. However, he smiled warmly as he held the elevator on stop. He raised his voice somewhat. "We're on the first floor."

"What?"

Obviously, he hadn't spoken loudly enough. The woman continued, looking at her husband and relaying the exchange like a UN interpreter through a PA system. "We're on the first floor, Dear."

"One, eh?" the old man asked.

"Yes," Bobby tried again. "What floor would you like?"

"What?"

"He wants to know what floor we want, Dear?"

The old man gazed at his wife. "What floor do we want, Mother?"

"We want three, Dear."

The old man looked at Bobby. "We want three."

Nodding, Bobby pushed the button for the third floor.

"Thank you," said the woman.

"Thank you," echoed the husband.

We rode in silence to the third floor. After the couple had departed, Bobby turned and looked at me. "What floor do you want, Sonny?"

I put my hand to my ear. "What?" Bobby laughed, and I looked at him more seriously. "You know, we shouldn't make fun of them; we'll be old some day, and at least they're together."

"I don't plan on getting older," he said.

"What, you're going to discover the fountain of youth?"

"Maybe."

We reached the sixth floor, stepped off the elevator and turned right toward the entrance of MICU 6. The various floors inside the towers were referred to as pods, and like all the pod sections, the MICU curved around in an arc. There were twelve individual rooms that curved around the outer wall, with inside walls of glass so that the nurses could watch the patients closely. Like the bays in the ER, each room had an ECG monitor mounted on the wall behind the bed, which connected to a central monitor located behind the large nurses' station in the center.

When we entered the unit, we were met by Shekinah Ingram, who was the head nurse and went by the nickname Shay. She was a black woman who was in her late twenties or early-thirties and young to be a head nurse, which spoke to the kind of grades she had attained in school.

She took her job seriously and brooked no nonsense, though she could be very funny. I'd noticed a sense of professionalism tinged with humor seemed to be a trait in most of the women in positions of authority here. I supposed that had a lot to do with why they were in positions of authority.

She approached us wearing a perplexed expression, something I hadn't seen on her face before. "Am I glad to see you guys. Something strange is going on around here."

"What seems to be the trouble, lovely lady? Bobby asked unctuously.

"Can it, Bobby, I'm not in the mood," Shay answered curtly. She turned and addressed me. "I've tried to run IVs with every pump we have and every damned one of them is running way too fast. I've never seen anything like it."

"Have you called central supply for replacement pumps?" I asked.

"They're on their way. I hope to hell that *they* work. I've got half a dozen critical patients in here and the docs are starting to scream.

Gravity-fed IV just isn't as accurate as an IV pump, at least one that's working right."

"Let's have a look at a couple of the bad machines," I said.

She led us into the equipment storage room that was located behind the nurses' station, and there along one wall were four of the small, blue pumps mounted on their silver IV poles. I grabbed the first one that I came to and threaded the test tubing from our equipment cart through the machine. I hung an IV bag from the hook on the pole and partially filled it with water from a nearby sink and inserted the end of the tubing into a graduated cylinder. I set the pump for fifty milliliters an hour, started it, and began timing it with a stopwatch. As the three of us looked on, the graduated cylinder filled to a hundred milliliters in less than five minutes.

"Good God!" exclaimed Bobby, "I've never seen one run that fast!"

"Listen to the damn thing whir!" I observed. After performing thousands of equipment inspections, a tech got used to the normal operating sounds that various machines made, and this machine was definitely not normal.

"Tell me about it!" Shay said. "If my nurse hadn't been on her toes this morning, her patient would have gotten one hell of a dose of potassium chloride, a fatal dose!" Shay was visibly upset, which was something else I'd never seen before and completely understood.

I unhooked the machine and hooked up the next one in line, only to get the same results. One after the other we hooked up every pump on the unit; they were all running the same way. The new machines had arrived from central supply and, upon testing them, we found they were working properly, so we substituted them for the bad ones.

Bobby used a phone at the nurses' station and called Dan in the shop. "Can you send somebody up here with a cart, Boss? We've got some pumps to bring downstairs... thirteen of them." Bobby held the phone away from his ear, and I could clearly hear Dan from four feet away.

Dan was still going when we got back to the shop. He'd called all the techs back in, junior and senior, and they were all looking concerned. "Jesus Christ, who did the inspections on these things last?!"

"I checked the stickers on them, Dan," I told him. "There are several different initials on them. They were up to date. A couple of them were just done last month."

"Well, forget these for now. We have a little job to do before we'll have time to look at them." We all knew what was coming, but no one wanted to voice it. "That's right, Kids, every damn last IV pump in the hospital needs to be checked again before it can be used, all fourteen hundred of them! Grab your carts and get hustling!" No one said a word; we just set about the job at hand.

I was working in surgical intensive care unit 4a, or SICU 4a, trying to get ahold of an IV pump that was alongside the bed of an elderly gentleman who was on a ventilator. I'd helped a nurse swap out the pump for one that I'd thoroughly checked out. I was somewhat used to the sight of people hooked up to machines to sustain their life functions, but sometimes it bothered me more than others.

The old man looked so frail as I stood next to the bed looking down at him. The spirometer on the ventilator moved up and down, and his chest rose and fell in concert, as the IV pump fed his veins what they needed to keep him going.

His eyes were shut tightly as if he were desperately trying to block out the pitiful existence he was now experiencing. He looked so alone, so helpless. I wondered about his family and the friends that he must have made during his lifetime. Were any of them still alive? Were they all gone to leave him behind by himself? I couldn't imagine a circumstance that would make a person feel more isolated and forgotten, more set adrift waiting for the inevitable end.

I was standing next to the bed leaning over the tubes and wires trying to reach the pump, when I looked down and saw that the old man's eyes were open. They weren't just open; they were as big as saucers and very clear as if they were focused on something. He looked straight ahead, and I turned to look in the same direction. There was nothing to be seen but fluorescent lights and ceiling tiles.

As I turned back toward him, he sat bolt upright, ripping the ventilator tube loose from his mouth and grabbing me tightly by the arm. I was shocked into immobility. His eyes suddenly looked right at me as if he recognized me and then he fell back in the bed still gripping my arm.

I heard the nurses running into the room before I saw them. The head nurse of SICU 4a, another seasoned nurse named Grace North, stood on the other side of the bed. She looked at me as she placed her fingers on the side of the old man's neck, feeling for his carotid pulse.

"What happened?" she asked me.

I felt numb with shock. "I... I don't know. I was trying to get to the IV pump when his eyes suddenly opened, and he sat up. He was looking at me like he knew me and then he fell back down." I felt like I was beginning to babble. The old man still had a tight grip on my arm, and it was beginning to hurt.

"He's dead," Grace said.

"What?!"

"He's dead, Jay. Gone."

"Aren't you going to do something?" It seemed to me they should be calling a code blue... or something.

Grace looked at me as if to study my face. "He's a DNR. The instructions are simple and explicit, do not resuscitate. He was ready for his life to end."

I didn't know what to think. My arm hurt, and I was beginning to feel dizzy. I think that I swayed, for I heard Grace issue a sharp command to another nurse, "Catch him!" I felt several pairs of hands grip my shoulders, and someone pried the old man's hand from my arm.

A few minutes later I was sitting in the nurses' lounge with a hot cup of coffee on the table before me. Grace sat across from me. She was at least twenty years my senior, with medium-length brown hair that was tinged with gray. She was a pleasant looking woman with a depth and an ageless wisdom that I found quite appealing in less stressful moments.

She looked at me with concern. "Are you okay, Jay?"

"I think so. What the hell just happened, Grace?"

"You nearly fainted. It's okay, it happens to a lot of us at our first experience with death."

"Do all the patients sit up and stare at you just before they die?"

She took a sip of coffee, and then sat back gazing at me with an expression that I couldn't quite read. "Honey, when you've been a nurse as long as I have, you've seen a lot of strange things at the end. I once had a patient detach himself from the monitors, walk to the family waiting room, sit in front of the TV, and die."

"You didn't see him walking?"

"They can move pretty fast, especially when you have your hands full with another patient. Luckily it was the middle of the night and no one else was in the waiting room."

I thought for a moment. "I guess he didn't want to miss the late show," I offered.

"Or maybe he was a Johnny Carson fan," she added. We both laughed a little, and I began to feel a little more relaxed. I realized that Grace had probably sat here like this with many staff members.

"Does it still bother you?" I asked.

She looked thoughtful, and I could see that she was looking back into her past. When she spoke again it was with a subdued melancholy. "Sometimes it still bothers me. You get hardened to it, you have to in order to do your job, but death is something that you never get completely used to. Sometimes I'd think that I was used to it, and then we'd get a patient that I'd get attached to and we'd lose them, and my heart would break all over again."

"Why do you do it? Why do you continue to put yourself through that?"

"I suppose it's like the old saying, it's a dirty job, but someone's got to do it."

"It can't be that simple. The stress has got to drive you up the wall from time to time."

"It does, but I get a lot of satisfaction out of helping people. That may sound cliché, but it's not just the sick ones in the bed, the family members out in the waiting room need a lot of support too. If I can ease their suffering just a little, then I have purpose, I feel like somebody who's needed."

"I guess it's not every job that you can say that about."

"Not the ones that truly make a difference. So, I keep going, and I try to concentrate on the positive aspects and not let the negative ones get to me any more than I can help."

"I suppose that attitude comes with... experience."

She gave me a sidelong glance. "You meant to say age, didn't you?"

"Now you're putting words in my mouth. You don't honestly think I'm going to answer that question one way or the other and expect to walk away unscathed, do you? Besides, there's chronological age and there's mental age, and one doesn't necessarily have anything to do with the other."

She was laughing now. "My, aren't we the little diplomat?"

"Uh oh, something tells me that I just painted myself into a corner."

"It's okay honey, a woman of my *experience* learns to deal with these things."

"I think that I'm going to quit while I'm behind and get the hell out of here while I still have my head." I didn't get up immediately, there was still something that I wanted to say. "Grace, I..." I wanted to express my appreciation to her for not making me feel self-conscious and for helping me to understand more than I did before, but everything that came to mind seemed trivial after watching the old man die.

She reached over and put her hand briefly over mine. "It's okay, Jay, I know. You're welcome."

I got up, kissed her lightly on the cheek, and left.

Early the next morning, we were all sitting around the shop having coffee from the machine located on a small table just outside Dan's office door and contemplating our day. The door opened and three very serious looking men in three-piece suits were ushered in by Genevieve Madas, the Director of Nursing Services. Behind her back, Madas was known to her nursing charges as 'The Ice Queen', and at the moment she truly looked the part. Dan came out of his office immediately and herded them in, closing his door behind them.

Everyone looked to Will Stanski. "What's going on, Will?" I asked.

Will shook his head slightly. "Those three distinguished gentlemen represent the J.C.A.H.O., the F.D.A., and P.H.I.C.O., the hospital's insurance carrier. If Dan doesn't answer their questions about the IV pumps to their satisfaction, we'll all be up S.H.I.T. creek without a paddle."

"Is there anything we can do to help?" Trevor asked.

"Just get out there and keep checking those pumps. It's the only thing we can do right now." Will said, and we finished our coffee and grabbed our carts.

On the way out the door, Bobby indicated his cart with one hand. "I'm gonna get me a flashing red light for the front of this thing and maybe a siren so people will get out of my way. Whadda you think?"

"I think people already avoid you when they see you coming," said Trevor.

"Thanks a lot, Trev," said Bobby feigning hurt.

"Don't mention it," said Trevor, clapping him on the shoulder as we left.

Trevor and I spent the morning checking pumps around the same area together. All the pumps we'd checked were working fine. We took a mid-morning break and returned to the shop where we found Will Stanski sitting at a bench scratching his head. Bobby was seated on the stool next to him looking on. On the bench was an IV pump that had been completely disassembled, and in Will's hand was an integrated circuit or computer chip.

"What's up, Will?" asked Trevor.

"This is the damnedest thing." He held the chip up so that we could see it. "This is the wrong chip, according to the schematic. This one isn't even listed for this board."

Bobby took the chip from Will's hand and studied it closely. "If it's not listed for this board then how did it get there?" he asked.

"You tell me and we'll both know," Will said.

Dan came out of his office and walked over to Will. "What have you got?"

"I've got a chip from the driver section of this pump's board that doesn't belong there."

"Have you checked any of the other malfunctioning pumps yet?"

"No, this is the first one."

"Open up another one." One after another we opened up all of the bad pumps, and one after another we found the mysterious chip that didn't belong. Dan was beside himself. "How in the hell did this happen?" He turned and looked at me. "Jay, do we have any of these boards in stock in the storeroom?"

"I'll go check." I walked to the back of the shop and into the large storeroom where I found a half a dozen spare boards which I took out to Dan. "Here you go, but I don't see the mystery chip on any of them," I told him.

Will took the boards from me and placed them one by one under the lighted magnifier on the bench for a closer inspection. "These are all normal, Dan," he said.

"Well, that rules out a manufacturer's defect," Dan said. "Besides, if that were the case, we would have caught them on initial inspection." We inspected every piece of patient care equipment that came into the hospital before it was put into use.

"And why were they all in MICU 6?" Trevor added.

"Let's see what we have in the computer," I said. All of the repairs done by our department were written up and entered into the department computer. I walked over to the computer and started pulling up service histories for IV pumps. Within seconds I had the information that I wanted. "We replaced boards in two pumps last week and in one the week before," I said, reading from the screen.

"Three's a long way from thirteen," said Trevor. "And why did they all malfunction at the same time?"

Dan looked thoughtful for a moment as he picked up the chip from the bench where Will had placed it. "What I want to know is, where in the hell did these come from?"

Suddenly the shop door flew open and in walked Dennis Lebon carrying his customary push broom. "Hi guys, are they keeping ya busy?" he asked as he always did.

Dennis was mentally handicapped, not severely, but he could never function completely on his own. He was part of a work program instituted by the hospital in conjunction with a local home for the mentally challenged. He did janitorial work and odd jobs around the hospital and he doted on Dan, for Dan had taken it upon himself to look out for Dennis.

Dennis also thought of himself as quite a comedian and loved to stop in the shop and regale us with his latest joke, which he always thought was uproariously funny. We always went along with him, for he was a kind-hearted soul, and no matter how dumb the joke, he always cracked himself up, which had a way of lifting our spirits.

"Hey, guys, I've got one for ya. Why does a chicken cross the road?"

Dan usually jumped in enthusiastically at this point, but Dan was still in deep thought, contemplating the mystery chip in his hand, and seemed not to hear. So I jumped in with Dan's usual response. "I don't know, Dennis. Why does a chicken cross the road?"

Dennis got the same impish look on his face that he always got just before he delivered his punchline. "To buy eggs at the Seven Eleven!"

At this point, as usual, Dennis became doubled over with laughter, and Trevor, Bobby and I pretended to enjoy the joke and chuckled along with him until he regained his composure. "Well, guys, you've been a lovely audience, but I've gotta go. See ya!" he said as he opened the door.

"See ya, Dennis," we replied. Then we turned back to our little mystery.

By our third day of IV pump inspections, we were thoroughly sick of them. One thing about IV pumps that made them difficult to inspect was that they were highly mobile and could be difficult to find—they could be anywhere. They could be stuck away in any storeroom or equipment closet, any cubbyhole, nook, or cranny. The only thing to do was to look absolutely everywhere, leaving no stone unturned, as it were.

Trevor and I had teamed up, and Dan had assigned us to labor and delivery, or L&D as it was called. L&D was located adjacent to the main OR corridor on the fourth floor. I had seen the publicity literature that the hospital had sent out promoting the Labor and Delivery Department.

The slick photographs the pamphlets contained depicted warm moments of new family togetherness: mother holding newborn baby and smiling while a smiling nurse in an immaculate white uniform looks on; proud father holding his child for the first time, wearing surgical scrubs that looked like they had just been starched and ironed; the group shot of mother, father, and baby in the center, with nurse and obstetrician in the background all looking relaxed and cozy and happy. All in all, the pictures reminded me of something that you might have seen in a Norman Rockwell painting from the fifties.

The L&D department consisted of twelve labor rooms, not much more than cubicles, where prospective mothers could knit baby booties, whiling away their time until their offspring decided to make their grand entrances into the world. These grand entrances were made in four large delivery rooms that housed all of the equipment that might be required in bringing forth these little bundles of joy. At least, that's what the brochures said.

On this particular day, Trevor and I showed up wheeling our equipment cart looking for IV pumps only to find they were stacking them to the rafters. Everywhere we looked we saw women in labor.

They had filled the labor rooms and lined the halls on gurneys, there were even two in the nurses' lounge. I managed to flag down Vicky Henderson, who was the head nurse of L&D, as she ran down the hall headed for one of the delivery rooms.

Vicky was cute and petite, with fiery red hair and green eyes that smiled most of the time; however, at this moment they held a darting harried look.

"Vicky, what is going on up here?" I asked, using my arms to indicate the mass of confusion around us.

"Hell, I don't know, Jay. There must have been a full moon last night."

"Trevor and I need to check out your IV pumps, okay?"

"Be my guest," she said as she opened the door to a delivery room.

As she opened the door, Trevor and I could see a woman on the delivery table with her legs up in the stirrups. Her distraught husband stood beside her, practically wringing his hands and looking as helpless as a small child who knows that he's done something terribly wrong.

The woman's hair was soaking wet and hanging down from the back of her head like a used mop. She was screaming at the top of her lungs. "You bastard! You miserable son of a bitch! Look what you've done to me!"

The man was ashen-faced with a look of pure panic in his eyes, like a prisoner about to be executed by a firing squad. The woman reached up and grabbed him by the front of his surgical scrubs, pulling him down until his face was inches from hers. "If you ever come near me again, I'll kill you!" she was screaming as the door swung closed.

Trevor and I stood stunned for a moment, looking at each other. Finally, he spoke. "If I ever say anything about becoming a father, don't even say anything, just punch me in the head as hard as you can."

"I will, if you'll do the same for me."

As we walked through the hallways lined with waiting women on gurneys, it struck me as a scene from a war movie. All around us was chaos; women were moaning softly or crying outright. It seemed to be a veritable den of human suffering. They looked like casualties after some momentous battle fought between opposing groups of large-bellied women. The nurses all rushed around looking weary as if they'd been there for days; some of them undoubtedly had been.

We progressed slowly, picking our way through the carnage and trying to stay out of the way. We eventually arrived at the central nurses' station where Linda, the unit clerk, was frantically running back and forth trying to answer the phone, which seemed to ring constantly, tend to doctor's and nurse's requests, and monitor the patient rooms with the use of the nurse-call intercom system.

Linda seemed like someone who had weathered a life that was sometimes difficult. She had an air about her that spoke of hard experience, and a toughness that was tempered with wry humor. I guessed that she was in her late forties, though at the moment she looked older, no doubt due to the considerable strain that her department was presently under.

"Hi, Linda," Trevor said. "Are you guys having a two-for-one sale? You look like you have your hands full."

Linda looked at him incredulously. "I'd have my hands full if I were a goddamn octopus; this is impossible!

Over the intercom we could hear a woman crying in a voice that was somewhat different from the rest. She had an accent, and over and over she called, "Oh God, oh sweet Jesus, oh God, help me!"

"Well, she certainly sounds the religious one," I remarked.

Linda looked at me with exasperation in her eyes. "You don't know the half of it. She has a huge gold-framed picture of Jesus sitting on the night table, and rosary beads hung all over the back of the bed. She's been keeping that wailing up for hours. She's tying up the intercom system, and I'm going out of my frigging mind!"

"Can't you just turn her intercom off?" asked Trevor.

"Oh, no," Linda replied sardonically. "That's against hospital *policy.*"

As we listened, the wailing seemed to achieve a fever pitch. "Oh Jeeesus! Oh Goood!"

Trevor turned to me and murmured under his breath, "We've got to get out of this looney bin."

"Come on, we're almost done. Just a couple more rooms and the storage closets."

Trevor went to check the next room, and I went across the hall to a storage closet. As I opened the door, I saw a row of tall shelves that went back about fifteen feet. From the back of the closet came a strange noise, a shuffling and a rattling of things. My curiosity piqued, I walked to the rear of the closet and poked my head around the last shelf unit.

There, seated on some boxes, was a nurse. Her scrub pants lay discarded on the floor, and her legs were raised and spread wide. There was a man in a white coat atop her with his pants down around his ankles. His buttocks moved rapidly up and down as he pumped away like a dog in heat, oblivious to the world. She was digging her fingers into his back and moaning something unintelligible that I didn't really want to understand. They hadn't noticed me, and I backed up as quickly and quietly as I could and exited the closet.

When I got back to the hall, I met Trevor coming out of the other room. I could tell by the puzzled look on his face that I must have been wearing a strange expression on my own. "Well, were there any pumps in the storeroom?" he asked.

"Plenty of pumps, but not IVs," I said, then I realized that I'd forgotten to check. "Actually, I'm not sure."

"You're not sure? What the hell is wrong with you, Jay?" He started for the storeroom door. "Forget it, I'll look for myself."

I started to let him go and then thought better of it and put a hand on his shoulder. "Trevor wait, don't go in there."

"Why the hell not? What is going on?"

"There's a doctor and a nurse in there."

"So, what? Are they having a conference?"

"You might say that. You might also say that they're trying to drum up more business for this department."

"What?!" Trevor paused, then slowly like mist rolling over a pond early in the morning I saw understanding come into his eyes. "You're kidding. In the storeroom...?"

"Well, you know what they say about any port in a storm."

Trevor looked at me for a moment, and then, "Is it lunchtime yet?"

"Close enough for me."

"Let's go."

The mood at lunch that day was subdued, mainly because Dan was subdued, which was something we rarely saw. He was usually the one making the rest of us laugh. We knew that he was having a tough time dealing with the various agencies involved in the investigation of the IV pump incident, as well as the hospital administration, which as rumor had it, was coming down on him hard.

No attempt at humor seemed to have any effect on him. The story about the couple I had seen in the storeroom, which normally would have given him at least a half-hour's worth of material, only drew a half-hearted chuckle from the top of his throat.

It was disheartening. We all knew how serious the situation was, and we were all doing our best to get to the bottom of it. But humor was the weapon we had used to combat the stress we dealt with on a daily basis, and now that seemed to be slipping away.

We were nearly done with our lunch when the door to Dan's office opened abruptly and Dwayne Dorfly poked his head in. Dwayne was the Director of Building Services as his title was called, or maintenance as everyone else called his department.

It was widely known around the hospital that Dan and Dwayne were mortal enemies. This animosity had developed years before from something that had happened between the two of them. As hard as we had tried, we hadn't been able to pry the story from Dan, and the only thing we had been able to get from Will Stanski was that it had involved a woman. Dan and Dwayne had both been married for a long time, but whatever had happened had been severe enough to make them hate each other for years after the fact.

Dorfly was about five and a half feet tall, with a paunch that was becoming prominent. He was mostly bald with his remaining hair looking like Brillo pads that had been glued around the sides and rear radius of his head. He wore a cheesy mustache whose black color didn't match that of his remaining hair, and it hung limply from his upper lip.

At the moment his face held a sour expression, but, looking back, it's the only expression I can ever remember seeing on his face. It was as if someone had slipped him an alum and lemon cocktail, and his face had frozen in that position.

"Dan, I need a decision on those beds," was all that Dorfly said, but the rise in tension level in the room was immediately felt by all.

The matter of the beds that Dorfly was referring to was an ongoing dispute between the two of them about whether the maintenance or the biomed department would handle the inspection and repair of the electric hospital beds. There were more than fourteen hundred beds in all, and informally we had always worked with the maintenance guys on them as a sort of joint venture, but we all figured that an official placement of the responsibility for them gave Dan and Dwayne something more to fight about, and that was an opportunity not to be missed. The decision, however, was certainly nothing that Dorfly needed to interrupt our lunch over.

The sudden tension in the room was sharp-edged. Not only did no one speak, I was certain that everyone in the room was holding their breath waiting for Dan's reaction.

Dan fixed Dorfly with a stare that seemed to carry the intensity of a laser beam. "We'll talk about it after lunch, Dwayne." He didn't raise his voice, but the undertone was sheer power and contempt.

Dorfly, although far from the brightest man I had ever met, seemed to get the message immediately. "After lunch then." He turned and left, the door clicking shut behind him.

For all intents and purposes, lunch was over. We finished up and got back to work.

It had been a week since my defibrillator accident. I hadn't seen Debbie since, though I thought about her a lot. I thought it best that I not change my usual routine to look for her; Michael's warning was all too true: the hospital had a gossip machine that never broke down. Trevor wasn't the only one who wanted to keep his private life private. I hadn't seen her the few times I had been in the ER so assumed she was working night shift this week.

For the moment the ER was relatively quiet. This was a rarity, as it was usually a struggle trying to get to all of the equipment that was due for preventative maintenance. We often played a game of grab it before they need to use it again, and we nearly always wound up with several pieces unchecked at the end of the month that we had to try to hunt down. Most of the bays were empty, and the housekeeping staff had a chance to give the place a thorough cleaning now that they didn't have to work around patients.

The morning sun was streaming through the eastern facing windows, and it sparkled as it was reflected off the highly polished floor. It was as quiet as I had ever seen it as I checked a defib for power output. Although our inspections of the IV pumps was far from finished, Dan had assigned Trevor and me to regular PMs of other equipment so that we wouldn't fall too far behind our regular schedule.

I had the paddles in my hands and was just about to push the charge button when I looked up and there she was. She was standing there leaning against the wall looking at me with a soft little grin that just touched the sides of her mouth. God, she was cute! I couldn't take my eyes off her.

"Don't you think you should be paying closer attention to what you're doing?" she asked. "I'd really hate to see you flat on your back in here again. Not that it wasn't interesting, mind you, but I think once was enough."

I placed the paddles back in their holders on either side of the machine and looked at her intently. "Can I talk to you for a minute?"

Her face had assumed an impish look; it fit her well. "I believe you're talking to me now, aren't you?"

I quickly looked around the ER, and whether or not it was my imagination, I thought that I noticed one or two of the staff giving us covert glances. I picked up my clipboard with the checklist on it and tried to look casual.

"I thought maybe you were on night shift this past week; I haven't seen you around."

"I had two days off, but I've been here the rest of the time. How are you doing?"

I relaxed a little. Since she had been one of my nurses after my accident, it made sense we would have a casual conversation.

"I'm feeling fine. No after effects." I looked down at my clipboard again. "I'd be feeling even better if you'd go out with me."

I raised my eyes to meet hers and saw a puzzled look in them.

"Are you asking me out or your clipboard?" she asked with a hint of a smile.

I felt myself blush. Not good. I quickly scanned the ER. Nobody seemed to be paying any attention to us. I looked back at her.

"I'm trying to avoid the gossip machine, if you get my drift."

Her expression changed instantly to a professional mode. "Of course. I definitely get what you're saying."

"Would you like to go to dinner or something?" I held my pencil over my clipboard as if to check something off.

"I didn't bring my prop," she said, "and I'm not sure about the 'or something', but dinner would be nice."

"Tonight?"

"I can do tonight. I get off at six."

"Then how about eight?"

"That's fine."

"I'll pick you up," I said.

"I'll look forward to it."

"Uh, Debbie?"

"What?"

"I don't know where you live."

She grabbed my pencil and clipboard, scribbled on it and handed it back to me. "I'll see you then." She gave me a brief smile and walked toward the nurses' station.

I tossed the clipboard onto my cart and pushed it to my next piece of equipment. I'd have to get a clean sheet and hide the one she wrote on. I glanced down and saw an address and phone number. I smiled to myself, then got back to work.

I had trouble concentrating on my job, as I was walking on air for the rest of the day. I kept thinking about my impending date. I chided myself for thinking like an adolescent. After all, it wasn't the first time that I had asked a girl out, or the first time I had been accepted.

I had my share of experience with women during my days as a road musician, but there was something about this cute, soft-spoken girl that got to me. I really wanted her to like me. I wanted to hold her and get to know all there was to know about her, and I wanted to tell her about myself.

Evidently what was going through my mind must have shown on my face, because Dan picked up on it almost as soon as I set foot back in the shop. Things must have improved for him with the IV pumps, because he'd been acting more like his old self the last two days. I had drifted through the door with my cart and set about taking care of some paperwork at the bench when I became aware that he'd sidled up beside me.

Bobby Gilford was seated at the bench perpendicular to the one I was using, and Dan addressed him. "Wooooo, boy. Who do you think got to him?"

I knew immediately that I should have done my paperwork elsewhere and stayed away from the shop. Dan was too good at reading people to miss something like this.

Bobby picked it up quickly. "I don't know, but I think maybe I'd better go to the kitchen and get some ice. We may need it to cool him down."

Dan grasped my chin in one large hand and turned my head to look into my eyes. "Mm, mm, you've got it bad, don't you?"

I swatted his hand away. "What the hell are you talking about, Dan?" I tried to sound firm, but I knew that the hint of a smile was sneaking its way across my face. I couldn't seem to help it.

Dan looked at Bobby again. "Looks like you may have some competition, tripod." He turned to me again. "What do you say, kid? You want old three legs to give you some romance pointers?"

"No, thanks. God knows where those pointers have been."

Bobby feigned affront. "Hey, you watch what you say about my pointers. Besides, I haven't gotten any complaints."

Dan looked at me semi-earnestly, which was about as serious as he got in these kinds of situations. "Come on, tell Uncle Dan who she is."

Ceaseless teasing, albeit good-natured, presented itself in my imagination. Endless days and weeks of off-hand remarks and side comments that would dig at me in tiny increments until I was laid bare. Trevor was definitely smarter than I was, he wouldn't have come back so soon. I shook my head defiantly, "No way. I'm not saying anything."

Bobby had worked his way up to my other side. "Come on, Jay, you can tell your old buddies who the lucky lady is."

Dan didn't miss a beat. "What makes you so certain it's a lucky *lady*?"

Bobby raised one hand, bent at the wrist, and touched his index finger to the side of his mouth. "Thurely you don't think heth that kind of a boy?"

"I'm beginning to wonder," Dan said.

I had enough of the conversation at this point. "Christ, it's like being in elementary school around here. If a guy doesn't try to jump on every female he sees, you think he's gay! My personal life is none of your business!"

"Well," said Dan. "If you're going to be that way about it, why don't you go PM the dragon's lair? It's due this month."

"Oh, come on, Jay," Bobby pleaded. "Anything's better than the black dragons! Tell us who she is!"

I hesitated only a moment, weighing the choices. Which was worse, the black dragons or endless ridicule and torture? "No," I said. "I'd rather deal with the dragons than you two vipers!" With that I stood and wheeled my cart to the door while a chorus of oooooos where emitted by Bobby and Dan.

I have witnessed open-heart surgery on more than one occasion. I have heard the sobs and even screams of those in pain. And I had now seen death at its moment of occurrence. All of these experiences have had profound effects on me, but nothing I have experienced gives me the willies like the GI lab.

Dan, of course, picked up on my feelings the first time he sent me up there. "Watch out for the black dragons!" he had exclaimed with that familiar glint in his eye.

"The what?" I'd asked, feeling an apprehension I hoped didn't show.

"You can't miss 'em. They're about three feet long, jet black, and they have eyes on the end like a cyclops."

"What the hell are you talking about, Dan?"

"The black dragons. The endoscopes. You know, the things they shove up your ass to go spelunking through your innards!"

I remember I'd felt my stomach constrict. And as I'd pushed my cart towards the lab, I'd realized that my hands were sweating, and I was suddenly very glad that we hadn't had lunch yet. "Make sure that you inspect all the devices in there," Dan had said. "Look in every closet, crack, nook and cranny." I could swear the rest of the guys in the shop were snickering as I'd turned to make my hasty departure.

So, my choice of PMing the GI lab over telling the guys about Debbie should give you an idea of just how relentless they could be.

Two well-seasoned nurses named Greta and Shirley ran the GI lab. It was obvious that they had been doing whatever it was that they did for a long time just by the way they handled the patients with ease. They got the patients to do whatever authority dictated. The patients often seemed to look to me like lambs being led to slaughter, though it was probably just my imagination.

Greta and Shirley were both in their late forties or early fifties, and both had dark hair that was tinged with gray; Greta's hair was short, and Shirley's was long. Greta was a rather masculine woman, big-boned and large, while Shirley was petite. They must have worked together for quite a while, because their actions as a team seemed so well coordinated. It was as if conscious thought wasn't needed; they seemed to move around each other by instinct.

The GI lab was on the second floor. From the hall you entered a large prep and holding area, with half a dozen bays containing gurneys separated by curtains. The lights were slightly dimmed, and elevator music played softly in the background. The atmosphere struck me as pleasantly ominous, as if the idea was to get you to lower your guard before a demon suddenly jumped out from behind a curtain and dragged you kicking and screaming into the nether world.

As I walked through, I saw that there was a single patient in attendance, a middle-aged, somewhat balding man on the gurney in bay one. He was a bit on the hefty side, and the hospital gown that he wore seemed to fit even worse than they usually did. It was pulled tightly across his middle as if it were two sizes too small and, given the way that they opened in the back anyway, I was sure that his was covering nothing. It was the perfect way to remove any shred of dignity that a person may have had left at this point.

Maybe it was my state of mind whenever I came here, but it seemed to me that all the patients wore looks that I can only describe as barely disguised terror. The man had a hand on each of the rails on either side of the gurney, and his knuckles were turning white from the pressure of his fingers. I gave him what I hoped was a reassuring smile as I passed, and he looked at me with a stony, unwavering gaze—a man, however reluctantly, resigned to his inevitable fate.

I began my rounds in room one, the first of the three treatment rooms, trying not to think about what the 'treatment' entailed. I finished the inspections on the first three machines with relative ease. I moved on to the electric examination table and found that it needed a new plug. I replaced the plug and moved on to the remaining pieces of equipment in the room and found no more problems.

I then needed to double-check for hidden equipment. I opened the doors to a long wall cabinet and there, in all of their gleaming, evil splendor hung half a dozen black dragons. They seemed to glow in the softly dimmed light, looking like a nest of eerie alien snakes ready to strike at any second without a moment's warning. I involuntarily took a step back.

At that particular moment, I heard a gasp and then a deep moan coming from the treatment room next door. I realized that both doors to the connecting restroom had been left open. I walked to the sink and grabbed several paper towels to wipe my forehead, which had become quite damp.

I stood for several moments waiting for my breathing to even out, and then exited room one and proceeded to treatment room three. For the moment, I bypassed room two where I had heard the sound effects coming from, knowing that it was in use.

I set about my assigned tasks, trying to focus on the job at hand. For the sake of thoroughness, I began doing inspections by the numbers like a green tech—analyzer hooked up properly, ground resistance okay, forward leakage seventeen micro amps, reverse leakage twenty-one micro amps...

As I worked, I heard an elderly woman from one of the bays in the outer room say, "My glasses, what shall I do with them?" She must have been hard of hearing, for her voice sounded louder than it should have. "When I had an x-ray, they gave me a little case to put my glasses in." I heard Greta answer in a raised voice to match the woman's, "Don't worry, Honey, we're not going to work on that end."

Calm. I was determined to remain calm and finish my job. I went on to the next inspection on a light source that was used to illuminate the tips of the black dragons when they were in use.

I needed to reach my hand all the way to the back of the machine to get to the plug. It was hard to reach, and I was on the verge of losing my balance. In order to steady myself, I placed my other hand on the counter next to me without looking, right on top of a large glob of something soft and mushy.

I shuddered and took a deep breath, trying to quell the awful thoughts that were jumping up and running through my head.

I stood for what seemed like a long time, not daring to look at the landing point of my hand. Suddenly Greta was standing beside me, looking at me with a bemused expression on her face. "What's the matter, Honey? You look like you've seen a ghost," she said.

If only that were it. If only Fred had come down from the sixth floor and materialized in front of me. That, I could handle. I was afraid to look and afraid to ask, but I had to know just what was going on. "Greta, what did I just put my right hand in?"

She picked up my hand and looked. "KY jelly... why? What's the... " Suddenly a look of understanding came over her face. She started laughing as she called, "Hey, Shirley! Come here a minute!"

Shirley came into the room to see what was going on, and Greta explained it to her, "He thought we'd leave shit laying around on the counter."

"We assure you we put it in the refrigerator for safe keeping," Shirley said, as they both started laughing harder.

I went to the sink and washed my hands, and then I collected my cart and left without looking back. I didn't care what Dan said; he could jolly well send somebody else to finish the job.

As I was heading down the hall towards the shop, I happened upon Dennis Lebon. Dennis was busily mopping floors with a determined look on his face while he hummed a nameless tune to himself. I had no doubt that when he was finished, the floor would gleam as if hand polished.

As I neared him, he saw me, stopped his mopping chores, and gave me a big smile. "Hi, Jay! Are they keeping ya busy?"

I smiled back. "Yeah, Dennis, they're keeping me pretty busy. How about you?"

"Oh, yeah, lots of floors to mop. I'm busy all right." He looked around and then gave me a conspiratorial look. I knew from long experience what was coming next, it was inevitable. "Hey, Jay. Do you know how you can tell if there's an elephant in your refrigerator?" His voice had gotten louder as he started his joke, as if playing to a large audience. There were several people in the hall that paused, as if they were expecting to see something out of the ordinary.

"No, Dennis. How can you tell if there's an elephant in your refrigerator?"

Dennis paused as he always did at this point, taking a quick look around to see how many people were listening to him. When he was satisfied they were paying attention, he winked and poked me in the arm. "You can't get the door closed!"

As always, he finished with gales of raucous laughter, and as always, I found myself laughing in spite of myself. Most of the other people in the hall sort of shrugged and walked away.

Something, maybe seen in my peripheral vision, caused me to look down the hall and the laughter died in my throat. Standing at the next corner were Genevieve Madas and Jerry Louis, the chief financial officer for the hospital. I hadn't noticed them before, and I wondered how long they'd been standing there. They were both staring at us with what felt like stark disapproval, as if they'd caught us doing something wrong.

Today Genevieve wore her hair pulled severely to the back of her head so tightly it looked as if it were stretching the skin of her face. Her angular face itself looked as if it were carved from granite, and her gray eyes were fixed on me so intently, I was sure she could see right through me.

Jerry Louis looked to me like a stereotypical CPA. He was small and round-shouldered, with short, thinning gray hair that he wore slicked back. He wore small, round, wire-rimmed glasses that made his eyes look about two sizes too big. They spent a lot of time together, and there was some speculation about them having an affair, though I couldn't imagine two people who looked more sexless. Dan had once remarked that they looked like poster children for the constipation society of America.

They gazed at Dennis and me with obvious distaste, as if they had been offended. After a few moments they abruptly turned on their heels, she giving a little snort that I wasn't sure was real or imagined, and walked in the other direction. I decided that it was a shame there were so many people in the world who just couldn't appreciate a good joke.

"Thanks Dennis, I needed that," I said, and I meant it. "I have to get back to work, I'll see you later."

"See ya later, Jay, and thanks for being such a lovely audience."

I had a rare lunch by myself in the cafeteria, as I had no intention of going back to the shop. Dan usually assigned us to general areas of the hospital, but he also gave us a lot of leeway to take self-initiative and do inspections where we found they were needed.

I spent the rest of the day wandering around looking for things to do to occupy my mind, anything to keep myself from watching the clock. But as the afternoon wore on, I found myself looking at my watch every few minutes.

I tried not to think about Debbie by concentrating on my job, but it didn't seem to help. By the time four o'clock came, my brain felt exhausted, and I still had several hours to go before I saw her. I drove home and let myself into my very quiet apartment.

I liked my apartment. It was a one bedroom with a den where I kept my musical equipment, including my small collection of guitars and a four-string banjo that my grandfather had given me for my seventh birthday.

In the living room, across from my couch, I had a thirty-six-inch television with a VCR on which to play my considerable collection of movies. I watched movies a lot when I wasn't listening to music on my stereo or playing music in my den.

Off the living room were sliding glass doors that opened onto a small deck that overlooked woods and a creek. It was a very peaceful place to sit and think or to visit with friends when they came by.

At the moment it felt to me like I lived a very lonely life. I supposed in some ways it was burnout, to a certain extent, from my years as a road musician. But then I had always been somewhat of a loner; maybe I was getting tired of it.

The only sound I could hear was the windup clock that I had inherited from my grandfather. It was about a hundred years old, nearly two feet tall, and made of wood with an ornate glass front and a brass pendulum. It sat atop a wooden bookcase I had built myself, with the pendulum patiently swinging back and forth... tick tock, tick tock. I was sure that I was going out of my mind.

I got a beer from the refrigerator and went back through the living room to the sliding glass doors. I opened the doors and went out and stood for a few minutes on the deck. It was a very nice view, and there was a pleasant, gentle breeze blowing. What was she thinking? Was she looking as forward to tonight as I was? Was she acting like a lunatic too? I began pacing back and forth, I couldn't seem to stay still, so I went back inside.

I took a shower, dried my hair, and then lay on my bed just thinking, fantasizing about how the date would go. How suave and debonair I would be. I would sweep her off her feet with my witty repartee and thoughtful, gentle humor. There was no way she'd be able to resist me as I gathered her into my arms at the end of our perfect evening.

I snapped awake and looked at the clock—seven twenty-five. Oh my God! And I had at least a twenty-minute drive to get to her place if the traffic was with me!

I practically jumped into my clothes and then began to search frantically for her address. I was sure I had put it in my wallet... no wait, a pocket, what pocket? What the hell pair of pants had I been wearing?! No, not pants, I knew I would lose them if I left them in my pants... my jacket, that was it! I had transferred them to the pocket of the light jacket I had worn! Jacket... closet, the jacket was in the closet!

I raced down the short hallway to the closet, knocking a framed poster off the wall in my haste, the glass front shattering as it hit the floor. I nearly ripped the closet door off its hinges and began rooting through the pockets of my jackets.

Triumph! There at last was the small piece of paper with the address. I turned, prepared to rush to the bathroom to brush my teeth, and promptly fell over my coffee table, banging my knee badly in the process.

Somehow, I managed to limp to my car, a fifteen-year-old blue Volvo, and at last was on my way. Mercifully traffic was light, and I found my way to Debbie's apartment complex with relative ease. My heartrate was beginning to return to normal as I pulled into the parking lot and found an unoccupied space in the visitor's section.

It was a large complex that was not new but seemed to be well maintained. I found her building and walked up the two flights of stairs to her door, still limping slightly. There was new-age music drifting into the hallway from her apartment, a pleasant mix of electronic strings and horns. I rang the bell, and in a few seconds, I heard the volume of the music drop and I experienced a rush of anticipation as I heard the door being unlocked.

I had never seen her in anything but scrubs, and as she suddenly stood before me, I had an involuntary intake of breath. She wore a white, cotton-knit, short-sleeved, V-necked top that buttoned down the front, and showed just a hint of cleavage, and a tan mini skirt that showed off her shapely legs. Her short, chestnut brown hair shined lightly, complimenting her large, blue eyes. I don't know how long I stood there admiring her.

"Are you going to come in or do you just want to take a picture and go home?"

"Sorry, I didn't mean to stare."

"Yes, you did, and thank you, I'm flattered."

She stood to one side, and as I passed her, I caught a whiff of her coconut shampoo. As she closed the door, I stood looking around at what must have been the tiniest apartment I had ever seen. The room I entered was a combination living room/dining room/kitchen, and I assumed the door to my right led to a bedroom and bath.

A couch took up most of one wall and, other than that, a coffee table, small bookcase and a nineteen-inch television were the only other pieces of furniture. Bright, colorful posters hung on much of the wall space, all of them seemingly devoted to one musical group or the other. There was a light odor of lemon in the air.

"Nice apartment," I said.

"No, it's not. It's a dump, but thanks for pretending."

"I'm serious. It's not at all what I expected. I think it's quite charming."

She looked at me curiously. "What did you expect?"

What had I expected? I wasn't sure. "I don't know. Something more nurse-like I guess."

"What do you mean, nurse-like?"

What did I mean? Why was I talking like an idiot? "I don't know. I guess I expected something a little more antiseptic." What the hell was I saying? "No, I don't mean antiseptic, I mean... " What did I mean? Had my brain suddenly gone south for the winter?

Debbie looked at me appraisingly. "Do you mean cleaner?"

"Yes." What are you saying, idiot? "I mean no... I guess I expected something more hospital-like."

Debbie's eyes were laughing. "Yuck! That would be like living at work!"

"Yes, I suppose it would." Very good, Jay. This is some witty repartee you've started off with. You're a real charmer. Why don't you just save time by reaching down, grabbing your foot, and shoving it into your mouth.

I stuck out my hand. "Hi, Debbie, I'm Jay. It's nice to meet you."

This time she did laugh as she took my hand. "Hi, Jay, it's nice to meet you too."

"I just meant to say that I think you have a nice place."

"Well, if you say so. I'd ask you if you wanted a drink, but to tell you the truth, I'm starving. Do you mind if I'm rude and ask if we get started?"

"Not at all. I'm hungry too."

She locked her door, and I ushered her to my Volvo. "Nice car," she said.

"No, it's not. It's a wreck, but thanks for pretending."

"Touché, " she laughed, and I realized that I very much liked the sound.

We drove to a small Chinese restaurant I had patronized many times called House of Ming. Debbie took one look at the sign over the door and I could almost sense her rolling her eyes in the darkness. "Where do they come up with the names for these places?" she asked.

"In this case it's named for the family that owns and runs it."

She turned to me. "I take it you've been here before?"

"Quite a few times. You'll love the owner and his family. He's a little old man named Mr. Ling."

"Mr. Ling Ming?"

"You've got it."

Debbie started to laugh and so did I. "You're putting me on."

"No, I swear, that's his name," I assured her.

We got out of the car and walked in the front door. The interior was pretty much standard Chinese kitsch. Paper lanterns hung from strings of tiny, white lights that crisscrossed the ceiling. Prints of Chinese Junks and Asian people wearing huge conical straw hats standing in rice paddies hung on the velvet tapestried walls. Along the rear wall was an enormous mural depicting the Great Wall.

A young girl of about twelve stood at the small counter just inside the door. "Hi, Sukki," I said to her.

"Hi, Jee. Table for two?" she asked, eyeing Debbie speculatively.

"Yes, please," I said to her. Sukki showed us to our table and left to get menus.

Debbie looked at me smiling. "Well, Jee, I see you have been here before. Do you get a special discount for bringing in new customers?"

"Why do you think I brought you here?"

Sukki brought us menus, cups, and a pot of green tea, and then she retreated to the kitchen where the faint rattling of pots and pans and other sounds of cooking could be heard through a pair of double doors. The aromas of food wafting through the doors was making my mouth water.

In a few minutes Mr. Ling came shuffling out to greet us. He stood beside our table beaming at Debbie with his wizened eyes. "Ah, Jee, I see you have a new friend. And who might this lovely young lady be?" he asked. Debbie looked slightly uncomfortable as she bore the appreciative gaze of this little old Chinese man.

"This is Debbie, Mr. Ling. She's a nurse at the hospital where I work."

Mr. Ling actually bowed to her. "Welcome lovely blossom of spring."

Debbie rolled her eyes slightly, and I could swear I saw her blush. "Thank you, it's nice to meet you."

Mr. Ling then reached out and took the menus from us. I had learned from experience that he considered it a great honor to orchestrate dinner, and he had never come close to disappointing me. But Debbie gave me a curious look, and I tried to communicate with my eyes that she should just go with it.

"Jee, you shall have my most special Moo Shu pork with fried rice. Miss Debbie, you shall have my Canton Shrimp with snow peas," Mr. Ling said.

Debbie still had that curious expression on her face. "Okaay?" she said.

Mr. Ling retreated back to the kitchen and we were alone once more. Debbie looked at me questioningly. "Does he always order for you?"

"Unless he's too busy. It's kind of his thing. Don't worry, I think you'll be pleasantly surprised."

I took a sip of tea, and as I set the cup down, I looked up and our eyes met. I had always felt slightly uncomfortable meeting someone's gaze for more than a few seconds, as if doing so would give the person a view into the depths of my soul, a look into a place that I kept reserved for myself. But suddenly I felt as if I could sit here all night gazing into her big, blue eyes.

"I have to say, I thought you'd never ask me out." She said as she looked down at the hands in her lap. "I've been watching you for months when you'd come to the ER, but you never seemed to notice me. And when I came to see you after the accident... well, I just figured you weren't interested."

"I... I, ah," she'd caught me off guard. She sat quietly, waiting for me to say something. Okay, Jay, this is where you need to not sound like an idiot. "I've noticed you too, but I figured a woman as pretty as you would already be spoken for. After you left my room that night, I asked Michael Evans if you were single. Since then I hadn't seen you until today."

It looked like I said the right thing, because she smiled, rested her elbows on the table and cradled her chin in her hands. "So, tell me something about Jay Barlow."

"What do you want to know?"

"What do you do when you're not trying to electrocute yourself?" she asked.

I wouldn't have thought it possible; framing her face in her hands made her even cuter. "I like to play guitar and sing. I used to be a musician."

"Used to be?"

"I mean I used to do it for a living before all the traveling started to burn me out. Now I just play for fun."

"Well, it's good that you're not doing it for a living anymore," she said playfully.

"Why is that?"

"My father warned me about musicians."

"What did he say?" I was enchanted.

"He said that if I ever fell for one, I'd probably fall hard," she said, still wearing that playful expression. Was she trying to tell me something?

Sukki suddenly reappeared at our table. "More tea, Jee?" she asked.

I wasn't sorry about the interruption; it gave my head a few moments to stop spinning. Sukki replaced the pot and was gone again.

I poured Debbie some more tea, and she picked up the sugar holder and added some. "So, what kind of music did you play for a living?" she asked.

"Anything but country-western or opera, although I probably stepped over the line once or twice."

She shook her head. "I can't picture you doing opera."

"Why, what has Pavarotti got that I haven't got?"

"A fifty-five-inch waist?" We laughed, and then her expression turned more serious. "Most people would give a lot to be able to play music for a living. Why did you stop?" Before I could answer the impish smile was back. "Were the groupies wearing you out?"

"You might be surprised to know just how far from the truth that is. The fact is I got tired of constantly waking up in a different place all the time. You can only wake up not knowing where you are so many times before you realize it's not worth it."

"You must have missed your family."

"My Dad left to find himself when I was five; he's still looking as far as I know." It was a subject that I would have been just as happy avoiding, but it didn't really bother me all that much anymore.

"I'm sorry," she said immediately, and I was afraid she thought she'd upset me.

"Don't worry about it. I learned to live with it a long time ago. As a precaution my Mom has sewn address labels in our clothing ever since." That earned me another smile.

"You said *our* clothing?"

"I have a sister, Jenny, who's studying marine biology in Jamaica."

"That's interesting. Is your mom there too?"

"No, she lives in Pittsburgh."

"That's nice."

"Pittsburgh? Have you been there?"

"No, I mean you must get to see her once in a while."

Her face looked genuinely warm with the thought; she wasn't just making small talk, and I wondered how she felt about her own mother. "Actually, it *is* nice. The older I get, the more I appreciate my mom and what she's had to deal with. What about your family, do you and your mom get along?"

She got a strange look on her face. "My mom died when I was a baby."

Now I felt uneasy. "I'm sorry."

She gave me a small, wry smile as she placed her hand over mine. "Don't be. It wasn't your fault; it just happened. Besides, it was a long time ago."

I turned my hand over and our fingers entwined. "Time doesn't really change the feelings. I told you I learned to live with my dad leaving a long time ago, but that doesn't mean there isn't an empty place in my heart. I guess there always will be."

"Yeah, you're right. We just keep going on, don't we?"

I thought it might be a good idea to change the subject. "So, tell me, why did you become a nurse?"

"Wow, that was an abrupt change of direction!" She sat up straighter and nearly let go of my hand, but I held on relishing the feel of it, and she settled in again and returned my grasp.

"I don't mean to be nosy; I'm just curious."

"What's the difference between nosy and curious?"

I felt myself blush a little, and her expression changed again. She put her other hand on top of both of ours. "I'm sorry, that didn't come out right. Sometimes my mouth moves faster than my brain."

"That's a feeling I know well," I told her.

She thought for a moment. "Do you want the long or short version?"

"I want to hear whatever you'd like to tell me."

"I'd like to say all the noble things about wanting to help people, but it really wasn't like that. I mean, helping people means a great deal to me now, but in the beginning, I think that I was rebelling against my father. He was an engineer, and he wanted me to be an engineer or a scientist or something like that. I suppose that I wanted to be something that was as far from his plans for me as possible."

"How did you decide on nursing?"

"I've always been interested in medicine. My mother died of leukemia, and I suppose subconsciously that had something to do with it. If I were to start over again though, I think I'd become a doctor."

"Why don't you? You're young, you still have plenty of time."

She gave me a sidelong glance. "Don't you know that dealing with effluvium and bedpans builds character?"

"I think I read that somewhere."

She gave me another of her wonderful, warm smiles. "It's been mainly a question of time and economics. If I could find the time to go back to school and still make money, I'd do it in a heartbeat."

"I thought that nurses made pretty good money. Surely, you're not paying that much in rent... " As I realized what I had just said, I felt the heat begin to come to my face again.

Debbie started laughing. "Are you kidding? A palatial estate like mine doesn't come cheap!"

"I'm sorry, I didn't mean... It's not that," I briefly paused and took a breath. "There goes *my* mouth moving faster than my brain."

"It's okay, Jay, I know what you mean and you're right. I could afford to save for school, except... "

The hesitation in her voice piqued my curiosity, and I could see that she was having trouble continuing, so I tried to lighten things up. "Oh, my God! You've accrued a massive gambling debt, and you're on the run from the mob!"

Her smile was back. "Yeah, they almost caught up with me in Albuquerque." Her expression changed again. "Actually, I'm supporting my little brother."

"He lives with you in that phone booth apartment?"

"Not hardly. He has Down Syndrome, and he lives in a community for the mentally handicapped in upstate New York."

I suddenly felt stupid. "I'm sorry, I didn't know."

"It's okay. It's a beautiful place and he's very happy, but it's not cheap."

"I thought you said your father was an engineer."

"He was a chemical engineer and a damned good one. He had at least a dozen patents to his credit, but he was naive. He went through life not seeing anything but what was on his lab table, while the company he worked for applied for and received the patents for his work. After he died last year, they didn't even acknowledge the existence of my brother and me."

"Isn't there anything you can do legally?"

"Against a team of highly-paid corporate lawyers? I tried at first; it cost me more than five thousand dollars and a whole lot of sleepless nights. You may win, or you may lose, but one thing's for sure, the lawyers always make out."

"I hear that."

We paused briefly, and then she looked at me curiously. "So, why do you do what you do? Are you answering some higher calling?"

"At the time I started, I needed a job."

"That sounds like a high calling to me. How did you get started in electronics?"

"My mom insisted that I have something other than music to fall back on. As it turns out, she was prophetic. I have always been interested in machines and electricity and electronics, so I went to trade school for it. I wound up using the electronics training a lot with music—working on amplifiers, sound systems, audio engineering, that kind of thing. Anyway, after I decided to stop playing music on the road, a friend came to me—you know Trevor—and told me the hospital was hiring technicians. I applied and, to my surprise, got the job. My mother was ecstatic that I'd finally gotten a real job. The rest is, of course, history."

"Do you ever miss being a road musician?"

"Sure, everything seems better in retrospect, but I don't miss the feeling of being unglued all the time. And there's a lot to be said for getting a steady paycheck. Besides, I haven't given it up entirely; I still play whenever I get the chance."

"I'd like to hear you."

"You will." I was sure of it.

We were interrupted by Sukki, who came to our table bearing wonton/egg drop soup and shrimp rolls. We were both hungry and dove into those, and then the food just seemed to keep coming. During the course of our meal, I think we must have sampled everything on the menu. Mr. Ling was really outdoing himself.

Debbie was also introduced to every member of the family during the meal. She seemed to relax and enjoy herself more and more as the evening went on. The Mings were going all out to make our dinner a special one, and I silently patted myself on the back for bringing her here.

At last the end of our meal had come and Mr. Ling was standing beside our table. Debbie had eaten all but a couple of snow peas, a fact that did not escape Mr. Ling's notice.

"Miss Debbie does not like my snow peas?"

"Honestly, Mr. Ling, they're delicious, but I couldn't eat another bite."

"You should eat snow peas, Miss, they beddy beddy good for you."

Debbie rolled her eyes at me, then grudgingly picked up a snow pea with her fork and put it in her mouth. Mr. Ling nodded to her slightly, then turned and retreated to his kitchen.

When she looked at me again, I was wagging a finger at her. "You should eat snow peas, Miss, they beddy beddy good for you."

With one hand she covered her mouth with her napkin, the other hand she held up with the back to me and raised her middle finger. I laughed and got up to go pay the check.

Back in the car she turned her head toward me. "I don't think I've ever felt so stuffed in my life."

"I take it you liked the House of Ming?"

"It was wonderful; a Chinese food junkie's dream. Thank you for bringing me."

"You're welcome. Now that we've eaten, would you like to take a walk?" It was something I had been thinking about.

"That sounds like a very good idea. Where would you like to go to walk?"

"I have a special place I like to go when I want to think and feel close to nature. I've never taken anyone else there."

"I feel honored, I think. Where is this place?"

"Oh, no, I'm not telling. You'll just have to trust me."

"Mr. Mystery. Okay, I guess I can trust you."

We drove down back roads through moonlit countryside for what seemed like miles. The evening air was warm, and I felt very much at peace with this woman.

We came to a small wooden bridge that spanned a stream. I drove over the bridge and pulled into a small parking area that was surfaced with gravel, and stopped the car facing the riverbank. There were only two other cars in the parking lot, but they were a distance from us, which couldn't have been more perfect. Debbie just sat there for a few moments, looking puzzled.

"Where in the world are we?" she finally asked.

"I told you, it's a special place. I like to come here and walk and think."

"Is thinking what you have in mind?"

I couldn't help but smile. "Sort of."

"Uh, oh. You would tell me if you were a secret axe murderer, wouldn't you?"

"Of course, I'd tell you. Come on, I promise to behave."

We got out of the car and stood looking around. The moon was full and cast ample light to be able to see clearly. The small river the bridge spanned moved by us with a quiet rush, while pine and oak trees stood solemnly all around. I went around to her side of the car and took her by the hand, leading her down the trail that followed the river.

We walked for a while without speaking. I was content to walk and enjoy the night air in her company. I hoped she felt the same. After a while we stopped, and she turned to face me.

"So, why did you really bring me here if you never bring anybody here?"

"I'm not totally sure; I just wanted to."

"Why haven't you brought anyone here before?"

"I never trusted anyone enough to share this place."

"You trust me?"

I nodded my head, took her hand, and we walked on.

"You're a strange man, Jay Barlow."

I felt she needed an answer to the question I thought she was trying to ask. So, I stopped us again and turned to face her.

"I'm afraid." There, I had said it.

"Afraid of what?" There was surprise in her voice.

"I'm afraid of you."

"Why in the world would you be afraid of me?"

"I like you." She looked puzzled again. "You see, I was too young to remember when my parents split up. I can't help thinking there must have been something missing. Did they like each other? Were they ever in love? And what the hell does that mean?"

"Haven't you ever been in love?" she asked.

I thought about it briefly. "When I was in ninth grade, I had an English teacher I was in love with. She was the most sophisticated lady I had ever seen."

"That's not what I mean."

"I know it's not. No, I don't think that I ever have. Not really. I've had a couple of relationships, but as soon as I tried to get too close, they were over, and I was left standing there, scratching my head and wondering what I did wrong. How about you? Have you ever been in love?"

"Yes. Once I was in love," she said flatly.

Her answer surprised me for some reason. "What happened?" I asked, softly.

"He turned out to be an asshole." She said abruptly.

It was clear she didn't want to discuss the matter further. So, we turned and headed back to the car. When we reached her side of the car, she turned to me.

"So, you like me." It was not a question.

I nodded and started to open the door when she pulled me to her and kissed me. I wrapped my arms around her and kissed her back. She stepped back and looked at me. A minute passed. Then Debbie spoke first.

"It's getting late. I think we'd better head home, we both have to get up in the morning for work."

My head was still spinning. "Yeah, I guess you're right."

When we were in the car, I couldn't help myself. I leaned toward her and our lips met again. No resistance, no comment, just warm and eager acceptance.

She held my head in her hands and pulled back sounding breathless. "This can't go any farther, not yet... come on, let's go."

I smiled and kissed her nose. "Yes, ma'am.

I sat up in my seat, reached down and turned the key, and ...nothing. The engine didn't even click. I looked briefly at Debbie and smiled. "Just a glitch," I said and turned the key again. Nothing. "Shit," I said more emphatically. I pumped the gas even though I knew it wouldn't help and tried the key again. Still nothing.

"Stay here," I said to Debbie and opened the door and got out. I walked around to the front of the car, which was no easy task because the ground sloped down toward the river. I used the car for support and made my way to the hood latch. I flicked it to the side and opened the hood. Unfortunately, the arm that supported the hood was on the passenger side of the car. I rested the hood down and walked around the car. Debbie had wound down her window and spoke as I passed her on my way to the front of the car.

"Is there anything I can do?"

"No. I'm just going to check things out. Maybe I can figure out the problem." The full moon cast considerable light, but as I looked in the engine compartment, I realized it was too dark to see much detail. "Well, maybe you can," I said to her. "There's a flashlight in the glove compartment. Can you get it for me?"

She opened the glove box and rummaged through papers and stuff and found the flashlight. I walked back to her window and took it from her. It wasn't the greatest flashlight, but it would have to do for now. Note to self—get new flashlight. I opened the hood and secured it with the arm and turned on the flashlight, perusing the engine compartment. I looked around and checked the obvious—battery terminals, connections to alternator and starter. I knew the gas tank was full when I left home. There had to be a loose wire or line somewhere. I started to walk around the car to check the other side of the engine, when I banged my knee on the bumper. The car rocked slightly and seemed to move forward an inch.

Just then, Debbie opened the door and flew out of the car right into me and we both went sprawling on the grass. The flashlight fell from my hand and rolled down the bank.

"I'm so sorry," Debbie said as we picked ourselves up. "I thought the car was rolling down the hill and didn't want to be in it."

"That's okay," I said. "The car is fine. There are some rocks along the edge of the lot, so they should hold it if it moves any more.

We brushed ourselves off and Debbie started walking to the bank. "I'll get the flashlight," she said, and started gingerly stepping down the bank to where the flashlight lay in some reeds.

"Okay," I said. "I'm going to check the other side of the engine. I didn't see anything on this side." I started walking around the car. Just then, the car gave a lurch forward. I ran to the front of the car and saw one of the rocks had given way. I looked down at Debbie. She had retrieved the flashlight but was walking up the bank in front of the car.

"Debbie!" I called frantically. She looked up and saw the front of the car lurch again as it leaned down toward the river. She quickly moved to the left out of its path, watching the car and not where she was walking. She promptly tripped over a rock that threw her onto her side, and I helplessly watched as she started rolling down the bank toward the river. I immediately jumped into the driver's seat and pressed my foot on the brake. My foot went right to the floor. No brakes. My inner technician realized that something must have flown up from the road and severed brake and electrical lines. But the more pressing problem was Debbie rolling closer to the river.

I jumped out of the car, leaving the door open and started running down the bank, waving my arms and shouting her name over and over. I watched in horror as she rolled into the river. The swift current began to quickly carry her downstream. I panicked and ran faster, slipping on the wet, muddy bank and landing on my ass. I quickly got to my feet and continued shouting. The noise and commotion had attracted the attention of the other people in the park, and I saw several people running toward us.

Debbie managed to keep her head above water and tried to grab branches along the river's edge. She finally found one and grabbed it. I could hear the car coming behind me, so I tried to swerve out of the way. Suddenly something slammed into me and I fell onto the bank face down, my head almost touching the water, and watched helplessly as my car plunged headfirst into the river while Debbie hung on to a tree branch several yards away. The wind had been knocked out of me, so by the time I got to my hands and knees, someone else had reached Debbie and was helping her out of the river.

The river wasn't deep here, so Debbie managed to get to her feet and slip and slide up the bank hanging onto the hand of a stranger. My car was on an incline—the front in the water and the rear on the side of the bank. I got up and hurried over to Debbie. She was covered with mud and soaked through. She did not look happy.

"Are you all right?" I asked as I reached her. She stood on the bank, dripping. "Just great," she said, sounding none too pleased.

"Thank you," I said to the man standing next to her. "Thank you so much."

"Bill Best," he said putting out his hand.

I wiped my muddy hand on my pants and shook it. "Jay Barlow," I said. "I'm so glad you were here."

"Listen," Bill said. "I have a cell phone. I can call for help."

"That would be wonderful," I said.

Debbie hadn't said another word. I took her arm and led her the rest of the way up the bank. "I think I may have a towel or something in the trunk." I led her to the back of the car, keeping as far away from the edge of the bank as possible, and opened the trunk. There was no towel, but I did find my gym bag. I opened it, praying it wasn't rank and was pleasantly surprised when it wasn't. I pulled out a sweatshirt that had seen better days and handed it to her. She looked at the sweatshirt that was full of holes and stains and then looked at the car.

"I should have stayed in it," she said flatly. I looked at the car again too. Although the engine was in the river, the front seat looked more or less dry. I noticed the driver's door still open and guessed that was what had slammed into my back.

Debbie had started toweling her hair when Bill came jogging back to us with his cell phone in his hand. "I just called 911, so we should have some help soon. Can I do anything else?"

I shook my head. "No, you've helped enough already. Thanks again, Bill. We'll be fine once the tow truck gets here." I turned my attention back to Debbie as Bill walked back to his friends.

Debbie was shaking water out of her clothes. "Guess I should freshen up for company," was delivered in the same sarcastic tone. I wanted to help her but didn't know what to do. So, I stood there helplessly, relieved when we started hearing sirens coming our way.

"That sounds like a fire truck," I said surprised. Just then a parade of vehicles turned into the parking lot, with a police cruiser in the lead. It was followed by a fire truck and ambulance. It looked like hundreds of lights flashing everywhere. "What's the fire truck going to do?" I asked stupidly to no one. The only vehicle that hadn't shown up was a tow truck, the one we could have used the most.

A cop exited the patrol car and walked slowly over to us. Either he surmised that no one had been seriously hurt, or he had already decided we were too dumb to deserve quick action.

"This looks like an interesting story," he said, as he pulled out a notebook and pen. Great, we had a cop with a sense of humor. Just what you need in an emergency.

As I explained the incident to the cop, who periodically jotted down notes, I saw one of the ambulance guys had approached Debbie and she followed him back to the ambulance.

I interrupted my story, saying, "Shouldn't we be getting a tow truck?"

"Already called it in," the cop said flatly. The EMT walked up to the cop and he turned away and they had a brief conversation I couldn't hear. The cop nodded and the EMT walked back to the ambulance and got into the passenger side. The ambulance turned off its lights and headed out of the parking lot. The fire truck followed. Debbie had obviously turned down their offer for medical help; she was still standing in the parking lot, now with a blanket wrapped around her. She looked so pathetic it made my heart ache.

"Anything else to add?" the cop asked me. I shook my head, watching Debbie, who was watching us with no discernable expression. "I'm going to talk to the young lady now," the cop said and walked over to Debbie. I assumed he was going to ask her the same questions to see if our stories jived.

Just then, the tow truck arrived. The driver got out of the truck and came over and perused the car for a few minutes and started to laugh.

"This is a good one," he said with mirth. "I've seen worse, but this one won't be fun. Looks like we've got wet ground and mud to deal with." I nodded in agreement, not knowing what else I could usefully add.

I stayed with the tow truck driver and my car, as it was hooked up to the truck in preparation to pull it out of the water. Debbie was still talking to the cop and I saw her nod to him.

The cop walked back to me. "I think I have everything. You'll get the report in a day or two. I'm taking the lady home before she freezes to death."

"Okay," I said helplessly, looking over at Debbie who was climbing into the police cruiser. My last view of her was sitting in the back of a cop car as it pulled out of the parking lot. With the blanket wrapped around her, she looked like a criminal. She turned to look at me with a weak smile, as I waved. I looked up at my waving hand and quickly brought it down feeling foolish. Somehow waving my hand seemed to be a stupid way to send her off in a police car.

As the tow truck engine whined and the winch cranked, my car was pulled slowly out of the river. It moved steadily backwards for a foot or two and then stopped, as if in protest. There seemed to be a momentary battle as my car seemed to refuse the effort to dislodge it. Finally, with a pronounced sucking sound accompanied by the smell of a swamp, it was pulled free and up the bank. It was clear the car was totaled. The whole front was mashed in and covered in weeds and mud.

"I'm thinking the junk yard is the most painless ending for 'er," the driver told me. "But if you have somewhere else you want me to take 'er, just say the word."

"No, I agree," I said, sadly looking at what was left of my car.

"Want a ride there?" he asked, as if I had so many choices for a ride here. I nodded my head and hopped into the passenger side. This was not the way I had hoped this night would end.

It took about twenty minutes for us to arrive at the salvage company. The driver directed me to the office where I could find a phone and told me he'd be along with the paperwork shortly. I thanked him as I wondered what kind of paperwork he was referring to. A death certificate for my car, no doubt.

I sat in the office staring at the phone for a few minutes thinking, and I was struck with the realization that I didn't have any friends that didn't work at the hospital. I knew one person who was likely to be home and would be glad to help me. With a heavy heart and an even heavier hand, I picked up the receiver and dialed.

"Hello, is Dan there?"

The next day I walked into the shop feeling like I had lead weights hung around my neck. Besides the aches and pains from the various physical insults from the night before, there was the emotional toll. I couldn't believe my luck. To get a dream date with a girl I really liked, to spend such a perfectly romantic evening, only to have my car attack us at its conclusion. I felt like an idiot. A couple weeks before she had seen me after I nearly killed myself on the job, and last night I could have killed us both with my car. Life sucked; there was no other term for it. Why would she want to spend time with such a loser? I wouldn't blame her if she refused to speak to me again.

Jimmy from maintenance didn't live too far from me, and he was kind enough to agree to give me a ride to and from work until I could get another car. I intended to go shopping for one as soon as possible since I was stranded, for all intents and purposes, until I did. To my great relief, he only asked a few basic questions about my accident and we spent the commute talking about work and sports. Or rather, he talked about sports and I nodded when appropriate since I wasn't a big sports fan.

The shop was empty except for Papa Joe who sat at his bench space peering through his large, lighted magnifier at a printed circuit board. Cloaked in self-pity, I mumbled "Morning," as I passed by him.

He looked up from what he was doing. "Good morning, Jay. It sounds like you had quite an evening last night."

I grunted something or other and proceeded to my own spot. There, sitting on my bench, was a child's diving mask with a snorkel attached and a sign reading, 'To help you find your car in the parking lot'. I sat down and buried my head in my hands.

In a few moments I felt a hand on my shoulder and looked up to see Joe standing there. "You want to talk about it?" he asked me.

I sat up and looked into the old man's eyes. "Papa, I met a girl that I really like, and now she thinks I'm a fool."

"Did she say that?"

"No, but she must. I think I'm a fool."

"There's a big difference there, Jay. Just because you think you're a fool doesn't mean she does. If you don't go and talk to her about it, then maybe you're a fool."

"I started to get to know her after I had knocked myself out with a defib. Then on our first date my car rolled into a river and could have killed us both. Do you think she's going to want to see me again?"

Joe made a clucking sound with his tongue and sat down on the stool next to me facing me. "Listen, Jay, don't ever imagine you know what's in a woman's mind before she tells you. Trust me, you don't. No matter how much you think you do."

"I'd like to believe that's true, Joe, but I just don't know."

Joe looked at me for a moment, and then made a barely audible sigh. "Okay, my young friend. At the risk of sounding like something right out of an old movie, I'm going to tell you a story."

"Uh oh. This story doesn't have anything to do with Mrs. Travello by any chance, does it?"

Joe shook his head and smiled. "It does, and I swear to God it's true. When I met Lillian I was smitten, I was head over heels. In those days, where we lived, it was customary for a suitor to meet the family before escorting a young woman on a date."

"Chaperoned, of course," I said.

He gave me a wink as he patted my arm. "We weren't *that* backward, boy. Anyway, I wanted desperately to make a good first impression. I took about two weeks' worth of my salary and bought a new suit, and I made reservations at the fanciest restaurant in town." His eyes were suddenly alight and glowing with the memory, and as bad as I felt, I couldn't help being drawn into his story.

"You were going to show her a good time."

"That was the idea, but on the way to her house across town my car had a little problem that altered my plans."

"Flat tire?"

"Not quite. The whole left front wheel fell off."

"What?! How did that happen?"

"The center nut somehow unscrewed from the spindle, the bearings fell out, and that was it. I was riding down the street anticipating my date one moment and the next BANG! The left front of the car dipped down to the asphalt, and my wheel went rolling down the street ahead of me."

"What did you do?"

"I chased the wheel down and I put it back on. The thing was, by the time I had hunted the parts down and wrestled the wheel back into place, I was covered with mud and grease from head to toe."

"All over your new suit."

"I didn't have any choice," he shook his head. "I was already quite late. There was no time to go back and change, so I just went on. I showed up at the house of the woman I so wanted to impress looking like a bum. I was covered with dirt and grime, and one sleeve of my jacket was half ripped off."

"What did she do?"

"She introduced me to her parents, who didn't seem to be too favorably impressed with me, and then we went to dinner."

"At the fancy restaurant?"

"No, I doubted they'd let me in the front door looking the way I did. We got a couple of hot dogs from a street vendor and ate them on a park bench. I was sure she would have nothing more to do with me after that, but after forty years of marriage, three kids, and five grand-kids, I guess she proved me wrong."

Dan had told me that Joe's wife had died of cancer. "How long has she been gone?" I asked him gently.

"Three years in April. There isn't a day that goes by when I don't think about her and miss her. After all these years, I still don't really know what she saw in me, but I'm damn glad she saw whatever it was." He paused and sighed again, taking in a breath before he looked at me once more. "If you've found your special lady, Jay, don't worry about a little dirt and grease or anything else. Just be yourself. After all, that must be what she likes. And hold onto her for as long as you can."

I didn't know what else to say to him. Everything that came to mind seemed stupid and trivial. He had shared something with me that meant a great deal to him in the interest of cheering me up, and I was touched. I appreciated what he had tried to do, and I did feel a little better. Then the rest of the guys came into the shop.

Bobby sauntered over to his bench and sat down, then he turned and faced me. "Hey, Jay, you gonna ask her out again? Next time, why don't you take her to Sea World? Or maybe one of those water parks where you don't have to actually park your car in the water."

I endured several more examples of sparkling wit. I could see Papa Joe shake his head sadly and bury himself back in his work.

Trevor made his way over and sat on the stool next to me. "We have PMs to do. You want to get out of here?"

"Good idea. I don't mind if I do." We grabbed a cart and left.

"Thanks for getting me out of there, Trev. I really didn't want to hear any more about my date," I told him as we pushed our cart down the hall.

"I could tell, Jay. I only heard your car wound up in a river. What happened?"

"I'm a moron. That's what happened. I got a date with Debbie Farrell and I blew it."

"Accidents happen. I'm sure you're being too hard on yourself. Why don't you take a few minutes this afternoon and go talk to her?"

I stopped the cart in the middle of the hall and looked at Trevor intently. "Have you ever watched your date roll down a river bank and into the water while your car was bearing down on her like a taxi from a horror movie with no one driving?"

He looked at me like he wasn't entirely sure whether or not I was putting him on. "I can't say as I have. That must be quite a story."

"It is, and I'll tell it to you later, but right now I'm tired of thinking about it. So, where do you want to do PMs?"

"The pathology lab is right here; let's start with that."

"Trevor, you do remember that the pathology lab is adjacent to the morgue?"

"What's wrong with the morgue? At least the patients are quiet."

"True. Okay, the pathology lab it is."

As soon as we entered the path lab, Trevor stopped so abruptly that I ran into the back of him with the cart, though he seemed not to notice. Candy Richards was working at a microtome on a table across the room.

"So, this is why you wanted to PM the path lab," I said to him quietly.

Candy was a tall, leggy, blue-eyed blonde, almost a stereotypical Nordic beauty, except for the fact that she had a strong Bronx accent. I knew for all his talk about not wanting to become involved with anyone from the hospital, Trevor was totally smitten with Candy. Whenever we were working together and she happened to be nearby, he got a goofy schoolboy look on his face and started stammering every time he tried to talk to her. Fortunately for Trevor, no one else seemed to have noticed his infatuation.

As fate and biology would have it, Candy didn't seem to be at all interested in Trevor. Most of the women in the hospital seemed thrilled when Trevor talked to them and would get all gooey-eyed when he was in the room. But Candy seemed as if she couldn't care less, which of course seemed to fuel Trevor's ardor all the more. As was Trevor's way, he tried to act as nonchalant about it as possible, but I knew him well enough to know that the situation was eating at him.

We were still standing by the door when Candy got up and walked toward us. She smiled politely and said, "Excuse me," as she moved toward the door. Just before she left, she turned back and announced to one of the other lab techs that she was going to the file room and then to the morgue to prepare for an autopsy.

Out of the corner of my eye I watched Trevor longingly watch her go, and as she did, he let out an audible sigh.

"She's something, isn't she?" I prodded, keeping my voice to just above a whisper so that no one else heard.

"Oh man, that just boggles my imagination."

I pulled at my shirt collar with one finger. "Yeah, I think the temperature in here just rose by ten or fifteen degrees."

He looked at me and grinned, but his smile quickly faded. "Jay, I don't know what to say to her."

"I've noticed she makes you a little tongue-tied."

"Yes, but I mean it's like she won't give me a break. At all."

"What have you tried saying?"

"Just hi, how're you doing? Nice weather we're having. It doesn't seem to matter what I say; she just gives me the cold shoulder."

"Maybe you just haven't used the right approach yet."

"Like what? Hi, you're the sexiest woman I've ever seen, would you be interested in bearing my children?"

"Maybe you just haven't presented yourself as being the kind of man that interests her."

Trevor shook his head and sighed once again. "If I could only figure out what kind of man that is... I could adjust."

"Find out what her interests are, if you have anything in common."

Suddenly I saw a gleam come into Trevor's eyes, and he grabbed my arm and practically dragged me through the room. I was somewhat apprehensive, being fully aware of the powerful effect that rampant hormones can have on the male psyche. The usually reserved Trevor was wearing a somewhat demonic look as I and our cart were swept along.

"I don't like the look on your face, Trevor. What have you got in mind?"

"Come on, Jay. I haven't had any luck with conventional methods. I think it's time to try something more... dramatic."

"I definitely don't like the sound of that."

"You're not thinking of deserting your old buddy in his time of need, are you?"

"That depends on what you're planning to do."

"Just a little substitution, that's all."

I didn't know what he had in mind, but I had the distinct feeling that it was going to mean trouble. "What kind of substitution?"

"Come on. I'll show you."

We went out the back door, which led to a short hall leading to the morgue. As we got closer to the morgue my apprehension continued to grow. "Trevor, what the hell are you planning?"

"Just follow me, oh faithless one."

He peeked around the corner, and seeing the coast was clear, quickly pushed the cart into a storage closet and pulled me into the morgue. Though it was innocuous enough, the morgue always had a vague underlying smell of formaldehyde that seemed to permeate everything in it, and it seemed a strange place for whatever overture Trevor had in mind.

We walked through the morgue with its rows of refrigerated body storage units to one of the three autopsy rooms, which seemed to be the only one prepped for use. In the middle of the room was a stainless-steel table with drainage gutters on all sides. On the table was a black body bag with a tag on it that stated simply 'Johnson, Robert'.

There was a gurney next to one of the cinder block walls, and Trevor wheeled this next to the table. "Come on. Give me a hand, will you?" he asked.

I was standing completely still, stunned, not believing what he was doing. "Trevor, you have lost your mind!"

He was struggling with the body, which was quite large, trying to move it onto the gurney. He stopped for a moment and looked at me earnestly. "Look, Jay. I've tried almost everything. Maybe if I hit her where she lives, she'll pay attention."

"And maybe she'll have you arrested."

"For what?"

"I don't know. Isn't there some law against disturbing a corpse?"

"Who are we disturbing? I really don't think he's going to mind a great deal. Now will you please give me a hand?"

I was convinced that my friend was going off his rocker, but I guessed that was what love was all about. I took a deep breath and moved to the opposite end of the bag. We both heaved, and the body slid over onto the gurney.

"Now what?" I asked.

Trevor looked quickly around. "Where can we hide him?"

"Hide him?"

"Yes, hide him."

"Why don't we just wheel him out into the hall and tell everyone he's just waiting for a downtown bus?"

"Come on, Jay. Get serious."

I shook my head. "Get serious? You've got to be kidding?!"

There was a small holding area through a pair of double doors at the back of the room. At the back of this was a second set of double doors that led to the outside to provide the morticians easy access. We wheeled the body into the holding area, and Trevor started going through drawers in the autopsy room.

"What are you doing?"

"I'm looking for a body bag."

I guessed I had experienced a lapse in my thinking, because up until now I hadn't realized what he had in mind.

"You've got to be kidding?!"

"I wish you'd stop saying that. Do I look like I'm kidding?"

I had to admit he had a very determined look on his face as he rooted through cabinet after cabinet. I shrugged and started looking through the cabinet closest to me.

"Eureka!" I looked up to see Trevor triumphantly holding up a black body bag as if he'd just discovered a pot of gold. "Help me get into this thing, will you?"

"I don't believe I'm doing this," I said as I held the bag open for him on the autopsy table.

"Doing what?" he asked. "I'm the one who's going to be in the bag."

We got him into the bag, and I zipped it up leaving a small open space at the top so he could breathe. Once he was situated on the table, I joined Mr. Johnson in the holding area. I discovered a small crack where the doors came together which allowed me a good view of the autopsy room. I suddenly realized that, as weird as this was, I was looking forward to seeing what Candy's reaction would be.

I didn't have long to wait. She came into the autopsy room and began retrieving and assembling the various instruments the pathologist would need. When she had done that, she picked up a chart and spoke in an accent that was pure New York. "Robbit Jawnsen. Well Mr. Jawnsen, let's see what we cun do for you."

She reached up and pulled the zipper halfway down, at which point Trevor sat up abruptly. "How about a date?!"

I hadn't realized a person could go into a dead faint so quickly. It was as if someone had just switched off a light. She was standing there one moment, and the next moment she was falling to the floor. I leapt from my hiding place in the hope of catching her before she hit the concrete, and as I did my foot knocked over a heavy exam light. The light fell against the gurney on which Mr. Johnson lay, which slammed into the outer doors, which popped open with a loud bang.

Trevor was still sitting on the autopsy table with his lower half in the body bag, and we watched in fascinated horror as the real Mr. Johnson rolled down the ramp and across the rear parking lot in search of adventure.

Trevor summed up our feelings perfectly with two words. "Holy shit!"

He scrambled the rest of the way out of the bag, and the two of us went tearing across the parking lot in hot pursuit, leaving poor Candy forgotten on the floor. We were catching up to the gurney, closing the distance rapidly, when a car came out of a side lane moving pretty fast. There was a squeal of brakes as the driver suddenly saw the gurney and made a desperate attempt to avoid hitting it.

He almost succeeded, but the right front bumper grazed the gurney and sent it in a whole new direction, which happened to be toward a deep gully with angled concrete sides at the edge of the parking lot. At the bottom of the gully was a drainage ditch which was, unfortunately at the moment, full of water from recent heavy rainfall.

I don't believe I had ever run so fast in my life. I was up on my toes, sprinting and wind milling my arms to maintain balance. In my peripheral vision I could see that Trevor was doing the same thing.

We were almost there, reaching out, stretching forward, our fingers only inches from the gurney. Somewhere in the back of my mind it occurred to me what we must have looked like to anyone in a position to watch—two men desperately trying to chase down a runaway corpse in a body bag, like something out of a Charlie Chaplin movie.

We had almost reached him when the gurney came in contact with the curb and abruptly stopped. Unfortunately, Mr. Johnson obeyed the laws of gravity and didn't stop, but went rolling down the side of the ditch and into the water. The air in the bag caused it to be buoyant, and the breeze caused a current. We stood there for several seconds, staring unbelievably as Mr. Johnson bobbed to the surface and began floating downstream as if he were being borne on the river Styx straight to hell. I had an immediate flashback to Debbie on our date.

Trevor had jumped to the other side of the ditch, and the two of us were running along on either side of Mr. Johnson trying to encourage him to pull over to one side or the other. As I looked up, I could see we were almost to the stream the ditch emptied into. If Mr. Johnson got to the stream, he would be floating along a body of water that was at least a dozen yards across as opposed to several feet.

Panic was setting in. We knew that we were already in deep trouble. If the body got to that stream and got away from us, we were probably going to jail.

Trevor kept jumping back and forth across the ditch. He even ran into me a few times, so I started running partially up the bank every time he jumped back in my direction like a sandpiper avoiding the waves on the beach. We kept shouting instructions to each other that didn't make much sense, but it didn't matter because neither one of us was listening to the other anyway.

We ran like that for what seemed like an awfully long time, babbling incoherently at each other while Trevor jumped back and forth, and I ran up and down. We were about a yard away from the stream when Mr. Johnson got caught on a tree limb, and we scrambled to drag him out of the ditch and up the bank.

Trevor went to retrieve the gurney, while I stayed with Mr. Johnson to be sure that he didn't try to get away again, though at this point I suspected he must have been winded. I knew I was. Trevor returned, and with considerable effort we got Mr. Johnson back onto the gurney and began wheeling him back whence he came.

The driver of the car that had redirected Mr. Johnson's attempted flight to freedom was standing by his driver's door with a very curious expression on his face. As we came abreast of him, Trevor looked at him with an apologetic shrug. "He keeps trying to leave the hospital against medical advice by sneaking out the back door."

"Uh huh." Seemed to be all the guy could manage to say.

"Trevor, I can't believe we did this." I said. "What if Candy's awake when we get back?"

"We'll tell her we took him out for some fresh air."

"Great. Wonderful idea."

When we got back to the morgue, Candy was still out cold. We put Mr. Johnson back where he belonged, and I quickly brushed off his bag and put the bag that Trevor had used back in the drawer where he had found it. Trevor went to a sink and dampened a cloth which he applied to Candy's forehead.

Soon she began to come around, and Trevor helped her to sit up. "Ohhh, muy head hurts. What happened?"

"We heard a crash and came in here to find you on the floor. Are you all right?" Trevor asked as he sponged her forehead with the cloth.

"I... I think so." Trevor helped her slowly to her feet. She stood shakily trying to regain her bearings. She looked down and seemed to focus intently on the body bag. I looked at it and realized to my chagrin that I hadn't gotten it cleaned off quite as well as I had intended.

"Why is Mr. Jawnsen covaad with sand?" Candy asked.

Trevor looked up. "It must be dust falling from the ceiling tiles. We've been doing repair work on some of the cables up there."

She seemed to accept this explanation, at least for the moment. She moved to a corner of the room where there was a chair and sat down, still looking a bit unsteady.

Trevor went over and knelt beside her. "Are you sure you're okay?" he asked.

"Yeah, I think I'm okay. I just need to sit heaa for a minute." She sat another few moments, then she looked toward the autopsy table and back at Trevor. "Say, you didn't notice anything odd about that bag, did you?"

"No... no. Nothing odd." Trevor shook his head and looked at me, and I shook my head as well.

"I mean..." She shook her head gently as if trying to clear it. "Oh, never mind."

I looked at the table and realized that there was a puddle slowly forming beneath it on the floor.

"Maybe I should come back and check on you in a little while." Trevor was not wasting any time or opportunity.

"No, really... I'll be all right," Candy assured him.

"But you never know with these things," Trevor continued. "Maybe I should come by your place tonight and see how you're doing." Oh brother, here we go, I thought.

"That really won't be necessary," Candy told him a little more forcefully.

"It's no trouble, really, I don't mind."

"Thanks, but no, that won't be necessary," she insisted, seeming to get herself back together.

Trevor seemed to be thinking about what tack to take next when the senior pathologist walked in, ready to begin the autopsy. He said nothing, but just gazed at us with a curious expression.

"Uh, we'll catch up with you later," I said to Candy. Trevor seemed to have lost his voice. "Let's go, Trev." I grabbed his arm and ushered him out of the morgue. We retrieved our cart and cut quickly back through the pathology lab. Neither of us spoke.

Trevor and I had just finished checking out a telemetry system in the cardiac care unit after lunch, when we saw Dan and Will Stanski down the hall. Will was up on a stepladder with his head poking through the suspended ceiling where he had removed one of the ceiling tiles. Dan was standing next to the ladder, handing Will tools when he asked for them.

Dan's expression was stern, and I felt a lump in my throat wondering if our little escapade with Mr. Johnson had been discovered already. My accident the night before was still very much on my mind, but at least I'd been distracted from it.

"Where have you two been? I've been looking for you." His voice was uncharacteristically short and somewhat angry.

"Fishing?" Trevor said hesitantly.

"What's wrong, Dan?" I asked.

Dan threw his hand up toward the ceiling. "The goddamned nurse call system is fucked up again! Whoever wired this thing didn't know his ass from his granddaddy's corn pipe!" Inwardly I breathed a sigh of relief. Dan didn't know about our race with the corpse.

I looked at Trevor and saw his shoulders relax. He was so relieved he sounded positively upbeat. "Is there anything we can do to help?" Trevor asked and Dan glared at him.

"Not unless you can tell me why the call light comes on in the hall but not at the goddamned nurses' station!" I started to ask if they had checked the bulbs in the nurses' station call lights but thought better of it. Trevor looked at me and rolled his eyes. It was time for us to remain silent and tread lightly. "Can you see anything, Will?" Dan asked.

The ceiling hid most of Will's upper body, and his voice sounded muffled, as if he were shouting from the next room. "Well, I've got a gold wire here that doesn't look like it belongs, but I can't tell where it's going. It seems to disappear into the plenum abruptly. Is there anything mounted on the wall down there?"

The three of us looked and saw nothing but a little box painted the same color as the wall with a button recessed in it. It didn't look like any of the normal switches that could be found throughout the rest of the hospital.

"There's some little box with a switch mounted in it. I'll be damned if I know what it's for," Dan said, calling up to Will. I was surprised. I didn't think there was anything in the hospital that Dan didn't know about.

Will seemed to be straining to reach farther up into the plenum to the point I was afraid he was in danger of falling off the ladder. "Well, ask somebody what it's for, will you?" His voice was even more muffled.

I could see that Dan was becoming more frustrated by the moment. "You want to know what it's for? I'll find out what it's for!" He reached over and pushed the button. With that, blue lights on the walls on both sides of the hall began flashing. An electronic gong began sounding, not overly loud but urgently, and the recorded woman's voice that was used for fire drills came over the p.a. system saying, "Code blue, cardiac care unit step-down... code blue, cardiac care unit step-down."

I looked at Dan. I had seen him in all kinds of situations, but I had never seen that same look on his face before. It was a mixture of the apprehension on the face of the child that gets caught with his hand in the proverbial cookie jar and the excitement on the face of the same child who knows that he had better come up with a good excuse, real fast.

A nurse came running down the hall, and when I say running, I don't mean that she was walking fast or that she was jogging; she was moving at full tilt, head-on ramming speed. She was possibly five feet tall and tiny, but when she came upon six-foot, two inch, one hundred ninety-pound Trevor standing in the doorway of the nearest room, she practically bowled him over.

She ran into the room, and half a second later stuck her head back out. "Where's the patient?! Where's the code blue?!" I would never have believed such a tiny person could have such a powerful, commanding voice.

Hurrying up the hall behind her were a half a dozen nurses and other medical personnel pushing a crash-cart with a defibrillator on top. It rode before them like some sort of figurehead, a standard, preceding an army about to march onto a battlefield.

Dan never missed a beat or batted an eyelash. He reached out and pressed the button again, and the alarm stopped. Then he put his arm lightly around the nurse's shoulders and asked in the sincerest voice I had ever heard him use. "Please, for our records, what is your name?"

She was totally confused now, and wore an indignant expression as if to ask what in the hell is going on? But instead she looked into his warm, green, soulful eyes and answered, "Kelly... Pat Kelly."

Dan continued, "Well, Nurse Kelly, that was excellent response time." He looked at Trevor and indicated the clipboard on our cart. "Make a note, Trevor. Nurse Kelly, excellent code blue response time."

Trevor quickly picked up the clipboard and pretended to write. I looked up and could see Will trying not to laugh. Nurse Kelly couldn't see his upper body at all, but I could. His shoulders were shaking up and down and he had a hand clamped over his mouth.

Dan was now walking her back down the hall with his arm still around her shoulders. "We in the biomedical department must check alarm response times every six months, Nurse Kelly."

"But why haven't I heard about it before?" she asked, still sounding confused

"New directive, just handed down from the J.C.A.H.O. Your time was the fastest we have seen so far." He wasn't lying about that. I wondered as he walked her up the hall if she was really buying it. We could still hear him thirty feet away. "Yes ma'am, this is sure gonna look good on your record!"

Trevor looked at me. "I can't believe this. Do you really think she's falling for it?"

"Time will tell, Trev, time will tell."

Dan gave nurse Kelly a fatherly pat on the shoulder, and then turned back toward us. His expression rapidly changed from one of compliment to one of anger with each step that he took.

"You," he pointed to Trevor. "Go down to maintenance and tell Dorfly to get his ass up here. You," he pointed to me. "Find Orville and start pulling that cable." I hurried off, relieved that I wasn't the one who had to fetch Dorfly.

I found Orville in the electrician's shop. Fortunately, it seemed I had managed to miss Trevor and Dorfly. Orville Coleman was the hospital's senior electrician, and though he was technically a member of the maintenance department, the jobs he performed often tied in with things under the jurisdiction of the biomed department, so we often worked together.

When I got there, he was sorting big rolls of cable. Orville was very tall, at least six-foot five or six, with a lean and lanky build, easy-going disposition, and long hair pulled back in a ponytail. My first impression had been that he looked like a leftover from the sixties, but as I got to know him, I came to believe that Orville was the kind of person that would have fit into any time or place.

As soon as he saw me, he gave me a big smile. "Hey, Jay! Give me a hand loading these on that cart, will you?"

"Sure, Orville. I see you already got the word about the cable."

"Yeah, Will Stanski called me from upstairs." We set about loading the rolls of cable onto a cart that was sitting in a corner of the shop. We were nearly finished when Kelley, another one of the maintenance guys, walked in.

"Hey, Jay," he said to me.

"Hey, Kelley."

He turned to Orville. "Dorfly's looking for you."

"Great. What does the bald-headed boy wonder want this time?"

I looked at Orville inquisitively. "Boy wonder?"

"Yeah, we wonder about that boy."

I looked over and saw a grin on Kelley's face. "I don't know. He was babbling something about the on-call beeper not working."

"Well, Jimmy's on call this week. They must not have been able to get hold of him last night for some reason, probably because Dorfly didn't do anything about the busted on-call beeper that I told him about."

As if on cue, Dwayne Dorfly came stomping into the shop. He set on Orville immediately. "There you are, you pencil-necked geek! Why the hell didn't you tell me the on-call beeper wasn't working?!"

Orville looked like he was calling on every reserve he had to keep himself in check. "Dwayne, I told you last week the on-call beeper wasn't working." I thought his answer was incredibly subdued.

"The hell you did! I just got my ass chewed out by Genevieve Madas because the goddamned night staff couldn't get hold of Jimmy last night!"

"Dwayne, I told you last Thursday the staff had to call me at home because they couldn't get me with the beeper."

"Bullshit! This is just another example of the piss-poor attitude you've had lately. I don't know what your problem is, Coleman, but if you don't shape up, you can hit the bricks!"

I could see that Orville was seething, and I didn't blame him. It was plain for me to see what the problem was.

Unfortunately, Trevor picked that moment to show up in the doorway. Dorfly stared at him for a moment and then yelled, "What the hell do you want?!"

"Ah, Dwayne?" Trevor stepped back slightly from the door. "Dan wants to see you on the second floor by the CCU."

Dorfly's face turned to stone and he started for the door, but he stopped before he got there and turned back to Orville.

"And another thing, beanpole, you look like a goddamned hippie! Get a fucking haircut!" With that he continued out the door.

As soon as he had left, Orville picked up a screwdriver and flung it at the wall. With a dull 'thunk', it became embedded shaft first in the wall right next to the door.

"That bald-headed bastard! One of these days..."

Kelley clapped him on the shoulder on his way out. "Yeah, man, I know."

I stood perfectly still, having no idea what to say. When Orville's breathing returned to normal, he looked at me again. "Well, you ready to pull some cable?"

"Uh... sure."

He laughed a little. "Don't look so shocked, Jay, I'm used to it."

"If you say so." We took the cart and headed out the door and up the hall not saying anything more until we got on the elevator and the doors closed. At that point I couldn't stand it anymore. "How do you put up with that?"

Orville looked momentarily baffled. "You mean Dorfly?" I couldn't believe how calm he sounded.

"Yeah, Dorfly. How can you listen to him talk to you that way?"

"Well, sometimes he bothers me more than others, but there's always one thought I keep in the back of my mind."

"What's that, pray tell?"

"Dorfly's an idiot, and if I let him get under my skin too much, then I'm not much better than he is.

I was amazed he could be so philosophical about it. "Doesn't he make you mad when he spouts off like that?"

"Of course, he makes me mad; I'm human, probably more than he is, but as soon as he's gone, I try to put him out of my mind."

"How in the world do you do that?"

"I remind myself that, Dorfly aside, I like working here. I try to think of the several hundred other people that work here that I really like. And, of course, I've got my balloon." Orville owned a hot air balloon. Although he had told me about it many times, I had yet to go flying with him. "Looking at the world from above has a way of changing your whole perspective." His expression turned mellow with the thought as he spoke, and then turned to one of curiosity. "So, what's Dan want to see Dorfly about?"

"The state of the wiring for the nurse-call system in CCU."

"Orville threw his head back and laughed. "I feel better already! I'd love to be a fly on the wall for that conversation."

I decided I'd better try to see Debbie. The accident was two days ago, and I'd not talked to her since. I tried to call her the evening before, but there was no answer. I hadn't left a message; a message on her answering machine didn't feel like the right way to go.

Instead I walked about a half-mile to Eskimo Ed's Used Cars where I hoped to find a decent car in my price range. Ed told me he went by Eskimo Ed because he was from Basin Creek, Alaska. After talking to him for five minutes, I suspected the real reason for the nickname was he could sell a refrigerator to an eskimo.

After an hour of negotiations, I wound up buying a white 1987 Hyundai Excel hatchback. It wouldn't have been my first choice, but it seemed to run okay, and we were able to agree to a price I could afford. It had been a long time since I'd driven a stick-shift, but the technique came back to me by the time I drove it home.

I had decided to wait to ask Debbie out on a date again until I had new wheels, it hadn't been long since the last fiasco. Maybe we could have lunch together. That would give me the opportunity to apologize properly.

I didn't see Debbie when I got to emergency, so I walked to the nurses' station where Betty was working on some paper work. She looked up as I approached and smiled.

"Hi, Jay, how's our favorite shock jock doing?"

I winced inwardly, but outwardly I gave her a smile. "Okay, Betty, I'm just trying to stay out of trouble. Is Debbie around?"

Betty got an odd look on her face as if something had just occurred to her. "She went to lunch... with Dr. Scott."

There was something about the look on Betty's face. Suddenly I was dizzy, and my heart seemed to drop to my knees. I managed to keep my composure as I said, "Oh, well, I'll catch up with her later."

I turned and left thinking, so what? So, she's having lunch with Scott. So, she's having lunch with a handsome single doctor, one of the most eligible bachelors in the hospital. We had only been on one date, and a disastrous one at that. I certainly had no claim on her. It was clear I wasn't having the same luck as Papa Joe.

I didn't feel very hungry, so I skipped lunch. I was practically worthless after that, as my imagination began to kick in. I kept seeing Debbie and Scott having lunch, first in an expensive French restaurant where they dined on escargot as they stared lovingly into each other's eyes. Then I saw them having a picnic lunch in the park by one of the lakes, sipping champagne from long fluted glasses, while they lay on a red and white checked blanket and she fed him grapes. Then they were eating hors d'oeuvres while they sat naked in a hot tub back at his place. At that point I knew for sure that I was losing my mind.

Skipping lunch had only served to turn my confused mood into an angry one. I had always been told that my thoughts and moods showed on my face, and I decided it must be true because people seemed to be avoiding me.

When I returned to the shop, Dan started to ask me where I'd been, but "Where..." was as far as he got before he saw the look on my face and changed the subject. "Grace North wants to see you in SICU," was all he said. I took my cart and left without a word.

When Dan told me that Grace wished to see me, I didn't think anything of it, because she frequently requested me when she had an equipment problem. This was a situation that Dan encouraged when he could. If a manager or department head requested a particular tech, Dan went out of his way to honor the request. He felt it promoted trust and confidence in our department, and I felt he was right.

Ever since our conversation about death, I had felt a special rapport with Gracie, as I and the rest of the staff called her. She was one of the few people I didn't mind the thought of seeing right now, because she always had a way of making me feel better.

Grace was seated at her desk in her office working on paperwork when I got to the department. Since she was alone and not on the phone, I entered and sat in the chair before her desk. "Hi, Gracie, what's up," I asked cheerfully.

She looked up and my heart dropped. In place of her usual smile was a look of grave concern.

"What's wrong?" I asked, all pretense of cheer forgotten.

When she silently rose and closed her office door, I knew for sure something bad had happened.

She sat back behind her desk and folded her hands on top of it. "Jay, we had a patient on an enteral feeding pump this morning that over-delivered." I suddenly felt an awful sense of dread.

"What happened?" I asked, hearing the apprehension in my own voice.

"The machine bolused the patient." Terrible images suddenly flashed before me as I imagined what it would be like to have a machine force feeding formula down your throat.

"Did the patient aspirate formula?" I shuddered at the thought of it being forced into someone's lungs."

"Some. We have him on a ventilator under observation for the time being. But that's not what bothers me the most."

There was something in the look in her eyes that made the hair on the back of my neck stand up. "What bothers you the most?"

"The patient was my brother."

It took a half second to sink in. "Oh my God, Gracie! He could have drowned on his formula!" The look on my face must have been one of grave concern, for her demeanor changed slightly. She looked sad more than anything else.

"He could have," she affirmed.

"Where's the pump?"

"In the dirty utility room." Grace looked haggard and tired, and I realized how scared she had been. I also knew veteran RNs didn't scare easily.

"Are you okay?" I asked with concern.

"I'm fine," she said weakly.

"You don't sound fine. Is something else wrong?"

"Jay, the pump has one of your inspection stickers on it. You looked at it the day before yesterday." My knees suddenly felt weak, and I realized I was involuntarily squeezing the arms of the chair.

"Oh my God!" I didn't know what else to say. I felt numb all over. "Grace, I swear... if it had my sticker on it..."

"I know. I don't doubt it was working properly when you looked at it, but it's not working now, and that's not going to look good for you."

"I don't know what to say."

"Why don't you take the pump down to your shop and check it out? Let me know as soon as you know anything."

"There's nothing complicated about this one." Will Stanski pushed his stool away from the bench slightly and began holding up parts of the feeding pump for the rest of us to see. All of the techs were standing behind him in a semi-circle. Dan had called everyone in to witness the findings.

"This stop was removed from the rotor shaft, and then the rotor just worked out from the tubing guide allowing a free-flow condition," Will continued.

"How do you know that the stop was intentionally removed, Will?" Dan was studying Will's analysis intently.

Will held the shaft up again so that we could get a better look at it. "These scratch marks around the shaft; look, it was gouged here." He indicated a place on the shaft with a pencil. "The stop was cut off, probably with a pair of dykes or maybe a small hack saw."

"The pump has Jay's initials on the sticker. Has anyone else been in SICU in the past couple of days?" I doubted Dan would get anywhere with the question, but he had to ask. He was answered by shakes of the head and mumbled negatives until Will Stanski spoke up.

"I took a call up there yesterday, Dan."

Trevor spoke up also. "I had a call up there the day before," he paused a second, "and Alan was with me."

Alan's eyes got big behind his glasses, and he began to shake his head vigorously. "That doesn't count; we were together!"

Dan looked at Will again. "Will, how long would you estimate this little job would take to perform?"

Will looked thoughtful for a second. "For someone good... less than five minutes. Of course, you know these pumps are all over the hospital. Someone could have doctored a pump and then replaced a good one with it, or they could have removed this one from SICU, doctored it, and put it back."

Dan had a disgusted look on his face as he began shaking his head. "Son of a bitch! Well, boys, it looks like it's time to drop back and punt. Every enteral feeding pump is gonna hafta be checked out!"

There were groans in abundance from all of the techs except Alan. "I don't see why we all have to check pumps. The faulty one had Jay's sticker on it; let him check them out."

Bobby walked over and placed a hand on his shoulder. "Alan?"

"What, Bobby?"

"How would you like an enteral feeding tube stuck up your ass?"

Dan looked angry. "That's enough of that shit! Now get going!"

We all grabbed carts and set out in different directions. I knew immediately where I was going to begin.

Grace was still at her desk when I got to SICU a few minutes later. "Gracie, did you see anyone up here in the last two days that could have gotten to that pump?" I then explained Will's findings, as well as the rest of the equipment incidents to her. I was desperately hoping that maybe she had seen something... anything."

"God, Jay, you know what it's usually like around here. People go in and out all the time. Someone could have easily gotten five minutes alone in the storeroom, and if one of Will's other scenarios were true about someone making a switch... hell, that'd be easy."

"I know. I was just hoping that maybe you'd noticed something that just wasn't right, even if it didn't strike you at the time."

"There's nothing I can think of; I wish that there was. I'll keep trying though." She looked determined.

"Will you do me a favor?" I asked.

"If it has something to do with finding the asshole that altered the machine that could have killed Bob, you bet I will."

"Will you start making a list of everyone you can remember seeing in the department in the last two days?"

"That's a tall order; you'll have to give me some time."

"Of course. And Grace?"

"What?"

"We will find whoever's responsible."

"I hope so. Now go and let me get busy." She had already started to write, so I got up and left quietly.

Despite all the weird machine problems at the hospital and all the uncertain drama being played out, Debbie was almost all I could think about. She was the first thing that came to my mind when I woke, after having dreamed about her. She was the last thought of my day before I fell asleep with her beautiful face beckoning me. I kept telling myself it was ridiculous, that she shouldn't have such an effect on me.

I knew it was only a matter of time before my work began to suffer, if it hadn't already. I was getting depressed, more at my lack of self-control than anything else. I wasn't a child, dammit! I was well past the age of schoolboy crushes, wasn't I?

I was jealous of Craig Scott. Why? Because she had lunch with him? I didn't know for sure there was anything going on between them romantically. There was nothing rational or even reasonable about my feelings. I only knew they were seriously disrupting what, up to now, had been a very well-ordered life.

I had to talk to her about it before I went out of my mind. I had to be honest and tell her how I felt, and if she didn't feel the same way, then I'd just have to learn to live with it. But how... Now there was a cosmic twist of fate if ever there was one. How could I, who had so carefully avoided commitment, now be so terrified of rejection? It was time to bring things out into the open, to let the chips fall where they may. Even if I regretted it later, it was time to stand up and be a man! God, I hate clichés.

There were inspections to do in the ER, so I volunteered for the job.

"Let me get this straight. You're volunteering to do PMs?" Dan didn't really sound surprised; it was more like he'd been waiting for it. He *would* have to make a big deal out of it; I should have waited until later to tell him. We were all sitting around the table in Dan's office having just finished our weekly shop meeting.

"No pleading? No begging? No claiming to have a bench project that needs to get done first?" It was obvious he wasn't going to let me off the hook easily.

"Well, Dan, it's a job that has to get done, and I don't have anything on the bench at the moment."

"I see." Dan addressed the rest of the techs. "Now boys, this here is the kind of dedication we at Kirkwood like to see. Here is a man who puts his own likes and dislikes aside for the good of his department." No one was laughing, but it felt as if they were on the verge. Dan wasn't done. "This man is totally ignoring his own desires, and of course the possibility of getting laid, to go in there and do those inspections regardless. I think we all owe him our gratitude." A loud round of applause broke out as I slipped out the door, grabbing my cart.

The ER was fairly quiet when I got there. I didn't see Debbie, so I started into the job and kept an eye out for her. I had my patient simulator hooked up to the bedside monitor in one of the bays and was taking readings, when Tom Nellum, an ER doctor and guitarist that I had jammed with a few times, left the paperwork he had been working on at the central station and came over to say hi.

"Jay! What's new and exciting?" he asked.

"Hi, Tom. Well, I hear you can join the navy and see the world.

"No, thanks, I did my five years," he said with a disdainful look.

His comment surprised me. "What? Were you really in the navy?"

"That's where I became a doctor."

"No kidding? You never told me that before."

He batted his eyes coquettishly. "Well, a boy's got to have some secrets."

I laughed at his expression. "Why did you get out? Did you have enough of the world travel?"

"Don't get me wrong, I loved every minute of it, but being the sole master of one's own destiny has its advantages." Tom made a sweeping gesture with his arm that took in the whole ER.

"It looks pretty quiet in here; aren't you getting bored?"

"Not hardly. Looks can be deceiving, and just because it's quiet in here now doesn't mean that it will be in five minutes."

"Yeah. I've noticed you don't usually seem to get much warning."

He lowered his voice to a conspiratorial level. "Hey, I hear you're going out with Debbie Farrell."

"How in the hell does news travel around this place so fast?"

"How do you think we keep from getting bored?"

I just shook my head. The gossip mill had been in full force again. "I wouldn't really say we're going out. She agreed to a date with me, we went out once and I tried to drown her with my car."

"Now there's a novel way to get a girl to remember you."

Tom's attention was suddenly drawn elsewhere as two paramedics wheeled a very large young woman into the bay next door. Tom began talking to one of them, a medic named Steve, to get a report and find out what the problem was.

"She's complaining of severe abdominal pains in both lower quadrants. Her BP is one, forty-five over ninety-five, and her pulse is ninety-two. I suspect a possible urinary infection?" Steve looked puzzled.

Tom took the woman's hand. "How are you feeling?" he asked.

"I got terrible pains in my belly doctor!"

She began grunting and groaning while Tom tried to get more information. "How long have you had these pains?"

"All mornin', doctor. And they gettin' worse. Oooohhhh!"

"Have you been able to go to the bathroom?" he asked.

"Number one or number two?"

I bit my tongue and silently admonished myself for eavesdropping, but it was difficult to help. I was fairly sure that I was going to hell anyway.

"Number one."

"Oh, lord yes, I can't seem to stop going number one."

"Does it burn?"

"Not really. I just feel like a garden hose that won't shut off."

"Do you have any back pain?"

"Oooohhhh. It feels like somebody's stickin' a knife in me!"

I decided that I couldn't stand here inventing things to do, so I moved to the defib that was sitting on a crash cart by the nurses' station. After a minute or two, Tom came up to the counter and spoke to a nurse on duty named Jenny.

Let's get a catheter in the woman in bed three. I think she may have a kidney stone and I'd like to get a clean specimen."

"Sure, Tom."

Jenny went to get her supplies, and I spoke to Tom briefly in a lowered voice. "Would you really get that much pain with a kidney stone?"

The woman's moaning and sobbing was growing louder by the second. The few other patients present were beginning to look apprehensive about what was happening to the woman behind curtain number three.

"You certainly could if that's what it is," Tom told me.

"What else could it be?"

Tom had a bemused expression on his face. "Well, the mothers that I know that have had kidney stones have compared the pain to labor."

Jenny had returned, and she and Tom disappeared behind the curtain. In less than a minute Jenny came bolting out of the bay and up to the counter and grabbed a phone and dialed. "Get Dr. Nicholas down to the ER stat! We've got a woman delivering. No, I mean right now!"

Jenny returned to the bay, and I watched, fascinated, as she and Tom rolled the woman's gurney into one of the trauma rooms like they were running time trials for the Indy 500. They were huffing and puffing to either side while the woman held her abdomen, rocking back and forth.

In another minute Dr. Nicholas, the obstetrician, came bolting through the double doors. He looked at me and I pointed to the trauma room and he went rushing in after them.

I had finished with a good part of the ER when they emerged again. Tom had gotten a cup of coffee and was busily filling out reports at the desk.

"Are you telling me that woman didn't know she was pregnant?" I had to ask him about it before I left.

He put his pen down, leaned back in the chair, and grinned at me. "It was a hell of a urinary blockage, about eight pounds." He got a more serious look on his face. "She knew alright, Jay; she already had a name picked out. There are a whole lot of people out there like that woman. The only medical care they receive is in here. They know we'll treat them whether they can pay or not." He took a sip of his coffee and his smile returned. "Besides, that's the kind of thing that makes the job interesting."

"I don't know," I told him. "I still think it might be easier to join the navy."

"It happens there too, Jay. Not all sailors are men, you know."

"Are you going to tell me you delivered a sailor's baby?"

"Actually, it was a sailor's wife's baby. I'll never forget it. I was wearing bowling shoes at the time."

I looked at him for a moment before I spoke. "Okay, okay I'll bite. What were you doing delivering a baby wearing bowling shoes?"

"I was wearing the shoes, Jay; I don't think they would have fit the kid." The little ironic smile that he seemed to favor was back.

"Are you going to make me drag the story out of you?"

He took another sip of coffee. "I was standing weekend watch at a remote base in Georgia when a woman came in obviously in the eleventh hour. The bowling center was right next door, and as it was frequently slow, I spent a lot of on-call evenings over there. I was on my third strike in a row when the call came, so I rushed over and delivered the baby still wearing my rented bowling shoes. I never could figure out why they didn't want the shoes back. I still have them."

"It could have been worse, you know?"

"How so?"

"You could have been into baseball. If you'd shown up wearing a catcher's mitt and mask the mother might have gotten even more upset."

"I suppose you have a point."

I changed the subject. "Are we still on for a jam on Thursday night?"

"I hope so; I could use a little musical distraction."

"Well, I'll see you then."

He waved a hand at me as another patient was wheeled in and someone called his name.

My next stop of the day was PICU. I had gotten somewhat used to the suffering I often saw in the hospital. I don't suppose I was becoming used to it so much as I was becoming inured to it. It was necessary to become at least partially hardened, for if you didn't, then you couldn't perform your job effectively, and if you couldn't perform your job effectively, then you only perpetuated more suffering.

This is true of nearly everyone who works in a hospital—doctors, nurses, housekeepers, dieticians, respiratory techs, everyone who comes in contact with patients. It's important to be as pleasant and friendly as possible, but if you don't maintain a certain detachment sooner or later it's going to affect the way you do your job.

There was only one place other than the GI lab that really got to me—the pediatrics unit. To see adults trying to deal with the hardships life had dealt them was one thing. To see children suffering with what I see as life's gross unfairness was quite another. I haven't determined exactly what the difference is, after all, pain is pain no matter who feels it. But there's something about seeing innocent children afflicted with ills they can't possibly comprehend that makes me angry. If you ask me what I'm angry at, I cannot tell you. It's a nameless anger. After all, who can you blame, God?"

The pediatric intensive care unit was laid out the same as all the other intensive care units. It curved around the fourth-floor pod of the westernmost tower. As I pushed my cart around the unit going from room to room, my heartstrings were pulled a dozen times.

In the first room a girl of about nine or ten lay in traction. Her right arm and her left leg were in casts raised by a frame attached to the bed frame, and there was a large bandage around her head.

She was watching cartoons on television when I entered the room, and she turned her head toward me as best she could and smiled. She was pretty, with blonde hair—what I could see of it around the bandage—and brown eyes full of intelligence and curiosity. I wondered what had happened to put her in such a predicament.

I smiled back and said, "Hi," and then proceeded to do an electrical safety check on an ophthalmoscope hanging on the wall.

"What is that?" she asked.

"This is an ophthalmoscope," I answered. Then I thought that I really should be accurate with the child. "Actually, it's an ophthalmoscope/otoscope. I'm sure that the doctors and nurses have looked in your ears and eyes with this, haven't they?" I held up one of the two handpieces on either side of the unit so that she could see the light go on.

"Oh, yes. Doctor Smith shined it in my eyes and made me look around the room. Is it broken?" she asked.

"No, it's not broken. I just have to check the hospital's machines once in a while to make sure they're working right."

"Oh. What do you check for?"

Here we go, I thought. I steeled myself to play twenty questions. Not that I minded. I liked talking about what I did, and the challenge of explaining it to a young mind appealed to me. "I check them for electrical safety and proper operation."

"So they won't shock people?"

This kid is sharp, I thought. "Yes, that's part of it. I also have to see if they do what they're supposed to do."

She had a thoughtful expression as she asked, "What do you do if you find a machine that would shock somebody?"

"I take it apart, find out what's wrong and fix it."

Now she assumed a look I had seen on the faces of teachers at school just before they handed out a test. "How do you fix it?"

I could plainly see there was no way around it. I took the ophthalmoscope down from the wall and got a screwdriver from my cart. I took the back off the unit and took it over to where she could see inside. "What's your name?" I asked her.

"Katie," she said.

"I'm Jay," I told her. "Well, Katie, you see these wires that come in from the back?" I asked her.

"Which ones, Jay? It looks like spaghetti in there." It still sounded as if I were being tested, and it looked like she was enjoying playing the proctor.

I pointed out several wires. "If any of these wires was to come loose and touch metal inside the machine, a person could get shocked. I would have to find out where the wire was supposed to go and put it back into the right place."

"Is it fun finding out where the wire is supposed to go?"

"Sometimes it is, and sometimes it can be a little frustrating, but after you get it fixed and working right it feels pretty good."

"I guess it does." That seemed to satisfy her. She went back to her cartoons, and I put the ophthalmoscope back.

"Would you hand me my cup?" she asked a minute later.

"Sure." I retrieved the cup of juice from the bedside table and handed it to her, and she took it with her good hand. "Are you doing okay?" I asked.

"Yeah, I fell off my bike," she said as if it were a normal course of events to fall off your bike and wind up in the hospital.

"It must have been quite a fall."

"Yeah, it knocked me unconscious. Mama said she found me laying in the back yard all banged up. I guess it scared her pretty bad."

"I'm sure it did."

"Did you ever fall off your bike?"

"A few times."

"Did it ever knock you unconscious?"

"Not that I remember. Of course, if I had been unconscious, I don't guess that I'd remember, huh?"

She laughed at that, a light, airy, lovely laugh. Then suddenly she stopped, and a somber look came over her. "I don't remember falling off my bike. Doctor Smith says it's because I banged my head."

"Yeah," I said. "I noticed your turban." I indicated her bandage.

"What's a turban?"

"It's a headdress worn by some people in different parts of the world."

She mulled that over for a moment and then tried the word again slowly. "T-u-r-b-a-n, I like that."

"Now you have a new word to impress people with." I had finished with a suction pump that had been standing in the corner, and it was time to move on. "I have to get back to work, Katie. I'll see you later, okay?"

"Okay, Jay, bye."

I was working a few rooms down when I met Amy, one of the PICU nurses. "I was talking to Katie in room one," I told her. "That must have been some spill she took from her bike."

Amy shook her head sadly. "That's what she tells everybody."

"That's not what happened?"

She looked at me with weariness. "Her mother pushed her down the back deck stairs, Jay."

I felt as if I'd been slapped. As if all the air had been sucked from my lungs. "How could anyone do that to such a beautiful child, let alone her mother?"

"She's been removed from her mother several times. Somehow she always winds up back there."

"Can't they place her with a foster family?"

"They've tried. She keeps running away and returning to her mother."

"Why would anyone return to something like that?"

"I guess even an abusive family is better than no family at all."

I thought about my own family and about the holes that I felt in my life. My parents had divorced when I was young, and my sister and I had been shuffled around. Although I had never been physically abused, I could relate to the little girl up the hall. I supposed the feeling of wanting to belong to something outweighed the suffering that she had to endure to belong. I felt I understood her, at least on some level.

There were brightly colored animals and alphabet blocks painted on the walls of the PICU hallways. I looked at these as I passed through the unit, and for some reason I felt even more depressed. There was a sad irony seeing such gay scenes in a place of such suffering. Of course, I supposed the walls looked cheerier than they would have if they were gray or olive green.

This place did such weird things to my head. It took me back to times I would just as soon have forgotten. I had spent a great deal of my own childhood in places just like this one, having had severe ear problems. I couldn't come here without some memory or impression of that time presenting itself to my consciousness, usually without warning.

I could be in the middle of doing a job and catch a scent of alcohol or the strange antiseptic smell of plasticized rubber like that used in anesthesia masks, and suddenly I was seven or eight years old again. I would gaze at my surroundings with the eyes of a child, recognizing even then the stark contrast between the gaily painted walls and the very serious expressions that I often saw on the adults, most of them dressed in white.

I remember at one point in my young life I came to believe that pain was God's way of testing little children. I couldn't have been more than six or seven when my ear doctor snuck up on me and performed a myringotomy. This procedure involved the doctor using a thin wire with a tiny ball on the end to pierce the eardrum, which relieved the pressure that had built up behind the eardrum. The pain it caused was excruciating.

I remember this doctor as a kindly older man with white hair. He had always taken great care to explain things to me, not speaking to me as an adult would speak to a child, but as a teacher might explain to a student he cared about. I always think of him as a compassionate man.

I remember understanding he snuck up on me so I wouldn't suffer the anxiety of expectation, but I got mad as hell and I told him so. When there was going to be pain, I wanted to know about it. He always respected that wish afterward.

I can remember visiting his office when he would look in my ear with his otoscope, and then place his hand on my shoulder saying, "I'm sorry, Jay." At this point I knew what was coming, but at least I knew. I sometimes wonder if it would be better for adults if we knew when the pain was coming. Probably not. I tend to think we lose much of our resilience after a certain age.

I thought about the images of the hospital that remained with me from that time. The sound of things on wheels and feet on linoleum had rung in my ears... echoing, sounding so much different than home where carpeting muffled noise. The sound of adults speaking with suppressed urgency... quiet desperation... trying not to upset the children. The confusion of trying to wake up after being anesthetized. The sickly-sweet smell of the gas they used pervading my nostrils and mouth... the room spinning each time I tried to open my eyes... the sounds, the voices that would ring in my semi-consciousness, coming quickly into clarity, and then fading away again.

I had endured surgery after surgery and earaches the intensity of which made me shudder with the memory. Eventually I had gone deaf in my left ear. But the pain had finally stopped, and I considered that I had gotten the better end of the deal.

I had to snap out of it and return to the present. I entered another room where there was a child of maybe two, standing up in a crib and holding on to the rails and bawling his head off. I set about doing my job and finished as quickly as I could.

In the next room a young mother sat in a rocking chair rocking a baby. The child wasn't crying, but the mother was. I moved on, resolving to come back later.

I came to an empty exam room that held two portable ECG monitors. Finally, some peace and quiet. I set about putting the monitors through their paces. I was about halfway done when an Asian doctor that I had occasionally seen around the unit came in carrying an infant. She had a nurse in tow, and neither one of them acknowledged my presence as they laid the child on the exam table.

The doctor reached into a drawer, took out a syringe, and began to extract a blood sample from the child. I was watching out of the corner of my eye. It was no big deal; I had seen it before. Somehow, when the syringe was nearly full the doctor managed to pull the plunger free. It was such an ordinary procedure, one that I had witnessed many times both on other people and myself.

The doctor had seemed so calm and so confident, she had seemed to know what she was doing, and all of a sudden, the plunger came out of the end of the syringe. Blood gushed out of the open end of the little plastic tube.

The doctor was trying to remain calm, but I could tell that she was getting very upset very quickly. The baby was lying on the table kicking and writhing, with what seemed like an unbelievable amount of blood beginning to soak the table cover. The doctor looked at me and started to speak rapidly in what I assumed was Chinese. I couldn't understand a word, but I gleaned from her gestures that she wanted me to hold the baby down while she went to get something.

I remember the nurse saying to her over and over, "He's not medical personnel!"

Medical personnel or not, I quickly put my hands on the kid who was squirming quite a bit, while she crossed the room to get bandages... or something. I was beginning to get light-headed. The sight of blood had never bothered me before, but I had never seen it pouring out of a baby either.

I remember being terrified I might pass out and let the kid go. It took considerable effort, but somehow, I held on.

They managed to stem the tide, and I managed to stagger back to the shop. As I walked in the door, I saw Trevor and Bobby Guilford working on something on the bench. They both looked up and Trevor spoke first.

"Jesus Christ, Jay. You're white as a sheet!"

"I'm not in the least bit surprised; you would be too."

I sat down and spent the next half-hour trying to regain my composure as I told them the story.

By the time I got home that night I was really bummed out.

I awoke with a start and lay staring into the darkness. I was lying in my own bed at home, I knew that, but what had caused me to awaken so suddenly? I heard knocking. Someone was knocking on my door. I looked at the clock on my nightstand. Three o'clock. Who would be knocking on my door at three o'clock on a Saturday morning?

I pulled back the sheet, slowly swinging my naked body out of bed, and put on my slippers and robe. I groped for the light switch and winced as the sudden brightness hit my eyes. I groggily made my way to the door and opened it with the chain still on. There stood Debbie, leaning against the doorframe wearing her scrubs under her coat.

"Well, are you going to let me in or are you going to make me stand out here in the cold all night?" I clumsily fumbled with the chain and finally the door swung open.

"Debbie, I..." I didn't get the chance to say anything more, for she abruptly clamped her mouth onto mine and I got the distinct impression she was not about to let me go anytime soon. There wasn't anything to do but hold her tightly and return her kiss. I'm not sure how, but somehow, we managed to move farther into my living room and shut the front door as she dropped her coat onto the floor.

I don't know how long we stood locked like that; I didn't care. She was soft and lovely, and I'd dreamed of her for so long like this. How many nights had I lain in the dark fantasizing about making love to her? How many times had I been somewhere, anywhere, and wondered what it would be like if she were with me?

My nostrils were filled with the light scent of her, and my body ached even as I held her close, for I wanted her completely. I wanted her more than I'd ever wanted anything in my life, and I felt I would surely burst if I couldn't have her.

She pushed me down onto the couch, and then stood up and slowly pulled her scrub top over her head. I was aware of the old clock ticking away on my bookcase, but time seemed to slow to almost nothing. Neither one of us uttered a word; it wasn't necessary.

She removed her scrub pants and stood before me wearing a white lace bra and panties. My breath caught in my throat; I couldn't believe it. I'd had fantasies like this, but here it was happening right before me. I was aware of a tight feeling in the pit of my stomach, a feeling of wanting to move quickly and at the same time a feeling of barely wanting to move at all, taking time to savor everything.

She removed her bra, dropping it with the rest of her clothes and I drank her in with my eyes. She had firm breasts, not large but full, just right for her build. Her nipples stood hard and erect, and I felt my mouth go dry as I thought about how much I'd like to touch them.

Wearing a mischievous grin, she slowly pulled her panties down and then off, and playfully tossed them aside. Her pubic hair was sparse and trimmed, as perfect as I had imagined it would be and erotic as hell.

I looked down and saw my erection pushing up the fabric of my robe. She knelt before me, opened my robe, and took me inside her mouth. As I watched, a sense of unreality came over me. Here was this adorable, incredibly sexy girl, doing to me what I couldn't believe... to me! Pleasure washed over my entire body as she teased me with her mouth until I couldn't stand it anymore.

I pulled her off me and rolled her over onto her back on the living room floor, burying my face between her soft, warm thighs. I wasn't about to be undone, and I wanted to communicate to her what I was feeling. Besides, her musky natural scent had me completely turned on.

I licked her playfully while I cupped her breasts in my hands gently, working her nipples lightly between my thumbs and forefingers. She moaned softly as she gently bucked her hips until she reached a fever pitch and came, quivering against my mouth.

With a hand on either side of my head, she pulled me up on top of her. She guided me inside of her, and I pushed, ever so slowly, until I had filled her completely. I held there for a time just relishing the moment, unable to believe how good and complete I felt, then I began thrusting into her faster and faster.

She dug her fingers into my back as she wrapped her legs around me urging me on. I was lost as if in a dream, my head swirling in and out of the realization of what was happening between us. Our momentum built until we reached the peak and began coming together in wave after wave.

I had never experienced anything like it. I hadn't imagined that it could be that good with anybody. My experiences before had been more or less half-hearted attempts to quell a biological urge; this was different. I had achieved a feeling of completeness with this woman that I didn't even know was possible. There was no other way to put it; it just felt right.

We lay wrapped together on the floor for a long time afterwards just holding each other. After I had regained my breath I turned and looked into her eyes. "I think I've just been raped."

She smiled at me. "So? Are you going to report me to the police?"

"Naa, I guess I'll overlook it just this once."

She grabbed a nearby pillow and beaned me over the head with it. "You guess you'll overlook it? You wouldn't make the first move, so I figured I had no choice but to do something drastic."

"Well, you certainly got my attention."

"I would hope so. I'm not normally so easy you know."

"Does that mean if I ignore you again, I can expect another visit?"

She was smiling when she said, "Fuck you."

"Yes ma'am." With that I rolled her over and we started all over again."

I lost track of how many times we made love that night. We'd revel in each other until we couldn't go on, fall asleep, and then one of us would wake and we'd start again. We couldn't get enough of each other, as if we had waited so long for this, we were afraid it would disappear like a pleasant dream. Finally, exhaustion took its toll and we fell asleep on my bed entwined in each other's arms.

When I woke again, the clock on my nightstand read eleven AM. I felt a sudden loneliness as I realized that Debbie wasn't with me. At first, I wasn't sure if I had dreamed the whole thing. Momentary confusion gave way to relief as I heard sounds, quite a bit of bumping and banging, coming from my kitchen. I swung myself a little shakily out of bed and went to investigate.

When I peeked into the kitchen, Debbie was on all fours looking through my lower cabinets. She was wearing one of my tee shirts, and her bare ass was in plain view. Electricity shot through my groin as she realized I was there and stood and turned.

"Where the hell do you keep the coff... uh oh." She was looking at my crotch, and I looked down to see my old friend standing at attention. There was a big grin on her face as she walked over and took me in hand. "No, no. Mister Lucky is just going to have to wait until I get my morning caffeine."

"Sorry, I can't help it; he has a mind of his own."

"Well, I've always admired free thinkers."

"Have I told you that you look much better in that tee shirt than I ever have?"

"No, *you* haven't." She looked down again, still keeping a hold of me, and addressed my penis. "Can you tell me where the coffee is?"

"He only thinks about one thing, and I guarantee you it isn't coffee. I, however, can be bribed."

"Okay, but coffee first."

I made us each a cup, and we sat on the living room couch slowly sipping it. I still couldn't believe she was really here with me like this. I reached over and began stroking her hair just to make sure she was real. "Tell me something?"

"What?"

"Why did you come by last night?"

"I'm not completely sure; it was an impulse... I had to know."

"You had to know what?"

"I had to know if you were what I thought you were."

I thought for a moment, trying to understand just what she was saying to me. "After our first little adventure together, I would have thought you'd think I was an asshole."

She gave me a coy little smile. "You really don't know much about women, do you?"

"I'm trying to learn. Maybe I should go ask Bobby Guilford for some pointers." Debbie started laughing. "What?"

"Bobby Guilford? God's gift to women? Now there's an asshole." She turned to me and looked at me intently with those big blue eyes. "Jay, you're a nice guy. You make me feel good when I'm with you; you actually listen to me. Do you have any idea how rare that is?" Her eyes softened a little. "By the way, you're also a damned good lay."

I took her empty cup and set it on the table. Then I took her in my arms and held her. "God, I've waited for you for so long. Now about the other matter."

"What other matter?"

"I believe there was something mentioned about a bribe?"

"Oh, yeah. I'd almost forgotten."

I kissed her as I slipped my hand under the tee shirt, and we were soon oblivious to everything else again.

It was late afternoon when she finally rose to leave. "I have to work tonight, and I need to pull myself together first." She indicated the wrinkled scrubs that she was now wearing.

"Then you'll be back?" I pleaded as I held her tightly.

"We'll see." She gently kissed me, and then pushed me back onto the couch and let herself out the door.

I promptly fell asleep.

I had just finished checking for pumps in the two ER trauma rooms and was making my way down the hall past the on-call physicians' rooms. The on-call rooms were where the ER doctors on duty slept when they were lucky enough to get a few free minutes.

They were made up as bedrooms with a bed, night table, and a small desk. I glanced through the open door to a room and stopped dead in my tracks. Dr. Scott stood with his back to me, as he and Debbie were locked in an embrace. Debbie didn't see me because her eyes were closed, but I could see that she had a peculiar look on her face.

I felt a strange sensation in the pit of my stomach, and my knees felt weak. I felt my face flush, as I fought to retain my composure and continue to walk down the hall as if nothing had happened. I was beyond conscious thought, as I began wandering the halls pushing my pathetic little cart before me.

I don't know how long I wandered like that, dazed. When I awoke from my reverie (catatonic state?) I found myself sitting in the library, staring at a bookshelf. I was totally confused. Hadn't we just spent the previous night and yesterday morning making love? And now she was with Dr. Scott? Again?

I felt a hand on my shoulder and, startled, I turned to see Trevor looking down at me. "Hey, are you all right?" He sat down in the chair next to me looking concerned. "I saw your cart out in the hall. Not the best place to leave your equipment, you know?"

I just looked at him and shrugged.

"Can I assume that Debbie Farrell's the reason you go around looking like the cat that swallowed the canary one minute and three miles of bad road the next?" he asked.

"And I just saw her stuck to Craig Scott like he was covered with superglue." I described the scene I had witnessed a short time earlier and about their going to lunch together. I decided it best not to tell anyone about our night together.

He looked thoughtful for a moment. "That's lousy, but how do you know there's anything going on between them?"

"Come on, Trevor, I just told you what I saw."

"That doesn't necessarily mean anything, Jay. You could have misconstrued what you saw. You've got to go and talk to her."

"I can't compete with Dr. Scott."

"What are you going to do, sit around staring at bookcases? If she isn't interested, then I guess you'll just have to pick one of the other two thousand available women in this place!"

"Yeah, you're right," I said to end the conversation. There was no way he could understand how I felt right now.

"Come on, let's get some work done before Dan fires us both."

On our way back to the shop we passed through the main lobby. This was indeed a grand entranceway with a gray marble floor, columns, and huge plate glass windows that looked out over the hospital grounds.

As we neared the lobby, I was struck with the thought that something looked different. It took me a few moments to realize the rubber mats that usually lined the main concourse were gone. Through the windows we could see it was raining furiously outside, and several of the maintenance guys, including Orville and Kelley, were standing in various spots in the lobby. Off to the side were two security guards named George and Jim who had been around since Kirkwood opened. They had a reputation for being easy going, to put it mildly. Rumor had it that they were occasionally seen taking naps while on duty in out-of-the-way spots.

Orville motioned us over. "You see what that asshole has us doing now?" I assumed he was talking about Dorfly.

"Orville, what happened to the mats?" I asked. I didn't really care, but the diversion helped take my mind off things.

"Dick brain had them taken up and sent out to be cleaned," Orville told us.

"He sent rubber mats out to be cleaned?" Trevor asked. "Don't you guys have a hose and a mop?"

"Why are you guys standing around up here?" I asked.

"Our illustrious leader never heard of a weather report," Orville explained. "As you'll notice it's raining outside. An interesting phenomenon occurs when a person's wet feet come in contact with a marble floor."

As if to illustrate his words, a man came walking in from outside. As soon as his feet contacted the marble his legs went flying out from under him. The closest man, Rick, made a spectacular diving catch and broke the man's fall just before he hit the floor. Trevor and I both watched with our mouths practically hanging open.

"Yes, that's right, folks," Orville said like he was announcing a ballgame. "Our latest mission is to play Brooks Robinson with the hapless clientele of the hospital!"

I looked at George and Jim and saw they were definitely enjoying the spectacle. I indicated them as I asked Orville, "What are Kirkwood's finest doing here?"

"They're here to act as witnesses in case someone falls and wishes to sue the hospital."

"Witnesses for the plaintiff or the defendant?" asked Trevor.

"Whatever," Orville told him. "Come to think of it, I suppose they're also here to do double duty and quell any unrest that might occur. You never know when a riot might break out."

"Rioting under these circumstances would be interesting," I mused.

Orville looked into space, framing his hands as if he were reading a marquee. "I can see it now. Rioting on ice. We could sell the idea to the ice capades. Whadda ya think?"

A young lady came through the door and Kelley began following her with his arms low and slightly outstretched, like a spotter at an Olympics gymnastic competition. She cast him a wary glance and tried to move away from him, but at that moment she slipped, and he made a very neat and inspired catch.

Orville gave him a thumbs up and then turned back to us. "Just you wait. Next week we're going to have a nurse-toss in the cafeteria."

Trevor looked at me. "Do you know, by any chance, is there going to be a full moon tonight?"

I just shook my head and shrugged, and we continued on our way.

Dan was on the phone when we got back to the shop. We could tell by the strain in his voice that he was not having a good day.

"I swear to you, Donna, I got rid of that dammed thing! How could he have possibly gotten it back?... was the patient hurt?... son of a bitch... I know... let me find out what's going on and I'll get back to you." He hung up the phone and turned to Trevor and me. "Either of you two have any idea how Linville could have gotten hold of another outdated electrosurgical unit?"

I couldn't believe what I was hearing. "Don't tell me he did it again."

"You've got it," Dan confirmed. "Doctor shock strikes again. Only this time the patient was burned." He paused and ran his fingers through his hair. "Where the hell could he have gotten the thing?"

Trevor cleared his throat and spoke reservedly, as if he were unsure of the depth of the water he was wading into. "Uh, Dan?"

Dan looked at him apprehensively. "What?"

"The last time I did PMs in the OR I noticed an old ESU sitting in the back of a storeroom. It hadn't been used or inspected in years. I didn't think anything of it. I'm sorry."

"Christ, Trevor, why didn't you say something?"

"Dan, it's not Trevor's fault," I told him. "I'd seen the old ESU up there myself. Who the hell would've thought that the old bastard would dig it out and try to use it? How badly was the patient burned?"

"Bad enough to create an incident report and leave us open to possible legal action down the road."

"What do you want us to do?" Trevor asked.

"I want you two to go upstairs and get it."

There was an audible groan and I wasn't sure if it came from me or Trevor, or both of us simultaneously. "Can't you send somebody else this time?" I asked.

"Look around, do you see anybody else?" We were alone in the shop. "Besides, you two have experience now."

"Lucky us," said Trevor.

"I don't need any grief from you two! Now get your butts upstairs!" As soon as he said it, I could see Dan regretted his words. "Sorry, guys, this whole thing just has me pissed off. Linville's gonna do his best to deflect the blame. He's gonna try to make us look like incompetent jerks, and I'm not sure there's anything we can do about it."

"It's okay, Dan, we'll take care of it," I said.

We started to go, but he stopped us. "Just do me a favor?"

"What?" I asked.

"Try not to piss off the old fart?"

"I don't think that's going to be a problem this time," I said.

We left and headed up to the OR. "What's with Dan these days?" I could tell that Trevor was upset by Dan's outburst. I was bothered by it myself.

"I don't know, Trev. I know that he has a lot on his mind these days with the pump investigations going on. He doesn't need any more major equipment problems right now. I get the feeling that administration is coming down on him harder than we know."

"What do you think's going to happen?"

"With which problem?"

"The pumps."

"I have no idea. I just hope that they resolve something soon. I don't relish the idea of living like this with Dan much longer."

When we got to the main entrance to the OR, Trevor reached over and pushed the button on the wall for the electric doors. The big double doors opened with a whirring of their motors, and there at the front desk stood Genevieve Madas. All thoughts of Debbie left me. Madas did not look happy, not that she ever did. Donna was standing behind the desk and she didn't look happy either. Madas was her boss, and my immediate thought was oh, boy, the shit has hit the fan and there isn't a mop in sight.

Madas was standing with her left hand on her hip, reminiscent of a gun fighter from the Old West. Her steely gray eyes bore into us as we advanced and stood before her. Neither of us said a word, and I wasn't sure if it was because there was nothing to say, or because I probably couldn't have remembered my name at that point.

"Dr. Linville has filed an incident report, and I expect some answers." I realized once again how appropriate the nickname Ice Queen was for her, for her voice could have frozen an active volcano.

I decided to give it my best shot. "Ms. Madas, the unit that Dr. Linville used was in storage. If he wished to use it, we should have been contacted to come and check it out first." I hadn't a clue as to what was going through her mind, for her face showed nothing but contempt, and that was normal for her.

"I want to know what it was doing in this department period!"

Though I couldn't say it, that's exactly what I wanted to know. As far as our department was concerned, this machine as well as Linville's other old machine should have been discarded years before. The only reason they were kept around was because of Linville's insistence.

"Ms. Madas, this machine was used for parts for Dr. Linville's other old machine." Trevor had decided to wade in, and I was glad for the reinforcement.

Madas wasn't having it. "If it was being used for parts then why wasn't it kept in the biomed department?"

This was a good question. The answer was that the hospital had not allotted us sufficient storage space for such spares. Of course, I couldn't put it like that. "Ms. Madas, our storage space is somewhat limited."

"Then why was it in the hospital at all?"

Bingo. She was beginning to get the idea. Unfortunately, there was nothing for us underlings to do but grovel. I was beginning to get angry with Dan for not handling this himself. "I'm sorry, Ms. Madas. We will remove the unit."

"Your damn right you will and tell that so-called boss of yours I'm going to take him to the rails on this one!"

Trevor had moved around to the side of the desk where the ESU sat, and we began wheeling the unit downstairs.

On the way back to the shop Trevor turned to me. "I just don't see the point."

"What point?"

"The point of living when you go around all the time looking like you just sucked a lemon."

"Maybe she just needs to get laid," I speculated. I was immediately sorry I said it, for thoughts of Debbie came rushing back to me.

"Please, we haven't had lunch yet. You're spoiling my appetite."

"Sorry."

When we walked into the shop Dan was just hanging up the phone.

"Thanks a lot, boss." I was angry now, about Madas *and* Debbie.

"Jay, I'm sorry. I didn't know that old ice britches was up there. If I had, I'd have gone myself." I knew immediately that he was being straight with me. He was more apologetic than I had ever heard him.

"She's on a roll," Trevor said.

"What'd she say?" Dan looked worried.

"She said she was going to take you to the rails on this one, whatever that means," I told him.

"Great! What that means is that she's going to initiate an incident investigation. That's just what I need with all the other shit that's been coming down. Goddammed Linville ought to be strung up by his balls!" Dan marched into his office and abruptly slammed the door.

"Gee," said Trevor. "This used to be such a fun place to work."

I opened my eyes and looked at my alarm clock—four-thirty. The phone was ringing. I hadn't been able to sleep very well since Debbie had been over. I missed her in my bed and my arms felt very empty. I must have finally dozed off because my first thought was of Debbie, but then I realized that was not happening.

I wasn't on call, was I? There was only one way to find out. I reached over and grabbed the receiver without bothering to switch on the light. "Hello?"

"Jay?" said a voice that was way too cheery for four-thirty on a Saturday morning.

"Yes?"

"It's Orville. You looked kind of down when I saw you yesterday. I thought you might be able to use a change of perspective."

"Orville, what the hell are you talking about?" My brain wasn't functioning too well yet.

"I've been promising you a balloon ride. How about it?"

I had wanted to go, but it was so early. "Orville, it's dark. How are you going to see where you're going?"

He laughed. "The early bird catches the wind right, Jay."

I reached over and switched on the light. Why not? I was awake now. And I could certainly use the diversion. "Sure, Orville. Where do you want me to meet you?"

"The field on the east side of the hospital. And Jay?"

"What?"

"Why don't you call Trevor and see if he wants to go?"

"Sure. Why should we be the only people up at four-thirty on Saturday morning?"

Trevor sounded about the way I probably had to Orville, but after he got his brain cells functioning, he agreed to come along to lend a hand or to watch me become a 'spot on the ground', as he so eloquently put it.

Orville pulled up in his brown Ford pickup truck, pulling a trailer with a large wicker basket and the rest of his equipment in it. In the passenger seat was Vicky Henderson from L&D. I was somewhat surprised to see Vicky with him, as the two seemed to make an unlikely couple. At the time I wasn't sure they were a couple, but I knew that Orville was frequently full of surprises.

"Hi, Jay. Are you ready to gain that new perspective?" he called as he stepped out of the truck.

"As ready as I'll ever be," I told him.

Vicky stepped out of the passenger side. "Do you know Vicky Henderson?" Orville asked.

"Sure. Hi Vicky," I said.

"Hi, Jay. Hi, Trevor," she called to Trevor who was on the other side of the trailer where he had gone to check out the equipment. He waved to her. "Will this be your first time up?" she asked me.

"Yeah, and I'm really looking forward to it." I was beginning to feel anticipation.

"You'll love it; it's not quite like anything else," she assured me as she gave Orville a knowing smile. I was sure I detected something between them, something private. Orville winked at her, and then turned his attention back to me and Trevor.

"Vicky will be driving the chase vehicle. Trevor, you can come with us if you want."

Trevor was still inspecting the trailer. "I think I'll just watch for now," he said.

"Suit yourself. Jay, give me a hand with this, will you?"

We unloaded a huge, green canvas bag from the trailer and carried it several yards away. We then went back and got the basket and carried it over to the bag. When Orville opened the top of the bag, I saw some of the brilliant red and blue fabric of the balloon envelope. He reached in and pulled the skirt of the envelope out with its attached wires and cables and attached it to the framework that extended beyond the top of the basket, which was now laying on its side.

Trevor seemed to grow more curious by the second, hovering not far from where Orville was working. Under Orville's direction the three of us grabbed hold of the big bag and began walking it away from the basket, paying out the fabric of the envelope as we went. We had gone at least fifty feet before we reached the end of the fabric, at which point Orville began walking back toward the basket pulling the fabric out and spreading it evenly on the ground.

I followed suit on the other side until the envelope was completely spread out. It was red and blue with two large white stars on either side, and I knew that it was quite striking after it was inflated and in the air, having seen him flying several times.

Orville went back to the trailer and returned with a gasoline powered fan that was approximately two feet in diameter. He placed it just to the side of the basket and positioned it so it would blow air up into the skirt of the envelope, and then he pulled the starter rope and the fan coughed into life. The diameter of the skirt was as tall as I was, and I held one side while Trevor held the other.

The envelope began to quickly fill with air, and as we held on to the lines, Orville continually circled, making sure it filled evenly and none of the various lines snagged. When it was about three quarters full Orville shut the fan off and fired up the burner which was on gimbals attached to the top of the basket frame.

He aimed the burner at the center of the skirt and pulled the trigger on the blast valve. With a tremendous 'woosh' flame shot up into the envelope, and the balloon finished its inflation even more quickly. In less than a minute Orville shouted for us to "hang on," and the envelope snapped upright as we struggled to keep the basket on the ground.

Now that the balloon was inflated, things seemed to settle down as Orville did his preflight checks. He took several toy balloons from a locker in the trailer and inflated them from a helium tank that was strapped into place next to it.

"This is how I determine what the wind is doing at what altitude," he explained as he let a balloon go and watched it ascend. After he had done this several times he seemed to be satisfied. "Vicky, it looks like we're going to be starting out going northwest," he told her.

"I'm ready when you are," she said as she climbed into the driver's seat of the pickup.

Orville climbed into the basket and indicated that I should do the same. Once I was in, he looked at Trevor. "Last chance," was all he said.

Trevor seemed to be weighing the thought, though he looked excited. "Oh, what the hell," he said and climbed into the basket with us.

"Now, before we go there is one very important thing I'm going to tell you." He was holding a red rope that stretched out of sight up into the envelope. "Whatever you do, don't touch the red rope."

"Why, what does the red rope do?" I asked.

"It lets the air out of the top of the envelope. If that were to happen before I'm ready for it, we could crash."

"You couldn't tell me that before I climbed aboard?" Trevor asked.

"You'll be fine Trevor, just don't touch the red rope," Orville said.

"Gotcha!" Trevor told him.

Orville triggered the burner with the blast valve again for a few seconds, and we waited expectantly for the moment we would lift off. We didn't.

"You guys must be heavier than you look," Orville told us.

"I keep telling Jay he should go on a diet," Trevor said.

"Hey, I'm not the one who cleaned out the taco bar at lunch yesterday," I told him.

"Tacos are light," he told me. "Besides, I left a few."

Orville fired the burner again while Trevor and I were practically on tiptoes trying to will us off the ground. At last, very slowly, we felt the basket swing free as we began to glide upward. I watched with fascination as the ground began to drop away beneath us. It was like being in an elevator. Albeit an elevator that was outside and completely unattached to anything else. We floated across the field to the northwest, toward the trees that bordered the lake on this side of the hospital.

"Uh, Orville?" asked Trevor.

"Yes, Trevor?"

"You do have a plan for getting over those trees, don't you?"

"What trees?" Orville asked.

"Those trees that are directly in our path."

"Trevor, did anyone ever tell you that you worry too much?" Orville asked. "Besides, I can't think of everything."

"Terrific," said Trevor.

Orville triggered the burner again briefly and as if by magic we rose just enough to clear the tops of the trees before we came back down and moved just over the surface of the lake.

"You've done this once or twice before, haven't you?" I said.

Orville gave me a grin. "I call this contour flying," he said.

We had moved across most of the lake when he triggered the blast valve again, and we just cleared the trees on the other side.

"That's a pretty neat trick," Trevor told him.

"Next time we'll do a touch and go on the lake. I just thought that you might not like getting your feet wet on the first trip."

"Very thoughtful," Trevor told him.

Orville did another burn, a little longer this time, and we gained enough altitude to get a good look at the hospital grounds from above before we moved on.

"I see what you mean about perspective," I told him. "It looks pretty and peaceful from up here." I was beginning to feel better.

"Deceptive, isn't it?" he said with another grin.

We continued to gain altitude until we could see for miles in all directions. For all his earlier reticence, Trevor looked like he was thoroughly enjoying himself.

"Well, Trevor, are you glad you came?" Orville asked him.

"This is great! It's like looking at a huge train layout." Trevor looked like a kid at Christmas time, and I knew how he felt because I felt the same way.

"I can't believe how quiet it is," I said. "I've been up in small planes before, but this is so different. It's like floating on a cloud."

"That's how I've always thought about it. There's nothing quite like it for leaving stark reality behind."

"I definitely need to leave stark reality behind for a while," I said.

"Has life been getting you down, Jay?" Orville asked.

"You could say that." I didn't want to talk about Debbie right now. It would ruin the feeling of calm that had come over me.

"He took Debbie Farrell out on a date and wound up driving his car into a river in the middle of it," Trevor offered helpfully.

"Technically, I wasn't driving at the time," I said.

"Well, that sucks," said Orville. "Is she okay?"

"Yeah, she's okay. Just a little damp."

"Have you asked her out again?"

I needed to redirect this conversation now.

"I found out she's seeing someone else," I said and turned to Trevor. "At least I didn't make the apple of my eye faint," I said to Trevor sarcastically and immediately regretted it. I could feel Orville's curiosity peak, and nobody else knew about Candy and our adventure in the morgue.

"You made somebody faint?" Orville asked him.

I didn't know how Trevor was going to react, but I needn't have worried because he didn't hesitate to talk to Orville either.

"I've had my eye on Candy Richards," he said.

Orville got an odd look on his face. "You mean Candy Richards from pathology?"

"Yeah. Tall, blonde, beautiful Candy," Trevor said with a dreamy look on his face.

Orville started to laugh. He laughed until he was holding his sides and tears came to his eyes.

"What?" Trevor's dreamy look had turned mystified.

"I'm sorry, Trevor," Orville said as he regained his composure. "It's just that..."

"What, Orville?" Trevor asked again.

"Trevor, Candy Richards is a lesbian."

"No way!" Trevor said in disbelief.

"I swear," Orville told him. "I thought it was common knowledge. Candy Richards likes girls. I'm afraid you don't have the proper equipment to pique her interest."

Trevor looked like he had been hit with a two by four. "I didn't know," Trevor said, innocently. "Why didn't somebody tell me..."

With the baffled expression on Trevor's face, I couldn't help it. I started to laugh which started Orville going again. Trevor just looked mystified.

"Well, that certainly explains why she wasn't interested, Trev," I said, nearly choking. Trevor stood still for a moment and then he cracked up too. "You sure can pick 'em, buddy," I said as I clapped him on the back and wiped the tears from my eyes.

"Look, a flock of geese!" Trevor was pointing excitedly, his misadventure forgotten for the moment. They were slightly higher than we were and just a couple of hundred yards away as we watched them fly by, honking to each other.

I couldn't get over how peaceful it was. The only things we could hear were each other when we talked, and we talked less and less as the flight went on, content to savor the moment and feel the light breeze. There was so much to see as we floated over farms and roads and housing developments. As we flew higher, I marveled at the seeming patchwork of the land. It reminded me of a hand-made quilt with its various colored squares and patches of material.

"Where's Vicky?" I asked as I gazed over the side, scanning the roads.

"She can't be far," Orville said. "There she is." He pointed, and we could see the brown pickup with the trailer making its way slowly along behind us.

We swung slightly more to the north as we hit a new gentle wind, and I wondered how Vicky was going to follow us. Orville seemed to be reading my mind. "It gets a little tricky sometimes. You can't really anticipate where we're going to go from down there. If she doesn't see us land, I'll put a call in to my service telling them where we are, and they'll tell Vicky when she calls in."

"Wouldn't it be easier to carry a radio?" Trevor asked.

"Trevor, you're in the oldest type of aircraft known to man," Orville told him. "The balloon was invented hundreds of years before the airplane. Would you really want to take so much of the adventure out of it with modern technology?"

"What about using the telephone after you land?" asked Trevor. "That's modern technology."

"I hate to point this out, but so's your truck with its internal combustion engine," I added.

"You guys are just no fun," Orville said with mock seriousness. "Hey, you want to pick some corn?"

I looked in the direction we were headed and saw a cornfield coming up fast. We were much closer to the ground than I had realized; I hadn't even been aware we'd been losing altitude. "I hope you know what you're doing," I told him.

"Oh, ye of little faith," he said. "You guys look around and see if you can find my flight manual. I know I dropped it in here somewhere."

"Great," said Trevor.

We could hear and feel the tops of the cornstalks as they brushed the bottom of the basket, and then we were clear and rising again.

"Well, it's time to find a spot to land," Orville said, looking at his watch.

"Already? It seems like we've only been up for a few minutes," I said.

"We've been aloft for nearly an hour," Orville said. "I don't want to cut it any closer than that with our fuel. I'd rather have control over our descent."

"Controlled descent sounds like a good idea," Trevor said.

In another minute or so Orville pointed ahead. "That house has plenty of open ground around it." The house was a large, old brick farmhouse that sat on a slight rise.

Orville did one more short burn to maintain our altitude a little longer, and then we began to slowly drift down toward an open, grassy area that was several hundred yards from the house. The word had evidently gone out, for soon there were several adults and a half a dozen kids out in the yard by the house watching us come down. "Okay," Orville said. "Put your feet against the front of the basket and lean back, and don't forget to hold on."

"Don't worry, we won't," I assured him.

Orville was holding the red rope, and he gave it a gentle tug. There was a light bump, and then the basket dragged along the ground for a few yards before coming to a stop. I looked over and saw the kids running for us at full speed.

"Uh, oh, welcoming committee at ten o'clock," I said.

"It's okay; it happens all the time. For some reason people get curious when a balloon lands in their back yard." Orville was smiling. "How about you two jumping out and grabbing those land lines while the envelope deflates." He was indicating two white ropes that went up the outside of the envelope.

The adults had caught up with the kids by now, and Trevor and I waited patiently while Orville talked with them for a few minutes.

"Okay," Orville said when he returned. "Walk those lines out while I let out the rest of the air." We pulled gently while Orville pulled on the red rope, and soon the envelope was deflated and laying on the ground once again.

Under Orville's direction we detached lines and rolled up the envelope while he answered a barrage of questions from the adults. I could tell he had done so many times before by the ease with which the answers came.

We were just about finished when we saw Vicky making her way up the long driveway in the pickup. Obviously, she'd been able to track our landing. She pulled off the drive and onto the grass and stopped with the trailer next to the basket. Then she got out and joined us.

"Well, what did you think?" she asked me.

"You were right. It's not like anything else I've ever done. I couldn't believe how peaceful and quiet it is up there."

Orville had gotten a battered old attaché case from behind the driver's seat in the pickup. "You guys think you can handle loading the trailer?" he asked Trevor and me. "I want to go give these people some souvenirs."

"Sure, Orville," said Trevor.

We set about loading the basket and other equipment while Orville went to talk to the people who had watched our landing. I looked at Vicky.

"What does he mean by souvenirs?" I asked.

"He always gives something to the people whose property he lands on. He has cards made up as mementos for the adults, and badges for the kids. It's a way of maintaining good relations with the public. At least, that's what he'll tell you."

"That's not what he's doing?"

"He's maintaining good relations all right, but he's also enjoying his few minutes in the spotlight."

I understood what she meant. The one good part of being a road musician was always the attention you got from your audience. "I guess he's earned it," I told Vicky. "What do the cards and badges look like?"

"The cards are made up as documents certifying this as an official balloon landing site; they're always popular. There's a place for him to fill in the address, and he signs and dates them. The badges are balloon lapel pins, and before he goes, he'll give them a seedling tree."

"Why a tree?" asked Trevor.

Vicky's eyes were smiling as she answered. "Orville is one of the most thoughtful people I've ever known. Can you think of a better present for a land owner than a tree?"

I had to admit I couldn't. I also knew now without a doubt that Vicky and Orville were a couple; there was no mistaking the look in her eyes when she talked about him.

The trailer was loaded, and Orville had returned. Trevor and I offered to take them to breakfast, and they took us up on it. We piled into the pickup and headed down the road to a little restaurant Orville knew called Betty's.

Betty's had wooden, blue-painted tables with red and white checked tablecloths and offered the 'finest home cookin' in the state. It was by no means fancy, but it was very comfortable and seemed to fit the relaxed mood that we were in after our balloon ride. We ordered breakfast and a pot of coffee and settled in.

"I almost forgot to give you these," Orville said as he produced two cards, each approximately three by five inches, and was busily writing on them. When he had finished, he handed one to each of us:

This Genuine Bragging Card
Certifies that _Jay Barlow_ at great risk to life and limb,
ignoring the perils of noxious atmospheric gasses and
other possible dangers, did leave the bounds of earth,
ascend in a balloon and return to terra firma on this
date _5/11/92_

Signed, _Orville Coleman_

Trevor turned to me with a big smile. "I guess this means we're official."

"It's about time you were declared legitimate," I told him.

"Next you'll have to go for the mile-high club," Orville said as he poured coffee for everyone.

"How do you do that?" Trevor asked.

Vicky let out a short laugh as soon as the words left Trevor's mouth.

"I'll give you a hint," Orville said as he raised his cup hiding a grin spreading across his face. "I could be wrong, but I don't think you two would want to qualify together."

"Why not?" I asked.

Orville lowered his head and his voice conspiratorially. "Well, the idea is you get somebody that you really like, you go a mile aloft, and then you... "

It only took a second for us to realize what he was talking about.

"God, in a balloon!?" Trevor's face had turned beet red. "Isn't that uncomfortable? I would think you could get splinters from wicker."

"Maybe I could offer it as a special ride at the hospital fair," Orville said. "We'd probably break records for ticket sales."

"Maybe Genevieve Madas and Jerry Louis would like to take you up on it." I was sorry as soon as I said it, for whatever laughter there was died at that moment.

"What's going on with Dan lately?" Vicky asked, changing the subject. "He's always been such a sweetheart, but the other day he almost bit one of my nurse's heads off when she called down about a problem with an incubator. He accused her of not using it properly. He called back and apologized, but it's just not like him to go off like that."

"He won't talk about it, but we're pretty sure administration is giving him a hard time," I explained.

"A hard time about what?" asked Vicky.

"Did you hear about the thirteen IV pumps in MICU that malfunctioned?" I asked her.

"Yeah, Shay Ingram told me about it. But that wasn't Dan's fault."

"We can't explain whose fault it was," said Trevor. "Somehow some computer chips got switched in them, but we don't know how or by whom."

"And there was the feeding pump that was tampered with in SICU," I said.

"Not to mention the defib that could have killed Jay," said Trevor. "We can't find anything wrong with it, and we can't explain how it happened."

"And administration is blaming Dan?" Vicky asked.

"Something like that," I said as I took a sip of my coffee.

"Sounds like the kind of crap that Dorfly gives us," Orville said. "The other day he told Kelley that he didn't know shit about air conditioning. Kelley has twenty years' experience in heating and air conditioning. Dorfly wouldn't know an air conditioner if it snuck up and bit him on the ass!"

"How do you really feel, Orville?" Vicky asked, and he smiled at her in spite of himself.

"All things considered, I'd rather have my boss under pressure than yours on his best day," I told him.

"Speaking of pressure," Orville continued, "guess what our latest project is? We're using pressure treated lumber to put new frames up in the ceiling in recovery to hold the curtain rods."

"And you're using pressure treated lumber?" I asked in amazement.

"That's right."

"But whatever it's treated with kills bugs, mainly termites, which means it can't be good for people," I said.

"You've got it."

"Who made the decision to use the stuff?" Trevor asked.

"I'll give you three guesses, and the first two don't count."

"Dorfly?" Trevor guessed.

"That's right."

"But what happens if it burns?" I asked.

"According to our fearless leader, pressure treated lumber doesn't burn."

"You're kidding. He said that?" I shook my head in disbelief.

"Do I look like I'm kidding?" Orville had a sort of sad, tired aura about him that I had noticed more and more in the maintenance staff lately. These men were professionals. They each had their specialty, be it electrical, plumbing, heating and air conditioning, welding, locksmithing; whatever needed to be done to maintain a building these guys could do. It seemed to me they had been pushed beyond the brink of absurdity too many times.

"I can't believe this," I said. "Where did this wood come from?"

Orville stared into his coffee cup for a moment. "While we were unloading it, I saw a couple of stickers on the lumber that read Billings Wood Treating, Inc. So, I called them and talked to Mr. Billings himself. The lumber is meant to be used to build decks and porches. He couldn't believe we were using it inside, and in a hospital of all places! The stuff is treated with arsenic among other things. When it burns, it gives off toxic fumes. It's expressly not for indoor applications. He faxed me information on exactly what the treatment contains."

"So, what are you going to do?" Trevor asked.

Orville looked at Trevor, then at me, then dropped his gaze back to his coffee cup. "What can I do?" It came out as a half sigh.

I knew what he was thinking, and I knew what his choices were. He could go to administration, but even if he were able to get something done about it, Dorfly would make his life even more miserable.

"I hate to mention this," Vicky said, "but you guys are starting to be a drag."

"You're right," I said, "sorry." At that moment our breakfast arrived, and I realized how hungry I was. "Good timing!"

Orville switched gears immediately. "Alright, it's a party, dig in!"

We spent the next few minutes working on eggs and biscuits and sausage and bacon, and it was almost gone in no time. I flagged the waitress down and ordered more food.

"Orville, you mentioned the fair. Are you going to have your balloon there?" Trevor asked him.

"Absolutely. I'm hoping the wind will be mild enough to give some rides."

"What if it isn't?" I asked.

"If it isn't, I'll just have to bring out my cooler sooner. I've got a great spot for a party all picked out."

"There's a surprise," said Vicky dryly as she rolled her eyes at him. Orville evidently pinched her under the table, for she jumped with a little yelp that made us laugh.

"Speaking of the fair, are you guys playing this year?" Orville asked Trevor and me.

"Oh yeah, we wouldn't miss it," Trevor said eagerly. "We're gonna have the biggest amplifier system we've had yet!"

"Gonna rattle some windows, are you?" Orville asked.

"That's the idea," I said.

"We're gonna rock 'til we drop," vowed Trevor.

"That's going to leave Candy a little disappointed, isn't it, Trevor?" Orville needled.

I looked at Trevor and saw that he was turning red again.

"What are you guys talking about?" Vicky asked.

Orville and I both looked at Trevor. "Oh, go on and tell her," he said. "Everybody else in the hospital will probably know about it soon anyway."

I started telling the story about our adventures in and around the morgue, and by the time I had finished Vicky was gasping for air. Trevor sat smiling, obviously having resigned himself to hearing it told time and time again.

Orville looked at him. "Trevor, if you're interested, I'm sure that we can find some more lesbians to date." We laughed, and this time Trevor joined in.

It was getting late, so Trevor and I split the check and we piled into the pickup and rode back to the hospital to retrieve our cars.

Beep...beep...beep...beep...beep...beep

Ugh, what a lousy way to be awakened from a deep dreamless sleep. The ride in the balloon had definitely helped with my ability to sleep. I'd forgotten I was on call.

I reached over and turned on the light, then I picked up the beeper and pushed the button on top to see where the call was coming from. It was the exchange for the ER. My clock read 12:30 AM as I reached for the telephone and dialed.

It rang a few times before it was answered by one of the nurses I knew. "ER, Kathy speaking." Kathy was the head nurse for the ER. I wondered briefly why she was working night shift but assumed that she was covering for one of her staff.

"Hi, Kathy, it's Jay. What's up?"

"One of our nurses was shocked by a piece of equipment."

Alarm bells immediately went off in my head. "Who was shocked?"

"Debbie Farrell."

My heart jumped into my throat. "Was she hurt?!"

"She was shaken up, Jay. She's lying down now."

"I'll be right there, Kathy."

I bolted out of bed and began to dress hurriedly. I couldn't believe this; it was extremely rare for anyone to be shocked by a piece of equipment. Outside of my own experience, I'd only heard of it happening once. I'd be concerned about it happening to anyone, but the fact it had happened to Debbie made it that much more difficult to accept.

It had been several days since we had made love, and I couldn't forget about her and Scott in the on-call room. I had started to get the irrational feeling I was being used. Why else would she have come over when she was clearly involved with another man?

When I got there, I grabbed the on-call tool bag off the passenger seat and went to see what was going on. The ER looked like a disaster scene. I had thought L&D was chaotic the other day, but people were not lying around bleeding in L&D. I arrived just as the paramedics were bringing in a family that had been in a car wreck. I walked past the ambulance as they were wheeling what must have been the mother out on a stretcher. She was moaning and rocking back and forth against the confines of the stretcher straps.

Her face was cut badly, and I guessed that she must have struck the windshield. The father limped back and forth between her and two children, a boy and a girl, who were also stretcher bound, though they didn't appear to be as badly hurt as their mother. The man was the only one walking, and I read the guilt and anguish he was feeling on his face.

As I walked into the ER waiting room, I saw sick and injured people everywhere. There was a little girl who sat on her mother's lap, crying. She had a bandage wrapped around her head, and every few seconds she would lift her head grabbing at her ear and crying louder. The mother was trying her best to console the child, but it seemed to be of little help.

There was a young black man sitting in a corner with a white towel wrapped around his arm that was rapidly turning red. He sat motionless, staring straight ahead like a bleeding statue. There was an older man sitting with him who seemed to be madder at him than concerned about him. "I told you not to run with those fools, didn't I? I told you they'd lead to nothin' but trouble. But do you listen?" he admonished.

There was a young woman of about twenty. She was blonde with what looked like the remnants of an expensive hairdo, although now it was mostly undone and hung loosely around her face. She was wearing an evening dress that I could see beneath the hem of a man's dress coat that was wrapped tightly around her. A young man sat with her who I assumed was her escort. He had an arm around her shoulders as she sat shaking and quietly sobbing.

I met Kathy coming out of one of the bays. "Where is Debbie?" I realized as I said it how much concern was in my voice. I saw Kathy's eyebrows arch ever so slightly, but I really didn't care.

She pointed to her right. "In on-call room one," was all she said.

I walked to on-call room one, knocked lightly on the door and opened it. Debbie was lying on the bed with a damp cloth on her forehead. As I walked in, she looked up at me with no expression and my heart dropped. I wanted to take her in my arms or at least touch her, but the look on her face immediately quelled that thought. "How are you doing?" I asked as I closed the door behind me.

"I'm okay, just a little shaken." Her voice was as cold as her eyes.

"I can understand that," I said, trying to sound professional. "I've been zapped before myself, you know?"

She nodded. "I remember."

I looked at her a moment. She wasn't looking at me directly; her eyes were gazing somewhere beyond me. I cleared my throat and decided to try to go by the book here. "What happened?"

"We had a kid come in with something in his eye. I needed to take a look at it, and when I grabbed the ophthalmoscope and switched it on, it shocked the hell out of me."

"Did someone unplug it?"

"Yeah, it's in bay three."

"I'll go take a look at it." I paused a moment. "You're sure you're okay?"

"I'm just fine," she sounded angry now. I wasn't certain, but it felt like the anger wasn't directed at the ophthalmoscope, but at me. "How about you? Are you just fine?"

Now I knew the anger was directed at me. All the confusion and agony of the past few days came down on me, and I was now angry too.

"No, I'm not *just fine*," I said.

"What's your problem." It was not a question.

"What do you mean 'what's my problem'?"

"What's your problem? I don't appreciate being used."

"*You* don't appreciate being used? What about me?" I could see my statement had confused her. Good, I thought. I'm not the only one confused.

"I come by your apartment and throw myself at you after you take me out on a date and then don't call me for two days. And then I don't hear from you for days after that! And now you're telling me that *you're* feeling used?"

"Why did you come over and practically rape me when you're clearly having a relationship with Dr. Scott!"

She looked totally confused now. "Why do you think I'm having a relationship with Dr. Scott?"

"You had lunch with him two days after our date, and the day after you spent the night, I saw you in this very room in each other's arms."

"And you just assumed that we were having an affair and I'm nothing more than a cheap slut?"

We both stopped. It was starting to dawn on me that I had made a terrible mistake. I should have asked her about Dr. Scott days ago.

"I'm wrong," I said quietly.

"You most certainly are." She seemed to feel our conversation had ended, because she sat up and gathered the cloth and water on the table beside her. "Don't you think you'd better check out that ophthalmoscope?" she asked, looking at the floor.

"Debbie, I'm sorry..."

She looked up at me again. "Just so you don't think I'm a total whore, I'll tell you what you saw, though I don't think you deserve an explanation. Craig pulled some strings and helped me get my brother into a very good handicapped adult community and I was grateful."

She paused, and then her voice softened. "You should have just asked me, Jay." And then she rose and opened the door.

Kathy was standing in the doorway with her hand raised, ready to knock. She looked at me, then at Debbie, but said nothing.

Debbie looked at her. "What is it, Kath?"

Kathy stepped through the door and then closed it behind her. "We just got a biker type in here. I need your help if you feel up to it."

"What's his problem?" Debbie asked.

"Well, it seems he and his old lady, as he put it, had a falling out. As best we can determine, he had been drinking heavily before this spat occurred and he fell asleep. When he woke up, he found she had gone, but before she did, she'd left him a little something to remember her by."

At this point Kathy had started laughing a little. "What did she leave him?" Debbie asked, sounding distracted.

"It's not what she left him as much as *how* she left him," Kathy said.

"Okay, *how* did she leave him?" Debbie asked.

"She super-glued his penis to his leg."

Debbie looked confused, but soon the corners of her mouth began to turn upward.

I looked at Kathy. "Sounds like you guys see some interesting things," I said.

With that, Kathy got up and walked to the desk. "If you think that's something, take a look at this." She reached into a drawer and pulled out an x-ray film. "This guy came in here a couple of weeks ago, and believe me, he was walking funny too."

It was an x-ray of a pelvis; the hips were unmistakable. In the center I could see a vague outline of a cylindrical shape, and in the middle of that I could plainly see the lettering '7-up'. "What's this?" I asked, and then it dawned on me what I was looking at. When I looked up, Kathy and Debbie were both laughing. "You're kidding, right? A 7-up bottle? I guess he was walking funny."

Debbie looked at me momentarily and then turned to Kathy. "They used to say things go better with Coke."

"I guess I see why they changed their slogan," I said. "You keep this in a drawer, and you imply *he's* weird," I teased Kathy.

"Well, it cheers us up when things get bad around here," Kathy said, slipping the x-ray back into the drawer.

Debbie and I stood awkwardly in the doorway. She didn't look at me. "I'd better go check out the ophthalmoscope," I said, picking up my tool bag. "I'll leave you two to Mr. Super Glue." And I left.

I walked to bay three and saw the little boy I had seen them taking from the ambulance when I arrived. He was about nine or ten years old, thin, with dark hair and eyes. I couldn't see any visible signs that he was injured, but he looked very confused and very scared. He didn't move a muscle or utter a sound, and I smiled at him as I moved behind his gurney to the ophthalmoscope on the wall underneath the ECG monitor.

As I was removing the unit from the wall, an intern came by and started to examine the boy. He was about my height, with impeccably coiffed sandy blonde hair and a mustache. I hadn't seen him before, but there was something in the way he carried himself, back ramrod straight, head high that made me think, another one of God's gifts.

ER doctors essentially live at the hospital when they're on call. It's normal, I think even comforting, to see them somewhat disheveled, for personally I would rather think they were more concerned about what they were doing than how they looked while doing it.

"You see what happens when you don't wear your seatbelt? Always remember to buckle up. If your parents had, they wouldn't be hurt right now." The boy started to cry. I couldn't believe my ears. Here was this child who had obviously just been through a very traumatic experience, and this idiot, this colossal moron was giving him a safety lecture.

I could barely contain myself, but of course it wasn't my place to say anything to him; I could lose my job. I had to do something. I was still angry with myself about Debbie and this jerk was only adding to the fire.

He was in the process of hooking the boy up to the ECG monitor, still jabbering away about the dangers of not wearing a seatbelt. I was still in the process of getting the ophthalmoscope off the wall, though it was a simple matter of lifting it up a quarter of an inch to clear the hook in the back. As he reached over me to adjust the monitor, I feigned a last mighty tug on the wall unit. It easily came loose, my arms reeled back, and I managed to jam my elbow into the intern's crotch.

He stepped back with a deep-throated ooof, as all the air went out of him and he proceeded to turn a light shade of purple. I put the ophthalmoscope down and took him by the arm, leading him to a chair.

"Doctor, I'm sooo sorry. Can I get you a glass of water or something?" I asked.

He mumbled something unintelligible and I went in search of a cup. When I returned a few moments later, he was still sitting in the chair breathing irregularly.

"Doctor, I really am sorry. I don't know how I could have done that. I guess accidents will happen." I didn't know what sort of repercussions I might experience from my little stunt, but I felt better.

I headed downstairs to the shop. As I walked through the darkened hallways, I thought, as I always did, about the almost sleeping giant that was the hospital at night. I could hear a barely perceptible deep rumble, more of a vibration really, coming from some unidentified area in the bowels of the hospital. It was as if the beast were lying there with one eye open, ready to pounce at the first provocation.

I rounded a corner and stopped abruptly. Before me stretched a two-hundred-foot hallway that ended in a corner that opened onto another long hallway. At night the fluorescent lights were turned off and low wattage night-lights embedded in the walls were turned on. The night-lights were spaced farther apart than the fluorescents, and they cast shadows on the concrete floor and gray-painted cinderblock walls.

In the middle of the hallway at the next corner stood a person in partial shadow. In the dim light at this distance I couldn't tell who it was, or even if it was a man or a woman. It was not unusual to meet someone in the hallway regardless of the hour, but this person stood completely still, looking in my direction.

It was the complete eeriness of the situation that caused me to stop and stare myself. I reached for some explanation as to who this person was, and why he or she would be standing as still as a statue looking at me like that.

We stood for a few moments facing each other, not a sound to be heard except for the building's vibration, that deep-throated hum that pervaded everything. With uneasiness I began to move forward to see just who it was that was watching me.

Suddenly, the figure turned and rapidly moved to its right down the next long hallway. I moved as quickly as I could to the next corner, tightly gripping the ophthalmoscope in one hand and my tool bag in the other.

I reached the corner and peered around the edge of the wall down the next hallway. Nothing. It was empty.

The doors that opened onto either side of this hallway were all closed, and I hadn't heard any of them shut. Because of the type of doors they were you could always hear the doors close and the bolts click shut. I had heard nothing. I put the ophthalmoscope and bag on the floor and turned left and walked along the hallway trying doors as I went. All locked... except the last one on the right that was marked 'Stairs'.

I had never been through this door before. There was no window in it as there was in many of the others along the hall, so I couldn't see if the person was on the other side. I slowly pushed it open and stepped into the stairwell.

Unlike other stairwells in the hospital, this one had no stairs leading up, only down into darkness. I could see because the stairwell was lit, though dimly, by a small light recessed in the wall behind wire mesh.

It appeared to be some sort of a service access because the walls were unpainted and there was no drop ceiling overhead. Pipes and conduit crisscrossed the space over my head and disappeared into holes in the bare cinderblock. I thought about going back to my tool bag and retrieving the flashlight it carried, but my curiosity was making me impatient, so I began to descend the stairs.

The low rumble, barely audible above, was growing louder as I slowly moved down into the gloom. There was a dampness in the air I could feel on my face, and a slight musty odor pervaded my nostrils. I clung to the railing with one hand descending one, then two flights of stairs. The light decreased with each step until it was dark.

As I got to the bottom, I could see a dim glow off to my right, so I began to cautiously move in that direction. I abruptly banged my left knee on something hard that made a dull metallic thunk, and I cursed as I grabbed my now throbbing knee. I reached out with my other hand until I felt the offending object and traced it to the edge; it seemed to be a large metal box. Moving gingerly around it, I continued toward the glow, which was becoming a little brighter as I moved closer.

My eyes were becoming used to the darkness, and I determined the light was coming from the other side of what looked like large cabinets of some kind. I moved to the end-most cabinet and peeked around the corner.

There was a single naked lightbulb hanging down from the exposed pipes and conduit overhead, and it swung slightly from side to side as if someone had just been here. Underneath the light was a wooden shipping crate turned upside down and on top of the crate were two screwdrivers and a pair of needle-nosed pliers. I took a step closer to the crate, and in the next instant I heard a sound over the rumble, a sudden intake of breath, and I was immediately aware that there was someone behind me.

I was violently shoved from behind before I had a chance to react and went reeling forward, putting my hands out in a desperate and futile attempt to regain my balance. I hit my head on something on the way down and saw stars, as the light went out and I heard footsteps fleeing in the direction in which I had just come.

I lay still for a few moments waiting for my head to stop spinning, and then I pushed myself to my knees, suddenly and painfully remembering the sore left one. I rose unsteadily to my feet, then gathering my wits as best I could, I began retracing my steps.

I found the stairway and ascended, soon coming to the door which I had entered from the hall with the recessed light on the wall. I tried the door handle—locked. I was trying to think about what my next move should be when the light went out. I hadn't heard it break or a switch click off.

I stood for a moment in the darkness wondering what was going on and wondering just what the hell I was going to do now. I had no idea what the layout was down below, and the only illumination had been from that single bulb that was now gone.

I tried pounding on the door, but it was a heavy door and I doubted the sound carried very far. I also had no idea when security made their rounds down here in the middle of the night, or even *if* they came down here. After a short time, my hand hurt and I decided that the best thing to do was to go back downstairs and look around, or actually feel around as the case was.

I groped around until I felt the railing for the stairs, and then I cautiously made my way back down moving slowly, like a blind man who's lost his white cane. Eventually I got to the wooden crate with the tools on it. Just what had I stumbled on? Whose little work area was this? Who had I seen in the hall, and who had pushed me down? The whole thing seemed unreal, as if it were something that I had dreamed.

I realized if I was going to get out of here anytime soon, I needed to find some source of illumination. I felt all around the crate; nothing. I felt around the large cabinets that surrounded the little work space on three sides, but I thought they were probably electrical cabinets full of wiring and I wasn't about to open them and go feeling around in the dark.

I began exploring the backs of the cabinets surrounding me, figuring that I was safe as long as I limited my search to the outsides. I hadn't gone far when my hands rested on something hanging on the wall. I recognized the shape almost immediately; it was one of the rechargeable safety lights that were placed in some areas of the hospital in case of a power outage—salvation! Relief swept over me. I had been getting desperate and a little claustrophobic, and now I could find my way out. I pulled the light from its bracket on the wall and hit the switch—nothing.

Dammit! How could they let the batteries go bad on a light down here where you really needed it? But of course, that was the answer in itself—nobody ever came down here... well, almost nobody. I decided to go back and make my way through the darkness.

I have read that over time blind people develop an ability to sense air density with their faces, that they can tell when a wall is before them. I found I possessed a similar ability, though I had to actually walk into the wall nose first to tell it was there.

After that I moved more slowly, stretching my arms out to their full length and moving them constantly back and forth. I thought how nice it would be to have a pair of night-vision goggles such as I had seen in movies and on TV. The thought occurred to me that anyone nearby with a pair of night-vision goggles would have an amusing spectacle to observe as I bounced myself off of walls, pipes, and metal cabinets as I made my way through this dark subterranean world.

After what seemed like hours of banging my shins, bumping my head, and tripping over objects on the floor, I ran into something that hit me squarely in the midriff. All the air left my lungs in a sudden rush as I automatically put my hands down in a belated attempt at defense. They rested on something cold, hard, and round; a railing! I moved around the railing and my foot bumped up against a step. I didn't know where the stairs led, but I knew they led out of here, and at the moment that was good enough for me.

I walked up two flights of stairs and feeling around in the dark found a door—locked. But this stairwell, unlike the first one that led down, continued upward. I walked up two more flights of stairs and came to another door—locked. I walked up two more flights of stairs and came to another door—locked.

Frustration and claustrophobia began to weigh heavily on me. I sat down on the stairs for a moment. Why the hell did they have to lock all the doors in the stairwell? What if there was a fire? How do I get myself into these situations? I could have just taken the dammed ophthalmoscope down to the shop, but no, I have to play

Sherlock Holmes and go following mystery people through strange doors down into dungeons. Get a grip, Jay! You're never gonna get out of here that way. Oh Christ, I'm starting to rhyme, I thought.

I pulled myself together and continued up another two flights of stairs. I could feel the door before me, but I was almost afraid to try it. What if this one is locked too? Oh, go on, don't be an idiot, I chided myself.

To my incredible relief this one opened to the pressure of my hands. When it did, I stumbled through it and nearly fell to the floor, but I regained my balance just in time. When I looked up, I was standing no more than a dozen feet from the nurses' station in labor and delivery. Vicky Henderson and the other nurses on duty were standing there looking at me with surprised expressions.

"What the hell happened to you?" Vicky asked.

I looked down to take inventory and saw I was covered with dust and dirt. My pants were ripped in several places as well as my shirt. My left knee was bleeding, and my right eye felt swollen where it had come into contact with a wall. All in all, I must have presented quite a spectacle.

"Vicky, you wouldn't believe me if I told you. Would you please be so kind as to page security for me? Tell them I'll be in the ER."

I limped back downstairs to the ER, and when Kathy saw me, she gasped. "What the hell happened to you?!"

"You know, the more I work in the hospital, the more I seem to need to *be* in the hospital." I proceeded to tell her about my adventures in the basement while she patched me up.

She was nearly finished when Frank the security guard walked into the treatment room. "What the hell happened to you?" he asked.

Kathy was just finishing a bandage that she had wrapped around my damaged shin. "He just can't seem to stay out of trouble," she told him.

I briefly told Frank the story while he wrote in a little spiral notebook he carried. "Let's go have a look at this little workshop you found," he said after Kathy had finished her ministrations.

We walked downstairs the way I had gone just a short time before. I showed him the place in the hall where I had seen the mystery person, and then I showed him the stairway door. He tried the handle; it was unlocked. He opened the door, and the first thing I noticed was the light on the wall behind the wire mesh was back on. He took a large flashlight from the utility belt he wore and led the way down the stairs. At the bottom he shined the light around for a few seconds, and then he hit a switch and the basement was bathed in light.

It looked different from the image that I had conjured in my mind; it was smaller than I had imagined. The electrical cabinets that ringed the workspace were only about fifteen feet from the stairs. In the dark it had seemed at least twice that far. I walked to them and then around to the other side and saw... nothing.

No light bulb hanging down, no crate, no tools, nothing. There was just a small, empty space between electrical cabinets. "What the hell is going on?!" I said more to myself than to Frank.

"Are you sure this was the spot?" Frank sounded skeptical. His skepticism made me angry, which I'm sure only made me more difficult to believe.

"I know damn good and well this was the spot!"

"Well, there's nothing here now."

"I can see that, Frank. Somebody's playing games; they've moved the stuff."

"Well, I can't file a report about something that isn't here. At least, I don't think you'd want me to."

The gentle, veiled threat was there, blatantly apparent even to my agitated mind. "Frank, I had not been drinking and I don't do drugs. I know what I saw!"

"But it was dark down here, wasn't it?"

I could see that he wasn't convinced. "What about the ophthalmoscope, Frank? I brought an ophthalmoscope down from the ER to check it out."

"Where is it?"

"I left it and my tool bag in the hallway."

"I didn't see them on our way down."

He was right. They hadn't been where I'd left them. "Debbie and Kathy saw me with the ophthalmoscope in the ER."

"Let's go back upstairs and look around."

We walked back to the ER to bay three where the intern had been giving the little boy the seatbelt lecture, where I had pulled the ophthalmoscope from the wall. The bay was empty at the moment, so I pulled the curtain completely open. I turned to Frank. "There, take a look, it's..." I turned my head toward the wall as I spoke, and there it was as if it had never been removed. I didn't know what to say. "I... it... I took it down."

Frank shook his head slightly. "It's there now, Jay."

"But... ask Debbie, ask Kathy, they saw me take it down."

When we found Debbie, I repeated the gist of the story to give her an idea of what had happened to me. She looked apologetic and somewhat puzzled as Frank asked her about the ophthalmoscope. "Well, I saw him with it, but we were busy with a patient. I don't know, Frank, I thought he had it with him. But it's here now. I don't know..." She looked at me. "I'm sorry, Jay."

I felt as if someone had dropped a brick on my head. She was right; I knew it. She hadn't actually seen me leave with it, neither had

Kathy. They were on their way to deal with the superglue patient; they'd had their minds on something else.

Frank sounded apologetic also. "Go home, Jay. Get some sleep. As far as I'm concerned none of this happened."

"I'm not going home until I've checked this thing out." I took the ophthalmoscope from the wall once more and headed back downstairs. When I got to the shop, the first thing I did was to turn all of the lights on. For some reason this afforded me some measure of comfort, at least until I noticed the on-call tool bag sitting on the workbench.

After checking the tool bag to make sure nothing was missing, I set the ophthalmoscope on the bench and began taking it apart. A short time later the device lay in pieces and I had found nothing out of the ordinary. I knew it was the same unit I had first taken off the wall because the control number was the same. All devices that came into the hospital were assigned a number as a means of tracking them, and by force of habit it was one of the first things I had checked.

I pushed the stool away from the bench and sat looking at my handiwork. What the hell was going on? The events of the past few hours were like a dream, a bad one.

The next morning, I promptly marched into Dan's office and told him the whole story. I was sipping coffee, trying to recover from the night's adventures.

"You couldn't tell if it was a man or a woman?" he asked.

"No, it was too dark."

"Big or small?"

"Like I said, Dan, the person was a couple hundred feet away and in shadows. I just couldn't tell. I wish I could." I knew besides Trevor, Dan was probably the only other person who would believe me. At least he was the only other person I felt I could trust with the story. I wasn't sure where I stood with Debbie right now.

At the moment he seemed to be struggling, wanting to believe, but I had to admit the whole thing was so strange, I was having trouble believing it myself.

"And when you went back to the ER you found the unit hanging back on the wall where you had found it?"

"Yes."

"I assume you checked for damage?"

"Yeah. It looked fine, but you know those things are built to take a lot of punishment." In the ER where events often happened unpredictably and the staff had to respond quickly and without benefit of time to be careful, a lot of the equipment was of an even sturdier construction than in other parts of the hospital.

We were sitting in Dan's office with the door closed. I had asked to see him privately as soon as I'd arrived at work. He'd taken one look at my face and ushered me into his office to one of the chairs in front of his desk. Before he had closed the door, he'd gotten each of us a cup of coffee, and he took a sip now as he sat mulling over the story I had just told him.

"Who the hell would screw with medical machines and why?" he mused.

"Those are the two questions I've been asking myself."

"As far as who, it must be an employee," he posited. "Who else would know their way around this place well enough to avoid detection?"

"That seems to make the most sense. Of course, thousands of people worked on the construction of this place. I suppose one of them might know their way around well enough," I said.

"I don't think so. I can't think of any scenario that would explain why a former construction worker was that disgruntled. Besides, too many changes have taken place inside since it was built. Whoever the culprit is, they'd have to be familiar with the way things are done here. If they stuck out at all, someone would have noticed."

"It's an awfully big place," I said.

"I still think it would have to be an employee," Dan said thoughtfully.

"It wouldn't necessarily have to be a *present* employee." I offered. "Can you think of anyone who's been fired or laid off recently who might hold a grudge?"

"Not off-hand. I'm going to look into it though; it would explain why."

"Of course, present employees might have reasons as well."

"Such as?" Dan asked.

"Revenge?"

"Revenge for what?"

"Oh, I don't know. Someone's pissed off at the boss because their last raise wasn't big enough?"

Dan gave me the eye. "Are you trying to tell me something?"

The realization of what I had just said hit home. Dan wasn't smiling. "Hell no, Dan, I'm very happy here. I'm just trying to figure this thing out. Besides, I *am* the one who brought it to your attention."

Dan's face softened immediately. "Yeah, Jay, you did. Sorry, it's just that this whole thing is so crazy."

"Tell me about it. If you think it seems crazy from here, you should have been down in the basement."

"Speaking of which, why don't you show me where this little workshop is you found?"

"There isn't much to see, but sure, I'll show you."

We walked down the hall to the first intersection and turned left to the door I had so recently discovered. Everything seemed so different in the daytime. The bright fluorescent lights were on, and people were busily going about their usual routines. The deep-throated hum was barely discernable with all the activity taking place.

I had brought a flashlight with me this time, and I switched it on as we began to descend the stairs. At the bottom I shined the light around and located the wall switch just as Frank had done. I switched the overhead lights on and as I looked around, I was struck once again with how much smaller the space seemed when it was bathed in light.

Dust covered everything in a thick layer except on the floor where it had been disturbed by passing feet, both mine and Frank's and the mystery person or persons we were trying to discover. With the electrical cabinets situated here and there, it looked for all the world like some ancient Egyptian tomb.

Dan stood looking around also. "Hell of a place for a workshop."

"Isn't it?"

"Where did you find the workbench?"

"Over here, between these cabinets."

We walked over to the spot, which was just as bare as it had been when I had been here with Frank, and began taking a closer look around. Once again dust covered everything except for where it had been disturbed on the floor.

"Something was definitely here and then moved," Dan said.

"At least you're seeing some evidence to back me up."

Dan looked at me intently. "I believe you, Jay."

"Thanks, Dan."

I had begun to walk around the back of the far cabinet when I stepped on something that rolled and nearly lost my balance. I managed to get a handhold on the closest cabinet and prevented myself from falling, though I ended up in an awkward stance.

Dan looked up at the sudden sound. "I really don't think this is the time for gymnastics, Jay."

"I found something, Dan!" I bent down to retrieve whatever it was.

"What is it?" Dan asked hurrying over. "What have you got?"

We both looked as I stood up with the object. It was a small pocket screwdriver emblazoned with the logo 'E-Z Engineering Products'. I recognized it and so did Dan. It was a souvenir from a digital electronics seminar some of the biomed techs had attended a few months prior.

Dan stared at it without speaking, then he looked at me. I had been mentally counting the techs from our department who had attended the seminar. "Six," I said, and Dan nodded. The look on his face was not a happy one.

"Alan, Bobby, Trevor, Will, you and me," I said, naming the group who had attended the seminar. "We're the only ones I know of who would have one of these."

"So, what does that mean?" Dan asked rhetorically.

"I'm afraid it might mean something I don't want to think about," I said.

"This is turning into a nightmare."

"I wish we could wake up."

Dan issued a small sigh. "Well, there's nothing we can do right now. Why don't you go home? You look like you could stand to get some sleep, and maybe a shower and some first-aid."

"Do I look that bad?"

"Yes."

I nodded, suddenly feeling fatigue wash over me. I had barely managed to nod off for a little over an hour after my night adventure, and sleep sounded really good right now.

I returned to the shop and gathered my things. I headed to the ER. Maybe I could catch Debbie before she ended her shift and talk to her. I had to make things right with her and I couldn't let this go several days.

When I got to the ER, I learned that Debbie had already left and wouldn't be back until the day after tomorrow because she was going back on day shift. She would be tired, and I definitely needed some sleep before I faced her again, so I headed home and fell into bed fully dressed and was asleep before my head hit the pillow.

When I awoke again the sun was shining brightly. I was confused, what day was it? I looked at the clock on my nightstand—it was after four. So, it had to be late afternoon; I hadn't slept round the clock. That was some relief. At least I didn't have to go to work until the next day.

I took stock of myself before getting up; my right eye was sore, and my left leg hurt where it had been bandaged. I was sure that there were a few more scrapes and bruises that I hadn't yet discovered, but I didn't feel too bad.

I got out of bed, realizing I was still in my dirty clothes. Great, I'd have to do some wash soon because the sheets would definitely need to be changed. I stumbled into the bathroom.

My face didn't look as bad as it felt. There was a bruise on my right cheek near my eye, but my eye wasn't nearly as swollen as I'd feared. I pulled off my filthy clothes and started to toss them in the hamper, but then thought better of it and dropped them on the floor. I'd decide later what I could keep and what I'd have to throw away. I got into the shower and let the hot water soothe my body.

I felt considerably better after a long shower, and I changed the bandage on my knee. Naked, I walked into my small kitchen and started some coffee, remembering the morning I found Debbie in here looking for coffee with her bare ass exposed beneath my shirt. At once I knew what I had to do.

Leaning on the counter, I sipped my coffee and made a list. This was probably going to be my last chance with Debbie, so I had to get it right.

I quickly dressed—khaki's, button down shirt. I wanted to look casual, but not too casual. I grabbed my keys and my jacket and headed to my car.

It took me more than an hour to get to Debbie's because I made several stops along the way. I parked out front and picked up my gifts and walked to her door. When I reached her door with my arms full of candy, flowers and Chinese food, I tried to reach the doorbell with my elbow, but couldn't quite manage. I couldn't knock with my hands, so I ended up kicking at her door. Swell, I thought, this is not the impression I was going for.

It took me two rounds of kicking, when the door finally opened a crack and Debbie peered out at me through the slot allowed by the chain.

"I'm really sorry about trying to kick your door down, but my hands are kind of full," I said hopefully.

"I can see that," she said, and we stood there for a moment.

"Can I come in?" My voice was meek, and I was really trying not to beg.

"I'm thinking about it," she said.

"Well, while you're thinking about letting me in, can you take the flowers before I drop them?"

She eyed me for another minute, and then the door closed. Just as I was beginning to panic, I heard her slip the chain and she opened the door wide enough for me to enter, but I hesitated.

"You're sure I can come in?"

A small smile appeared. "Yes, you can come in now."

I walked into her tiny apartment and over to the counter that separated her living room from the kitchen and put down the candy and Chinese food. "Do you have a vase for the flowers? I forgot to get a vase..."

She was still standing by the door, which was still open. She was wearing sweat pants and a sweatshirt, no makeup, and her hair was tousled. She obviously had spent her day sleeping too. And she looked sexy as hell.

"Or do you want me to just leave?"

She closed the door and walked to the kitchen and rummaged in a cabinet until she found a wine carafe. She ran some water into the carafe, took the flowers from me and placed them in it and put them on the counter next to the candy and Chinese food. She hadn't said another word.

I had expected she would be angry, but at least willing to hear me out. This reaction totally threw me. We stood on opposite sides of the counter and she looked at me expectantly. All the things I had planned to say left my brain. I had an apology all ready to go, but when I opened my mouth, no words came. I could only think of how beautiful, sexy and vulnerable she looked. I had to say something. I sifted through the blockage in my brain for some remnants of my apology speech, but instead I blurted out, "I love you."

She continued to stare into my eyes, and I could feel myself start to blush. I held my breath. This was not the way I had planned this at all. I waited for her to tell me to leave.

When she finally spoke, it was not at all what I was expecting.

"I know," she said softly.

I felt a little dizzy and realized I was still holding my breath. I breathed. "You know? How could you possibly know after the way I behaved like such a jerk?"

A slow smile crept across her lips. "Because you behaved like such a jerk."

I suddenly recalled my apology speech. "I was afraid; I never felt this way about a woman before. And when I saw you with Craig

Scott, I figured I couldn't compete with a rich, handsome doctor. And I never thought you were a whore..."

While the words gushed out, she slowly walked around the counter and at the word 'whore', she took my face in her hands and kissed me.

She pulled back, her hands still holding my face.

"But I treated you so horribly," I said, relieved but confused.

"Jay, there are jerks who know they are jerks and then there are jerks who don't." She kissed me again and this time I put my arms around her and held her close, kissing her back.

When the kiss ended, she said, "Promise me that now you know you were a jerk, you will never be a jerk again."

"I promise," and I kissed her again tightening my arms around her.

After a minute she pulled away and walked back around the counter. "Are you going to take your jacket off and stay?" she asked. She picked up the bag of Chinese food and started putting containers into the refrigerator.

I took off my jacket and hung it on the coatrack standing next to the front door. "I thought we'd have the Chinese food for dinner..." I said.

She finished putting the containers into the frig. "Do you want to have dinner now or later?" she asked with a mischievous look on her face.

I immediately took my foot out of my mouth. Mr. Suave, I thought, and hastily agreed, "Later."

She closed the frig and walked over to me taking my hand and leading me the four steps to the bedroom.

I ended up spending the night. We ended up having the Chinese food as an early breakfast. We both had to work this morning, and

I decided it was best to go home, shower and change before work so my attire would not raise eyebrows at the shop.

I kissed her goodbye at the door and left her standing there in a short robe tied at her waist. I didn't want to leave, but she smiled and said, "See you at the office," and closed the door behind me.

I was alone when I entered the shop, so instead of hanging around, I decided to just grab my cart and get to work. I was not in the mood for the usual morning banter. My thoughts were totally focused on Debbie, which was not good; I needed to focus on what I was doing.

I pushed my cart, heading to the third floor to start my inspections for the day. As I stepped off the elevator on three, I heard the call.

"Code Blue, east wing, room thirty-four, twenty-four... Code Blue, east wing, room thirty-four, twenty-four."

Several doctors and nurses passed me moving rapidly toward room thirty-four, twenty-four. A patient had gone into cardiac arrest, and I knew there would be a defibrillator on a crash cart standing by. This was a prime moment for a BMET to suffer an acute attack of anxiety. A person's life was probably going to depend, at least in part, on the performance of a machine, and if you were the last person to work on that machine, you couldn't help but be a little nervous about it.

I always found myself asking, did I check everything? Did I put it through a rigorous enough inspection? If all the answers were yes, you still knew the machine's performance might depend on something that was done several months earlier, and you really had no control over it. There was nothing you could do now but watch and pray. I had never actually seen it happen, but you knew that if it failed, someone was probably going to die.

I fell into step with the medical personnel heading down the hall and we soon arrived at room thirty-four, twenty-four. The scene was one of organized chaos. It seemed every doctor, nurse, respiratory technician, and ECG technician in the area was on the scene to lend whatever assistance they could. I even saw Donna Fielding from the OR there.

Trevor was standing just outside the door to the room, and I suspected from the look on his face he had been the last tech to work on the defib. I walked over and stood next to him.

"How's it going, Trev?"

"It doesn't look good, Jay. I was just a couple of rooms down when the nurse went into this room and found the guy not breathing."

"You worked on the defib last?"

"Yesterday. I inspected it and replaced the batteries. They sounded weak while the defib was charging, squealing, you know?"

"Yeah, I just replaced the batteries on one the other day." Defibrillators made a distinctive sound when their batteries became weak. The batteries charged a large capacitor, and when they were insufficiently charged or on the verge of wearing out, the capacitor sounded like it was straining to reach full power.

"I just hope the new batteries charged fully."

"Relax, Trevor. It's been more than twenty-four hours; they'll be fine.

I tried to sound encouraging, but I knew there was nothing I could say that was going to ease his anxiety at this point. We could see the patient through the glass beside the door. He wasn't old—maybe late forties or early fifties.

His skin looked gray and pasty, and a doctor was performing CPR on him, counting as he applied compressions to the man's chest. The room seemed strangely quiet as this was going on. All those medical people stood around the bed, and the only sound that could be heard was the doctor counting.

After so many counts the doctor would pause, and a respiratory tech would ventilate the man with an ambu-bag while the doctor checked for a pulse. This went on for several minutes until the doctor paused, listened to the man's chest with a stethoscope, and nodded to a nurse that was closest to the crash cart. She wheeled it closer to the bed, and the doctor removed the paddles from their holders and said, "Two hundred joules."

The nurse turned the knob to the requested setting and hit the charge button. The machine gave a healthy whine as the charge capacitor strived to achieve full power. I could sense Trevor holding his breath as he stood next to me. Even before the doctor said, "Clear!" the people around the bed had taken a step back in unison, as if the scene was being orchestrated by some unseen director.

The paddles came down onto the man's chest as if in slow motion and made a slight slapping sound as they contacted his skin. The doctor pressed the discharge buttons, and the patients back arched once and then settled back onto the bed. Immediately the doctor palpated the man's carotid artery feeling for a pulse, and then he listened again with his stethoscope while everyone else in the room stood staring at the ECG monitor on top of the defib. It remained in V-fib.

The doctor grabbed the paddles once again. "Three hundred joules," he said as the nurse reset the machine. She pushed the charge button... and nothing happened.

"Get me another defibrillator in here stat!" The doctor did not sound happy.

Three nurses ran out the door and headed in different directions. The doctor had resumed CPR, as I stole a glance at Trevor. His face was a mask of shock and disbelief, and I felt a growing horror as the unreality of what was happening hit me all at once. Seconds seemed to drag on forever as the doctor frantically continued to work on the patient.

Finally, one of the nurses returned carrying a portable defib which was hastily set in position. The doctor shocked the man, searched for a rhythm that wasn't there, and then shocked him again. In another few minutes all that could be tried was done, and the doctor angrily slammed the paddles back into their holders on the machine.

"Pronounce him!" was all that he said, and then he turned and left the room without looking at anyone.

I turned to Trevor; he was gone.

I returned to the shop to see if Trevor had gone there. As I walked in, Dan and Will Stanski were sitting at a bench talking. By the looks on their faces I knew they'd heard the news.

"Dan, have you seen Trevor?" I asked.

"No, Jay, but you'd better go find him." His voice was sad and concerned, with a certain air of foreboding as if he knew what was coming.

"Is Trevor in trouble?"

"There will be a formal inquiry."

"Dan, you and I both know there isn't a BMET in this shop that cares more about what he does than Trevor."

"I know, but I want to talk to him before they do. Find him, will you? You're his buddy, Jay. I don't care how long it takes, find him and bring him here."

It took me more than two hours. I checked the maintenance wing, the cafeteria, the lounges, the library. I was going through the patient floors becoming worried he had left the hospital, when I looked out a window and there he was. I could barely see him for the foliage, but he was sitting on a rock looking out over one of the lakes.

I hurried out the nearest exit and ran across the grounds to the lake. I approached him from the side, I didn't want to startle him by walking up from behind. He never looked up at me, but as I got closer, I could see there had been tears streaming down his face.

My heart ached for my friend, for I had been close enough to this situation myself to understand what he must be feeling. Doctors and nurses lived with life and death situations all the time, and we respected them for it immensely, but at least they had some control over the situations they encountered. The machines we maintained were often involved in these encounters, but we couldn't physically make them work when the time came.

When you knew the machines well enough to realize all the intangibles, all the reasons why they might not work, it became a scary, helpless feeling when you knew they were being pressed into vital service. It was abundantly clear to me that to see a device you had been responsible for fail with such dire circumstances could be devastating.

I didn't know what to say to him; everything that came to mind seemed stupid and meaningless, so I just sat down beside him figuring he'd talk when he wanted to. We sat for a long time just gazing at the lake. I felt I could sense his confusion and frustration.

"Life's funny sometimes." He said it so quietly I could barely hear him. I wanted to keep him talking to get his feelings out where they could be dealt with.

"How do you mean?" I asked in the same quiet tone of voice that he had used.

"You think you know what you're doing and then..."

I was trying to weigh my words carefully; I still wasn't sure what to say. "Trevor, there are so many possible things that can happen, you can never be completely... "

Suddenly he shouted with all the desperation I knew he was feeling. "The guy died, man!" His face was turning red. "I didn't make him late for an appointment, I didn't screw up and piss him off! The guy is fucking dead!"

I realized that although I thought I understood what he was feeling, I hadn't actually lived his experience. I could empathize, but there was nothing I could say or do to make him feel any better. Maybe listening was the best I could offer my friend.

"Yeah, Trev, he died."

He got up abruptly and walked a half a dozen paces away and stood with his hands on his hips, his back to me. After a few moments he turned and there was an intensity on his face I had never seen before.

"Do you understand what that means? Do you? He'll never laugh, or love, or cry, or work, or play again. There will be people who love him, whose hearts will break because of me. Because of me!"

I felt a great frustration myself. On one hand I understood why he felt the way he did, but on the other hand I knew he must be made to see it wasn't his fault. I stood up and walked toward him, stopping when I was about a foot from him. It was hard to look into his eyes, for they held such gut-wrenching despair, but I looked at him hard none the less.

"Look, Trevor, all that you say about the man's life ending is true, but you cannot blame yourself. I know of no one else who cares more about what they do. I know of no one else who pays more attention to detail. I know of no one else who tries harder to feel right about what he does than you do. You told me you checked that machine out. I know damned good and well that you did everything you could. I know you. You trained me, remember?"

He shrugged and turned away as if afraid to look me in the eye. "Yeah, I guess I did, didn't I?" His voice was quieter, sadder. "Well here's your latest lesson; learn it well. Give it everything you've got and then don't look back." He turned to look out over the lake again.

"You don't mean that, Trev. If you don't look back, then you gain no perspective on where you're going. You didn't kill that guy, life did."

He looked at me again. "What the hell are you talking about, Jay?"

"Maybe it wouldn't have made any difference what you did or didn't do; maybe it was just the guy's time. When all is said and done, life is terminal."

"But the machine failed! When it was really needed it wasn't there."

"When you did the inspection did you do everything you could to check it out?" I asked.

"Yes... I think so. I've been over it in my head a thousand times. I can't think of anything I forgot to do."

"Do you believe in God?"

He looked at me strangely with my sudden change of direction. I was beginning to wonder about what was coming out of my mouth, but I had already decided to trust my instincts and go with the flow.

"I used to, when I was a kid. I guess... yeah I guess I do."

"Maybe God just decided it was time for the guy to die and it wouldn't have made any difference what you did."

"Maybe. They still have to analyze the machine. Jay, what are they gonna do to me?"

His demeaner had changed. I sensed the fear and apprehension of having his ability as a BMET called into question had caught up with him. I wished I had some comfort to offer him, but I didn't. I knew no matter how hard we tried, to someone it wouldn't be good enough.

"We don't know what they're going to find, Trev."

"That's what scares me. With all of the equipment problems that have been happening, you know they're going to be looking for a scapegoat."

"And you think it will be you?"

"Who else? Administration is going to want a sacrifice, and I'm afraid it's going to be my head on the chopping block. If they fire me over this, I'll never be able to get another job in the field. My career will be over."

"Come on, let's go talk to Dan. He's been worried about you." I put my hand on his shoulder and guided him in the direction we needed to go. He offered no resistance.

I went home that night feeling totally despondent. Trevor had refused a drink and/or company, so I left him at his car. I worried about him and what he might do. I didn't think his life was in danger, but I was afraid he would consider quitting, and that could start a downward spiral that would be difficult to pull out of.

After sitting on my couch sipping a beer and staring at the TV, I decided I needed to talk to somebody. I walked to the kitchen and lifted the receiver from the phone on the wall and dialed Debbie's number.

She answered after the fourth ring, sounding tired. "Hello?"

"Hi, it's me. Did you just get home?"

"Yeah, about fifteen minutes ago. I was just going to change and find something to eat."

"Can I come over? I'll bring something to eat," I asked hopefully.

"Jay, I don't think I'm up for anything tonight. It was not a good day..."

"No, I don't mean that. I really need somebody to talk to. That's it. I just need to see you," I said earnestly.

She didn't respond immediately. A minute passed and I tried to wait patiently. She finally said, "I heard about the code and Trevor." She sounded sad.

"That's why I need to talk to you," I explained.

"Okay, you can come over. But we'll just talk, is that alright? I don't think I can..."

"Neither can I. I'll be there as soon as I can."

I arrived at her door with a pizza and a bottle of wine. This time I knocked properly, and she opened the door and gave me a tired smile when she saw what I'd brought.

She was wearing her sweats again and looked beautiful. I put the pizza and wine on the counter and proceeded to open the bottle. She got two juice glasses from a kitchen cabinet and I poured some wine in both and we each took a sip.

"I know white wine doesn't go with pizza..." I said apologetically.

She shook her head. "I don't care." She found some paper plates and we took our wine and pizza over to the couch and sat down. We ate for a minute, and then she said, "So tell me what happened."

I launched into a detailed description of the code and looking for Trevor and our conversation. She said little, but listened intently, and as it poured out of me, I started feeling better. When I finally stopped talking, I realized I'd barely eaten any pizza.

"Let me warm some up for you." She took my paper plate into the kitchen, loaded it with pizza and put it in the microwave. She brought the warm pizza back. "Here, eat something." She poured us both more wine.

"Thank you," I said sincerely.

"For what?" she asked.

"For listening."

She leaned over and kissed me on the cheek. "I think it's sweet you're worrying so much about Trevor. It says a lot about what a decent person you are."

I didn't know how to respond to that, so I kissed her back lightly. "I didn't intend for you to spend your evening listening to me," I told her.

"It's all right, you needed to talk about it."

I suddenly felt hungry, so ate my pizza and we had some more wine.

"So, what happened to make your day bad?" I asked between bites.

She sighed and put her wine glass down on the small table next to the couch. "We had a seven-year-old boy come in today with a broken back."

She paused, and the look in her eyes was a combination of sadness and anger. Her hands were in her lap folded tightly.

I put down my plate and wine glass and moved closer to her, removing one of her hands from the death grip and putting it between both of mine. "Tell me what happened," it was my turn to say.

Tears ran down her cheeks as she explained to me the extent of the child's injuries. "I don't know yet if he'll be paralyzed. He went to surgery and I didn't hear any more news before I came home."

"I certainly understand how that would upset you, it's hard enough to hear second-hand." I remembered the girl I saw in the pediatric department who had been a victim of child abuse and how hard it was to fathom someone doing that to their own child. "Do you know how he was injured?" I asked, almost afraid to hear the answer.

"Someone hit him and knocked him down a flight of stairs onto a cement floor in the basement," she said with disgust.

"I'm guessing I know who the 'someone' was," I said, beginning to feel her pain.

Her eyes met mine and we shared an understanding and she nodded. "It was the boy's father, Jay. His own father. One of the people he's supposed to be able to trust."

I leaned over and took her in my arms. " I know. It's so hard to believe a parent could do that."

"It's not just that. The boy has Down Syndrome and it reminded me of *my* father and how he didn't understand my brother. He seemed to believe it was my brother's fault he was mentally handicapped, and felt God was punishing him for something. I don't know what, but he didn't always treat my brother well..." Her voice broke off as the sobs came. There was nothing I could say, so I just held her until her crying ebbed.

"I'm sorry," she said, reaching to the end table to get tissues to wipe her face and my wet shirt.

"Whatever are *you* sorry for? Here I am going on and on about the defibrillator and Trevor, when your day was so much worse. And you just sat and listened to me. I'm the one who should be sorry."

She shook her head and her lips formed a small, tired smile.

"Nothing to be sorry about. We both had bad days," she said.

"I didn't know about your father and brother," I said, expecting more to the story.

She shook her head again. "Of course you didn't, but I'm too tired to think about that now. I'll tell you the whole sad tale later."

I looked at my watch; I was surprised to see it was almost midnight.

"I'd better go and let you get some sleep," I said rising from the couch and putting the plate in the trash along with the wine bottle. She rose and locked the door and stood in front of it. We looked at each other a moment.

"But you said..."

"Yes, I did, and I meant that. But you've had too much wine to drive. Come in and lay down with me and just hold me."

I followed her into the bedroom and we both got under the quilt on her bed fully dressed and promptly fell asleep in each other's arms.

Three days later the atmosphere at lunch was funereal. It seemed like every regulatory agency and insurance investigator in existence had beaten a path to our door.

We were all treading lightly around Trevor. His nerves had obviously had enough; he was edgy and nervous, practically afraid of his own shadow. All of us in the shop empathized with him. Even Alan seemed to treat him with deference and an attempt at understanding.

Trevor had one more interview to endure after lunch, and then Dan was sending him home for a badly needed week off. Dan had first proposed this the other day as we sat down to eat. Trevor had at first protested, thinking he was being suspended, but we all jumped on the idea telling him to take a little time for himself. He seemed to accept the idea with a reluctance that soon turned to gratitude as he thought about it.

We were about halfway through lunch when Dwayne Dorfly stuck his head in the door. "I need a decision on those beds, Dan," he said.

We sat stunned. No one could believe Dorfly's pettiness, coming to Dan with something so trivial at a time like this. We all waited with bated breath, eyes somewhat averted, to see what Dan's reaction would be.

We didn't have to wait long, for suddenly a half-full carton of chocolate milk went flying over our heads and landed squarely in the middle of Dorfly's forehead. Chocolate milk covered the wall and the open door, but Dorfly didn't move a muscle as it ran profusely through his eyebrows, over his nose, through his mustache, and dripped off his chin forming a brown puddle on the floor.

The room was eerily quiet as we sat there watching Dorfly's face turn bright red under its coating of chocolate milk. We waited for an explosion, but it never came. Dorfly simply said, "We'll talk about it later," and he left.

Nobody said a word; we were too shocked to speak. We had all witnessed, and occasionally experienced a dressing down from Dan. With a look and a few words, he had the ability to make even the most aggressive person cower, but we had never seen him get physical with anybody, let alone another department head. I felt there was something at play here we didn't understand and maybe never would.

The silence was broken by a gagging sound coming from my right-hand side where Trevor was sitting. When I looked at him, I saw that his face had turned an even brighter shade of red than Dorfly's. His shoulders were heaving up and down and his hand was clamped over his mouth in an unsuccessful attempt to stifle the laughter that was beginning to rock his body. All of the tension that had been building up in him seemed to be trying to get out at once.

It was contagious. The room was suddenly filled with laughter as the tension that had built up in all of us began to seep out. My eyes were so full of tears I could hardly see. Dan was doubled over onto the table holding his sides coughing and laughing as Will Stanski clapped him on the back.

The laughter would ebb and then someone would start to giggle, and it would start again. I don't know just how long we'd have kept it up if the phone hadn't rung.

Papa Joe was closest to the phone, so he answered it with a chuckle escaping his lips. His expression immediately changed, and the laughter died as he listened. "Okay," he said, looking at Dan, "I'll tell him." Papa Joe replaced the receiver and turned back to Dan. "It's Dennis. He's in the ER. He had a bicycle accident at the loading dock."

Dan didn't say a word, didn't even stop to ask questions. He got up and hurried out the door.

Papa Joe looked after him with his mouth half open. "I didn't even get a chance to tell him it wasn't serious," he exclaimed.

"It wouldn't have mattered," Will told him. "He would have left just as fast anyway to see for himself."

I looked from Will to Papa Joe with a question I did not ask. It was clear that lunch was over for the day.

Dan didn't return for nearly three hours. I was the only one in the shop when he came through the door looking haggard. He went immediately into his office and sat behind his desk. Figuring he could use it, I got a cup of coffee from the machine and took it into him.

"Thanks, Jay."

"Sure. Is Dennis okay?"

"Yeah. He's scratched and banged up a little, but he's okay. They stitched his head, and I took him home and put him to bed. It wasn't easy. He knows he's supposed to be at work now, and trying to change his schedule is like sword fighting with Zorro."

"You think a lot of him, don't you?"

"Yeah. He's a sweet kid. He just needs a break, that's all."

"Well, boss, I'd say he's found a good friend."

He looked at me and the barest hint of a smile came to his face. "Yeah, yeah. Don't you have somethin' to do?" And he waved me out of his office. Not really knowing why, I closed the door behind me.

Alan and I didn't go on many calls together. Alan didn't go on many calls with anyone. For the most part he preferred to work alone, and since he was a loner anyway and an excellent tech, Dan usually went out of his way to accommodate him.

We had gotten a call from GICU, the geriatric care unit, step-down section on the fifth floor, about a telemetry malfunction. The intensive care unit took up part of the southern pod and the step-down unit took up the rest. While all of the intensive care units had bedside monitors to keep track of the patient's vital signs in detail, all of the step-down units had telemetry systems to keep track of the less critical patient's ECG waveforms.

A telemetry 'set' consisted of a transmitter about the size of a deck of cards the patient wore, usually on a lanyard around their neck, and a receiver located out of sight in a storage room.

Before we were in the elevator, true to form, Alan started to get upset. I don't know why; I couldn't understand why he couldn't just relax and go with the flow as it were. As usual, the more upset he got, the gassier he became.

"I don't know how many times I've told those nurses to prep thoroughly (thbbt). Do they listen? Of course, not (thbbt). I've told them not to use alcohol but to clean with soap and water, abrade the skin, and then put the electrodes on (thbbt)." His flatulence was beginning to sound like punctuation.

The elevator stopped at the first floor as it usually did, and several people got on. I tried to get Alan to calm down. "Come on, Alan, we haven't even looked yet. It could be a legitimate problem."

"Yeah, right (thbbt). You just know those dumb nurses probably put the electrodes over the hair and all (thbbt)."

The people who had joined us on the elevator began to look uncomfortable. There had been some conversation between them, but that died quickly.

"Well, how about if we take a look before we jump to any conclusions?" I tried to console him again.

Alan had retreated to a corner of the elevator and began muttering to himself. "Damned nurses (thbbt). Still don't know how to prep a patient (thbbt)." Maybe it was my imagination, but I could swear there was a cloud forming in the elevator car.

The elevator stopped at the fourth floor and everyone else on it seemed to jump at one time, trying to be the first off. Alan was oblivious to them, still muttering away in the corner and farting with abandon.

I was glad of the fact we only had one more floor to go and there wouldn't be anyone else joining us. We arrived at five and stepped off the elevator, turning left toward GICU.

As we approached the nurses' station, I saw an old man sitting in a geri-chair behind the counter. This was not unusual in itself. Patients, especially older long-term patients sometimes become lonely, and the nurses would sit them in the middle of their activities for a while to make them feel a part of something.

What got my attention was that this old man was stark naked. Nurses moved back and forth around him checking charts and ECG strips and he just sat there babbling away, sometimes to them and sometimes to someone nobody else could see. The geri-chair had a tray attached, and the old man had his lunch in front of him.

"What do you mean you don't like it?" he asked an imaginary person on his left. "How do you know unless you try it?"

"Eat your lunch, Mr. Eldrich. He'll just have to get his own," one of the nurses said to him as she passed.

"Goddamned lousy service in this place. I don't know why I come in here," he said as she went by.

"Because you love the ambiance," said another as she went in the opposite direction.

"Yeah, but the food stinks!" Then to his imaginary friend, "Don't eat the corn, it gives you gas."

I walked up to a petite woman with short salt and pepper hair examining ECG strips.

"Hi, Lucy," I said.

She smiled at me when she looked up, though the smile faded somewhat when she noticed Alan.

"Hi, Jay, that was fast. I just hung up with Dan."

"All part of the friendly service ma'am," I said in my best attempt at a western drawl. Then I indicated the old man in the geri-chair. "Is this a new trend we're starting?"

She looked at him with an exasperated expression as she shook her head. "We can't keep clothes on him. We dress him, and two minutes later he's in the buff again. Finally, we just gave up."

"Well, I go through moods like that myself sometimes." I told her.

"I'll bet you do, lover," she said with a wink.

Alan looked at me disapprovingly and seemed to draw himself up as if preparing for a fight.

"What's the problem?" he said bluntly as I cringed inwardly.

Lucy was another of my favorites, and I couldn't imagine why Alan found it necessary to be such a pain. Of course, Lucy had been around a long time; she was no pushover, and I knew she wasn't about to take any crap from him. The warm demeanor that she usually addressed me with was gone and toward Alan she projected all the warmth of an iceberg.

"The problem, *junior*, is that number five telly is displaying artifact like a seismograph. Off-hand I'd say it needs to be tuned."

I could almost see the hairs going up on the back of Alan's neck. He was extremely sensitive about stature, and Lucy had zeroed in on the fact like a guided missile.

"Well, that will be for a technician to decide, not some *nurse*!" He spat the last word out like it was an obscenity.

Here we go, I thought. I knew there was really nothing I could do to smooth over the situation, but I figured it was worth a shot.

"Alan, Lucy is probably right. Why don't we just take the unit downstairs and check it out?" My suggestion fell on deaf ears.

Alan was on a roll. "I don't need to be told my job by some... lay person!"

"Only when I'm lucky, honey," Lucy said as she smiled at me.

"Just who prepped the patient?!" Alan demanded.

"I did, why?" It was as if Lucy had just drawn a line in the sand with her toe and dared him to cross it.

"I'll bet you prepped with alcohol, didn't you?" he snarled.

Lucy was cool. She didn't get angry, she didn't bat an eyelash, she just smiled sweetly. "Alan, do you suffer from hemorrhoids?" she asked.

"What?!" Alan said incredulously.

"I'll bet a nice ice-water enema would do you wonders. I could probably find a few volunteers to carry out the procedure."

That did it. I couldn't help it, a smile came to my face of its own volition, and of course that pissed Alan off even more. I glanced at him and saw he had turned beet red as he gathered himself rigidly to the full extent of his five-foot, two-inch frame.

"How... " he began while Lucy was still smiling, waiting patiently. "How... How dare you! (thbbbbbt)."

There was an old woman in a wheelchair sitting about ten feet behind Alan when the big release came. It could be heard plainly all over the area, but evidently, she was hard of hearing for she put her hand to her ear asking, "Yes?" as if someone had called her.

The naked guy in the geri-chair looked to his left and shouted, "I told you not to eat the corn!"

Lucy had an amused look on her face. Alan stood like a stone statue not knowing what to say after having the wind knocked out of him, so to speak.

I was trying to maintain a straight face and hoped it was working. "Alan? Why don't you go back to the shop and I'll bring the telly set down?"

Without a word Alan headed for the elevators, while Lucy waited to help me get the units I needed.

"What is his problem, anyway?" she asked.

"I don't know, Lucy, he's always like that."

"Maybe he was abused as a child."

"Maybe he was raised by wolves," I offered.

"Wolves, no, aardvarks maybe."

"Where is number five telly?" I asked her.

"Come on, I'll show you."

We walked back through the unit, and as we passed one room, I noticed that the nurse call light was on above the door.

"It looks like someone needs assistance," I said.

Lucy got that exasperated expression again. "That's Mrs. Browning. That light hasn't been off for more than two minutes since she got here."

I could hear an old woman's voice, one that was pure acid. "Nurse!... Nurse!... Where the hell are you?!... Nurse!"

"Excuse me a second, Jay." I watched Lucy walk into the room and tried to be inconspicuous as I waited in the hall, listening. "What's the problem, Mrs. Browning?" Lucy's voice was pure honey.

"Well! It's about time one of you layabouts got here; I could have been dead!"

"What do you need?"

"My pillows need to be fluffed!"

I couldn't believe my ears any more than I could believe how calm Lucy remained. She fluffed up the old woman's pillows and rejoined me in the hall.

"How can you listen to that and remain calm?" I asked her.

"Jay, if I was to get upset it would only make her more upset, and then it would get worse."

"I suppose it would, but I'll be damned if I could take it."

"The other thing you have to understand is the rest of her family is gone; she's the only one left and she's lonely."

"Are you sure the rest of her family died, or did they just go into hiding?"

That earned me a laugh. "As far as I know they've departed this mortal coil."

"As far as I'm concerned, I think you should be considered for sainthood."

"Well, before you start genuflecting you should know that Mrs. Browning's picture is featured on the board this week."

Lucy had explained this to me earlier. 'The board' was a dartboard that was kept in the nurses' lounge. Whenever they got a patient who was particularly difficult to deal with, the patient's picture went on it. When a nurse got upset or angry at the patient, she'd throw a couple of darts at it. I thought it was an ingenious and constructive way to deal with this particular stress, but I knew that administration didn't share my view.

"I thought Genevieve Madas made you get rid of the board."

"Funny thing about that. It keeps mysteriously reappearing on the wall. Of course, when the Ice Queen visits it seems to find its way to a closet." We had arrived at another room. "Telly five's in here," Lucy told me.

I followed her into the room and saw a pair of knobby-kneed bare legs sticking out from under the bed.

"Mr. Brickman, what are you doing?!" Lucy called.

A gnomish old man stuck his face out from under the bed. "Hiya, honey. I'm just changing the oil in the old Ford." With that he slid himself the rest of the way out, stood up, walked to the foot of the bed and grasped the hand crank adjustment for raising and lowering the bed. They didn't allow electric beds in here for some reason. He gave the crank a couple of quick turns. "Damn thing still won't start! Next time I buy a Chevy!"

"Come on, Mr. Brickman, sit down here for a minute." Lucy steered him over to the side of the bed, and he sat down. She reached into the front of his gown and unsnapped the wires from the electrodes on his chest, and then she handed me the telly transmitter. As I took it, I noticed that the casing was not completely together. Mr. Brickman was watching me examine it closely.

"You the radio repairman?" he asked.

"You might say that," I answered.

"That thing's a cheap piece of Japanese crap."

"You don't say." I got the distinct feeling that he had noticed the transmitter well before we arrived.

"All I wanted to do was listen to the ball game. The damn thing won't pick up nothin'. I took it apart, but I can't make head nor tail of it."

Lucy had a sudden look of grave concern. She knew that telemetry transmitters like this one went for well over a thousand dollars. "You took it apart?" she asked him.

"Sure. I've always been good with gadgets, but that one's full of cheap little Japanese parts. If I was you, I'd throw it away and go to Radio Shack for somethin' decent. They got some good American-made stuff."

Lucy was looking a little light-headed, so I took her by the arm, and we walked back to the hall.

"My God, Jay, I had no idea he took it apart. Please tell me you can fix it."

"I'll have to see just what he did, but from what I've seen so far it doesn't look like he did too much other than opening the case."

"I'd hate to have my pay docked over this."

I looked at her with amazement. "They'd dock your pay for something a patient did?"

"I wouldn't be surprised. Administration's been on a big money-saving kick, and there are some strange rumors going around."

"Don't worry, Lucy. I like a challenge." I told her as reassuringly as I could. "I'll figure it out and have it back to you in a little while."

"Thanks, love. You really are a darling man."

"I told you, it's all part of the friendly service."

We walked back to the nurses' station where I collected my cart and headed back downstairs.

I was on my way back to the shop when I passed the maintenance wing and heard Dan's voice raised in anger. "What the hell do you mean you haven't got any?! You got three cases in last week! What the hell are you doing with all that degreaser, Dorfly, using it on what's left of your hair?! You're an asshole!"

Dwayne Dorfly's office was the first one on the right as you went down the maintenance hall. As I passed by, I heard Dan screaming at him again. I think that everyone in the general vicinity could hear Dan screaming at him.

I paused for a moment, and as I did, the door to Dorfly's office slammed open and Dan stormed out. He was red-faced and didn't even glance at me as he went by, and I wasn't about to say anything to him under the circumstances. I wondered for the thousandth time what had happened between them to cause such anger and hostility.

I returned to the shop with the telemetry transmitter and receiver. As I walked in, I saw Papa Joe putting away some new supplies in a large cabinet in the back of the shop. I mumbled something in the way of a greeting as I set about checking out the transmitter on one of the back benches adjacent to the cabinet where we kept telemetry hardware.

"What's wrong, Jay? You look like your best friend just kicked your dog." It was a simple statement but somehow it seemed to describe exactly how I felt. Papa Joe had a talent for that.

"I just listened to Dan and Dwayne Dorfly going at it down the hall. Dan's never like that with anyone else, and Dorfly seems to delight in getting under his skin. Why do they hate each other so much?"

Joe looked at me for a few moments. He seemed to be making a decision, then apparently thought better of it and just smiled.

"Life would be pretty boring if you had all friends and no enemies, wouldn't it? Could you imagine going through life loving everyone all the time, never having anyone to get your Irish up once in a while?"

"No, it's more than that. Something happened between the two of them. I've heard rumors that it involved a woman."

He looked at me again as if he were appraising me. "Ah, rumors. You've got to be careful with rumors; they have a way of popping up and biting you in the ass when you're not looking."

"I can assure you that I'm not in the habit of believing all the gossip I hear, but in this case, I think there's something to it."

Joe still seemed to be measuring his words. "You can never know what Dan has lived, what experiences he's had or how he's felt in the past, any more than he can truly know your past. Sometimes it's better to leave things alone, to let sleeping dogs lie, to use an old cliché. I came to the conclusion at some point in my life that some people were put on the face of this earth to despise each other. Of course, some people do it with good reason."

The last sentence he said with a hard edge to it, something out of character for Joe. I looked at him and saw a firm set to his jaw, while at the same time there was a sadness in his eyes. I knew Joe had known Dan for a long time; I wondered just how long. "You know what happened, don't you?" I said quietly.

"What are you talking about, Jay? What happened to whom?"

"Come on, Joe, you know what I mean. What happened between Dan and Dwayne? What was it that made them hate each other so much?"

He looked at me in silence for a few moments more, then he cleared his throat and began in a low, almost mournful voice. "Yes, I know what happened. I suppose I'll tell you, but before I do, give me your honest word that you'll never repeat it."

I looked at him for a moment before I spoke. I had never seen him so serious about anything. "Yes, Joe, I give you my word. I won't repeat it."

"You're sure? If Dan were to find out I'd told anyone, he'd never forgive me."

Now my curiosity was really peaked. "I'm sure, Joe. I won't tell anyone."

He paused, thinking, as if waiting for words to come. Then he softly cleared his throat again and began in a voice that was barely above a whisper. "Dwayne Dorfly raped Dan's sister."

At first the words seemed to just bounce off me. Rape was such a foreign concept to me. It was something abstract, something you read about in the newspaper. Gradually the words began to sink in. "What happened?" I asked softly.

"It was a long time ago. Dan and Dwayne were friends in high school, and Dwayne dated Dan's sister for a short time. According to her, he had been drinking one night, things got out of hand, and when she said no, he knocked her around and raped her."

"Did he go to jail?" I asked with a sense of unreality.

Joe sadly shook his head. "No. She reported it, but the police didn't do anything."

"Why not?"

"The land this hospital is built on used to be part of an enormous farm. The owner donated it to the community for the purpose of having a first-class medical center in the area. Once the hospital was built, the land surrounding it increased in value many times over. I'm sure you never think about it when you pass the two hotels and the shopping centers just down the road, but they came to be because of a very smart business man, Dwayne's father.

When the incident happened between Dwayne and Dan's sister, the donation of the land was in negotiations with the county government. The elder Dorfly was a very influential man, and he used his influence to get his less than brilliant son out of trouble. There were never any charges brought."

"What happened to Dan's sister?"

"She wasn't the same person after that. A once bright and lively girl was suddenly afraid of her own shadow. She lives in another state, as far away from here as she could get."

"So, that's how Dorfly got his job?"

"And how he keeps it. The son didn't inherit the father's business acumen or sharp intellect. Dwayne flunked out of several colleges and wound up back here where his father had him installed as the head of the maintenance department... for life."

"That explains why he never seems to know what he's doing."

"Exactly. He doesn't."

"No wonder Dan resents him so much."

"He practically destroyed Dan's sister, and then he was rewarded with a very good job that he didn't earn."

"Is Dwayne's father still living?"

"No, he died years ago."

"How is Dwayne able to keep his job when his father isn't around to protect him anymore?"

"The land again. The land isn't owned by the hospital, it's leased to the hospital for a minimal amount of money. The land is owned by a trust fund, and in order to maintain what is for the hospital a very good deal, certain conditions must be met."

"What conditions?"

"I don't know everything, Jay; I can only guess."

"Then what's your best guess?"

"Oh no, I'm not going to venture into conjecture. There are some conclusions that you're going to have to make for yourself."

Just then we heard the door to the shop open abruptly and Dan called out. "Anybody back there?"

I hurried to the front of the shop, and as Dan came into my view, I realized I was looking at him with slightly new eyes. "I'm here, Dan."

"Jay, take twenty bucks out of petty cash, go down to the hardware store, and buy us a few cans of degreaser."

"Sure, Dan." I went to the computer desk and got the petty cash box out of the drawer where we kept it. I opened it, took out a twenty-dollar bill, and headed for the door. As I passed Dan, he put out a hand and stopped me. My first thought was he somehow knew that Papa Joe had told me about Dorfly and his sister, and I fought down a brief panic. "What, Dan?"

The hardness that had been on his face slowly eased, and he gave me a small smile. "*Please* go to the hardware store and buy us a couple of cans of degreaser."

I smiled back and gave him a quick salute, feeling relieved. "Sure, Dan."

As it turned out, I didn't quite keep my promise to Papa Joe. I told Debbie about Dan and Dorfly. But I didn't think that really counted, because I was beginning to tell Debbie everything, and telling Debbie felt more like telling myself than another person. Besides, I knew she wouldn't tell a soul.

I was spending the night at Debbie's apartment more and more. Although she would come to my place to eat or visit, we never had sex or spent the night there since that first night she paid me the surprise visit. Her place was too small for me to leave anything more than a toothbrush, which meant I was always driving home to shower and change before going to work. It made no sense to me. But the few times I brought up the convenience of spending the night at my place—more room for her stuff and closer to the hospital—she didn't seem to take me seriously.

Maybe I was going about this the wrong way. Maybe I should just be direct. So it was one night after we had made love in her tiny bedroom and were sitting in bed, my arm around her and her head on my shoulder, I decided to broach the subject.

"I want you to move in with me." There, it was out.

She didn't move. After a minute she said quietly, "Is that a question?"

"No. I'm not asking you anything; I'm telling you I want you to move in with me. I already told you I love you, and I'd like to be with you as much as possible."

"You're with me as much as possible now," she said sitting up and pulling the sheet over her breasts.

"But I always have to run home and change for work, and I feel like I'm sneaking around or something."

"You can get ready for work here," she responded.

"And where should I put my clothes and stuff? On the front stoop, or maybe in my car?"

"You're making fun of my apartment again," she protested.

I turned to her and took her face in my hands. "I'm afraid it's a fact your apartment is too small for two people. Mine isn't huge, but we could live there comfortably for a while."

"A while? What happens in a while?"

"I don't know. We could get a bigger place or a house."

"Jay, I don't know if I'm ready for all that." She had moved away from me and reached for her robe.

"Wait," I stopped her. "I'm sorry. I'm not sure I'm ready for all that either. My feelings are getting away from me." I took her hand. "How about we try it for a short time and see how things go?" I asked hopefully.

"What's a short time?" she asked.

"A month?"

"And what happens if it doesn't go well?" she asked.

"Then we'll just find out sooner if this isn't going to work," I said.

"Can I think about it?" she asked hesitantly.

"Of course, you can think about it," I said disappointed.

She leaned over and kissed me. I held her tightly, feeling deflated, like she had turned me down.

I could hear keys jangling from around the corner in front of me. I knew immediately it was a security guard, and I stopped so abruptly that Debbie ran into the back of me. I turned around quickly and put my finger to my lips, gesturing for silence before she could say anything and give us away, since I wasn't sure if she had heard what I had.

There was an office door with a dark window in it to our right with a placard that read 'L. Snodgrass, Food Services', and as I reached for the handle, I prayed that it wouldn't be locked. To our incredibly good fortune it wasn't, and I grabbed Debbie's hand, pulling her inside with me. I held the knob turned so it wouldn't click as I closed the door as quietly as possible, and we ducked down beneath the door's window. If the security guard heard us or tried this door it was all over.

We held our breath as we heard his footsteps pause right outside the door. I was sure we would see the knob turning at any moment and we would be caught. We heard his muffled voice through the door, "Say again sixteen. What's your position?"

I realized immediately he was talking on his radio. One of the other guards must have called him and he stopped to answer. We heard his footsteps receding down the hall, and with a mutual sigh of relief we were able to breathe again.

"That was too close," Debbie whispered to me. Are you sure this is worth it?"

I knew with all the problems going on at the hospital this was probably not a wise move on my part, but it was something I'd thought about doing for a while, and I felt I owed Debbie a little adventure. Besides, if we got caught, I seriously doubted they'd put us in jail, at least I hoped not.

"Trust me," I whispered to her.

"Yeah, sure. What could go wrong?" I hadn't known before that you can express sarcasm while whispering.

We slipped back out into the dimly lit hall and proceeded to the corner where we stopped, and I pressed myself tightly to the wall and peered around just like I'd seen in the movies. The next hall was also dimly lit, but the coast was clear, as they say.

We proceeded quickly down the hall, noticing the lights were off in the offices along it until we got to the last one on the left. Damn! There would have to be an industrious after-hour worker. Was this person out of his or her mind? It was eleven o'clock at night; was the mystery person bucking for a raise? Whoever this was sure was making this difficult.

We dropped down onto all fours and began crawling, as I hoped the occupant of the office wouldn't pick now to decide to go home. When we had cleared the window on the other side, we stood once again and made our way down the rest of the hall.

At the end of this hall was a small lobby with a couple of chairs for waiting patients. All of the lights were off, but there was enough light filtering in from outside for us to see a large poster on the wall declaring this to be 'Physical Therapy Month'.

I reached into my pocket and retrieved a key which I inserted into the lock of the door now before us. With a soft click the door unlocked, and I felt fortunate to have such a good friend as Orville, particularly one who knew his way around the hospital locksmith's shop. He had agreed to supply me with the key as long as I didn't tell him what I wanted it for.

"Plausible deniability," he'd said.

I opened the door to the physical therapy department, and we slipped inside. It was darker in here than it had been in the lobby, but I knew my way around well enough, having done inspections on the equipment many times.

There was a small amount of light reflecting in from the parking lot. I thought there would have been more since there were floor to ceiling windows along one wall, but there were curtains drawn across them I hadn't really noticed in the daytime because they were usually open.

"Where is it?" Debbie whispered to me.

"Right in here," I whispered back, turning into another room that was adjacent to the main one. I pressed a switch on the wall, and we heard a quiet bubbling and gurgling sound coming from across the room. "This is it."

"What happens if we get caught?" Debbie asked.

"We're not going to get caught; take your clothes off."

"I must be out of my mind."

"Of course, you're with me, aren't you?"

"Definitely out of my mind."

My eyes were becoming adjusted to the darkness, and I could just make out Debbie pulling her shirt over her head. I hurried out of my own clothes and slipped into the hydrotherapy pool and Debbie soon joined me. As we embraced, the feeling of her naked body against my own in the warm, swirling water was amazing!

"I've wanted to do this ever since I first saw this thing," I whispered in her ear.

"I must admit, this is nice."

"I told you it would be."

We cuddled for a few minutes then we separated, and I floated across the pool on my back. It was wonderful just floating there, as the water swirled around my head while I held myself in place with my hand on one of the rungs of the entry ladder. I thought maybe an interlude like this was just what was needed to convince Debbie to move in with me. We hadn't discussed it since the night I had broached the subject.

Suddenly, Debbie popped up between my legs and kissed me on the balls, and then, giggling softly, she disappeared again beneath the surface. She reappeared across the pool, floating on her stomach as she held onto a hand railing.

I slowly propelled myself back across the pool until I was next to her, then I stood up. The water was chest high, and I stood there for a long time supporting her legs with one arm and massaging her soft, sexy ass with the opposite hand. I knew without doubt that if there were a heaven, this is what it must be like.

My fingers proceeded into the cleft of her buttocks, and she moaned very softly and spread her legs to accommodate me. I played with her until she came, and then she turned and pushed me down onto the suspended seat the therapy patients used.

She was partially suspended in the water as she straddled me and guided me between her legs. The whole thing felt so kinky and just risky enough to be as erotic as hell. We were both extremely turned on as I held her and moved her up and down on top of me.

It was almost as if we were suspended in mid-air, as if gravity had ceased to be. My head reeled as wave after wave of pleasure rolled over me. It was much more than just sex, more than just a physical connection of our bodies, it was as if our minds were melding together as one. I was so in love with this woman I couldn't believe it. I had never known anyone that I truly trusted half as much or had half as much fun with.

Suddenly a blinding light assaulted my half-closed eyes. At first, I thought the light was inside my head, and then I came to the sickening realization the lights had been turned on in the other room.

Debbie flew off of me like she had been shot from a canon. I got off the suspended chair, and we did our best to hide behind the rim of the pool closest to the door.

I cautiously peaked over the rim of the pool. Through the glass that separated the hydrotherapy room from the main room, I saw a security guard moving cautiously around. It was Yusuf, a security guard I knew. He was from Iraq and was working his way through school.

At least it was someone I knew. That might prevent us from landing in serious trouble; then again, I didn't really know Yusuf all that well. I wondered briefly what the religion of Islam said about naked couples in hydrotherapy pools in the middle of the night. At the very least, if we were able to retain our employment, we would never be able to live this down with the hospital staff once the rumor mill kicked in. I had to do something.

While Yusuf was moving in the other direction, I quickly slipped out of the pool to the side where I had left my clothes. To my incredibly good fortune someone had left a towel on a chair nearby, and I was at least able to dry off enough to get my clothes back on.

Debbie looked at me with panic in her eyes, no doubt wondering what she should do. I didn't want us both to be seen, so I silently indicated that she should stay where she was and keep quiet.

I cautiously moved close enough to the door to see Yusuf; his back was to me. I slipped through the door and moved in the opposite direction and through another door that led into another room where the small hydrotherapy tubs used to treat arms and legs were kept.

There were no windows opening onto the main room here, so I flipped a switch on the wall and the room was bathed in bright light. I had worked in here enough to know that Sylvia, the woman who ran this section of the department, kept a small toolbox full of tools for tightening and adjusting the equipment in a drawer.

I reached into the box and took out a couple of screwdrivers and a wrench, and then I unplugged the nearest tub and removed the motor housing. I then dropped the wrench into the metal tub which made a very loud clattering noise. I moved around to the back of the tub and faced the door, which opened abruptly a few seconds later.

"Jaee, what you doing heer?" Yusuf asked in his thick accent. "It after midnight in the morning!"

I looked up feigning surprise. "Oh, hi Yusuf. I'm just trying to finish up this tub. Sylvia needs it first thing in the morning."

I prayed that he was buying it. In spite of his broken English, I knew Yusuf was not a security guard by accident; he was very observant.

"Why I never see you in here at night before?"

"This was a rush job, Yusuf; it just came in at the end of the day. It turned out to be more of a job than I had figured on." I could see suspicion written all over his face, and I hoped my own face didn't look as flushed as it felt.

Yusuf was looking down at my waist, and when I followed his gaze I saw, to my horror, the flowered shorts that Debbie had been wearing were caught in the belt of my pants. "What you doing with lady's shorts?" he asked.

I quickly grabbed them and began wiping my hands on them. "My mom's. She saves some of her old clothes so that I can use them for rags." I grimaced inwardly. Oh Lord, please let him think it's some strange American custom that he hasn't heard of yet.

"Why is your hair wet?" he asked. Oh shit, I hadn't thought of that.

"Valuable lesson, Yusuf. Don't ever try to run a hydrotherapy tub with the impeller housing off." I hoped the bullshit line sounded better to him than it did to me.

"I'm going to look around," he said, and turned back toward the main room.

Just after he turned, Debbie's panties came tumbling out of the shorts I held in my hands. I grabbed them and stuffed them in my pocket.

He headed for the door and I, my panic increasing steadily, followed him. "I'll come with you. I need a break." An understatement, I thought.

We walked back into the main room checking all doors and peeking into closets. Soon we came to the hydrotherapy pool room, and a lump rose instantly in my throat.

Yusuf walked over to the wall and turned on the overhead light. Here we go, I thought. I looked into the pool, no Debbie. I knew she hadn't gone far, owing to the fact I had her pants in my possession.

Yusuf was making his way around the pool until he approached the spot where I was standing. I looked down and saw the towel I had used lying on the floor. I knew if he picked it up, he would feel it was wet.

"Just what I've been looking for!" I said, sure I was sounding ridiculously exaggerated. I picked up the towel and began to vigorously rub my head with it.

"Why is there water on the floor?" Yusuf was looking down intently.

"Someone left the pool on," I said helpfully. "It must have splashed out." I walked over to the switch on the wall and turned off the whirlpool.

I was sure that Yusuf wasn't buying any of this. The way he was standing there looking at me made me feel like a teenager whose parents had walked in and turned the light on at the wrong time.

"How much longer you going to be, Jaee?" What was this?! Was he offering me a way out?

"I shouldn't be more than a few minutes, Yusuf."

"Well, you finish your job and I'll come by in half-hour and lock up."

"Sure thing, Yusuf."

He turned and left, and I was struck with a thought. Was he letting me off the hook, or was he planning on coming right back and surprising us before we could get away?

It didn't make any difference; we didn't have any choice. I immediately wondered where Debbie had gone.

"Debbie?" I called in the loudest whisper I could manage.

A closet door opened and Debbie, sans pants, emerged along with about a dozen prosthetic legs that tumbled out after her. I had seen her look happier.

"Is he finally gone?" she asked. "I was getting damned tired of being stuck in that closet with a foot up my ass!"

"Come on, let's get out of here before he comes back!"

I handed her pants to her and began gathering up the legs and shoving them back in the closet. That done, I hurried back into the tub room and put the housing back on the motor, and then I walked around the room making sure everything was as it should be. I rejoined Debbie, and we shut off all the lights and left as quickly and quietly as we could.

We were both quiet in the car on the way home. We were still somewhat shaken from our close call, though I, for one, was still excited. I reached down and took her hand and our fingers entwined.

I cleared my throat softly. "You know, the other day I checked out a brand new GYN table in an exam room on six West... the kind with the stirrups?"

It was too dark to see the look on her face, but I could clearly imagine it as she picked up my hand and flung it back on the seat.

"Oh yeah, right! Dream on, lover boy!"

We were both quiet for a split second before we both cracked up. We laughed most of the way back to her place, where we made love with no interruption until we fell asleep.

The next day in my mailbox there was an interoffice memo of some sort, and a note from Yusuf. In very simple and deliberate block letters it read, "The next time you want to take your lady swimming, why don't you ask me?"

That was the good news, and then I opened the other envelope.

My palms were sweating as I walked down the long corridor in the hospital administration section, and my nervousness grew with every step I took. I was on my way to see the Ice Queen.

My unease was due in part to the look of apprehension I had seen in Dan's eyes and on his face when he looked at my memo and told me I had indeed been summoned to her office, the time to be determined by her phone call.

I'd been at work at the bench, managing to immerse myself in a tough troubleshooting problem with a muscle stimulator, while occasionally thinking about my hydrotherapy pool session with Debbie the night before. I had been only vaguely aware of Dan's office phone ringing.

Shortly after that I became aware Dan was standing next to me. He didn't say a word until I looked up at him. "Genevieve Madas wants to see you," was all he said, but the look on his face caused my heart to leap into my throat.

"Can you tell me what it's about?"

"I don't know. All I do know is that you've been called to her office... stat." In a hospital 'stat' means don't ask questions, get your ass in gear immediately.

My usual brisk walking pace had been reduced to a reluctant saunter as I made my way along the carpeted hallway. This was one of the very few areas of the hospital that was carpeted, a deep maroon plush pile that absorbed sound like a vacuum.

There was dark mahogany paneling and molding that gave this section a weighty, corporate, business-like atmosphere. Expensive-looking oil paintings were hung on both sides along the entire length of the hall. To me they seemed to whisper, money... money.

I found this ironic in light of the fact the hospital administration was currently claiming to be in the middle of a budget crisis. I had even heard rumors they were considering scaling back our hours to help compensate for the financial crunch.

These thoughts flashed through my mind, but the one overriding thought was what in the world did the vice-president in charge of nursing want with me? Had she found out about the hydrotherapy incident already? Was the feeding pump coming back to haunt me? Or was there some other unspeakable horror that was as yet unbeknownst to me?

I came to the doors of her office suite, which were also of a rich, dark mahogany with polished brass hardware, including a plaque bearing the name and title of the occupant. I was vaguely surprised there weren't brass door knockers, but since there weren't, I held my breath, turned a knob and stepped inside.

I was standing in a large anteroom that was even more expensively festooned with objets d'art than the hallway. Ms. Madas' prim, austere secretary cast me a frigid glance as I stood there feeling like a schoolboy who's been summoned to the principal's office.

"Can I help you?" she asked, not sounding like she wanted to help me at all.

"Jay Barlow to see Ms. Madas?"

Without saying another word, she pushed a button on the intercom on her desk. "Jay Barlow to see you". I heard no reply, and then realized she was wearing an earphone. She looked at me stonily, "Have a seat." It was not a request.

I took a seat in one of several wing-backed chairs that looked like they had been designed to double as medieval torture devices. The secretary went back to whatever paperwork she had been doing before my arrival, and I sat listening to the soft tick-tock of a grandfather clock standing in the corner, which was the only sound to be heard.

I had heard Genevieve Madas referred to as a Nazi SS officer in a dress. I wondered for the hundredth time what she wanted to see me about. I also wondered how long she intended to torture me out here.

I didn't have to wait long, for five minutes later the door to the inner sanctum opened, and Yusuf the security guard stepped out looking like someone had just kicked him in the crotch. He was slightly hunched over, and his face was milk-white even with his olive skin. I gave him a barely perceptible nod, which was met with a very blank stare.

Oh shit! I thought, here we go. It was definitely the hydrotherapy incident. I swallowed hard and tried to think of the worst thing that could happen to me. That was something a friend of mine had once said. "If things look bad, try to think of the worst thing that could happen to you. It helps to put things into perspective and to shore up your courage."

Well, the worst thing that could happen to me was I could be fired. At least I thought that was the worst thing that could happen to me. Maybe she had torture devices back there, or maybe she could have me thrown in prison on some barren island to do hard labor by day and serve as some ax murderer's sex slave by night.

Come on, Jay, I told myself. Get a grip. You still don't know exactly what's happening. Although Yusuf's presence here gave me what I thought was a pretty good rough idea.

I watched Yusuf step robotically through the outer door and then turned back to the inner door involuntarily catching my breath as I did. There stood the Ice Queen herself wearing a gray business suit that looked all business, scowling at me.

"Come in, Mr. Barlow," she ordered flatly as she receded into her lair, expecting me to follow.

She walked around an enormous antique mahogany desk and sat in her crushed red velvet desk chair, indicating a chair in front for me. As I sat down, I tried to smile at her, but as I saw the determined set of her jaw and her steely-eyed gaze, I realized any attempt to lighten the gravity that I felt in the room would be useless.

"Mr. Barlow, what were you doing in this hospital at twelve o'clock in the morning last night?"

It briefly occurred to me to point out the incongruity of describing the early hours of the morning as night, but I mentally slapped myself and realized panic was beginning to set in. The cat was out of the bag as it were, and I knew I was taking too long to answer.

There was no reasonable excuse I could think of, and I didn't know how much she knew. I had to try to keep Debbie out of it if I could. I quickly decided a partial truth was the only tack to take.

I took a deep breath and tried to look as sincere as possible. "To be honest, Ms. Madas, I was using the whirlpool in physical therapy."

She didn't bat an eyelash. "And what makes you feel so privileged as to be able to waltz in here and use the hospital's equipment at will in the middle of the night?" She hadn't raised her voice in the slightest, but I felt as if an army drill sergeant were screaming at me.

"I don't, I mean... well." She wasn't looking at me expectantly, she was looking at me coldly, calculatingly, as if she were baiting me. I had to stop stammering. "I have arthritis in my legs, " the truth, "and I've been having trouble sleeping," also the truth, but not because of the arthritis. "I've inspected the whirlpool many times, and I just thought maybe it would help me... to sleep." I hoped this didn't sound as asinine to her as it did to me.

Her expression changed slightly at this point. It wasn't softer it was... different. I wondered what was coming. "Mr. Barlow, your job requires that the hospital bestow upon you some measure of trust. You have broken that trust."

There was nothing to do but grovel. "I'm sorry; I know I made a mistake."

I became alarmed by the look of triumph that came into her eyes. She was moving in for the kill. "How many other mistakes have you made, Mr. Barlow?"

"What do you mean?" I wasn't sure where this was going.

"How many other times have you snuck in here after hours?"

"This was the first, and last. I swear."

"There have been many strange things occurring with our medical devices lately."

Oh my God! She thought I was the one screwing with the machines. "Ms. Madas, I assure you I would never tamper with, or alter the functions of the hospital's medical devices. It would go against my entire nature."

"What kind of assurance can you give me, Mr. Barlow? As to your nature, you've just admitted you have no problem with breaking and entering."

The room was beginning to spin. "Ms. Madas, I believe I was the victim of one of the machines that was tampered with. I could have been killed!"

"Yes, I know. One of your little jokes went awry, didn't it?"

I didn't know how to respond. This couldn't be just Madas; she and Jerry Louis worked very closely together. It was inconceivable to me they could accuse me of such a thing as tampering with medical devices, but I guess I'd given them reason for their suspicion. I knew they were grasping at straws, because so far that's all they had.

"Ms. Madas, what possible motivation could I have for doing what you're accusing me of?"

"Your motivations don't concern me, Mr. Barlow. What does concern me is the Joint Commission on the Accreditation of Healthcare Organizations and the FDA have gotten wind of our strange little occurrences, and they're threatening to shut us down if they continue. What they need is a head on a plate, and if your head happens to be the one, Mr. Barlow, I have no problem with that."

I sat stunned for a beat. "What happens now?"

"For now, we shall wait and see. But remember, we're going to be watching you very closely." She punched a button on her intercom. "Marjoram, is my ten o'clock appointment here yet?"

"Yes, Ms. Madas."

"Well, send the dumb son of a bitch in here." She looked at me again. "You're excused, Mr. Barlow."

I rose and left, passing a funny little man with a handlebar mustache on his way in. As I passed Marjoram's desk, she gave me a cold, icy stare. I wondered how much Madas confided in her, and then realized there must be a good reason for the intercom earphone that Marjoram wore.

"She said what?!" Dan had been pacing back and forth in front of his desk for ten minutes while I sat at the table and tried to explain to him what had happened in Madas' office.

"She said the JCAHO and the FDA are looking for a head on a plate and if that head happens to be mine, she has no problem with that," I said.

"Jay, what the hell were you doing in here last night?"

I sighed briefly. "I think you know that I've been seeing Debbie Farrell?"

"Yeah, I've picked up on the fact." He was not sounding sympathetic.

"Well, ever since I saw the hydrotherapy pool, I've had this idea in the back of my mind..."

Dan sat with a blank expression for about three seconds, then he clapped his hand to his forehead. "Oh Jesus, Jay. You couldn't have picked a worse time to play bobbing for boobies. I don't know if I can get you out of this one or not." He sat down and rested his chin in his hand. "Yusuf saw you?"

"He saw me; he didn't actually see Debbie."

"You're sure?"

"Yes. It was close, but he only saw me."

"But in the note he left you, he mentioned your girlfriend?"

"Yes. I figured he assumed there was someone with me."

"Why would he assume that? Why wouldn't he assume the story that you gave old ice britches about using it yourself?"

With Dan voicing the thought, it struck me like a lightening bolt. Why would he assume there was someone with me?

"You said that while you were sitting in Madas' outer office, Yusuf came out looking like someone had raked him over the coals."

"Yusuf came out looking like he had just gone three rounds with Mohammed Ali."

"If he had reported what he had seen, why would Madas come down on him? What if he hadn't reported what he had seen? What if someone else had seen you, reported it, and Yusuf got caught looking the other way?"

"What about the note?"

"What about it?"

"If Yusuf didn't write it, who did?"

Dan had informed me later I was not the only person that had been accused of tampering with equipment, though he would say no more than the administration was on a fishing expedition. The investigation by the Joint Commission was ongoing, but everyone involved was very tight-lipped about it.

Evidently, Frank the security guard had never filed a report about my adventure in the basement since no one had asked me about it. Of course, I had told the whole story to Debbie. She and I had talked about the ophthalmoscope that shocked her, but since I hadn't found anything wrong with it, we decided it would be better to say the cord had frayed and I repaired it, which is exactly what I did say when they asked.

There had been an incident report filed for that and I had no choice. It seemed that to try to tell the story the way it had really happened would never have sounded believable, especially in light of my conversation with the Ice Queen.

What I knew of the investigation centered on the incident with the IV pumps in the MICU, the incident with the enteral feeding pump, and with Trevor's defib, although it still hadn't been proven the defib wasn't an accident.

The main topic of conversation in the shop was how long would the situation continue? There were actually two situations. How long would the incidents with machines continue to occur, and how long would the powers that be put up with them?

We all knew that time was running out in a hurry. Either the person or persons responsible would be discovered, or the administration would find a scapegoat, as Genevieve Madas had made so clear to me.

I didn't know exactly how blaming the wrong person would solve the problem, but given the sticky situations that I had found myself in, admittedly by my own fault, I had a good idea about whose head would be most likely to go on the chopping block. All in all, there was only one thing I could be sure about, I needed a vacation. Unfortunately, this was not exactly the time to ask for one.

That night I called Debbie and apologized for the way the night in the hydrotherapy pool had ended. I hadn't intended to tell her about my visit to the Ice Queen's office, but as usual, it was impossible for me to talk to Debbie without pouring out my soul. I thought she would be upset that news of our escapade had made it all the way to administration, but she seemed more focused on Madas' other accusation.

"She really thinks you're responsible for all the equipment malfunctions that have happened lately?" Debbie knew about the problems we'd had with medical devices because I'd been keeping her informed.

"I don't know if she really thinks I'm the one responsible, but she thinks someone is and because I'm a nobody, I'd make a perfect scapegoat."

"You're not a nobody," she insisted.

"I'm not saying I am; I meant Madas thinks I'm a nobody."

"She thinks that of everyone who actually works."

"I understand that. I told Dan about the hydrotherapy pool, I felt I had to, and he wasn't too happy with the explanation."

"I'm sure he wasn't. I still can't believe we did that." She paused for a moment and then said, "You know, the Ice Queen may be right."

"What?! You think I had something to do with all the malfunctions? I was a victim!"

"No, Jay, hear me out. What if it wasn't Fred or a crazy coincidence? What if there really is someone at the hospital who's sabotaging equipment?"

"You really think someone would do something so despicable?"

"Well, there are too many for it to be coincidence, and all these events are recent, correct?"

"Yeah, they've all happened within the last few weeks."

"So, someone is trying to get revenge, or someone has a problem with someone in your department."

I thought about what she was suggesting. There was one person who came to mind immediately. "Dorfly," I said.

"What?"

"Dwayne Dorfly."

"From the maintenance department?"

"Yeah. Dorfly and Dan are longtime enemies. They absolutely hate each other."

"You think Dorfly is doing this?" she asked.

I thought about it for a few minutes, then realized how unlikely that would be. "It couldn't be Dorfly. He can barely turn on a light switch." I thought about the strange chips we had found in the IV pumps. "It would have to be someone who knows what they're doing, who has an electronics background."

"Well, let me know when you get Gracie's list. I can help you look through it."

"Thanks. I'll let you know."

We said our goodbyes and hung up. She still hadn't decided whether to move in with me. After the hydrotherapy pool incident, I guessed that was less likely to happen, so I gave up thinking about it.

I got ready for bed but lay there thinking about what Debbie had said. I mentally reviewed every tech in the department but couldn't believe any of them would do such a thing. It had to be someone outside the hospital. But how would they know so much about our routine and where to look and how not to get caught? It took a while to fall asleep.

Three days after my meeting with Madas, Bobby Guilford and I were sitting at one of the benches working on a problem with a venous compression device. With this device a boot was placed on each of the bed-ridden patient's legs, and then each boot was inflated alternately, thus aiding circulation.

These devices were very effective normally. The one we had on the bench, however, seemed to insist on inflating both boots at the same time. This would not be a problem in itself, but not only did it inflate both boots simultaneously, it kept on inflating them past their safety cut-off point. The inflation pressure had gotten to several hundred millimeters of mercury before the patient started screaming and a quick-thinking nurse had the presence of mind to pull the plug.

We were in no particular rush, for even after we had found the problem and fixed it, we knew no one would be anxious to use this machine again. The staff would mark it and it would sit until things got busy, the physicians started yelling, and it was pressed back into service because it was needed and there was no other choice.

Dan came out of his office and walked up to us. "If you two can let that thing be for a few minutes, I've got an assignment for you."

Bobby grinned at him. "Come on, Dan, you know I can never let my thing be."

"So, I've heard," said Dan, pausing a moment and then continuing. "There's a defib up on the cardiac care unit the charge nurse claims wouldn't work when she checked it out at shift change. Go up and check it out, will you?"

Dan seemed preoccupied, as he had more and more lately. The jokes had become nonexistent, and we wondered once again how much pressure was being exerted on him from above.

"Sure, Dan," I said clapping him lightly on the shoulder. "We'll take care of it." I grabbed my cart and Bobby and I set out up the hall.

When we got to the CCU, we saw the defib sitting on a crash cart at the nurses' station. It was pulled out slightly from the wall and its paddles lay on the floor, their coiled connecting cables stretched to their fullest extent.

My conversation with Debbie was still in my thoughts and I found myself checking staff every time I went on a call, like a cop looking for a criminal who comes back to witness the scene among the spectators.

At the nurses' station desk sat Patty Louden who was the head nurse for the CCU. She was an attractive woman, tall and slim, in her late forties with blonde hair as yet untouched by gray. The other nurses for reasons unbeknownst to us, often referred to her as Peppermint Patty.

Bobby walked up to her smiling. "Hi, Patty. What did you break?"

I could tell immediately from the look on her face she was having a rough morning and Bobby's approach had been the wrong one. He knew it too, for his initial smile vanished under her gaze.

"I didn't *break* anything. That Goddamned machine doesn't work, as if I didn't have enough to worry about today!" she said with exasperation.

Bobby held up both hands defensively. "Woah, sorry. We're on it, stat." Bobby moved immediately to the defib and began inspecting the paddles which he'd removed from the floor.

I approached her delicately. "Ah... Patty?"

In response she looked up at me and smiled at me with a grotesque smile, like a jack-o-lantern with clenched teeth. "Yes, dear?" she asked with forced warmth.

"Did the machine do anything at all when you tried it?" I was watching Bobby out of the corner of my eye. Defibs still gave me pause.

She thought for a second and then answered in a mock-efficient manner. "It whined like it always does, and then its lights went out and it wouldn't do anything... it must be male."

I grimaced inwardly and wondered which doctor had gotten under her skin so deeply so early in the day.

I repeated to myself the words that she had just spoken. It whined like it always does... a thought hit me like a hammer. I looked up and saw Bobby still examining the paddles.

"Bobby!" I yelled and he looked up. "Watch for a residual charge!"

The words were barely out of my mouth when there was a loud POP! Bobby immediately slumped to the floor.

I practically jumped over the counter as I yelled, "Patty!" It wasn't necessary, for Patty had heard the noise and was already in motion.

She knelt beside Bobby and began searching for a pulse. She evidently couldn't find one, for she leapt for the phone as she commanded, "Get his shirt open!" She hadn't raised her voice, but her tone demanded immediate compliance.

Bobby's face was turning blue before my eyes as I began fumbling with the buttons on his shirt. I couldn't seem to make my fingers respond. They felt numb, and they just wouldn't do what I wanted them to.

Everything seemed surreal as I heard the announcement, "Code Blue, Cardiac Care Unit, Nurses' Station... Code Blue, Cardiac Care Unit, Nurses' Station."

I had gotten Bobby's shirt open somehow, and I just sat there dumbly wondering what else to do as I watched Patty alternately pumping oxygen into him and then doing chest compressions. I kept waiting for him to reach up, or protest, or at least cough, but he wasn't moving.

I remember being impressed with the large number of people who responded to the code. I vaguely remember being shoved out of the way, rolling a few feet across the floor, and then sitting up and trying to see around the knot of doctors, nurses, and other personnel that now surrounded Bobby.

A childhood memory came to mind of a schoolmate that had been knocked down on a playing field. I remembered parents, coaches, and other students all surrounding him like this. I remembered wondering, what should I do?"

They worked on him for what seemed like hours, though it was probably only minutes. They brought another defib from somewhere, and I watched as the doctor was handed the paddles. I heard the machine whine as it charged, and I heard the doctor command, "Clear!" I watched all the people gathered around as they took a step back in unison, thinking how clever it is that they do that. I heard the machine pop as it discharged, and I could vaguely see Bobby's back arch through the bodies around him.

I heard somebody say, "He's gone." Shortly after that I felt hands gripping me beneath the arms as I was raised to my feet and held steady.

Patty's face appeared in front of me. "Jay? Jay... are you okay?" I remember nodding dumbly and then I remember the room beginning to spin. I heard Patty say, "Grab that wheelchair!" and then I was lowered into it. I remember thinking, I've done this before.

Dan had called all the techs, junior and senior, off the floor and back to the shop to deliver the news about Bobby in person before they heard it through the rumor mill. All the techs sat on stools around the shop, Dan stood. His news was met with stunned silence. I still couldn't wrap my head around it, and from the blank looks on the more than a dozen faces around me I could tell I wasn't the only one.

"How could this have possibly happened?" Papa Joe asked rhetorically.

"Bobby is a damned good tech," Trevor said, and then reality kicked in. "I mean, he *was* a damned good tech. God, he can't be gone!"

"I was there, Trevor, and I can't believe it," I told him.

"This kind of thing is not supposed to be able to happen!" I could see that Alan was having as much trouble with the news as everyone else."

Dan looked at him. "It did happen, Alan. Whether we can believe it or not."

Will Stanski sat on a stool near Dan. "What happens next, Dan?"

"Damned if I know, Will. They're going to do an autopsy to determine the cause of death."

"Don't we know the cause of death?" I asked.

"They need to make it official," Dan said, letting out a breath. "After that I guess we're all going to a funeral."

"What happened to Bobby is unbelievably horrible," Papa Joe said. "I don't mean to be insensitive Dan, but do you have any idea what this is going to mean for the equipment investigations?"

Dan rubbed his head briefly with one hand and looked lost. "I surely don't, Joe. For the first time in my life, I think I'm out of answers.

That night I drove home on autopilot. My emotions felt completely raw and my mind was still blank. I opened the door, tossed my keys on the little table just inside and sat on the couch without turning on the lights. I didn't think about eating, and I couldn't seem to bring myself to shower and change my clothes.

I don't know how long I had been sitting like that when there was a knock at the door. I stood up and walked to the door and opened it. There was Debbie with a small rolling suitcase and a bag of something.

"Can I come in?" she asked gently.

"Sure." I pulled the door open and she walked past me with her things.

She put her suitcase on the floor by the couch and the bag on the coffee table turning on lights as she went. Then she turned to the door and walked back out. "One more trip," she said, and I stood by the door watching her get another suitcase and tote bag from her car and bring them up the walk and through the door.

"You can close the door now," she said just as quietly.

"What's this?" I had found my voice and motioned to the things she had placed on the floor while she picked up the bag and took it into the kitchen.

She didn't answer right away. I heard her rummage through the paper bag and then she peered around the partition. "Beer or wine? Or something stronger?"

"Something stronger."

She came back in with a tumbler of whisky on ice and a wine glass in her hands. She handed me the tumbler. "I thought you might like to have some company for about a month." She gave me a small smile and clinked her wine glass against my tumbler and we both took a healthy sip.

I put my tumbler down and walked over to her, taking the wine glass from her and sitting it on the coffee table. Then I took her in my arms and held on for dear life as the tears came. When I finally stopped crying, she pulled away and led me to the couch where we both sat down and had another sip of our drinks. I noticed that her face was wet too.

"There's going to be an inquiry," I said in a monotone. "And I'll have to testify because I was the only tech there." Dan had given me this little piece of information after everyone else had left.

"Not just you," she said. "Patty and the others on the code will be there too."

I nodded. "Do you think...?" I couldn't bring myself to say what I was thinking. Fortunately, I didn't have to.

She nodded back. "Yes. Now whoever it is has committed murder."

"Murder. Bobby. Bobby was murdered." I hadn't realized I'd said it out loud until she took my hand in hers. "It could have been me. I could have been the one to touch the defib first."

"God, I know," she said with a shudder as she put her arms around me and we hugged again.

"Why Bobby?" I said mournfully.

"Jay, it could have been anyone. Patty had checked it out; she could have been the one. Anyone could have picked it up before you guys got there."

"Patty, yes, but it would have been more likely a tech putting it through its paces."

She nodded.

"I brought something to eat," she said.

"I'm not really hungry," I said, finishing my drink.

"I know, but you have to eat something. I just brought sandwiches. Try to eat one." And she brought two sandwiches, chips and another whiskey to the coffee table.

I was surprised to find I could eat and was actually hungry. We finished our food and Debbie picked up the plates.

"I'll take care of this. You get a shower. We both need some sleep."

I did what I was told. She joined me in bed a little while later and, although we were both naked, we just went to sleep in each other's arms again.

"Mr. Barlow, will you please describe the events that transpired last Tuesday?" The man speaking was the middle of three men who sat across the immense, mahogany boardroom table from me. The table was in the middle of the immense mahogany-paneled boardroom, which was located in the heart of the administrative wing. I had never been in here before.

The lighting was soft and indirect, and the chair was well padded and comfortable, but nothing could lessen the gravity of the situation or the tension in the air. In fact, the surroundings only increased them.

I still felt a sense of unreality since Bobby's death. I still couldn't quite grasp what had happened. The man speaking seemed avian, with his owlish eyes and hawkish nose. A small pair of wire rimmed glasses sat perched on his nose, and he sat waiting for my reply.

"I will to the best of my ability," I said.

They all seemed to nod almost imperceptibly and then sat waiting.

I took a deep breath and then let it out. "Bobby Guilford and I were assigned to check out a defib."

"A what?" asked the man in the middle.

"Excuse me, a defibrillator." They nodded slightly again. "In the CCU."

"The what?"

"Excuse me, the Cardiac Care Unit."

"And who assigned you?"

"Dan..." Blank looks. "Dan Harris, Director of Biomedical Engineering." I cast a wary eye on the small tape recorder sitting on the table with its red record light on.

"What was the complaint you were answering?"

"The head nurse on the unit..."

"The Cardiac Care Unit?"

"Yes."

"Go on."

"The head nurse, Patty Louden, had discovered that the defibrillator at the nurses' station was not working properly at shift change."

"What time was this?"

I thought back and tried to remember what Bobby and I had been doing. "About nine o'clock."

"AM?"

"Yes."

"Doesn't shift change occur at seven AM?"

"Yes."

"Why the delay?"

"I don't know."

"Go on."

And so it went, seemingly hour after hour, question after question. Some of them seemed relevant and some did not. I knew Patty and the rest of the people involved were being interviewed like this, one at a time, but I had no idea who they had interviewed so far or exactly what they had said. There was nothing for me to do but be as honest and forthright as I could be. When it was over, I felt completely drained.

I walked back into the shop moving like Boris Karloff in Frankenstein. The shop was deserted. Dan was in his office seated behind his desk talking to Will Stanski who was seated in one of the two chairs in front. I walked in and slumped into the other one.

"How'd it go?" asked Will.

"About like you would expect. I felt like a Christian being interviewed by lions." I wondered if I looked as weary as I felt.

"It looks like the lions had lunch," said Dan.

"With dessert," added Will.

"Dan, what's going to happen now?" I asked apprehensively.

Dan looked haggard and tired himself as he leaned back in his chair, took a deep breath, and exhaled slowly. "I don't know, Jay. I'm afraid this may be the straw that breaks the camel's back."

"I still can't believe Bobby's gone. God, he died right in front of me. I sat and watched, and I couldn't do a damn thing."

Will reached over and put a hand on my arm. "None of us can believe it, Jay."

"If only I could have done something, anything!" Dan looked at me and I realized there were deep dark circles under his eyes. "I'm sorry, Dan. I know everyone feels the same way."

"That's okay, Jay, you were there. I'm not going to tell you not to do this to yourself. You shouldn't, but you're going to do it anyway. I guess I would too."

"I've never felt so helpless or useless in my life."

"I know about helpless and useless," Dan was staring down at the middle of his desk. "That seems to be part of my job description lately."

The job that I had found so interesting and full of adventure was now a burden to be endured. It had truly become a struggle to get out of bed and suffer through another day. I began to wonder how long I could continue, and I knew I was not the only one who felt that way. But I was luckier than a lot of the techs; I had Debbie.

True to her word, she had definitely moved into my apartment 'for a month or so', as she said. It felt more like 'or so', because I felt the apartment slowly changing. It was the same furniture and decor, but I could feel the feminine touch when I walked in.

I had lost closet space and a couple drawers, as well as space in the bathroom, but it was fine with me. Somehow the presence of her things made it feel more like home and I was hoping she would stay. She made all the pressure easier to bear.

Bobby's funeral was on Saturday. If there could be a perfect day for a funeral, that was it. It rained on and off all day, and if it wasn't raining, there was a thick layer of fog that hung just a foot or two off the wet ground.

Bobby's family was devout Irish Catholic, and it was hard to believe one man could have so many relatives. Between the family and the people who turned out from the hospital, the funeral procession must have stretched for a good mile or two. Will had a large van, and the guys from the shop rode together about midway in the procession. I had wanted Debbie to be with me, but she had to work.

We had made it through the viewing, and I vowed to myself for the hundredth time I would not put my family through one. Of course, I realized that Bobby had very little to say in the matter.

I supposed the viewing did have a practical function; I'd hate to think all that keening and wailing was for nothing. It was impossible for me to think of the shell of a man lying in the casket as Bobby; he had always seemed so full of life.

Everyone seemed to be in a daze. Bobby's death had been horrendous in itself, but the shock had been compounded considerably. Every regulatory agency in the medical profession, as well as the police, had demanded an interview. I found it disrespectful to begin the investigation before Bobby was even buried, but I had no control here.

I told the story of what happened that morning so many times it became automatic. I had no trouble with it being fresh in my mind because I relived it every night.

At first Debbie had dealt with my waking up in the middle of the night yelling for Bobby, only to find myself sitting up in bed and sweating profusely. But her job was demanding too, and she needed her sleep. The love seat in my den opened out into a single bed, so I took to sleeping in there. Debbie offered to sleep in the den, but I wouldn't let her. I was relieved she hadn't suggested going back to her place for a while.

My thoughts were interrupted by Dan. "I can't believe old tripod is gone." Dan's voice was strangely detached in the front of the van. However, it was the most we had heard him say all day. No one said anything for a while. We just sat listening to the windshield wipers as they swept back and forth.

"A hell of a way for a tech to die." Will Stanski gave a small shudder as he said it, and I knew everyone present agreed completely.

I had noticed early on most of the people I met that worked with electricity had an inordinately healthy respect for it. Not really fear per se, but they understood its potential better than most. I supposed it came after witnessing the power of electricity a number of times.

We had all seen short circuits and meltdowns on a fairly regular basis. When a technician finished working on a machine and it was time to plug it in to see if it was working, it was time for the 'smoke test'. We had all seen smoke tests on our own and on other tech's work that didn't go as hoped. It wasn't a great feeling to put your work on the line only to see it fizzle out, sometimes to a spectacular degree.

I'm sure that for most people who work with electricity, electrocution is their most feared form of demise. I could now appreciate just how close to death I had come myself. It could very easily have been me instead of Bobby.

"Must we dwell on Bobby's death?" Papa Joe asked. "Can't anyone think of a fond memory of the boy?"

As I looked around at my colleagues, I didn't think anyone looked capable of drawing forth fond memories. Trevor had begun to look more washed out all the time, as if the color and the life were slowly seeping out of him. Alan was fidgeting constantly, seemingly unable to sit still. Dan was beginning to look as old as Joe and didn't seem able to move without extreme effort. Will's eyes were glassed over, and he looked like he was somewhere else entirely. Papa Joe seemed to be handling it better than the rest of us, but then I guessed he had more practice at weathering adversity.

I didn't feel much like reminiscing myself, but I thought anything would be better than the mood we all seemed to be wallowing in. The pall that had fallen over us was as thick as the fog just outside the window.

"Do you guys remember the time Bobby was caught in the storeroom on the fifth floor with that student nurse?" I thought it was worth a try, but it got absolutely no reaction.

I looked at Joe and he continued. "You mean when he told the nurse that caught them he was just showing her where the supplies were?"

That got a small chuckle from Dan, so I continued. "As I remember, when they were found he had her skirt up around her waist, and his hands in her panties."

"Old tripod never did have any trouble remembering where the supplies were." Dan's voice was dry and cracked, but his involvement did rouse a half-hearted laugh from the rest of the van.

The mood had lifted slightly for a brief moment, but there was no momentum to keep it going. Everyone lapsed back into silence and remained that way for the rest of the trip.

It seemed impossible, but the cemetery was even drearier than I had expected. It had stopped raining for the moment, but everything was soaking wet and the fog made it look like something out of an old horror movie.

Bobby's mother, father and two brothers stood closest to the grave. Bobby's mother cried incessantly, while his father held his arm around her and tried to comfort her. His two brothers stood stone faced, but when I looked closely, I could see they were both shuddering slightly. There were about a dozen cousins, aunts and uncles behind the immediate family, and one of the men put a hand on each of the brother's shoulders in show of support. There were dozens of people from the hospital, and the crowd stretched back for ten or twenty yards. Everyone was quiet and somber as befitted the occasion.

We techs were situated behind the family and we all seemed to be struggling with the unreality of the situation. Nonetheless, we seemed to be okay right up until they sang 'Danny Boy'.

We had stood there listening to the priest deliver the eulogy, and then an Irish tenor started in with the old ballad. He got to the refrain before I noticed Dan's shoulders shaking up and down.

By the time the singer had finished there were tears rolling down all of our cheeks. We herded ourselves back to the van and left in silence.

"Garson? Garson! 'Nother round here!" Through the fluffy haze that seemed to surround my peripheral vision and the cotton I was sure someone had stuck in my good ear, I finally realized Dan didn't remember the bartender's name.

"Dan, the word is garçon. 'S French for waiter," I informed him, slurring my words slightly.

We had decided the best course of action was to hold a wake of our own. We had dropped Alan off at his car, he didn't care about going to a bar and had volunteered to cover the shop for the evening, and the rest of us had proceeded to the little bar, Paddy's, we knew Bobby had patronized occasionally.

"I never trusted the fuckin' French no how," Dan proclaimed. "Hey Garson, I need a drink!"

The bartender appeared with a fresh pitcher of beer and a bottle of whiskey from which he filled the shot glasses that were stationed in front of each of us. When he had finished, Dan lifted his shot glass.

"To our downed comrade of arms," Dan toasted.

"I think it's comrade *in* arms," slurred Trevor.

"That's only if you're kissing him, Trevor. It's comrade *at* arms," corrected Will. Although he'd had as much to drink as everyone else, he seemed to be the only one still in control.

"Who's Trevor been kissin'?" I asked.

"I ain't been kissin' nobody!" Trevor assured us. For some reason Papa Joe seemed to find this incredibly funny, for he suddenly burst out laughing.

"Are we goin' ta have a toast or what?" asked Dan. He raised his glass again. "Ta Bobby!" He upended his glass and set it down, and we followed suit. He sat for a moment looking somber before he spoke again. "At least where he is, he doesn't have ta listen to the fuckin' Madas and Louis review."

"They been givin' ya a hard time, huh Dan?" I asked.

"You don't know the half of it. They been sayin'... ah fug it. You don't want to know." Drunk or not, Dan suddenly had everyone's attention.

"Come on, Dan. What's they say?" Trevor was looking at him intently, as was the rest of the group.

Dan seemed to mull over his thoughts for a few moments before he continued. "They been sayin' we ain't no good, we don't know what we're doin'. They been sayin' they can do it better."

"They can do better? How?" Will Stanski's expression had changed almost instantly. He looked serious.

"I don' know," Dan said. "They don' know what the fug they're talkin' about. Hey, I'm hungry!"

"Yeah, me too," said Trevor.

"Hey, Garson! We need somtin' ta eat!" Dan called.

The bartender was only too happy to comply. In short order we had a table laden with onion rings, fries, mozzarella cheese sticks, and any other oily food they could find to slow down the effects of alcohol. They needn't have bothered, for we kept on drinking steadily.

I remember having an onion ring toss with Trevor. We sat for quite a while trying to toss onion rings around the neck of an empty whiskey bottle across the table. We were playing for money, and at last count I owed Trevor three and a half million dollars.

Dan and Will had discovered an old bowling machine in the corner. It had a short wooden lane and pins that flipped up out of sight when they were hit with a small, rubber bowling ball. We watched them play a few frames, and then got back to our ring toss.

I had gotten back one of the millions that I owed Trevor when we heard a long, loud yell. We looked up to see Will go running across the room and jump up onto the machine, sliding up the lane and burying his head in the pins. Evidently the alcohol had finally caught up with him, but it was a perfect strike!

A short time later the bar closed for the evening, but not before Dan bargained with the bartender for a bottle of whiskey. The bartender complained it was strictly illegal, but Dan explained to him we weren't leaving without it, and he finally gave in.

There was a three-foot stone wall along the highway outside the bar, and we sat on it drinking from our bottle and singing to the few cars that drove by. Sometime later someone called us a cab, and I don't really remember much else until I woke up on my couch the next morning with the granddaddy of all hangovers.

The interviews had gradually eased up, at least temporarily. There was the preventative maintenance schedule to be caught up with, and I was glad there were PMs to do.

The ER was on the list and I grabbed it immediately, hoping I might run into Debbie. Our schedules had prevented us seeing much of each other. She had been working nights until two days ago, and I was in interviews and official meetings when not working. I was still sleeping in the den, and I was afraid she might move back to her place if I didn't get my act together.

I was working in one of the trauma rooms, taking test readings from a pulse oximeter, when a nurse by the name of Suzy Quinton, who of course was known as Suzy Q, came through the doorway pushing a gurney bearing what was obviously a body covered with a sheet. I could tell it was a large body because of the sizable hill the sheet made in the middle. I was standing behind a large crash cart so she couldn't see me easily. She stopped and began pulling the sheet away, and then she looked up and noticed me for the first time.

"Oh, Jay, I didn't know you were in here. Listen, I have to get this guy ready for his family to see him and there doesn't seem to be any other out-of-the-way spot available. Do you mind?"

"Not at all, Suzy. Go right ahead." I had seen dead bodies before, even ones I hadn't chased across a parking lot. And as much as Bobby's death upset me, I couldn't really picture him dead. "I'll try not to disturb you."

"Yeah, right," she giggled. She proceeded to remove the sheet, and then she used a brush to begin brushing the guy's hair.

I believe there's no way a human being can be in the same room with a dead body without looking at it. It's the same morbid fascination that causes people to slow down and look at auto accidents. Of course, I looked. The guy was extremely overweight, but what really caught my eye was the fact that he was the deepest shade of purple I had ever seen on a human form.

"Suzy Q?" She was busily brushing his hair for some reason I couldn't quite fathom.

"What, Jay?" she said, not pausing her ministrations.

"Why is he that color?"

"Oh, that," she said with a matter-of-fact tone. "He's been dead for quite some time."

"Do tell?" I inquired with a tone to try to prompt more information from her. I knew there had to be more to the story.

"He died at ten or eleven o'clock last night," she said, still brushing. "His wife didn't want to disturb and distress the rest of the family, so she just rolled him out of bed and went to sleep," she said as if she were gossiping about a neighbor.

"How did she move *him*?" I asked, indicating the guy's girth.

"Oh, believe me, she's no petite thing either."

"Uh, huh." I tried to concentrate on what I was supposed to be doing. "Suzy?"

"What, Jay?"

"What's his name?"

She consulted a chart that was lying on the gurney. "Cheswald, Samuel A. Cheswald."

Suzy finished with his hair and left, and I was alone with Mr. Cheswald. I looked down at him and suddenly felt a sort of kinship with this unfortunate soul.

"Well, Sam. You don't mind if I call you Sam, do you?" He didn't object. "I think I understand what you've been through, buddy. As long as you're producing everything's fine, but just stop for a moment and you're a burden, you're dead meat... whoops, sorry." I realized I was in a very strange mood. I supposed it was because of Bobby and everything else that had been happening. I felt like there was a weight pressing down on me though I knew I was far from alone in that feeling.

Sam didn't say much, but I felt he really understood. "Take me for example. There I am feeling like I'm on top of the world. I've got a great job and the girl of my dreams and then, the next thing you know, wham! I wind up feeling as bad as you look. Sorry, Sam, but I have to be honest, you do look pretty worse for the wear. Nice hair though. It just goes to show you, man, shit happens."

"Now I know you've gone over the edge." I turned and saw Debbie standing in the doorway and felt my face flush. I didn't know how long she'd been standing there.

"Hi," I said, feeling self-conscious.

Debbie came to me and put her arms around my neck and kissed me. "What's this about the girl of your dreams?"

I put my arms around her and held her tightly, reveling in the feel and the light scent of her. "I've missed you."

Her answer was to kiss me again, hard. After a while we broke off and she looked at Sam. "Why is he that color?"

"You don't want to know." I looked at her face intently. "I want to make love to you. I think I'm ready to move out of the den."

She ran her hand over my hair and moved her face closer to mine. "Have the nightmares stopped? Are you feeling better?"

"Getting there. I'd feel better if you were there to hold onto." I put my arms around her again.

"I've missed *you* too, Jay. And it would be nice if you moved out of the den."

She kissed me again, and then we heard yelling. We both ran out into the hall to see a young man in his twenties who was obviously intoxicated, screaming at the staff at the nurses' station while waving an IV pole menacingly.

"You're not keeping me in here! I know what you do with your needles and your probes! You're not using them on me!"

Several people were moving, trying to get close enough to subdue him while avoiding the IV pole which the man handled like a staff. He was clumsily shunting it back and forth until one nurse managed to get close enough to trip the guy. He went down like a wet sack of cement and a half a dozen people moved in to hold him in place while a needle was inserted in his arm. The man suddenly went limp and quiet.

I realized I had been holding my breath, and I let it out with a rush.

"Are you okay?" Debbie asked me.

"I'm fine," I said and then my beeper went off. "I've got to get to a phone," I said.

"That's okay, I've got to get back to work," she said and kissed me again quickly. "I'll see you later."

"I hope so."

The number that had come up on my beeper was for the shop, so I used a phone at the nurses' station to call. The phone rang twice before it was answered by Dan.

"Dan, it's Jay, what's up?"

"Jay, I need you to get to MICU 6 ASAP. Shay Ingram's having a problem with an enteral feeding pump." I could hear resignation in Dan's voice.

"Oh, no."

"Oh, yes. It's running too fast."

"I'll go get it and bring it to the shop."

"I'll be here."

MICU 6 was relatively quiet compared to the last time I was here. Shay was doing paperwork when I got there, so I knocked on her doorframe and she looked up and waved me in. I took a seat in one of the chairs in front of her desk.

"Jay, what the hell is it with pumps running too fast around here?"

"I hear it was a feeding pump this time."

"Luckily the tube fell out of my elder patient's mouth, but by the time we got it shut off there was formula all over his bed. It was a mess."

"I'm sorry, Shay. This is the second time this has happened; we'll get to the bottom of it."

"Gracie North told me about the one in her department. What's going on?"

"I'll be honest, Shay. We believe someone's been tampering with machines."

"Why the hell would they do that?"

"That's what we're trying to find out. Where's the pump?"

"It's in the storeroom."

"I'll be right back."

"I'll be here."

I walked to the storeroom and found the pump attached to an IV pole. I didn't need to do much more than glance at it to see it had been doctored just like the last one. I removed the pump from the pole and carried it back to Shay's office where I sat it on the edge of her desk.

"You can see where the stop was cut off," I told her pointing out the defect. "It's just like the one from Gracie's department."

"Who would do such a thing?" she said, looking disgusted.

"Like I said, that's what we're trying to find out. There's something you can do for me if you don't mind."

"What, Jay?"

"Will you try to make me a list of all the people you've seen in your department in the last week?"

"Is that all?" she said with sarcasm. "I hope you don't want it too soon, that's a lot of people."

"I know it is, Shay, but we think it might help. Gracie's been putting together the same sort of list."

She looked doubtful, but it turned to determination. "I'll give it my best shot. If it helps it helps, but you'll have to give me a little time."

"Of course. How about if I come back tomorrow?"

"How about if you... smart ass."

"Sorry, Shay, we're running out of time."

She shook her head, but there was the hint of a smile on her face. "Go on, get out of here and let me get busy."

Whenever there was departmental business to discuss we had always taken care of it in the morning before everyone went off to do his job, or at lunch. No one could remember Dan ever having called a meeting before, and now he called the second one in less than two weeks.

I was in MICU 6 working on PMs when my beeper went off. The number it displayed was the shop, so I called down and Will Stanski answered the phone.

"Dan wants to meet with everybody."

"I'll be done with PMs up here in less than an hour. It can't wait until this afternoon?"

"No. He said, and I quote, 'Tell them to get their asses down here, stat.'"

"Dan said stat?"

"I heard him with my own ears."

"I'll be right there."

Dan didn't normally use words like stat. I wondered what could possibly be going on. I assumed it may have to do with the latest equipment failure, but he hadn't called a meeting for the others. A sense of foreboding immediately came over me.

I walked into the shop to find everyone else was already there, seated like they had been for the news of Bobby's death. Well, almost everyone; Alan still hadn't arrived. I took my place on a stool.

Dan was standing as he had been before. He looked around at us for a moment. "Where's Alan?"

Will was at his usual place near Dan. "He's finishing up in L&D. He should be down shortly."

As if on cue, Alan came through the door and took a seat.

Dan slowly looked around the room once more as if he was making mental notes and then he began. "I called you all together because I just attended a meeting where I received a piece of news I thought you'd want to know about immediately." He paused and cleared his throat. "In two months, this department will no longer exist."

For several seconds no one said a word; we just sat in stunned silence. Then everyone began to speak at once.

"What?!"

"You can't be serious?!"

"How are they going to do that?!"

"Who's going to keep the machines running?!"

"What happens when PMs are due?!"

Dan held up his hands for silence and waited until he had it. "The how is not complicated. They're going to bring in a biomedical service company called Medi-Max. They will run the department and do the repairs and PMs."

"What about us?!" Alan looked alarmed, which is something we hadn't seen before.

Dan fixed him with a hard look, and I briefly wondered what its cause was. I attributed it to the pressure he'd been under lately.

"Us?! There is no us no more!" Dan said loudly. "We get our pink slips! We get tossed out of here like yesterday's garbage!" He sounded disgusted, and I could feel his frustration.

"What about severance pay?" Trevor looked very strange. He had looked more haggard than anyone else had lately, and I imagined the sudden prospect of losing his job was weighing particularly heavy on him. The rest of us had done other things, but this was the only real job Trevor had ever known.

I was worried about him, but I was worried about me too. My God, two more months and no more job! To think I had wanted some stability in my life, and I had thought this was the answer. Shit, I should have stayed on the club circuit.

"Everyone will get two weeks' severance pay," Dan informed us, still sounding disgusted.

"What about retirement?" Joe had asked the question quietly, but I stopped thinking about my own situation when I thought about his. Papa Joe only had a few more months to go.

"I don't know, Joe, it wasn't discussed." Dan looked old and tired as he addressed Joe. He really looked as if he were bearing the weight of the world.

"Surely they can't touch Joe's retirement," I said. I just didn't want to believe that was possible.

"With the situation being what it is, I'd say they can do whatever they damn well please! Now, if you guys don't mind, I have some things to take care of."

The other guys got up and left, but I stayed behind. Dan went around and sat behind his desk without a word, as I closed the office door and took a seat in front. I had known Dan long enough to know that he probably wanted to talk, and if he didn't then he'd throw me out. He looked at me for a long moment, but he didn't tell me to leave.

"Who all was at this meeting?" I asked.

He seemed to be weighing his thoughts at first, but then he spoke. "Madas, Louis, and Harry Diamond."

"The big three?" Harry Diamond was the president of the hospital.

"Yeah. I couldn't help but think how much they looked like Moe, Larry, and Curly sitting on the other side of the table."

"What did they say?"

"Pretty much what you'd expect. With all the incident reports being filed on equipment failures around here, and the regulatory agencies breathing down everyone's necks, they feel they have no choice but to replace us."

"Dan, we haven't had anything to do with the equipment failures; they've all been due to things outside of our control."

"I know that, and you know that, but they don't want to hear it." He looked completely beaten.

"And I have a strong feeling they know that too. Something stinks!" I said, wrinkling my nose.

"Like a landfill in July. But unless you can tell me what that something is, we're just sword fighting with Zorro."

"Do you have any idea what's going on? Why they would shove us out the door so quickly?"

"Sure. Medi-Max came waltzing in here with tales about how much money could be saved. It doesn't matter if the equipment goes to shit, they'll do it cheaper!"

"So, why didn't they just fire us?"

"That's exactly the kind of thing the medical workers union has been waiting for; they've been on the fringes for years. Every so often the employees vote on whether to let the union in or not, and every time the union has lost by a narrow margin. Firing a whole department would give the union just the fuel they need."

"How can they do this to people?! Can't we blow the whistle on them?"

"With what? We have no proof of anything. And I've got news for you, Jay, you're talking about going up against professional politicians. They play hardball and they do it well. If they weren't running a hospital, they'd be running for congress."

"So, a few vital equipment failures give the hospital the justification it needs to get rid of our department."

"Yeah, funny how that worked out."

I thought about my conversations with Debbie and her suspicions. I didn't want Dan to know I'd talked about it with her yet, so I decided to pose my thought like it just came to me.

"Dan, do you have any thoughts on *who* has been *fixing* the equipment?"

"That's what's been bugging the hell out of me. Whoever it is knows exactly what they're doing."

"You don't think it's one of us?"

"I don't want to think that, but no one would be in a better position."

"God, after all we've been through together. And Bobby..." Whoever was responsible for tampering with the equipment was responsible for Bobby's death.

Dan looked as if he were struggling with great pain. "I believe Bobby's death was an accident. I have to believe that, or I'll go crazy."

"I can't believe one of us could be responsible for what's been going on."

"You don't know what might have gone on behind the scenes, Jay. You don't know what might have been offered or threatened. You don't know what arm-twisting has taken place."

He looked at me in silence for a few moments. "By the way, I hate to say it but you're not off my list of suspects."

I couldn't believe it had come to this, but of course logically he was right. "I understand. I guess you're on my list too."

"That only makes sense, though the whole idea pisses me off."

"List, damn! There's been so much going on that I forgot about Gracie's and Shay's lists!"

"What the hell are you talking about? What lists?" I quickly explained to him about the lists I had asked Gracie and Shay to compile of all the people they had seen in their departments around the time the IV and enteral feeding pumps had been tampered with. "Well, don't just sit there talking about it, get your ass upstairs and get them."

I had to face Gracie first. I felt like an idiot when I walked in to SICU 1. I had asked Grace to do a difficult, time-consuming job for me, and then I hadn't even bothered to pick the list up. She was with a patient when I got there, so I stood at the nurses' station waiting and tried to compose some sort of apology that didn't sound like a stupid excuse.

I needn't have bothered. When she had finished what she was doing, she came over and put her arms around me and hugged me tightly.

"I can't believe what happened to Bobby. How are you doing?" I almost felt like crying as I hugged her back, but I wasn't about to make more of a spectacle than we were already making in the middle of SICU 4.

"How about we talk in your office, Gracie?"

I noticed we were getting a few stares as we headed back, but I didn't really care. When we had gotten to her office and closed the door, I sat in the usual chair and started talking. It was like opening a floodgate, everything came pouring out at once. I told her about

Debbie and Madas and Bobby. I told her about my suspicions and fears and what Dan had just told us about being replaced.

When I had finished, I felt drained and no closer to solving what was going on, but I did feel better having let it all out. I also felt for at least the hundredth time what a special person I had sitting before me. She sat and listened to it all, offering small words of sympathy, understanding, or encouragement where they were needed.

"Gracie, it may sound corny, but all I really want out of life is true love and peace, and maybe a little respect. Does that sound unreasonable?"

"No, Jay, it doesn't sound unreasonable at all. I think those are the things most of us want. Unfortunately, it only takes a couple of true assholes to make those goals difficult to reach."

"So, how do you avoid true assholes?"

She laughed lightly. "You can't, but I'll tell you what you can do."

"What's that."

She reached into her desk and took out a couple of sheets of paper. "You can take this list. I'm glad you gave me the extra time, because I've been over it dozens of times and talked to all my staff. I don't know if what you're looking for is in here somewhere, but if it is, it's going to take you a while to find it."

I took a quick look at the list and saw there were probably well over a hundred names on it. "That may be an understatement."

She gave me a small, wry smile. "If it was easy, my dear, anyone could do it. The point is, you find the true assholes involved and make them pay. That's what you can do; score one for all of us. By the way, the Ice Queen's on the list; if you can nail her, you'd make a lot of people happy including me. That reminds me, I don't pay a lot of attention to the rumor mill, but the word on the street is there's something going on between her and Louis."

"I've heard that before. Do you really think they're a couple? The thought makes me a little sick to my stomach."

"Jay, the word couple can have more than one meaning, but I really don't know." Gracie had her brows furrowed for a moment, but then she gave me a small smile. "If there's anything else I can do to help, you know where I am."

I proceeded to MICU 6 where I found Shay supervising procedures being done on several patients at once. She was moving between cubicles when she saw me standing by the nurses' station.

"I'll be with you in a minute, Jay," she said as she ducked into the nearest cubicle.

"No problem," I called to her.

Soon she was back and led me to her office. She reached into a drawer and took out several sheets of paper.

"Here," she said handing them to me. "I interviewed my staff, and I took it home last night and racked my brain."

Her list was about the size of Gracie's. "Thanks, Shay," I said. "We'll compare your list with Gracie's and maybe we can get to the bottom of what's been going on."

"I hope so, Jay. I hear your department's in trouble. Maybe it will help."

"How did you hear about the department so fast?" She just looked at me. "Never mind."

By the time I had collected Gracie's and Shay's lists, I realized Dan had gone home. It was not quite the end of the workday, but Dan sometimes left a little early because he took care of some department paperwork at home where it was quiet and he wouldn't be interrupted. I realized he also probably wanted to tell his wife, Joyce, what he'd learned about the department being dissolved. I puttered around the shop for the next hour or so with the lists heavy in my pocket, my curiosity building as to who was and wasn't on them.

That evening, Debbie and I sat at the kitchen table with the lists spread in front of us. The first thing we had to do was eliminate all names not on both lists. This was tedious with the number of names on the lists, but it helped whittle the list of suspects down significantly.

Debbie had a pad of paper in front of her and began creating a single list. All patients and their families and visitors were automatically eliminated first, because none of them were in both departments during the timeframe the lists covered and also because it would be very unlikely an outsider would have the knowledge of the equipment or hospital procedures to sabotage anything.

Our list of suspects now included a handful of doctors, respiratory techs, and radiology techs who had worked in both departments, as well as me, Trevor, Will, Alan, Orville, two other maintenance guys, Dorfly, Madas, Denis Lebon, three junior biomed techs and two hospital volunteers. We didn't cross off any of these names because I still had to discuss the list with Dan, but we believed some of the names could be easily eliminated. Debbie wrote the names we thought could be eliminated in blue pencil and the rest in red.

"I seriously doubt we can call the respiratory and radiology techs suspects here. If a patient were harmed, or God forbid killed, it would be not only their jobs, but their licenses," Debbie said.

"Not to mention their freedom," I added. "But I agree. And I think the same could be said for the doctors. The feeding pumps could have been done by someone who wasn't an expert, but the defibs and the wrong chips in the IVs had to be done with electronic experience."

Debbie nodded. "I also think we can eliminate the two volunteers. They're seniors, and I doubt they had past lives as biomed techs."

"It seems unlikely, but it's easy enough to check," I said.

"What about the junior techs?" she asked.

"Again, the chips in the IVs makes me think it highly unlikely it would be one of them. Dan would have a better handle on the extent of their abilities. But that's true for all the techs. We have the same issue: besides the possibility of prison, we would lose our jobs and the ability to find another job in the field."

"Maybe we have a disgruntled employee situation?" Debbie asked.

"I've thought of that, but I have no reason to believe any of the techs are angry enough to kill someone," I said, thinking of my coworkers. "The most unhappy person is Alan, but I can't see him doing these things."

"How about Orville or the other electricians?" Debbie asked.

"Why would they want to get rid of our department? They gain nothing from that."

"Okay, so we're left with Madas, Dorfly, and Dennis Lebon," Debbie said skeptically, and put down her pencil.

"And Madas doesn't have a background in electronics." I said. "Or Dorfly or Dennis, for that matter?"

She shook her head. "Maybe we're looking at this wrong. Maybe it's not someone who's acting totally alone, but someone who's been blackmailed or threatened or offered money," she said.

I sat back feeling depressed and lost. "So, we're at square one again?" I asked.

"I don't know. I think we should sleep on this and you still have to take the list to Dan tomorrow. Maybe he'll have some ideas."

We stood up and Debbie turned toward the bedroom. I reached out and pulled her to me.

"I'd rather sleep on you," I whispered in her ear. "Are you too tired?"

She pulled back and looked at me. "I think I can stay awake a little while," she said with a small smile. Then she took my hand and led me to bed.

The next morning, I took Gracie's and Shay's lists as well as Debbie and my condensed one to Dan. He was seated at his desk, so I entered his office, placed the lists in front of him and sat down.

"I see you've already gotten to work on them," he said, looking at our list compared to the others.

"I had help," I told him.

"Oh?" he asked, quizzically.

"Debbie Farrell and I have been seeing a lot of each other."

His curious expression turned to one of amusement. "Is that supposed to be breaking news? She's moved in with you, hasn't she?"

"How could you possibly know that?"

"Jay, you should know by now that this place has a better information network than the FBI."

"I've been told that, but now I know for sure."

Dan's expression changed once again to one I hadn't seen before. It was softer yet serious at the same time. "From what I know about Miss Farrell, you'd better hold on tight, Jay."

"What do you mean?" I asked warily.

"I mean you're a lucky man; she's a keeper," he said with a small smile.

"I agree with you," I said, somewhat relieved.

"So, what does Debbie think?"

I explained our discussions of the night before and the purpose of the different colored pencils. When I had finished, Dan sat looking thoughtful for a couple of minutes before he spoke again.

"I think you may have been hasty with your eliminations," he said.

"How so?"

"We don't yet know about the motivations involved. That could drastically change the list of suspects."

"That's almost exactly what Debbie said."

"She's a smart girl."

"How do we go about ascertaining the motivations?"

"That's a question I wish I had the answer to."

I left the shop and wandered around for a while trying to think, without much success. I got on an elevator at one point and rode to the sixth floor where I got off and went to the nearest patient lounge. I stood looking at the lakes with their manicured lawns, trees and bushes. The sky was overcast, and the lakes were reflecting a deep shade of gray.

What had gone wrong? The guys that worked in the shop had always had a sense of belonging, of purpose, because we knew what we did was important. Keeping the machines running well helped to save lives, of that there was no doubt because we saw it all the time. Every time we saw a procedure being performed in the OR, or an emergency resuscitation taking place in the ER, we felt a sense of pride. It created a bond between us and boosted our confidence in our abilities, making us determined to do an even better job the next time.

What was going on? Could one of guys in the shop have been persuaded to take part in sabotaging the very thing that gave our lives the most meaning?

I thought of Alan. True, he could be difficult and downright abrasive at times, but he took his job very seriously. Sometimes I thought he took it too seriously. Alan clearly didn't much like the other techs, and I knew nothing of his financial situation. But could Alan be bought or threatened?

I thought of Papa Joe. Joe was one of the kindest people I'd ever met. I was glad he wasn't on the list. It was inconceivable he could ever intentionally hurt anybody. Besides, he was so close to retirement. He had nothing to gain and everything to lose.

I thought of Will Stanski. Will lived and breathed electronics. I seriously doubted he had ever even thought much about money. What sort of enticement could there be for him?

Dan Harris. Dan wasn't on the list either. Besides, his whole life had been devoted to the hospital and the biomed department. Without it, what did he have left?

Trevor... of them all, this was the possibility I wanted to believe the least. He was my friend and one of the most dedicated techs I knew. We were all under a lot of pressure lately, but it seemed to me this would only increase his resolve to do his job well. That was the way he thought, as he had demonstrated to us all time and time again. It didn't seem to me that it would be possible to betray that kind of trust.

None of it made any sense. The more I thought about it, the more absurd the situation seemed to become. After a while, I gave up trying to think anymore and headed back downstairs. There may only be two months left, but I still had a job to do.

As I walked into the shop, Trevor was just hanging up the phone.

"Good timing Jay. How about taking a call with me in the OR?"

"Sure, Trev. What's the problem?"

"Dr. St. John is in the middle of an arthroscopic procedure and he's having trouble with interference on the video system."

"We're going to trouble shoot it in the middle of a procedure?"

"That's the best time to catch the problem, isn't it?"

"I guess you've got a point. Let's go."

The OR was having a relatively slow day, and the atmosphere seemed unusually relaxed when we walked in. Donna Fielding was waiting for us.

"You said on the phone he's getting intermittent interference?" Trevor asked her.

"Yeah. The thing seems fine for a while, and then all of a sudden the picture starts breaking up."

"We don't usually pre-guess equipment malfunctions, but it sounds like a connection problem to me," I said.

"Well, you two go suit up and see what you can do," Donna told us.

"Where is he, and what procedure is he doing?" Trevor asked.

"He's doing a tubal ligation in room four."

We walked through the doctor's lounge, into the locker room and got into scrubs. I always liked this part; scrubs are comfortable. It's kind of like working in your pajamas, and since everyone else around you is also wearing them, you don't feel awkward. We transferred our beepers and pocket items to the scrubs, put on shoe covers and headed down the hall toward OR 4.

We left our cart in the hall since it wasn't sterilized; we'd come back for whatever tools we needed. We donned surgical masks and caps and quietly opened the door and slipped inside.

The patient lay on the table on her back with Max, the anesthesiologist, just above her head monitoring her vital signs. Max was another of our hospital favorites. He had a reputation for being off-beat, and he had proven it on several occasions at hospital functions. He had shown up at the hospital Christmas party the year before dressed as Santa Claus with a pretty nurse on each arm dressed in red bra and panties, garter belts and stockings, high-heels and a pointed green elf cap.

He was at work now, however, and his eyes looked very serious as they peered over the top of his surgical mask. He looked up and gave us a nod.

"Oh good, the cavalry's here," he said.

Dr. St. John had a fiberoptic scope inserted through the woman's navel, and he looked up at us briefly. "Ah, gentlemen, glad you could come." Dr. St. John was also a likable character with a keen, dry wit. "I do hope you can improve the operation of this thing."

"I hate to sound like a doctor, Doctor, but what seems to be the problem?" I asked.

St. John chuckled appreciatively. "Come around here where you can see the screen and I'll show you."

Trevor and I made our way gingerly around the table, being very careful not to step on or trip over anything vital. We had both been in ORs during procedures on numerous occasions, and we weren't particularly nervous about it, but when you thought about what was occurring on the table you tended to have a healthy respect for everything in the room.

The woman on the table was completely covered with surgical drapes except for her head and a small circle around her navel where the scope was inserted. As we got closer, we could see the video screen which had a perfect shot of the inside of her lower abdomen. I stood staring at the screen for a few moments, spellbound. To see this kind of image on TV was one thing, to see it while it was happening in front of you was quite another. My fascination was not lost on Dr. St. John.

"You've never seen a tubal before?" he asked me.

"I've never seen an abdomen before. I mean I've seen pictures, and I've had courses in anatomy and physiology, but this is a new experience for me."

"Well, by all means, let me give you the nickel tour." He moved the scope ever so slightly in an arc. "There's a lung." It filled most of the screen, pink and bulging as the patient inspired, and then shrinking away again as the patient exhaled.

I looked over at Trevor and saw a look of awe in his eyes that must have matched my own.

St. John moved the scope again, inserting it a little farther. "And there we have the heart."

And there it was, pumping away. I couldn't believe we were standing here watching this woman's heart as it worked, keeping her alive. Suddenly wavy lines appeared across the screen making it impossible to see any detail.

"Damn, there it goes again," St. John said. "You guys think you can do anything about that?"

"We'll sure give it a try," Trevor said, making his way to the back of the video cabinet. The cabinet, like most things in the hospital, was on wheels that locked into place. It was about five feet tall, three feet wide and two feet deep. There was a TV monitor in front at eye level, and a panel in the back that opened allowing access to the wiring that hooked the system together. Trevor opened the panel, taking a small flashlight from his pocket and began looking around. He touched something and the wavy lines intensified.

"That's it. You've got it," I told him.

"It's just a loose connector," he said. "Jay, hand me your pocket screwdriver, will you?"

"Where's yours?" I asked him, feeling a chill go up my spine.

"I don't know; I lost it somewhere. Come on, will you? I can't hold this thing open forever."

The sound and light in the OR seemed to intensify, and I didn't seem to be able to get enough air into my lungs. I knew I must have stood still for too long, for St. John looked at me expectantly. "Are you going to help him, Jay?"

"Sorry," I said. I reached into my pocket and then handed my E-Z Engineering Products screwdriver to Trevor. He tightened the connection and the picture on the monitor stabilized. With the job done we left, heading back to the locker room.

"What's wrong? Are you alright?" Trevor sounded concerned. "I've never seen a surgical procedure get to you before."

My legs were beginning to feel heavy as we walked down the hall, but I shrugged it off. "I'm okay, Trevor. Tell me something, will you?"

"Sure. What?"

"When did you lose your screwdriver?"

"I don't know; it disappeared from my bench a couple of weeks ago. What's all this about my screwdriver? It's not like I lost anything vital."

I didn't know what to say or what to think or how to feel. "I don't know. I guess the procedure *was* getting to me. There's a first time for everything." I didn't want to think about the irony of my last statement.

"Well, come on. Let's get changed and back downstairs."

That evening when I got home, I found that Debbie was already there, and the aroma of cooking wafted around the apartment. I poked my head into the kitchen and saw Debbie working on our dinner, wearing sweatpants and one of my shirts, looking as delicious as whatever she was making smelled.

"What are you doing here?" I asked, happy to see her because I really didn't feel like being alone right now.

"I live here, remember? Or is my month up?" she said lightly while stirring something on the stove.

I walked into the kitchen and stood behind her at the stove, encircling her waist with my arms.

"Whatcha cookin'?"

"Poor man's beef stroganoff," she replied, leaning against me.

"Do I want to know why it's called that?"

"It has ground beef instead of real beef," she explained.

"I always thought ground beef *was* real beef, or have I been eating fake beef all these years?"

She put a lid on the pot, lowered the heat and turned in my arms to face me. We kissed. She put her arms around me and kissed me again.

"I didn't want to be the one to tell you. It's like saying there's no Santa Clause," she said.

"There's no Santa Clause?" I asked.

"I'm sorry," she said and held me tightly. "You look like you really need him right now."

"No, what I really need is you," I said.

"You have me. What happened?"

"How do you know something happened?" I asked.

"I know." She pulled away. "How about a glass of wine or a beer?"

"Beer would be good," I said.

She turned to the frig. "Go sit down," she ordered.

"Yes, Ma'am," I said.

I went to the couch and sat, accepting the beer she brought to me. She sat beside me. We sat and sipped our drinks. She waited for me to decide when to talk. That was one of the things I loved about her; she always gave me room to gather my thoughts, never pounded me with questions.

"Remember the screwdriver I found the day after I made that crazy trip to the basement after you were shocked by the ophthalmoscope?"

"I remember you telling me about it," she said quietly.

"Well, today Trevor and I took a call in one of the ORs. It was interesting, actually. We got a tour of a woman's abdomen."

"Should I be alarmed?" she asked teasingly.

"No, it was an arthroscopic surgery," I explained.

"I figured. I Just wanted to be sure you weren't doing anything weird in the OR," she smiled.

I smiled back. "In the OR? Do you think I'd tell you if I did?" I asked.

"Yes, I do," she said.

"You're right. You'd see right through me if I tried to lie to you."

"You've got that right." Her face turned serious again. "So, what happened that has you upset? Did something happen with Trevor?"

"How did you know?" I asked surprised.

"I didn't, but I know how close you and Trevor are and the story started with the two of you going to the OR. What happened?"

"Well, we were working on the video system and Trevor asked to borrow my pocket screwdriver. I told you all the techs that got one at the seminar."

"I remember."

"Apparently, his has been missing for a couple weeks." Somehow saying it made Trevor seem more guilty.

"And you think the screwdriver you found in the basement was Trevor's? That Trevor was the person you followed into the basement and then shoved you?" she asked skeptically.

"I don't know. It's just that with the screwdriver, I can't eliminate Trevor from the list of suspects."

"I don't believe it's Trevor," she said with conviction.

"I don't want to either, but..."

"So, you think someone got to Trevor? You think maybe Trevor is being blackmailed or bribed?" she asked.

"No, I don't think that. I don't know what to think," I said, confused now.

"Who would bribe him, Dorfly?"

"No, not Dorfly. Trevor can't stand him anymore than the rest of us." I was sure of that.

"Madas?" she asked, sounding like she was beginning to get annoyed with me.

Madas' name reminded me about the rumor. I had forgotten to tell Debbie what Gracie had said, so I repeated Gracie's comment about the rumor of a relationship between Madas and Louis.

"Now that's something I can work with!" she exclaimed.

"What?" I asked puzzled.

"I feel helpless because all this stuff is going on and there's really nothing I can do to help. But that is something I can do."

I was now totally confused. "How does that help," I asked.

"Don't you see? If the head of nursing and the CFO have something going on between them, that's something I'm in a better position to investigate than you."

"I don't understand. Why would investigating them help our department?"

"Maybe it's related," she said conspiratorially.

"You think?"

"Well, it could be. If money is behind getting rid of your department. Maybe their relationship, whatever it is, has to do with that."

"I guess it's possible." The thought was beginning to make sense to me. "So, what do we do?"

"You don't have to do anything. It's better if I nose around. They don't really know me and wouldn't suspect my involvement in this."

"Okay." I gave her a hug. "Thank you."

"Don't thank me yet," she said, hugging me back. "I may not turn up anything."

"Thank you," I said firmly and meant it.

I looked at the digital clock on my nightstand for what felt like the thousandth time. It was three-fifteen. The last time I looked it was three-fourteen. Click. Now it was three-sixteen.

I can't go on like this, I thought. Bobby's dead. I'm losing my job. My best friend may be a murderer. If I had a dog it probably would have run off by now when they repossessed my pickup truck. It was either time to start singing country music, or it was time to get off my ass and do something. Of course, what can you do at three-sixteen. Click. Three-seventeen in the morning?

I could tell by Debbie's breathing that she was deeply asleep. I'd moved out of the den and back into what was now our bedroom, and we'd made love for a while to celebrate. It was Saturday morning and Debbie was off for the weekend for once, so neither of us had to work. I got carefully out of bed so as not to disturb her and went and sat on the living room couch, turning on the small lamp on the end table so I could see enough not to stub my toes.

My thoughts seemed to be all over the place with so many things happening of late. I was finding it hard to relax with so many disparate thoughts raging through my brain. The equipment failures we now knew were sabotage by someone, Bobby's death, the imminent loss of my job. I kept bouncing from one thought to the next and none of them seemed to make any sense.

Orville had invited us to go flying with him, but I had turned him down thinking that after our first night together in a while we wouldn't be moving that early. I wished now that I'd taken him up on the offer, as a change in perspective didn't seem such a bad idea at the moment. I'd told Debbie all about my experience ballooning and she'd seemed eager to try it. As I thought about it now, I wondered if he had found anyone else to go. I got up and walked into the kitchen to the phone.

"Hello?"

At three. Click. Twenty-one AM, anyone else would have let it ring a dozen times or more, and when they answered they would have sounded half dead. Orville sounded like it could have been the middle of the afternoon.

"Hi, Orville, it's Jay."

"Hey, buddy, what are you doing up this early?"

"Just having a little trouble sleeping. Listen, are you still going flying this morning?"

"Damn straight. I just thought that I'd wait awhile before I started calling around for a crew. People can get testy this time of day."

"You don't have a crew yet?"

"No. Why? Did you change your mind?"

"Yeah, as a matter of fact I did."

"Just you?"

"Me and Debbie Farrell, I think."

"One of those I think deals, huh? When will you know?"

"In a few minutes. I'll call you back."

"Do you both want to go together?"

"Oh yeah."

"We'll have to get someone to drive the chase vehicle. How about Trevor?"

I hadn't thought about that. "Orville, can you get somebody else?"

There was a momentary pause. "Sure, Jay. I'll take care of it."

Good old Orville. He knew when not to ask questions. "I'll call you back in a few minutes."

I got up and went to the kitchen to make a pot of coffee and plan my strategy. I had no idea how receptive Debbie was going to be to the idea on the spur of the moment. The fact it was three-thirty in the morning made it definite unknown territory.

By the time I'd finished my first cup it was four o'clock and I still had no idea how I was going to win her over. I decided what the hell, it's time to wing it. I poured us each a cup and carried them into the bedroom turning on the light in the hall so it wouldn't be too bright.

"Good morning, Miss Farrell. This is your wake-up call," I said, gently shaking her shoulder.

She mumbled something unintelligible and then turned and looked at the clock. "Christ, Jay. What's going on?"

"Would you like to ride in my beautiful balloon?" My singing voice wasn't at its best, but the tune was recognizable.

"What did you have to drink after I fell asleep?"

"Nothing, my dear, I swear. Your presence is intoxicating enough."

"Oh, brother..." At least she was starting to giggle a little. I offered her the cup of coffee and she sat up and took it, taking a small sip. "Are you going to tell me what's happening?"

"I was just talking to Orville. He's going flying this morning and we're invited to go along if we'd like."

"Jay Barlow, you're a nut. Doesn't anybody else sleep around here?"

"You've got to go early to catch the wind right. So, what do you say?"

"Put those leather gloves on and hold these lines back like this." Debbie was making a pretty good apprentice, but of course Orville had taught many new recruits because that was the only way he got to fly on a regular basis. The sun was just beginning to hint at its presence on the horizon, and our shoes were getting quite damp from the early morning dew that covered the field beside the hospital where we were preparing the balloon for flight.

"Is this far enough?" she asked.

"Yeah, that looks fine," Orville called from the front of the balloon where he was pulling the envelope out farther to spread it on the grass. I hurried to give him a hand, which wasn't easy because he always ran back and forth doing several things at once. This was out of necessity because he never knew from one flight to the next who his ground crew was going to be or how experienced they were.

He had brought a friend, Helen, who was an old hand at this. I had met her several times before, and she did a much better job of keeping up with him than I did.

"How's the wind looking?" I asked Orville.

"Perfect so far. I'll release a helium balloon in a few minutes, and we'll see what we've got, but I think we'll be good to go."

We had gotten the envelope spread out enough to begin inflation, and Orville took the gasoline powered fan and placed it above the basket. After a couple of pulls on the starter rope the engine coughed into life and began to blow air into the envelope.

Debbie was fully awake now, and I watched the fascination on her face as she watched the proceedings and remembered my own fascination the first time I had seen this.

The envelope was filling quickly, and Orville continued to circle the balloon, checking lines and making sure the envelope was not getting caught or bound up in any way. One of the big stars on the side was facing up, and we watched as it rose and seemed to become bigger by the second.

"Pull back now!" Orville shouted to Debbie and me. We were on either side of the basket holding the lines out of the way, and

Orville lit the propane burner and opened the blast valve. He aimed the flame up into the skirt, and we watched as the envelope finished inflating. With a sudden jerk the envelope left the grass on which it had been laying, and the basket became upright. We held on to keep it from leaving the ground prematurely.

"Go ahead and get in," he said to Debbie. She didn't need to be told twice; she eagerly swung herself into the basket.

Orville got in and began making a last-minute check of everything. He finished his checks and then nodded at me to climb aboard, and I hoped in and put my arm around Debbie's waist. I gave her a little squeeze just to reassure myself that she was actually there. She responded by giving me a little peck on the cheek, and I looked over to see Orville grinning at us.

Debbie's excitement was contagious, and I understood why Orville liked to take people up for the first time. He squeezed the blast valve again and the burner responded with a mighty whoosh as it shot flame up into the envelope, warming the air still further.

For a few seconds we felt the basket teeter on the edge of flight, and then suddenly we were off the ground gaining altitude. In no time we were skimming over the trees by the nearest lake.

I could feel Debbie's breath coming in short gasps, and I tightened my hold around her waist and felt her respond to my touch. I looked at her and saw joy on her face, and I knew I had done the right thing by bringing her. I also thanked providence for kind, wise friends like Orville, who was looking very much like an excited kid himself at the moment.

We were looking over the side enjoying the view. "Everything looks so different from up here. Neater, cleaner," Debbie said with a light in her eyes.

"It's funny," I said. "I have always been a little afraid of heights, but in this balloon, I feel no fear at all."

"Of course not, you're floating on air!" exclaimed Orville.

"Oh, look. People are waving at us," said Debbie.

"It happens every time," said Orville.

As early as it was, there were people out in a field looking up and waving to us, and we waved back. We flew over some woods and watched a small herd of deer directly below us as they scattered in different directions, their white tails flicking back and forth.

"It's so quiet. It's like a dream, just floating along with the clouds," Debbie said. She kept alternating between looking over the side and then straightening up and looking around. "This is wonderful!"

We floated along for miles, enjoying the scenery and the crisp morning air. We skimmed just over the top of woods, and then we came to a pond and Orville let the balloon descend until we were just over the surface. Before we got to the other side, he did another burn, and we ascended a couple of hundred feet and floated along like that for a while.

We saw many houses and were having fun identifying the ones of people we knew. "Look, there's Dan's house," I said pointing down to the small, quiet little neighborhood where Dan and his family lived.

"Oh, look. That's Kathy's house!" Debbie said pointing down to where her friend and boss from the ER lived.

"There's Dennis Lebon's house," I said pointing down to an enormous old farm house about a mile from Dan's. It was a group home for mentally handicapped adults that had been restored by volunteers. Dan was on the board of directors of the small organization that sponsored it.

"What the hell is Dorfly doing there?" Orville said pointing to a brown and white Chevy Suburban with cattle horns on the front of the hood that was parked beside the farmhouse. It was unmistakably the vehicle of Dwayne Dorfly.

"I don't know. Could he be picking Dennis up for work?" I asked.

Orville looked as puzzled as I felt. "No, Dennis always rides that old bike of his rain or shine. I've never heard of him accepting a ride from anybody. I think it's a matter of pride; you know how stubborn he can be." I made a mental note to bring it up with Dan.

All of a sudden, the cap that Orville was wearing went flying off his head, and we felt a very strong breeze from the side. I felt Debbie tense, and I followed her gaze to see one entire side of the envelope flattened.

"Wind shear!" shouted Orville as he swung the burner on its gimbals and began blasting away to get the envelope back open fully.

It wasn't until I looked down and saw the ground considerably closer than it had been that I felt panic. By then it was over.

"Damn, that was exciting!" exclaimed Orville. I noticed that Debbie had turned quite pale.

"Does it always do that?" she asked.

"No, you were just lucky!" Orville said with a big smile on his face. "I think maybe it's time to land though. There's not much fuel left."

"Maybe that's not such a bad idea," I said.

"We'll try for a clear spot on the other side of those trees," said Orville.

"Try?" Debbie asked, looking a little doubtful.

"It's just an expression," I assured her.

Orville hit the blast valve one more time and we rose over the trees. His timing was such that as soon as we cleared them, the balloon began to come down again.

"Show her how to brace, Jay," Orville said.

I showed Debbie how to wedge herself in the basket so she wouldn't fall out at landing. Orville was still jockeying with the few controls he had, pulling on the red rope to his right that let air out of the top of the envelope.

"Hold on!" he shouted.

There was a brief pause and then a bump as we touched down. The basket pitched a little as we slid for a few yards, and then it settled, and we jumped out to hold it steady.

Just as quickly as it had inflated, the balloon deflated, and we had it mostly rolled up and ready to go by the time Helen drove up with the truck and trailer.

"Well, what did you think?" Orville asked Debbie.

"That was fantastic!" she exclaimed as she gave him a hug and a kiss.

"Hey, how about me?" I asked. She gave me a hug and a kiss too, and we finished packing up and went to breakfast.

We went back to Betty's because it was still Orville's favorite breakfast spot and I knew how good the food was from last time. We placed our orders with the waitress and sat sipping coffee.

"I can't understand what Dorfly's car was doing at Dennis' house," Orville said between sips.

"There've been a lot of strange things happening around the hospital lately," Debbie said as she added cream to her coffee.

"So, I've heard," Orville said, then looked at me. "Jay, I don't normally pay much attention to the rumor mill, but I heard something about administration trying to do away with your department."

"They're doing more than trying, Orville," I told him. "We're supposed to be gone in two months' time."

He put his coffee cup down. "You're kidding."

"I wish I was. I'm soon to be unemployed."

"How can they do that?"

"We're more concerned with why they would do that," Debbie said.

"Who's going to service the equipment?" Orville asked.

"Dan says they're bringing in an outside contractor called Medi-Max that will do the job cheaper," I told him.

"There's no way they're going to do it better," he said firmly.

"Thanks for the vote of confidence," I told him. "One way or another, it looks like it's going to happen, and there's nothing we can do about it."

Orville shook his head. "They're worried about their damn bottom line. Anything to save a buck and to hell with the patients."

"The problem is, with all the equipment failures lately, we don't have much of a leg to stand on," I said.

"What's going on with that?" he asked.

"It seems someone has been sabotaging equipment in an effort to make us look bad."

"That's unbelievable," he said, putting his cup down again. "Who would do such a thing to patient care equipment?"

"That's what we're trying to figure out," Debbie told him.

"Do you have any ideas about who's responsible?" he asked.

Debbie told him about the lists and who was on them.

"So, you think it was one of the techs, maybe after being coerced in some way by someone?"

"We don't want to think that; it's too hard to believe," I said. "But that seems to be what we keep coming back to."

"Orville?" Debbie asked, "Have you heard anything about Genevieve Madas and Jerry Louis having something going on between them?"

"Again, I don't pay much attention to the rumor mill, but yeah, I've heard something to that effect," he told her.

"Have you heard anything about the nature of their relationship?" she asked.

He shuddered almost imperceptibly. "I've heard it's a romantic one, but who knows? Maybe they're into slaughtering chickens in a grave yard at midnight to appease Satan. It wouldn't surprise me."

Debbie smiled at him, as the waitress arrived with our food. We ate our breakfast making occasional small talk, and then we left to spend the rest of our Saturday.

I was alone in the shop, sitting at the bench. Everyone else was out on the floor tending to various jobs. I had been doing battle with one of the large electrosurgical machines they used in the ORs all morning, plying my knowledge against the machine in an attempt to troubleshoot its problem. This one didn't seem to want to go to full power and I needed to know why not. Troubleshooting is always an exercise in logic, and I usually considered it to be the fun part of my job. Though at the moment, it seemed to be the best way to keep my mind off everything else that was going on.

I plugged the unit in for what must have been the fourth or fifth time for the 'smoke test'. I flipped the switch to turn it on, and there was a loud popping noise and a blue spark jumped several feet in the air.

"Wow, that was neat!" I turned on my stool to see Dennis Lebon standing in the doorway, leaning slightly on his broom. I hadn't even heard the door open.

"Hi, Dennis. I'm glad you enjoyed it. This thing is driving me nuts."

"Well, I know just the thing to take your mind off your troubles," he said, stepping into the shop. I knew what was coming. "What's red and goes putt putt?"

I really wasn't in the mood, but I knew there was no avoiding the inevitable. "I don't know, Dennis. What's red and goes putt putt?"

The usual look of triumph came immediately into his eyes. "An outboard apple!" As usual he was doubled over with laughter in a second, and I chuckled mainly to make him happy.

"Thanks, Dennis. As always, your timing is perfect, but I really need to get this machine fixed."

"What's wrong with it?"

He had stepped closer and was now looking over my shoulder with interest. I didn't want to hurt his feelings by telling him he wouldn't understand, so I tried to think of a way to explain it to him on his level.

"Well, when you turn on the switch, the lights come on and everything, but when the doctor tries to use it, there's no power." I held up the ESU pencil and he seemed to study it with interest. "When you push the button on the side of the pencil there should be electrical power flowing to the tip, but there isn't."

He studied the pencil for a few more moments, and then looked into the open casing of the machine.

"Have you checked the driver on the power supply board?"

At first, I wanted to pound the side of my head to get my ear working again, but I realized that I had heard Dennis correctly. Then the rationalization came to me. He spent a lot of time in our shop and he was just repeating something he had heard one of the other techs say. I decided to play along.

"What makes you think it's the power supply driver?"

"When you close the switch on the pencil, you're asking the machine for power. If the driver's bad, it's not going to be able to give it and it will shut the circuit down."

Before I could react, he had reached his hand into the potentially live machine and plucked the power supply board from its slot. "And look. You've shorted this triac putting it in, that's why you got the fireworks!"

The fluorescent lights suddenly seemed brighter and my head reeled. This couldn't be happening. Dennis Lebon, the mentally handicapped janitor, couldn't be standing here telling me what was wrong with a sophisticated piece of medical equipment. I had to be dreaming.

He pulled the driver chip from its socket on the board and held it up. "Do you have another one of these?" he asked.

I was dumbfounded. I didn't know what to think, but I told myself he could still be repeating something he had heard. I knew one way to find out. I took the chip from him and walked back into the storeroom, and in less than a minute I was back with a replacement. He took it from me and looked back at the board.

"We'll need another triac too," he said.

I wrote the number on a scrap of paper and went back to the storeroom. By the time I had returned, he had desoldered the triac I had put in. He took the new one from me and installed it in the board, and then he reinserted the board in its proper spot. He turned the machine on, and it hummed back to life.

"Try it now."

I took the pencil and inserted the needle into my ESU analyzer on the bench. I pressed the cut button and the needle on the analyzer jumped up into its set range. I felt numb and more confused than ever.

"Dennis, how...?"

"How what, Jay?"

"How did you know how to fix this machine?"

"I like machines and they like me. Hey, that sounds like a song." He walked across the shop singing, "I like machines and they like me... I like machines and they like me." When he got to the door he paused and turned. "I want to thank you, Jay. You've been a lovely audience." He turned and left.

A short time later Trevor and Dan came into the shop. I knew I had been acting strangely around Trevor lately, and I knew he didn't know what to make of it. We usually spent a lot of time together, and suddenly I had been avoiding him.

I had told Dan about Trevor's missing screwdriver. At first, I wasn't going to, but after much deliberation, I decided it wouldn't be fair if I didn't. I felt he had the right to any information I discovered, and I hoped he felt the same way about me.

When they came through the door Dan had a big grin on his face. It seemed out of place because it had been so long since I had seen any kind of smile on Dan's face. Trevor kept looking at him oddly, and I wondered what was going on.

"Go on. Tell Jay what you told me." Dan was nudging him in the shoulder.

"Uh, Jay?" Trevor looked mystified.

"What, Trevor?"

"Dan says that I should tell you I found my pocket screwdriver." He held it up. "I left it in my locker."

I jumped off the stool I had been sitting on so abruptly that it made Trevor jump. I rushed over to him and, clapping him on the back, took the screwdriver from him and held it up in the air.

"Look, Dan, he found his screwdriver!" I practically shouted.

"I know. Isn't it great?!" Dan was nearly bouncing on his feet.

"It was in his locker the whole time!" The joy in my voice was barely contained.

Trevor looked like he was debating whether to attempt to run or just pick up the phone and call the psycho ward.

"Wait a minute," Trevor said. "I'll go look in my locker and see if I can find a pair of dikes, that ought to make you guys ecstatic!"

Dan and I settled down, and then we ushered Trevor into Dan's office and shut the door. We proceeded to tell him everything we had learned. At first, he was upset we could have believed he was responsible for what had been happening, but as we talked, he admitted that with all the strange things that had been going on lately, he could see how we came to such a conclusion.

Given my own and Dan's reaction to the simple fact of Trevor finding his screwdriver, we now felt sure we could trust each other. Now we were three.

I didn't tell Dan and Trevor about Dennis and the ESU. The event seemed so fantastic I wanted to look into it further before I did. Was sweet, lovable Dennis behind the strange occurrences that had been plaguing the hospital's machines? It was unbelievable, but then so was the talent he had demonstrated with the ESU.

Debbie and I had been making love nearly every night since our balloon ride. It was getting to the point where I couldn't bear the thought of spending much time alone without her. That night as we lay in bed together, I decided to confide in her about what I'd witnessed. I had to tell someone about my concern.

"Debbie, there's something I have to talk to you about." I had been putting it off all evening. I wasn't sure how she'd react to my suspicions about Dennis.

"What's wrong?"

"What makes you think something's wrong?"

She propped herself up on one elbow and took hold of my chin with her other hand. "Hey, this is me. I've known you long enough now to know that look in your eyes. You're uncertain about something and it's bothering you. I was wondering when you'd get around to telling me what it is."

"Lord, I think she knows me too well," I said to the ceiling.

"Come on, quit stalling."

"Okay. What would you say if I told you I think I know who's been tampering with the machines?"

"Who do you think it is?" she asked.

I told her about the amazing thing I had seen Dennis do. I knew she'd believe me, and she was, in fact, quite interested.

"He must be what's known as an 'idiot savant'. I've heard of it from the people who take care of my brother, and I've read about it." She snuggled a little closer under the sheets. "It's pretty rare but has been studied. He may barely be able to tie his shoes, but you put a broken machine in front of him and he relates to it on some level that we don't understand."

"It was eerie to watch. It was almost as if he became part of the machine, as if he could feel what was wrong with it."

"I suppose on some level he could. Like I said, it's been studied, but not a lot. There's a lot the scientific community doesn't know about it." I could feel her reassuring warmth against me and took comfort in it. "And you think Dennis has something to do with all that's been happening?" she asked.

"I don't know what to think. I just know there have been some strange things going on."

We were both quiet for a few minutes, each of us lost in our own thoughts as we lay in each other's arms. So many things swirled around in my brain all at once.

"Jay?"

"What?"

"Dennis couldn't have done it. At least, not alone."

"Why not?"

"Because, lack of motive aside, all of the things that have been happening would take fairly extensive planning."

"Yes, I guess they would."

"Dennis can work on machines because he can relate to them on a certain level, but he's not capable of the complex thought that was involved in the planning."

"I guess not." We were quiet again for a few more minutes. "Debbie?"

"What?"

"What if someone else did the planning for him?"

"Any idea who it might have been?" she asked.

"The first name that comes to mind is Dwayne Dorfly."

"We did see his car at Dennis' house from Orville's balloon," she mused. "But from what you've told me, he's not all that bright."

I thought for a moment. "But he might be bright enough, and I know he hates Dan."

"Enough to kill someone?"

"Maybe by accident."

"Dan, there's something I need to talk to you about." I had just gotten to work the next morning and Dan looked like he was on his way out the door. The shop was otherwise empty; no one else had arrived yet.

He stopped and looked at me briefly. "What about, Jay? I've got an important meeting in a few minutes."

"I found out yesterday that Dennis has abilities we never would have dreamed of."

He immediately looked wary. "What kind of abilities?"

"He has a talent with machines I would have thought was impossible, at least until Debbie explained to me how it could happen."

His face was suddenly unreadable. "Come into my office."

"What about your meeting?" I asked.

"Never mind my meeting. Come into my office."

I followed him into his office and noted that he closed and locked the door. This aroused my curiosity, as I had rarely seen him lock his office door before.

"Have a seat, Jay," he said as he walked around and sat behind his desk. I sat down and he looked at me intently. "What did you find out and how?"

I told him about Dennis and the ESU the day before and what Debbie had told me about how that could be possible. I decided not to tell him our suspicions about Dorfly's involvement since I had no proof. When I finished, he looked thoughtful for a few moments.

"Have you told anyone else?" he asked.

"Just Debbie."

"And has she told anyone else?"

"No, Dan, of course not."

He sat for a few more moments, thinking. "What are you two doing this evening?"

"Nothing in particular. Why?"

"Why don't you come over to my house where we can talk more easily?"

"Sure, we can do that if you like. What time do you want us?"

"Seven?"

"Seven should be okay. Do you want us to bring dinner?"

"No, we can feed you. I'll call Joyce and ask her to make extra." I knew from previous experience Joyce was an excellent cook.

"What are you having?"

"What?!" he said looking slightly confused.

I smiled at him. "I'm just messing with you, Dan. I know whatever Joyce makes will be delicious. Will your boys be there?"

"Naw, I'll tell Joyce to feed them early so the four of us can talk."

"I assume she knows what's been going on around here?"

This time I got a small smile. "You're not the only one with a lady confidant at home, you know."

Dan lived in a modest, half-brick, split-level house in a pleasant neighborhood built just after WWII. It looked like a nice place to raise kids, and Dan and Joyce were raising three of them. They had an older daughter who was away at school and early teen twin boys,

Jason and Jesse, both big like their father and both possessing his easygoing manner.

When we got to Dan's at seven, he met us at the door and ushered us to the kitchen where Joyce was tending to something on the stove that smelled fantastic. Joyce, like Dan, was in her forties. She was about Debbie's height with shoulder length curly chestnut hair and brown eyes. She was funny and quick-witted and a good match for Dan. I gave her a hug and introduced her to Debbie.

"What smells so good?" I asked her.

"It's nothing fancy, Jay. Just an Irish stew with beef and Guinness, and I baked some rolls to have with it," she told me.

"You put Guinness in the stew?" I asked.

"Yes, that's how I always make it. At least when I have Guinness."

"Well, Joyce, the aroma is making my stomach rumble," I told her.

"She didn't put all the Guinness in the stew," Dan said. "Would you guys like one?"

"I sure would," I assured him.

"Maybe Debbie would prefer a glass of wine," Joyce told him. I noticed she had one on the counter where she was cooking. "We have a nice Chardonnay," she told Debbie.

"Chard sounds good," Debbie said. "I'd love some."

Debbie and I took seats at the kitchen table and Dan brought our drinks. Joyce lowered the heat on the pot on the stove, picked up her wine glass, and joined us.

"Dan told me about what you saw Dennis do, Jay," Joyce said.

"It was amazing," I told her. "I was standing there watching and I couldn't believe it."

"I told Jay what I know about idiot savants," Debbie said. "Though admittedly, it's not a great deal."

"The kid's talents are... surprising," Dan said. Something in the way he said it sounded like he wasn't all that surprised.

"Wait," I said. "You knew what Dennis could do?" I asked him.

Dan looked at me silently for a few moments. "Yeah, I've known for a while."

"Why didn't you say something?" I said. "We might have been able to use him around the shop."

"That's what I had hoped at one time."

"Why didn't you bring him in?" I asked.

"I tried. I couldn't just bring him in without telling anyone, so I held a meeting to discuss it. I was overruled. They didn't believe Dennis could handle anything but being a janitor."

"Who was at this meeting?" Debbie asked.

"A few department heads and a representative from administration."

"Was Dwayne Dorfly one of the department heads?" I asked.

"Yes."

"Who was the representative from administration?" Debbie asked.

"Genevieve Madas," Dan told her.

"I met that woman once, at a hospital dinner for department heads," Joyce said. "I talked with her for less than five minutes before I realized why everyone calls her the Ice Queen."

I told Dan about us seeing Dorfly's car at Dennis' house from Orville's balloon. We could see suspicion immediately come into his eyes.

"When was this," he asked.

"Last Saturday," I told him.

"Dan, have you heard rumors about Genevieve Madas and Jerry Louis having a relationship outside of work?" Debbie asked him.

"Several times," Dan told her, "That one's been going around for a while."

"Do you think there's anything to it?" she asked.

"Anything's possible," he said.

"Let me ask you something else. I've heard from a few department heads that money has been disappearing from their budgets. Do you know anything about that?"

I could see Dan weighing how much to say before I saw resolve on his face. "Yeah. I thought it was just my budget to begin with, just added nails in BioMed's coffin, but I've heard other departments are experiencing the same thing. Why?"

"Wait a minute," Joyce said, "I think you guys are getting off track."

"How so?" I asked her.

"You were talking about Dennis' abilities and seeing Dorfly's car at his house. I think finding out if there's a connection needs to be the first thing you do before you go off on a tangent."

"That's a good point, Joyce," I said. "Any ideas how to do that?"

She took a sip of her wine and then put her glass down. "Why don't you ask Dennis? You know he never lies."

Dan looked at his wife with a small smile. "That's a good idea, Dear," he said, then looked at me. "I think you should talk to him, Jay."

"Why me?"

"Dennis likes you. He seeks you out often."

"He likes you too," I pointed out, "and you've known him longer."

"That's true, but I have more of a conflict of interest," he said, then he looked at Debbie. "It sounds like you've already been talking to department heads, Debbie."

"I have, why?"

"Do you happen to know anyone in the finance department?"

"No, but I think my boss, Kathy McMillan, might."

"Can you ask her?"

"I suppose. What do you want to know?"

"Anything you can find out," Dan told her. "Maybe if we have enough information, we can put all this together and figure out what's going on."

"Hello?" Kathy answered on the fourth ring. Not a good sign. Debbie decided to call Kathy as soon as she got home from Dan's house, because maybe Kathy's kids would be in bed and she'd have time to talk. Debbie had never called her boss at home before, and she was beginning to think this was not a good idea. But she had to say something.

"Kathy? It's Debbie Farrell. I wanted to talk to you about something. Is this a bad time?" She was hoping it was and she could forget this whole thing. It was a mistake getting her boss involved in this. Besides, they weren't even sure there was something untoward going on.

"Not at all." Kathy said. "What's up?"

Debbie hesitated. How do you explain a conspiracy theory without proof and without naming names? This was a *really* bad idea. She was about to respond with a noncommittal comment, when Kathy spoke again.

"What's wrong Debbie?" Now she sounded concerned.

Debbie took a deep breath. "Well, remember I was talking to you about a rumor that's been going around about Madas and Louis?" Debbie began.

"Of course, I do," Kathy interrupted. "Did you find out anything?" she sounded excited.

"Not directly about them, no. But do you remember telling me how money seemed to be disappearing from your budget?"

"I remember," Kathy sounded puzzled now.

"Well, I've been talking to a few department heads about the rumor and it turns out they're all experiencing the same problem with budget money disappearing."

"All of them?" Kathy asked.

"All of the ones I talked to," Debbie said.

"I know Gracie North has budget issues, but she's the only one I talked to about it. I rarely see other department heads, with our schedules and workloads. That *is* interesting."

"Yes," Debbie agreed. "We thought so." She added before realizing she had let that slip out.

"We?" Kathy had not missed the slip.

Debbie sighed. "There have been some strange things happening with equipment in the hospital, so Dan Harris and Jay Barlow have been looking into the cause. Then when we heard about the rumor involving Madas and Louis, we thought there may be some connection."

"I heard about the equipment failures. At the time I thought it was strange they could be due to incompetence of the biomed staff, especially when one of their own techs died." There was silence for a minute and then Kathy spoke more quietly. "Is it true the hospital is getting rid of the biomed department and bringing in an outside company?"

"Yes, I'm afraid that rumor is true," Debbie said.

"Not good," Kathy said. "I've heard nightmare stories about some of those outside companies."

"Dan and Jay are trying to get answers before that happens. All those guys will lose their jobs."

"You know," Kathy added thoughtfully, "That sounds like a financial scheme too. There may be more going on here than we think."

"Exactly, which is why I called you. You mentioned that you were friends with someone in the finance department. I was wondering if there was some way I could talk to them." Debbie waited, holding her breath. Everything she needed to do to help Jay hinged on talking to someone in finance.

After another moment of silence, Kathy said, "As a matter of fact, Laura and I are having lunch tomorrow. You could join us."

"Tomorrow?" Debbie asked surprised. "I, uh, have to work tomorrow. I don't get much time for lunch and I never know when that will be. Not sure I can do that."

Kathy laughed. "I know all about your schedule. I'm your boss, remember? I'm giving you permission to take a two-hour leave for medical reasons."

"Medical reasons? But I don't..."

"I'm the only one who needs to know why you're taking a long break. Meet us for lunch at the restaurant at the Holiday Inn at 1:30."

"Do you think Laura will talk to me?" Debbie still had doubts about the ruse.

"One way to find out. I'll see you tomorrow." And Kathy hung up.

Debbie put the phone down and turned to find Jay behind her with a glass of wine.

"I thought you may need this," he said. "It sounds like it went well."

"It went well. I'm going to lunch with my boss and her friend from finance tomorrow at the Holiday Inn." She sipped her wine and smiled.

I got to work the next morning by six thirty, because I knew Dennis always showed up well in advance of his seven o'clock starting time. As always, he was the first one there, and I managed to catch up with him outside the men's locker room. He was walking up the hall smiling and whistling some tuneless little ditty when he saw me.

"Good morning, Jay. What are you doing here so early?"

"Good morning, Dennis. I was wondering if I could talk to you for a few minutes."

"Sure. What do you want to talk about?" He didn't look surprised or even curious. His buddy Jay had appeared at six thirty in the morning to talk to him and that was just fine; a nice way to start the day.

"Well, why don't we go talk in the biomed shop? I think it would be better than here in the hall."

"Okay."

He followed me faithfully down the hall, and when we came to the shop, I took out my keys and unlocked the door. He followed me inside, and I indicated a couple of stools at the nearest bench.

"Why don't we sit down?"

"Okay."

We each took a seat and I sat looking at him for a few moments still trying to fathom the idea of harmless, trusting Dennis being involved in what had been going on. It was difficult. He just sat there smiling at me. I wasn't sure where to start, so I decided to just jump right in and see where it went.

"I was very impressed with the way you fixed that machine yesterday," I told him.

"Oh, that one was easy. I'm good with machines, you know."

"So, I've noticed." What now? I thought. What the hell, why beat around the bush? "Dennis, have you worked on any other machines around here?"

"Sure. Lots of them."

"What machines?"

"What?" He looked suddenly confused.

"What kinds of machines have you worked on?"

"Well..." I could see that he was concentrating hard, his eyebrows were knitted together. "There were the shocker machines."

"Defibrillators?"

"What?"

"You worked on defibs?"

He looked thoughtful. "Defibs?" Suddenly his eyes lit up. "Defibs! Yeah, shocker machines."

"What other kinds of machines have you worked on?"

"Well... there were the pump mach..." He stopped in mid-sentence and the smile quickly faded from his face. "I don't remember."

"What do you mean you don't remember, Dennis? You were about to say pump machines."

"I don't remember." He looked as though his resolve was set.

"Come on, Dennis, you're playing games with me now."

He seemed to be weighing his thoughts for a few moments, and then as quickly as the smile had left his face it returned. "Awwww, I can't fool you can I, Jay?"

"No, you can't. You should know that by now." I felt we were getting close.

"But you're going to spoil the joke," he said sounding mildly disappointed.

"The joke?" I suddenly felt numb, and at the same time icy fingers were crawling up my spine.

"Yeah. The joke we've been playing on you guys. You won't tell the other guys, will you?"

"No, Dennis, of course not."

"That's good, because it's been going good so far."

"Dennis, who's we?"

"What?"

"You said that we've been playing a joke on you guys."

"Yeah?"

"You and who else?"

"Me and Dwayne. And we sure had you guys fooled, didn't we? I thought you were going to catch me in the basement that night though."

"Dennis, you're the one that pushed me?"

The smile left his face and he looked apologetic and a little upset. "I'm sorry I pushed you, Jay. I was afraid you were going to see me and spoil the joke. I hope you're not mad at me."

"No, Dennis. It's okay. I'm not mad at you." His face brightened as I thought further. "Dennis, was that your workbench I found in the basement?"

"Yes, Dwayne set it up for me. He said it was my secret shop. Pretty cool, huh?"

"Yes, Dennis, pretty cool."

Debbie waited until Kathy left the ER before going to the locker room to change out of her scrubs. Kathy had arranged coverage for her, so that was one less thing she needed to take care of before leaving the hospital. She left her scrubs in her locker, grabbed her purse and headed to her car. It was only a couple blocks to the hotel, but she thought it best to not be seen walking there when she was supposed to be on a medical break.

When she arrived at the Holiday Inn restaurant, she found Kathy and Laura were already seated at a table near the kitchen. The location seemed to be the right one, because the tables on either side were empty. As she approached the table, Kathy raised her hand and indicated the chair to her right, opposite a young woman with long blond hair and brown eyes. She was dressed in business casual and looked nervous. The silky blond hair didn't fit her; she looked rather mousy. She was obviously Laura from finance.

Kathy made the introductions and Debbie shook Laura's hand before sitting down opposite her. Laura was seated with her back to the wall, so Debbie had little for her eyes to focus on other than Laura and the wall behind her. Laura's nervousness was beginning to affect Debbie and she wondered if this had been a good idea.

But Kathy didn't seem concerned and she smiled at both of them. "I'm glad I had the opportunity to introduce you two. It turns out you have something in common." She turned to Debbie. "Laura's boyfriend is a musician. I know Jay doesn't play professionally anymore, but I know he did."

This surprised Debbie. "You knew Jay was a musician?" she asked.

Kathy nodded. "The first couple years he was here he brought his band to play at the annual fair. I'm sorry he doesn't do that anymore; they were good," she added.

"They're planning on playing this year," Debbie said.

"Oh good. I look forward to hearing them," Kathy said.

"What does your boyfriend play?" Debbie asked Laura.

"He's a drummer," Laura answered, looking a little more relaxed.

"Does his band play in the area?"

"Sometimes, but he's on the road a lot and I don't get to see him as much as I did before I took this job," Laura answered.

Debbie nodded. "Jay said being on the road was hard and he finally stopped because it was getting to him. I didn't meet him until recently, so I haven't had that experience." She smiled at Laura.

"Well, said Kathy. "On that note, why don't we order some lunch?" They perused their menus. "Their sandwiches are pretty good, and they make excellent salads," Kathy added. After a minute, Kathy asked, "Are we ready?" Debbie and Laura nodded, and Kathy signaled the waitress. They placed their orders and the waitress left.

They chatted about the weather and the upcoming fair until the waitress returned with their beverages. Once she had left again, Kathy turned to Debbie.

"I told Laura that you were doing some detective work to find out why the biomed department is being closed down to be replaced with an outside company. Since we assumed it had to do with money, we thought your talking to Laura may uncover something to prove that to be true."

"Yes, that was originally my concern, but while talking to some of the nursing department heads about another unrelated matter, I found that all the departments seem to be experiencing unexpected budget cuts. The cuts are not being made with input by the department heads; what's happening is that purchase orders are not being honored while the department heads know there should be sufficient money in their budgets for the expenses."

Laura nodded. "I heard something about that. I have a friend in the purchasing division, and she's had some complaints about purchase orders being submitted but no orders being sent. She couldn't really help them. She collects the purchase orders, checks to see they meet budget requirements and then passes them on to another person who does the actual purchasing. For nursing departments, those orders need to go through the chief of nursing or her assistant. I don't know what happens to them really." She looked down at her hands before her eyes darted around the dining room again. The dining room was in the lobby of the hotel, so from her perspective, she could see the entire lobby. It seemed like she was trying to avoid someone.

"But what about biomed?" Debbie asked. "I didn't check with departments outside of nursing yet, but I'm suspecting some of them are experiencing the same problem. Who handles those?"

Laura shrugged. "Another person in purchasing, I suppose. I'm not sure of the approval process for them, but my guess would be the chief of operations or his assistant. But I'm not sure." She hesitated a moment and then looked directly at Debbie. "I'm not sure how much help I can be with your search. You see, I work in the gifts division; I handle donations coming into the hospital."

Debbie was visibly disappointed. It was clear this lunch was a total waste of her time and only making Laura nervous. A bell rang in Debbie's head. "Laura, I'm sorry and I know it's none of my business, but I feel I'm making you nervous asking you to come here and talk about the finance department. The last thing I want to do is create problems for you. Would you rather I leave?"

Debbie put her napkin down and picked up her purse from the floor beneath her feet, but Kathy laid her hand on her arm to indicate she should stay. "For one, I'm the one who asked everyone here. And two, nobody is going to get into trouble." She looked at Laura. "What's going on Laura?" It was obvious from her tone she and Laura were good friends and she was as concerned about her behavior as Debbie.

Laura looked down at her hands again and then her eyes roamed the hotel again before she answered. "There are some weird things going on in finance," she said. She looked at each of them in turn. "It's hard to tell if something's wrong because there are so many people involved."

"Involved in the weird things going on?" Debbie asked confused.

"No, I'm talking about the finance department. I don't know exactly how many people work in our department; you see, we take up two floors in the administration wing. There are about two dozen people on my floor. My friends in purchasing and accounts payable work on the floor above me, so we don't work together. We usually meet after work for dinner or a drink, and they've both been concerned about some odd things happening in their divisions."

Both Kathy and Debbie looked at each other. Kathy turned to Laura. "You mean odd like money disappearing?"

"Yes and no," Laura said. "It's like things shifting in and out of their departments, like money is moving more than just disappearing. But none of us know enough about the other departments or budgets to really know if something's happening or not."

"But what do you mean moving?" Kathy looked puzzled. "If they don't know where the money is moving to, why do they assume it's just moving and not disappearing?"

Laura opened her mouth to speak, then shut it again, as her eyes got big and she froze in place.

"Laura?" Kathy asked alarmed. She turned her head to follow Laura's gaze and saw Madas in the hotel lobby. She leaned toward Debbie and whispered, "Don't look now, but Genevieve Madas just walked in."

Laura tried to make herself shrink behind the table with her eyes downcast. Kathy put her hand on Laura's arm now. "It's okay. She's going to the check-in desk and now she's walking to the elevator. She's in the elevator now." She turned back to Laura. "You were expecting her here?"

Laura shook her head. "No, I was expecting Mr. Louis." Her eyes got big again.

"Let me guess," Kathy said. "Louis just walked in."

Laura nodded. She seemed less nervous now. "He got in the elevator too." She turned to Kathy and smiled. "Sorry, I should have told you about Mr. Louis."

"And Madas?" Kathy asked.

Laura shook her head. "I didn't know she was coming."

"Now I'm really confused," Debbie couldn't help saying.

Laura turned to her now. All her nervousness seemed to have disappeared. "Mr. Louis makes reservations here once or twice a week in mid-day. I thought it was for lunch with someone. I wasn't worried about him seeing me here for lunch, but I would have to be careful of the time and watch what I say if he should come in and see me."

"How do you know?" Debbie couldn't help asking.

"I'm friends with his secretary, Shirley, too. She sometimes joins us for a drink after work. She has two little kids, so she never stays for dinner."

"Did you know he was meeting Madas here?" Debbie asked, now excited that her search for proof of the rumor was at an end.

"I don't know about Madas. Shirley just makes reservations for two. I thought it was for lunch. But maybe it was for a room? She never said, but why would she? It's her boss after all."

Kathy looked at Debbie and smiled. "Looks like one of your investigations has ended successfully."

It was Laura's turn to be confused. Kathy turned to her. "Debbie was originally looking into the truth about a rumor that Louis and Madas are an item. She found out about the budget issues by accident. It looks like those rumors are true." She turned back to Debbie. "One question answered." She licked her finger and made a checkmark in the air.

"Mr. Louis and Ms. Madas?" Laura asked. "I heard those rumors too, but it never occurred to me that his lunch dates were with her."

"Well, that question is answered, but you left dozens of others on the table," Kathy said to Laura. She looked at her watch. "But I don't think we'll solve those today. I need to get back. If you ladies would like to stay a little longer, that's fine with me."

Both women shook their heads. Debbie didn't think it would be useful to her job to take a longer lunch than her boss, and Laura looked rather worn out. They rose from the table. Laura and Debbie shook hands again and Kathy gave her friend a hug. "Maybe we can meet again in a safer place and talk more about what's bothering you."

Laura nodded and looked at Debbie. "It was nice to meet you and I'll ask around about the purchase order issues you talked about."

"Nice to meet you and thank you. Any help would be appreciated." She really hoped Laura could provide more help. But what she learned today should be shared with the team, as she thought of them now.

"That no good lousy back-stabbing mother-fucking lying son of a bitch!"

"Dan, take it easy, the boys will hear you!" Joyce admonished her husband.

"I always knew Dorfly was an asshole," Dan continued, "but Jesus Christ, he got Dennis involved in this shit!"

Debbie and I had been invited to Dan's again and we were sitting around their kitchen table as before. I had just finished telling them about my conversation with Dennis Lebon and learning about the 'jokes' Dennis had been playing at Dorfly's direction.

"Dennis has no idea that what he's been doing is wrong, or what the consequences have been," I said.

"Yeah, but Dorfly sure as hell does," Dan said.

Joyce put her hand on Dan's forearm. "What you need to think about, Dan, is the questions you need to be asking."

Dan looked at her. "And what would they be?"

"What's Dorfly's end-game? What's in it for him? Why has he been doing the things he's been doing?"

"I think there's another question that needs to be answered," Debbie said.

"What's that?" I asked her.

"From what you've told me about him, Dorfly's not that smart. Who else is involved?"

"What makes you think someone else is involved?" Dan asked.

"I had lunch with Kathy McMillan and a friend of hers from the finance department, Laura Teller."

"What did you find out?" I asked her.

"There have been some strange things going on in the purchasing department." She proceeded to relate what she'd learned about money being moved around, purchases not being made, and budgets being slashed without input from the department heads.

"So, where's the money going?" Joyce asked her.

"Nobody seems to know," Debbie said. "The other thing I learned is that Jerry Louis and Genevieve Madas are evidently doing the horizontal mambo a couple times a week at the Holiday Inn."

"You're sure about that?" Dan asked her.

"While we were having lunch they came in separately, went to the lobby desk, and then boarded the elevator and disappeared upstairs."

"You saw them do that?" Joyce asked.

"Actually, I was facing the other way, but Kathy and Laura saw them and told me about it."

Dan sat silently thinking for a few moments. "As disgusting as that thought is, we need to take a step back."

"How do you mean?" Joyce asked him.

"What we really know is just conjecture. We have some vague suspicions about money being moved around and possibly disappearing and the chief financial officer may be involved. As far as Madas and Louis are concerned, there's no law against having an affair."

"But it places them together," Joyce said. "Surely that's something."

Dan looked at Debbie. "No offense, Debbie, but you didn't actually see them."

"Kathy and Laura certainly wouldn't lie about what they observed," Debbie said.

"I'm not saying they would," Dan told her, "but it wouldn't hold up under scrutiny, and it doesn't really tell us anything."

"But this can't be the end of it," I said. "We know Dorfly put Dennis up to tampering with the machines, and Bobby..."

"I didn't say this would be the end of it. It can't be. But we need proof," Dan said.

"What kind of proof?" I asked him.

He thought for a few moments more. "Jay, you've done a lot of work with microphones and sound equipment. How difficult do you think it would be to bug Dorfly's office and tape him incriminating himself."

"It wouldn't be that hard, but I might be able to use some help."

"Trevor can help you," he said.

"He probably could," I said. "But I'm thinking a listening device in Dorfly's office would best go above the ceiling tiles over his desk. In the plenum. And no one knows what's in the plenum better than Orville Coleman."

"That's probably true. But do you think we can trust Orville?"

"Absolutely, he hates Dorfly as much as we do. He'd probably get a kick out of the idea. But we're going to have to think of a distraction for Dorfly, I don't want to put Orville's job in jeopardy."

Dan smiled for the first time all evening. "You just leave that to me. Shit-for-brains has been yammering about bed maintenance for months. I think it's high time we had a meeting about the subject."

"But doesn't he know about our department being shut down?" I asked.

"Yes, but do you think he'd turn down an opportunity to argue with me?"

"Good point," I told him.

"And Debbie and I can go to lunch at the Holiday Inn with my old Instamatic camera and get pictures of Louis and Madas together," Joyce said excitedly.

"But Madas has met both of us," Debbie said to her. "What if she recognizes us?"

"I doubt she paid much attention to us peons when she met us," Joyce told her.

"But she still could..."

"I can get my hands on some old wigs and other stuff we can use," Joyce said. "We could wear disguises."

Debbie looked at me with concern. "I can't tell you what to do," I told her. "Our department is being closed down, but you still have your job."

Her concern evolved into a small smile. "Oh, what the hell. If it doesn't work out, maybe I can get a job with the CIA."

"Hello?"

"Hey, Orville, it's Jay. I hope I didn't get you at a bad time."

"No, Buddy, I was just working on my soap box racer."

"You have a soap box racer?"

"No, Vicky's son Todd does. He's eight. He's in Cub Scouts and he has a big race coming up next weekend. We're planning to win this year."

"Well, I wish you both good luck," I told him.

"What's up, Jay? I hope you weren't thinking about a balloon ride. The weather's gonna be crappy the next few days and I'm grounded."

"No, that's not it," I said, thinking about what I was about to ask him to do and what the consequences could be.

"It sounds like you're stalling, Jay. Why don't you just say what you want to say?"

"Orville, do you know Dennis Lebon?"

"Of course, everybody knows Dennis. He's a sweet kid, why?"

"You know about the equipment failures the hospital has been experiencing."

"I do. What does that have to do with Dennis?"

I spent the next few minutes telling Orville what I had learned about Dennis' abilities and how Dorfly was using the knowledge.

"That son of a bitch!" Orville said when I had finished.

"Dan had several additional adjectives for him."

"We all know ferret-face is an idiot, but who would have thought he could be so evil?"

"Evil's the word for it."

"So, what do you need, Jay? I know you didn't just call to chat."

"I want to ask you to help me do something."

"What?"

"If you don't want to do it that's fine, I'll understand."

"Now you really have my curiosity peaked. What do you want me to do?"

"I want you to help me bug Dorfly's office so we can hopefully get the goods on him."

I had to wait more than a minute for Orville's laughter to die down enough for him to speak again.

"If we should be caught it could mean your job," I pointed out.

"Do you really think I'd want to work in a place that could allow such unbelievable bullshit to happen?"

"I'm guessing no?"

"When do you want to do this?" he asked.

"ASAP. We need to work fast."

"We're going to have to find a way to keep Dorfly away from his office for a while."

"Dan's going to have it covered."

"How's he going to do that?"

"He's going to call for a meeting with Dorfly to discuss bed maintenance."

I had to wait again for Orville's laughter to subside. After that we discussed details of what we'd need to do. As it turned out, Orville had a voice activated cassette tape recorder that we could use. I didn't ask him why he had a voice activated cassette tape recorder.

Two days later, I was sitting in the shop at a bench working on a muscle stimulator when Orville walked through the door carrying a small leather case. I could tell by the look on his face that something was wrong.

"What is it?" I asked quietly, though all the other techs were working up on the floor.

"Is Dan around?" he asked just as quietly.

"The last I saw he was doing paperwork in his office."

"Come on," he said.

We walked to Dan's office door and he looked up from what he was doing. "What's up?" he asked.

We entered the office and I closed and locked the door. Orville reached into his case and pulled out a small cassette tape player.

"I changed the tape in the machine while Dorfly was in a meeting, and I thought you should hear this right away."

He pushed the play button and we soon heard Dorfly's voice. "Yes, I think we've done enough with the machines. We've definitely gotten the ball rolling." There was silence while the person on the other end spoke. "That's true, but now we've got another problem." Silence... "It's Dennis. He's been having fun playing his 'jokes' and he doesn't want to stop." Silence... "Do you really think we should go that far? That's a big step." Silence... "Couldn't we just have him fired?" Silence... "Isn't there some way we could have him put away?" Silence... "Yeah, I think I've heard that. Something about a danger to himself or others." Silence... "That's a good idea. I'll take care of it, Jerry." We heard the receiver being replaced in its cradle and Orville shut the tape player off.

I looked at Dan. A few seconds ago his face had held a look of horror, now his face was set in stone.

"Dan, what are we gonna..." I began, and then stopped when he raised his hand.

"The first thing I'm going to do is take Dennis home with me where I can watch him like a hawk.

Debbie had been keeping Kathy apprised of the developments pertaining to the missing purchase orders and the status of the biomed department, so Kathy was totally supportive of Debbie's role in solving the mysteries. As a result, it had been no problem for Debbie to get the afternoon off to pursue the Louis/Madas story.

Debbie arrived at Dan and Joyce's house around noon. They agreed that gave them plenty of time to prepare, because Laura had learned from Louis' secretary that he had an appointment at 1:30 that day. Joyce had selected two wigs for the lunch appearance—one was a blond shoulder-length bob cut and the other was short and gray. It was Joyce's idea that they disguise themselves as a mother and daughter visiting from out of town, spending the afternoon shopping.

Joyce wore the gray and Debbie wore the blond. Joyce also wore glasses and Debbie wore makeup that made her blue eyes look greener with green eyeshadow and mascara and a peach blush. Debbie laughed when she looked in the mirror. The wig, makeup and flowered spring dress certainly didn't look like her. Joyce, on the other hand, looked absolutely lovely in her gray wig and print suit. They stood in front of the mirror and Joyce swore.

"What's the matter?" Debbie asked. "We certainly look different."

"But we look good," Joyce sounded disappointed.

"What's wrong with looking good?" Debbie turned back to their reflections and then understood. "Shit, you're right."

"The last thing we want to do is attract attention," Joyce said. She turned side to side in the mirror. "Although I might keep this wig for Dan," she smiled.

"I think that's a good idea. I think I'll borrow this one to show Jay," Debbie agreed.

Joyce walked over to her closet and pulled a box out and started going through it, throwing clothes and wigs on the floor.

Debbie picked up a wig of long black hair and replaced the blond one. She walked over to the mirror. "I think if I wore darker eye makeup, this may do the trick," she said.

Joyce turned to look at her. "That's definitely better. Nobody would take a second look at you in that getup." She pulled another gray wig that was duller in color and a little shorter and placed it over her hair. "Maybe if the glasses are more dated, like these," she pulled out glasses that were more almond shaped with large frames. "Now we just need clothes with more neutral colors." She sorted through another box and pulled out a belted shirtdress for herself and an A-line for Debbie. "Try this one," she handed the dress to Debbie.

Once they had changed their costumes, they felt ready to go. Joyce looked at her watch. "We better call a cab; we're running later than planned."

They grabbed their purses and shopping bags Joyce had put together and went to the front door to wait for the cab.

Debbie looked in her shopping bag. "Nothing but empty boxes and bags," Joyce explained. "I have my camera and flash cubes, but that's it. I thought it would look better if the perception was that we'd been shopping all morning."

"Where did all this come from?" Debbie asked indicating her hair, outfit and purse.

"I volunteer at the local playhouse as a seamstress and prop assistant. So, I have a key to the place and access to the costumes and everything. I didn't think anyone would mind if I borrowed a few things."

"Oh," Debbie sounded disappointed. "I was hoping I could borrow the blond wig."

"You certainly may," Joyce said. "We women have to stick together after all, right?" She winked at Debbie.

The cab pulled up and they climbed in and rode the three and a half miles to the Holiday Inn. Joyce asked the driver to stop a block away, paid him and they climbed out. Joyce waited for the cab to drive off and then turned to Debbie. "Show time."

"Should we just go in?" Debbie asked.

"Heavens no," Joyce responded, looking at her watch. "It's almost 1:30. Let's do a little window shopping and try to arrive the same time our lovers arrive so we can get a picture of them going in."

"How do we do that?" Debbie asked.

"We'll take pictures of each other in front of the hotel as each one arrives, getting them and the hotel sign together." She reached into her bag and pulled out the camera and a flash cube. She showed the camera and flash cube to Debbie, instructing her on taking a picture while they strolled to the hotel, pretending to look in windows of the hotel's gift shops.

They lingered in front of the last shop window until they saw a cab pull up to the front door with Jerry Louis in the back seat. "You go first," Joyce said, motioning Debbie to stand in front of the hotel doorway. Debbie smiled for the camera as Joyce attached the flash cube and held the camera up. Just as Louis reached the door, Joyce took a shot. Louis didn't seem to notice the flash of the camera as he reached the door. "One more," Joyce said, and Debbie smiled again. Flash. Louis was in the door.

Debbie walked back over to Joyce. "We have two more flashes on this cube; try to get two shots," Joyce said as she held the Instamatic out.

Debbie took the camera. She pretended to fumble with it until a second cab pulled up to the curb with Madas in the back seat. Madas got out of the cab, frowned at the two women and walked to the door. Debbie pushed the button. Nothing. The flash hadn't gone off.

"Try again," Joyce called to her. Debbie quickly made sure she had the final flash of the four-shot cube ready to go and got a picture of Madas' back going through the door.

"Shit," she said.

Joyce hurried over to her. "Quick. Give me the camera. We'll see if we can get a picture of her inside." She took the camera and put a new flash cube in place, and they hurried into the hotel. Once in the lobby, they found Louis was nowhere to be seen, but Madas was heading to the Ladies' room. Joyce raised the camera and snapped a picture. The flash worked this time and as Madas turned around to see what was going on, Joyce jumped behind a planter, pulling Debbie with her.

Debbie peaked around the side of the planter. "I don't think she saw us taking the picture; she's going in."

They walked out from the behind the planter and casually strolled to the dining room. "Let's pretend nothing happened. We'll have lunch and see if we can find out when they leave," Joyce said.

Debbie asked the hostess for the table she had shared with Kathy and Laura, and they sat down. This time Debbie sat across from Joyce, so between them, the dining room and lobby were easily visible to both. The table behind Joyce was empty and just the kitchen door was behind Debbie. The dining room was pretty full, and a low din hummed throughout the room. Debbie picked up her menu and looked at Joyce.

"Where did you learn to be so sneaky? Were you a spy in a former life?" She smiled at Joyce.

"I guess I read too many books. I especially like detective stories and mysteries."

Their waitress arrived with glasses of water. "Can I get you ladies anything to drink?" she asked.

Joyce looked up at Debbie. "I think today calls for a glass of wine. How about a Riesling," she said to Debbie. It wasn't a question. Debbie nodded and the waitress left.

As they sipped their wine and waited for their food, Joyce asked Debbie about her job and background, and Debbie found herself talking about her brother. Joyce was sympathetic. They started talking about what was going on at the hospital, when Debbie's eyes got large.

"Don't look now, but Louis and Madas just entered the dining room," she whispered.

"What, no sex today?" Joyce asked.

"If there was, it was quick," Debbie said. "They're coming this way." The women waited quietly while the chair behind Joyce was pulled out and someone sat down and moved their chair toward the table.

"Who?" Joyce mouthed subtly indicating the chair behind her.

Debbie put the wine glass to her lips and mouthed, "Madas."

While Debbie drank her wine, Joyce started talking quietly about their plans for the afternoon. There was a museum they could visit, or they could do more shopping.

Debbie played along. "I'd like to get a pair of shoes to match the dress I bought," she said.

"That would be fun," Joyce said. "I love shopping for shoes. Maybe I'll get myself a pair." She picked up her purse and rummaged through it, pulling out a tissue wrapped around something. She surreptitiously laid a pen on the table, dabbed her nose with the tissue and returned it to her purse. She then took her paper napkin and opened it halfway.

"Waitress," warned Debbie.

Joyce slipped the napkin and pen onto her lap, and as the waitress placed their salads on the table, she asked for another napkin. They waited until the napkin came and the waitress left, then

Joyce placed the napkin on the table and took pen in hand. "Talk," she mouthed to Debbie.

As they ate their salads, Debbie talked about the new house she was looking to buy, with excruciating detail. Joyce wrote on the napkin and made nondescript remarks in response to Debbie's boring monologue. They had just finished their salads, when the waitress appeared again. Joyce had just enough time to drop the pen and napkin in her lap while their entrees were placed on the table. After telling the waitress they needed nothing further, she was gone, and the napkin was back on the table.

Debbie caught a few words here and there of the conversation taking place behind Joyce but trying to maintain the subterfuge of having a conversation, it was difficult for her to catch much of what was discussed. It appeared Joyce was having better luck, since she jotted words down frequently and her responses indicated she hadn't listened to a word Debbie was saying. By the time they were finished with their meals, Louis and Madas were still seated.

"We should have some dessert," Joyce remarked. "This is a special occasion, after all." The napkin and pen disappeared again, and she signaled for the waitress. "We'd like dessert," she announced. The waitress left and returned with dessert menus, which they perused while the waitress removed their plates. The table behind Joyce had been silent for several minutes.

"Call, Fred," Louis said. And Joyce listened intently, but only heard one other word, which she wrote down.

"Ok," they heard Madas respond. Then Debbie watched while pretending to read the menu as Louis rose from his chair, tossed cash on the table and walked away.

Debbie started to whisper that Louis was gone, when they both heard Madas talking on her cell phone. "Fred? It's Genie. One month. Will you be ready? Okay, sounds good." Then the chair pushed back, Madas rose from the table and walked away without looking back.

Debbie waited until they were both gone before she spoke again. "They both left the hotel."

Joyce put her pen back into her purse and pushed the napkin over to Debbie, who turned it around so she could read what Joyce had written.

L: to us...

    M: ...can't wait...out...here...

    L: ...little longer...Fred?

    M: ...when...should...him...

    L: ...need to...

    M: ...no one...told him...

    L: ...

    M: ...no...

    L: ...can't...chances...

    M: ...who's taking chances?

    L: ...lower your voice...

    L: ...

    M: ...

    (Louis orders another round)

    M: ...someone died...

    L: ...fault...

    M: I'm ready...

    L: ...no...first...wife...beach...

    M: ...wife?...What...

    L: ...excuse...

    M: ...been there?

    L: ...of course...ready...

    M: ...

L: ...call Fred...month...

M: ...ok...

(Louis leaves)

M: (on cell phone) ...Fred? Genie...a month...will you be ready? ...ok, sounds good.

(Madas leaves)

Debbie looked up as Joyce took the napkin, folded it and put it into her purse. "I heard her ask 'who's taking chances' and, of course, I heard the phone call. Do you think there's enough here to use?"

"We're not done yet," Joyce stated. She signaled the waitress again and requested the check. She placed cash on the table with the check and rose from her seat. "We need to make a phone call first."

"Who are we calling?" Debbie asked as they left the dining room.

"Medi-Max," Joyce replied.

"Do you have their number?" Debbie asked.

Joyce shook her head and walked over to a small bank of pay phones in a small space off the lobby. "No, but information does." She put change in the phone, dialed information and asked for the number for Medi-Max. She pulled out the napkin and turned it over, writing down the number. "Remind me to bring paper the next time I'm sleuthing," she said as she put in more change and dialed the number.

"Hello. This is Marsha Steele from the budget department of Kirkwood Medical Center. May I speak to the president?" She waited a moment. "Yes. This is Marsha Steele from the budget department of Kirkwood Medical Center. May I speak to Mr. Cooper?" Debbie heard the voice on the other end but couldn't make out any words. "We had questions about a recent contract.... That will be fine. I understand. Mr. Madas, you said?" she turned to Debbie, raising her eyebrows while she was apparently being connected to Mr. Madas.

"Hello. My name is Marsha Steele and I'm calling regarding a recent contract with our hospital, Kirkwood Medical Center.... I see... Which one?... Maintenance." She turned and looked at Debbie with a surprised look on her face. "No. I'll call back then. Thank you." She hung up the phone.

"Who is Marsha Steele?" asked Debbie.

"Hell if I know. I just made her up," Joyce said with a smile.

"What did you find out?"

"Well, it turns out Mr. Fred Madas is the senior vice president of sales. And the contract that's scheduled to be finalized this week is for covering both the biomedical and maintenance departments."

"Really?!" Debbie said with excitement. "So, Dorfly's head is also on the block but he doesn't know it yet. That's really big news."

"Yes," Joyce agreed. Debbie turned to go, but Joyce put her hand on her arm. "Wait. One more call." She dialed again.

"Hello lover," she said with a smile on her face. "No, not tonight, I'm afraid.... Because we have to call another meeting.... Dennis?" her face took on a look of surprise. "Of course, that's fine. I understand. Sounds like we all have a lot to talk about. We're heading home now.... Love you." And she hung up again.

She turned to Debbie. "Dennis is coming home with Dan. Apparently they think he's in danger."

"Danger?" Debbie asked.

"We'll soon know. Now let's get out of these duds." Debbie followed her out of the hotel to hail a cab.

We met back at Dan's house to discuss developments and, of course, stay for dinner. Dan had brought Dennis home, and he and Dan's boys joined us for dinner this time. Dennis was being quieter than usual, though he seemed comfortable and at ease with Dan's family, and it was apparent he had been here many times.

We chit chatted during dinner with the boys telling us what they were doing at school, while Dan, Joyce, Debbie and I listened attentively. I was impressed with their maturity in the way they presented themselves. Dennis concentrated on his meal of chicken and noodles with green beans, having become more animated at the prospect of Joyce's cooking. When we'd finished eating, Dan addressed his sons.

"Why don't you guys take Dennis upstairs for video games?"

Dennis brightened immediately. "Can we play Mario?" he asked. He was assured they could and the three of them left the table.

Once they were out of earshot, Joyce addressed the table in general. "I can't believe what they've done with Dennis and the fact he could now be in danger."

"I don't think any of us can believe it, Joyce," I said. "It's like we're in a bad B movie or something."

"I think it's more like an episode of 'The Twilight Zone,'" Debbie said.

Dan had been even quieter than Dennis, but he sounded resolute when he said, "If anything happens to that kid, I'll kill them."

Joyce placed her hand over her husband's. "Nothing's going to happen to Dennis," she said. "He's with us now."

We'd looked over the pictures from Joyce and Debbie's 'lunch' and saw that what we had was probably of little help. There was a decent picture of Louis in front of the Holiday Inn sign, but there was no picture that identified where Madas was. We tried to concentrate on the list of partial conversation between the two that Joyce had written.

L: to us...

M: ...can't wait...out...here...

L: ...little longer...Fred?

M: ...when...should...him...

L: ...need to...

M: ...no one...told him...

L: ...

M: ...no...

L: ...can't...chances...

M: ...who's taking chances?

L: ...lower your voice...

L: ...

M: ...

(Louis orders another round)

M: ...someone died...

L: ...fault...

M: I'm ready...

L: ...no...first...wife...beach...

M: ...wife?...What...

L: ...excuse...

M: ...been there?

L: ...of course...ready...

M: ...

L: ...call Fred...month...

M: ...ok...

(Louis leaves)

M: (on cell phone) ...Fred? Genie...a month...will you be ready? ...ok, sounds good.

(Madas leaves)

"Louis says 'to us'. He's obviously toasting the two of them for whatever they're doing," Joyce said.

"Then Madas says, something... can't wait, something... out, something... here," I said.

"Then Louis says little longer," Debbie said. "So Madas must have said she can't wait much longer for what they're planning to happen. And we know now, thanks to Joyce's quick thinking, that Fred is Fred Madas, Genevieve's brother. We also know that he calls her Genie."

"Does that really help us?" I asked her.

"Well it doesn't hurt," she informed me.

"We know from the rest of the dialogue they're becoming afraid of taking chances," Joyce said. "It also looks like they may be trying to advance their timeline."

"Their timeline for what?" Dan asked Joyce.

Joyce gave him a look as if it should be obvious. "We know Madas called her brother afterwards and asked if he'd be ready in a month. We also know they're planning to replace the biomed and maintenance departments both. That must be what she wants to know if he'll be ready for."

Dan rubbed his eyes with his hand. "I think we're relying too much on conjecture and not enough on fact."

"You can see right there Madas is concerned someone died, and Louis must tell her that it's not their fault," Joyce said.

"That's certainly the way I'm reading it," Debbie said.

"I think you need to call Jason," Dan said to Joyce.

"I assume you're not referring to your son," I said to him.

"No, he's referring to our Jason's namesake, my brother, Jason Cantrelli," Joyce said. "He's our lawyer."

"We need to find out if Jason thinks we have enough to act on," Dan said. "In the meantime, I'm going to confront Dorfly tomorrow."

"Are you sure that's wise?" Joyce asked him.

"We need to find out who all is involved in this." Dan told her.

"You can't tell him that his department is going to be out too," Joyce said.

"Why not?" Dan asked. "That would make my day."

"It would also tip our hand, Dan. You want Dorfly to be in the dark." Joyce told him.

"Dorfly's always in the dark," Dan said.

"Don't tell him." Joyce was adamant.

"Okay, okay," he said, holding up his hands in surrender.

"Kathy tells me that Laura has more information," Debbie said. "I'll meet with her and find out just what she's learned."

"That sounds good," Dan said. "We need all the information we can get."

"What do you want me to do, Dan?" I asked.

"I want you to get back with your buddy, Orville, and see what he thinks about the feasibility of bugging Jerry Louis' office."

"Shall I tell him what we've learned about the maintenance department?"

"Sure." He looked at his wife and seemed to read her thoughts. "But be sure to tell him not to tell Dorfly."

"That might not be so easy for him to do," I said.

"Tell me about it."

Dorfly looked surprised the next morning when he unlocked his office door, turned on the light and saw Dan sitting there next to his desk.

"What the hell?! How did you get in here?!" he sputtered.

"That doesn't matter, Dwayne. We need to talk." Dan's voice was perfectly calm and controlled and reflected none of the rage he felt.

"What do you mean talk?! You call and make a goddamned appointment if you want to talk to me! I'm calling security!"

Dan's internalized ire rose instantly. Dorfly reached for his phone, and Dan reached for Dorfly's jacket. Dan was not, nor had he ever been a violent man, but he grabbed the back of Dorfly's jacket with both hands and flung him headfirst into the wall, which shook and rattled considerably.

Dorfly was, needless to say, stunned. Both with the contact between his head and the wall and undoubtedly by the surprise. Dan grabbed the front of his jacket and pulled his face to within inches of his own, until he could smell the coffee and bacon on his breath.

"You're going to give me answers, Dwayne, and you're going to give them to me now!"

At first it looked as if he were going to give Dan trouble, as if he might try to bullshit his way out. But Dan was not in a mood to be argued with, and he was gratified to see a flicker of fear in Dorfly's eyes.

"Answers about what?"

"Answers about what the hell you've been putting Dennis Lebon up to and why!"

Dan could see Dorfly was shocked he'd been found out and could almost see the wheels turning as he thought about how he might cover things up to save his ass. "What has that dumb shit been telling you?"

Dan tried telling himself that further violence would accomplish nothing, but in an instant, he decided that was total bullshit. He had never felt more contempt for another human being. He was so enraged he couldn't help it, he hit him. He didn't just tap him, he hit him as hard as he could in the side of the mouth. He knew as soon as he did it that it was a mistake, his hand hurt like hell, but it was gratifying to see Dorfly knocked into the wall once again.

Dorfly sat there on the floor for a moment dazed, holding his face. "What the fu...?"

Dan didn't give him a chance to recover. He grabbed him by the jacket once again and partially lifted him onto his desk. His adrenaline was definitely flowing.

"What the hell have you been doing, asshole?!" Dan asked with utter contempt.

Dorfly sat perfectly still on the desk, his eyes glazed and his lip swelling and beginning to bleed down his chin on the left side where Dan had hit him. Then his eyes focused with a hard, dull look.

"Who's an asshole?" he asked through partially clenched teeth. "I'll sue you, dumb jerk!" Just like that he had become belligerent again. Of course, Dan must have seemed like a complete lunatic. At that point he probably was.

"You're going to sue me for what, Dwayne?"

"Assault, to begin with!"

"And where's your witness?" Dan asked, briefly indicating the rest of the empty office. "Who's going to corroborate your story?"

Dorfly had gotten a little smirk on his face. "Just wait until Louis hears about this."

"You mean Jerry Louis, the Chief Financial Officer? Why would he give a shit about you?" Dan asked.

The smirk had gotten even more pronounced. "You still don't get it, do you jerk-off? Louis is closing down your department. You're almost out the door now!"

Dan could see that Dorfly realized he'd said too much, and he saw the smirk begin to falter. "Thanks, Dwayne, that's all I needed to know." Dan let go of him and left.

Orville was more than up to the task of bugging Louis' office, especially after I told him what we knew about the maintenance department being axed along with the biomed department. Neither of us had anything to lose, so we decided to do the same thing with the recorder that we'd done in Dorfly's office.

Debbie was able to learn Louis had his afternoon 'appointment' the next day, so we were all set. Orville decided if he needed cover to retrieve the tape, he could always do so under the guise of working on the plenum wiring. He was one of the very few people in the hospital who could invent a reason to be up in the ceiling.

"Some woman claiming to be someone named Marsha Steele from the hospital finance department called Fred, Jerry."

"So what?"

"I checked. There is no one in hospital finance named Marsha Steele."

I stole a quick glance at Joyce and saw her and Dan exchange a glance. We sat in Dan's rec room in the basement listening to the recording from Louis' office that had caught a conversation between him and Madas.

Debbie sat on the couch between Papa Joe and me. Will Stanski and Orville sat on armchairs that were perpendicular to us as Orville operated his tape recorder on an end table between them. A large-screen TV that was one of Dan's prize possessions sat against the wall opposite us, its screen dark at the moment. Trevor and Alan sat on the floor in front of the TV, and Joyce and Kathy sat on kitchen chairs near the bottom of the basement stairs. After Debbie's latest revelation, Kathy had insisted on being involved. Dan, who didn't seem able to sit, paced back and forth.

"What did this mystery person want?" we heard Louis ask.

"She wanted to know about the contracts for taking over biomed and maintenance."

"And what did they tell her?"

"Not much, but it confirms our plans and leaves our asses hanging in the breeze."

There was a pause and I could imagine Louis mulling over the situation.

"I don't think we're going to have a month to wait," he said. "I think it's time for me to move the money we've garnered already. After that, I'll resign first. I've been prepping my wife, telling her about the new job I'll be getting. She's already been scoping out houses she might like to live in. The accounting books are such a mess, by the time they figure it all out, we'll be long gone."

"You mean you'll be long gone." Madas was starting to sound angry. "You'll be taking off with your wife to Timbuktu leaving me here to deal with the fallout!"

"I'm not leaving you, Genevieve. We just need to make some adjustments to our plans."

"Adjustments to our plans? I've got news for you, Jerry, I have no intention of being the fall guy here! A person has died, and if I go down, there won't be anywhere you can hide. I'll see to it!"

We couldn't hear footsteps on the plush-pile carpet and the sound was muffled, but we could hear Louis' office door being closed with force. Orville turned off the recorder.

"How have they been getting away with this?" Papa Joe asked.

"I talked with Laura, our friend in finance," Debbie told him. "Louis fired the internal auditor weeks ago."

"Who's doing the auditor's job?" Joe asked her.

"No one," she told him. "They haven't filled the position."

"So, the foxes are guarding the henhouse," Joe said.

"You've got it," she told him.

"We certainly should be able to use that, and the recording is pretty damning evidence," I said to the group.

"We can't use it," said Dan still pacing.

"Why not?" asked Trevor.

"I've been talking to Jason Cantrelli, our lawyer," Dan told him. "We're not law enforcement and we had no warrant. If we tried to introduce the recording as evidence, any lawyer for the other side would have it thrown out immediately."

"Can't we just go to the police?" Kathy asked.

"We don't know the scope of Louis' influence with the local department." Dan told her. "We don't know if they'd come up with some trumped up charges, or they could write us off as a bunch of paranoid loonies trying to cover our asses and save our jobs."

"What about going to the police in another jurisdiction?" Will asked.

"We can't be sure about going to the police in another jurisdiction because we aren't sure how willing they'd be to step on the toes of the locals." Dan said. "And what proof do we really have? Dennis is our only witness, and who knows if he'd be believed."

The more we talked, the more we became convinced that Louis was holding all the aces, that we really didn't have a leg to stand on.

Dan had gone upstairs to use the bathroom, and I had gone upstairs to help myself to a beer. I had just retrieved one from the fridge and was closing the door, when Dan came into the room on his way back downstairs. There had been a thought that kept nagging at the back of my mind, and I brought it up to him.

"Dan, there's something that keeps bugging me."

"No kidding?!"

"I mean besides all the rest of it. What's the connection between Dwayne Dorfly and Dennis?"

He said nothing for a few moments but stood absolutely still, and I waited, knowing from experience an answer was not long in coming. As he looked at me, I could see pain in his eyes, pain that had been there for a long time.

"Dennis is my nephew." The statement was barely above a whisper, but he might have shouted it from the top of his lungs for the effect it had on me.

"What?" Stupid, but it was all I could think of to say.

"Dennis is the child of my sister and Dwayne Dorfly."

Papa Joe's words came rushing back to me. 'According to her he had been drinking one night, things got out of hand, and when she said no, he knocked her around and raped her'. All at once I understood the intensity of the feud between Dan and Dorfly. I understood why Dan hated him so much. What I couldn't understand was how Dan had refrained from killing Dorfly.

I could think of many questions, but the most basic one came to mind first. "Why is Dennis' name different from Dwayne's?"

"Dwayne Dorfly has never acknowledged his responsibility for anything. So, he got Cindy pregnant, so what? The only thing that it meant to him is he proved his manhood. When the kid was born handicapped, that motherfucker denied it was even his."

"Does Dennis know?"

"As far as Dennis knows, his father is Jed Lebon, a very decent man who married his mother and lives with her in Ohio."

"How did Dennis wind up here?"

"Dennis was institutionalized at a very young age. When his talent with machines became known he was slated to enter an experimental work program. Since I was running the biomed department, I thought I could help him by bringing him in."

"But why didn't it work? Why wouldn't they want to use his talent?"

"I believe I wound up pushing too hard." Dan took a moment to rub his eyes with a tissue that he got from a box on top of the fridge before he continued. "I was trying to show him off. I thought that maybe if Dorfly could see what the kid could do, he might appreciate him at least a little. I must have been out of my mind thinking that Dwayne Dorfly could think of anyone besides himself. I had thought that maybe Dennis could work in the shop; after all, he has the talent. All he needs is supervision."

"What happened?"

"The hospital administration doesn't give a damn about talent. All they care about is aesthetics. It doesn't matter that the kid's an electronic genius; it wouldn't look good to the board of directors to have a retarded—God I hate that word—BMET working here."

"So, we have a retarded janitor instead."

"Welcome to Kirkwood. It's safe to have him working as a janitor."

I offered Dan my still unopened can of beer and got another one for myself. I couldn't think of another single thing to say and he seemed to be talked out, so we headed back downstairs.

We spent the next several hours knocking thoughts and ideas back and forth. The next thing we knew, it was one o'clock in the morning and we hadn't really gotten anywhere. Joyce excused herself and went upstairs to check on things. We were all getting tired when Joyce came slowly down the basement stairs. She looked at her husband with that non-verbal communication that only long-time married couples seem to possess. I looked at Dan's face and immediately knew that something was going on.

"What?" Dan whispered to her.

"Someone is outside," she whispered to him.

"What do you mean someone is outside?"

They were both speaking so softly that it was difficult to understand them. The rest of us had become absolutely quiet as we picked up on the fact that something was wrong.

"I mean just that. Someone is sneaking around outside."

"Are you sure?"

"Dan, we've lived here for twenty-five years. I know every shadow in the back yard, and I'm telling you that someone is out there."

I could see Dan quickly process the situation. "Joyce, go back upstairs very carefully and turn out all the lights like we're going to bed."

"But Dan, all of our cars are out front," I reminded him.

"So, we're having a sleepover."

Joyce went slowly back up the stairs, and we listened to the floor over our heads softly creak as she moved around turning out lights.

When she'd finished, she came to the top of the stairs and whispered down to us, "Okay, they're off."

One at a time we ascended moving as quietly as possible. We stood back from the windows peeking out very cautiously from the sides. There was a little light from a street lamp out front, but there was no moon and it was quite dark.

"I can't see a damn thing!" Alan whispered, peering out the front window.

"I saw him out back," whispered Joyce.

"Who would be snooping around out there?" Will whispered.

"I have a pretty good idea," whispered Dan.

"Dorfly?" whispered Papa Joe.

"Who else?" whispered Dan."

"But what's he trying to do?" whispered Trevor.

"What could he hope to gain?" I whispered.

As if in answer to my question, we saw someone strike a match through the front window. In the brief glare of the flame we could see a red gas can sitting on the ground.

"Oh my God!" Joyce wasn't whispering now.

"Get the boys!" Dan shouted to her on his way out the front door.

We all followed in his wake. I was the last one out, and I got to the door just as Dan got to Dorfly.

Dan had leapt out the door so quickly that he'd caught Dorfly completely by surprise. Dorfly dropped the match he'd just lit, and his right pant leg immediately burst into flame. He started yelling and running around the front yard in circles, the flames from his burning pantleg billowing out behind him.

Dan was chasing him yelling, "Keep him away from the house!"

We all stood along the front of the house blocking Dorfly from it like a bunch of demonic goalies, while Dan continued to chase him trying to gain a purchase on him. It looked for all the world like someone trying to catch a greased pig at a county fair, one that was on fire no less.

Dorfly kept yelling, "I'm burning, I'm burning!"

Dan kept cussing as he tried to catch the elusive Dorfly. Several of Dan's neighbors had come out of their houses to watch the show, and I wondered just what they thought was going on. It isn't every day that you see your neighbor trying to catch a squealing human Roman candle in his front yard.

Dorfly had made yet another mindless sharp turn and was coming directly back toward Dan. Dan stopped and moved his feet apart taking a firm stance. I thought I knew what was coming and watched fascinated as everything seemed to move in slow motion. Dan reared back and sent his large, meaty right fist flying with what must have been the accumulated rage of several decades.

The fist caught Dorfly squarely under the chin, and there was a sickening, POP! as he went flying backwards. He landed and rolled so far, the fire was extinguished. Debbie went over to him and felt for a pulse to make sure that he was still alive.

"Is he okay?" I asked her.

She looked up at me with an expression I could feel more than see in the darkness. "He's still breathing if that's what you mean. I don't think he's ever been okay."

"I wonder if anyone will listen to us now?" I asked.

"You'd hope so."

She stood up, and I walked up behind her and put my arms around her waist, nestling my chin on her shoulder. "Hell of a day, wouldn't you say?"

She reached up placing her soft hand on my cheek. "I must admit, Jay Barlow, since I met you, life has been anything but boring."

"I'll bet you say that to all the boys." She laughed and turned in my arms, and we held each other for a few moments until Dan came up behind us.

"I hate like hell to drive a wedge between you two—actually I think it may take a crowbar—but we have to do something about this carcass laying in my front yard," Dan said, rubbing his hand.

I pulled myself away from Debbie. "Is your hand okay? That was quite a pile driver you delivered to Dorfly."

"It's the best pain I ever felt," Dan said. "I've been aching to do that for years, and I got to do it twice in one week."

"Dan, I don't mean to be a party pooper, I know that must have been gratifying, but don't you think it's time we called the police?"

"Yeah, I do; I just wanted to hear somebody else say it."

As it turned out, one of Dan's neighbors had already called nine-one-one before we did. I don't know exactly what was reported, but when the cavalry arrived it made the response to my river accident look paltry. From the fire department there were two ambulances, the rescue squad, a tanker truck and a hook and ladder truck, as well as a medic unit from the hospital. Leading this entourage was no fewer than five state police cruisers. The emergency lights lit up the neighborhood like the Fourth of July.

The medics descended on Dorfly immediately, recognizing him as the most in need of medical attention. He was laying in the grass of Dan's side yard on his back, moaning and holding his jaw, while his right pant leg emitted small plumes of smoke.

They set about bracing his obviously broken jaw and tending to his burned right leg, and then the police had a few questions. I wasn't sure how the interrogation of a man with a broken jaw was going to proceed, especially since he hadn't recovered from the last time Dan clocked him the other day, but they asked away, as Dorfly more or less grunted his answers in between moans of pain.

The gasoline can and the gas all over Dorfly's hands, feet, what was left of his pants and the sides of Dan's house made for some pretty damning evidence. Also, on one side of Dan's house the police had found Dennis' bike. Dorfly had brought it from Dennis' house not knowing Dan had brought Dennis home with him.

"That son of a bitch intended to blame Dennis for burning my house! To have him declared a danger and put away," Dan said, holding a cold-pack the EMTs had given him against his hand. "I'm sure he thought if more people had been killed, it would just make the set-up more convincing."

"Keep your voice down, Dear," Joyce said to him. "Dennis is over there and he can hear you."

Dennis was standing at the corner of the house where his bike had been found. He occasionally peeked around the corner to observe what was going on. I would have expected him to be excited by all the emergency vehicles with their myriad flashing lights, but the look on his face was one of fear and trepidation. The rest of us were standing in a circle in Dan's front yard trying to process what we had all just been through.

"I hope they put Dorfly away until he turns to dust," Joyce said vehemently.

"At the very least he should be too old to have any kind of a life when he gets out," Papa Joe said.

Debbie lightly shook her head. "I doubt he's ever really had any kind of a life."

"Do you think anyone will listen to us now about what's been going on?" I asked again. "Maybe it's not too late to stop the dismantling of the departments."

"That depends on whether or not anyone looks into the finance department," Dan said.

"Do you think they will?" asked Kathy.

"That would involve a major outside audit and investigation," Dan said.

"Do you think that will happen?" Debbie asked him.

"I'm not holding my breath."

Joyce looked at Debbie. "Can you go see if you can get Dennis to come into the house for bed? I need to go see about our boys."

"Of course," Debbie told her as she walked to where Dennis was."

I'd noticed the Harris twins had been glued to the living room window watching the proceedings. I watched as their mother walked through the front door and shooed them back to bed. Debbie spent a few minutes talking quietly to Dennis, then put her arm around his shoulders and guided him across the yard and in the door.

The preliminary hearing was held the next week. The judge found enough evidence to try Dorfly for attempted arson. We had expected a charge of attempted murder as well, but it wasn't mentioned. The judge determined that there would be no bail, so Dwayne would have to await trial in jail.

All through the hearing Dorfly had sat as silent and immobile as a statue looking shamed and remorseful. I found one of the more interesting aspects to be neither Genevieve Madas nor Jerry Louis was mentioned once. Nor had they bothered to come.

All of the regulatory agencies had backed off, accepting the source of the equipment tampering had been Dorfly, and he was being dealt with by the law. The powers that be had decided the ongoing feud between Dorfly and Dan had been the motivation, and that was the end of it. It had also been decided that Bobby Guilford's death had been an accident. We all knew better, but what did it matter? It seemed to me that it must be nice to have everything wrapped up so neat and tidy; no need to look any further. Ah, politics.

After the hearing we all felt drained and disappointed. It didn't seem as though Dorfly's trial would cause any additional light to be shed on what really happened. Not only was justice not being served, but the replacement of the biomed and maintenance departments had been set in motion and were still proceeding as if nothing had happened.

We all met back at Dan's house to console each other and talk about what we might do next.

"I can't believe that son-of-a-bitch Louis is gonna get away with it!" Dan was once again unable to sit still and had been pacing back and forth in his rec room for half an hour.

The rest of us were seated the same as we had been the last time we met here, with the exception of Gracie North who was seated on a kitchen chair next to Joyce where Kathy had been. Kathy had to work. Somebody had to run the ER.

Dennis was back home. Dan had spoken with the couple that oversaw the group home in which Dennis lived and learned Dennis was not eating and sleeping normally since Dorfly's arson attempt. Dennis had always had a healthy appetite, but they told Dan he often picked at his food, and he kept waking up in the middle of the night crying. This knowledge only served to make Dan more furious than he already had been.

Gracie had called Dan to ask about new developments and when he'd filled her in, she'd taken some of her vacation time to attend the hearing. She had said very little so far, but she looked almost as angry as Dan. She looked up at him as he paced by in front of her.

"Dan, you've been around the hospital as long as I have. You know nobody in administration makes a move without a scapegoat to blame if things go wrong."

"Sure, why stick your own neck out if you can stick somebody else's out for you!" Dan hadn't broken his stride.

"You also know as well as I do Louis wasn't the only one involved. He doesn't have the balls to pull something like this without being goaded into it!" She practically spat the words out as she said them.

The rest of us were silent; no one had ever heard Grace North speak like this before. Dan stopped pacing and looked at her with a slightly bemused expression. It had been quite a while since any of us had seen such a look on his face.

"I guess I neglected to tell you Genevieve Madas is involved," Dan told her.

"That explains it," Gracie told him. "The Ice Queen's got balls enough for both of them."

"That's my take on it," Dan said. "The thing is, Louis is already talking about taking off with the money he's stashed away. Madas can't be far behind."

Gracie shook her head as she looked at Dan. "There's no way we can just let this go."

"What are we going to do about it, Gracie?"

"I don't know, but I know we've got to do something. The assholes could have caused my brother's death as well as any of my other patients. I'm not just mad, I'm pissed off!"

"Can't we go to the president of the hospital?" Trevor asked. "He'd have to be concerned about employees ripping them off."

"Harry Diamond is a slick operator," Dan told him. "If he's not involved himself, he would know if it came out that it happened on his watch, the board would toss him out the door."

"But it has to come out," Alan said. "There's no way they can keep it a secret."

"Diamond won't be in any hurry to spread the news," Dan told him. "He'll bury it as long as he can while he looks for another position."

"This is so wrong!" Gracie said. "There has to be *something* we can do; we just haven't thought of it yet."

Dan walked over and put a hand on Gracie's shoulder and addressed the rest of us. "Gracie's right. If we're going to get to the bottom of this, we need to trip Louis up. What we need right now are ideas. Put your thinking caps on people!"

They started with a trickle. Someone suggested rewiring his car so all the controls would do something other than the function for which they were intended. Someone else suggested drugging Louis and hanging him upside down from the flagpole out front. Soon everyone seemed to be talking at once until Joyce whispered something in Dan's ear, and he held up his hand for silence.

"No, guys, you're thinking pranks. We need something that will break everything that's been going on wide open so it can be plainly seen."

Everyone sat in silence until Papa Joe spoke up.

"I've never been a particularly religious man, but I do know the Bible says something about an eye for an eye. I think that's the direction we need to head in."

"That passage ends 'vengeance is mine, sayeth the lord'," Trevor told him.

"Well, Trevor," Joe said, "I haven't been to church in a long time, but I still think vengeance is what we have in mind, if the Lord will forgive us."

Before long the ideas were flowing again, but this time we had a direction. We kept going until well after midnight, and by the time we were finished, we had a plan.

"Have you got a picture yet?" Will's voice sounded tinny over the walky-talky set the maintenance guys had loaned us. With Dwayne Dorfly out of their hair, they had been more than happy to help after we had told them what was happening with the departments and what we intended to do. Orville in particular seemed to be highly motivated.

"Yes, I've got a picture," Trevor told him, "but it's fuzzy. Adjust the focus... no the other way. That's better, now move it to the left a little. There, perfect, that one's centered on the desk." Trevor was concentrating, as we all were, on the monitor in front of him.

There were a dozen monitors in all, set up on the bench we had hastily constructed in the storeroom. It was hard to believe we were doing this, but as I looked around the room the thought struck home, what choice did we have? Orville had done an amazing job running cable all the way down to our little control room in the short amount of time we had. He had gotten plenty of help, but it was still impressive. There were security cameras set up in various areas of the hospital and we had added to their number, figuring no one was likely to notice.

"Okay, let's check the microphones," I said to Trevor, who relayed the message. We had hidden a camera in Jerry's ceiling, and we watched Will walk around Jerry's office. He walked to several strategic spots, stopping at each one and saying 'testing, one, two, three, four'. The sound was my department, and I sat at another makeshift console making adjustments to tone and volume.

"Okay," I nodded to Trevor.

Trevor picked up the walky-talky again. "Okay, Will, we've got it. Come on back down; we've got a lot to do yet."

"Are you sure Jerry isn't getting back until tomorrow?" Alan was looking apprehensively at Dan.

"Relax, Alan, it's like I told you." Dan's voice was calm and patient. "The conference ends today, and Louis' flight doesn't get in until nearly midnight tonight."

"Okay, what do you want me to do?" If it had been a week earlier, I would have been sure I misunderstood or was losing my hearing, but this was really Alan Labinowitz asking what he could do to help.

Dan clapped him on the shoulder. "My man, I thought you'd never ask."

There had been a change in all of us. We had always functioned as a team, but now there was an added dimension that wasn't there before. Before we had just been co-workers, now we were fighting for ourselves and our livelihoods and for justice, and at least some measure of retribution.

We had decided that night at Dan's house that this kind of thing must not be allowed to happen no matter how much the bastards felt they had the ability to get away with it. Now we truly felt like a team, and we had no intention of just letting it go without a fight.

"He's pulling into his parking space." The voice of George the security guard came clearly over the radio. It was the next morning and it was go-time. We felt we were ready, and now we would put that assumption to the test. "Now he's out of the car and headed toward the building."

"Okay, George. Jim should be picking him up." Trevor was proving to be quite the director.

"Got him," came Jim's voice over the walky-talky. "He's heading down the hall and into the coffee shop."

"Does Alice have the doughnut ready?" Trevor asked Dan. Alice was the volunteer who ran the coffee shop. As we found out from Gracie North, she was an old friend of Gracie's mother and had easily been recruited for the cause once she'd heard about Gracie's brother.

"Yeah, she's all set," Dan told him.

"Good, let me know when he comes out." Trevor turned to Joe. "Papa, is your team ready?"

"Good to go." Joe said, using one of Trevor's favorite terms, which earned him a quick smile.

"He's out and heading for his office," came Jim's voice again.

"Okay, Jim, next station," Trevor said.

We watched the monitors expectantly, and a few minutes later we saw Jerry walk into the picture and sit at his desk. He took a sip of the coffee he'd bought and then took a bite of his usual glazed doughnut. He opened a newspaper and began reading.

"Okay, Jay, start the clock," Trevor said.

I pushed the button on the stopwatch that sat on the counter in front of me and watched as the second hand began its sweep of the dial. "Mary said fifteen minutes, didn't she?" I asked. Mary ran the hospital pharmacy. She was also a regular companion of Papa Joe. Joe had told me he had no more intention of being a lonely old man than he did of being a penniless one.

"Right. Fifteen minutes before the event," Trevor said, and then turned back to his walky-talky. "Orville, are you in place?" He really seemed to be relishing his role running things, and I decided he was just enjoying being in control for once.

"I'm here," came Orville's reply.

"Alan, are you ready?" Trevor asked.

"I'm ready," came Alan's reply.

We had ten minutes to wait, and with the anticipation, time seemed to drag as I watched the hands on the stopwatch. The minute hand finally rested on the fifteen-minute mark, and when the second hand hit zero, I told Trevor who picked up his radio.

"Okay, Alan, hit it."

As we watched the monitor, we saw a brilliant flash as the light over the wet bar exploded. We could see Jerry had dropped his newspaper, and he sat looking stunned for a few seconds before he punched a button on his intercom.

"Miss Riley, get the electrician in here, stat!"

"Yes, Mr. Lewis," came the secretary's voice.

Another few minutes passed, and then we heard Miss Riley's voice again. "The electrician is here, Mr. Louis."

"Well, send him in!" barked Louis.

The door opened, and Orville came strolling in. He was wearing a pair of coveralls—no one had ever seen him in coveralls before—and an absolutely blank expression.

"What's the problem, Mr. Louis?"

"Damn, he should have been an actor!" Dan said from behind my right shoulder. "Listen to that innocence."

"The problem is your wiring, you incompetent boob!" Louis sputtered.

"Uh, oh! Somwone's in twouble." Dan seemed to be enjoying this most of all. Many of the ideas had come from him, and I got the impression he was living out more than just one fantasy.

Jerry had stepped out from behind his desk, and the feverish pitch of his voice was rapidly increasing.

"Look at this mess!" He had begun shuffling his feet and kicking at the glass that littered his carpet. "Fix it! Clean this up, and then get out!"

"Mr. Louis?" Orville asked sounding clueless. He was playing his role to the hilt.

"It's not that difficult to understand, you moron! Straighten out this mess and then get out. You're fired!"

"Mr. Louis?" Orville wore a baffled expression and he hadn't moved an inch.

"That man should get an academy award." Dan was beaming. "He's definitely made my Christmas list!"

Jerry had reached exasperation very quickly, which happened to be according to plan. He was pacing back and forth swearing at Orville, who continued to stand as if he couldn't decide what to do.

Jerry stopped in his tracks. "I need a drink!" he exclaimed.

"But it's nine o'clock in the morning, Mr. Louis." Orville pointed out.

"Be ready, Alan." Trevor was practically whispering into his walky-talky.

"Fuck you!" Jerry reached for a bottle of scotch and as he did, he rested his hand on top of the metal bar counter.

"Hit it, Alan!"

There was a loud POP! and Jerry jumped back clutching his hand. We could see his face turning red even from our vantage point.

"You idiot!" Louis screamed at Orville. "You... You..." Suddenly Jerry let out a strangling sound and began clutching at his chest as he sank slowly to the floor.

We heard an ear-piercing scream come through the system, and I instinctively pulled the right earpiece away from my head. Evidently Miss Riley had stuck her head in the door to see what all the commotion was about.

"Call a Code Blue, call it now!" Orville commanded her with authority, the clueless act having disappeared. It must have made her move, for the phone we had put in here for the occasion rang and Dan answered it.

"It's Sharon from the switchboard, she called it in," Dan informed Trevor.

"Papa's team move!" Trevor directed.

We saw several very familiar medical people move in, wheeling a crash cart with a defib sitting on top. Debbie, Gracie and Tom Nellum knelt beside Jerry examining him. Tom had joined our group without a moment's hesitation after he heard what had been going on.

"He's out cold," Gracie said flatly.

"Okay then, move him," Trevor instructed.

We watched as the medical team including Michael Evans, Shay Ingram and Vicky Henderson, rolled Jerry onto a stretcher and then lifted him onto a gurney. They wheeled him out the door and down the hall. As soon as they were off the monitor, Trevor shifted his attention to the next one.

"How long do you think this is going to take?" I asked Dan.

"A good long time, I hope. You two have plenty of tape, don't you?" he asked.

I pointed to a box by the side of Trevor's console. "Enough for several hours at least."

"Good, we wouldn't want to miss any of the highlights."

"Get them to give me a sound check before they wake him up," I said to Trevor.

"You've got it."

In another few minutes they were wheeling Jerry into our special little trauma room. They got him into a hospital gown and prepped, and Debbie looked toward the camera.

"We're ready. Shall I wake him up?"

"Not yet." I said to Trevor. "We need to get the sound levels a little better."

Trevor relayed the message adding, "And turn the big exam light on, will you?"

George, who had been holding the walky-talky so they could hear Trevor, went around the room reciting nursery rhymes like I had instructed him to do while I adjusted my levels.

Someone turned on the exam light over the gurney and Jerry fairly glowed in the middle of the screen. By now they had him all set up with an IV pump to the side, a four-channel ECG monitor behind him beeping continuously, and a twelve-channel diagnostic ECG machine on the opposite side from the pump. His chest was covered with electrodes, and wires seemed to run everywhere.

"What's in the IV?" Dan asked.

"Just saline solution. Salt for the salt of the earth," I answered.

Trevor picked up his radio again. "Okay, Debbie, wake him up."

Debbie had a syringe filled with a clear fluid, and she injected it into Jerry's IV. Within thirty- or forty-seconds Jerry's eyelids began to flutter, and a minute later he was awake, albeit a bit groggy.

"W... where am I," Jerry managed to croak.

"You're in the ER," Tom told him. "You've had a heart attack, Mr. Louis. You're lucky we got to you as soon as we did."

Jerry tried to sit up, and as he did, he saw all the wires and tubes that were hooked to him.

"W... W... what's this?" The rising panic in his voice was obvious to all listening.

"How do you like it, you son of a bitch?!" Dan couldn't help himself as he voiced the sentiment we all felt.

Michael, who was not a small man, pushed Jerry back down onto the gurney asking him to, "Please lie still so that we may do our job, Mr. Louis."

Tom was looking at the twelve-channel ECG monitor and shaking his head.

"Call radiology and tell them we're on our way. I want an MRI done."

I had never had an MRI, but I was familiar with the machine. There was a specialized technician from the manufacturer that serviced it, and she had given Trevor and me a tour the last time she was here. She also told us some stories she'd heard about people who were claustrophobic but hadn't known it until they were placed in the long tube for a scan, panicked, and had to be immediately removed from it.

Tom was playing his role as well as any actor I had ever seen on TV. "Gracie, call the OR and have them ready as well."

"Yes, Dr. Nellum." I had never heard Gracie call a doctor by anything other than their first name. She was getting into her part too.

"Surely it can't be that bad?" Jerry's voice was pleading, almost desperate, but not desperate enough. Not yet.

"You've had a coronary, Mr. Louis, not a stubbed toe." Tom was really getting into it. "Let's move, people!" I almost expected him to clap his hands for emphasis.

They had him detached from the ECG monitors in short order and wheeled him out the door with the IV pump in tow. Trevor shifted his attention to yet another monitor, and a short time later we saw them wheeling Jerry into radiology. As he saw the open end of the MRI tube, we could see the growing panic in his eyes.

"The MRI was a nice touch," I said to Trevor.

"Thanks, I thought so," he said.

"I agree, Trevor," said Dan. "Great idea."

"When I thought of the tech that gave Jay and me a tour of the machine and told us her stories about people panicking in them, it seemed the perfect experience for Jerry," he said with a smile.

The team had loaded Jerry into the MRI tube and left the room. A technician in an orange space-aged jump suit that made him look like an astronaut told Jerry to lie very still while he went to take pictures. It was hard to hear him through the hood with its plastic face-shield that he wore.

I looked at Dan. "Where in the world did you find the suit?"

"Orville found it with the emergency hazmat equipment and thought it would make a nice touch," he said with a grin.

Jerry was now alone, and though we could only see his head and shoulders I could have sworn I could see him shaking, though it could have been my imagination. I mentioned it to the others.

"Oh, no, that's not your imagination," Dan told me, "I had maintenance turn the air conditioning in that room down to fifty-five degrees. Considering the protection that gown is offering him, his balls should be turning blue about now."

We let Jerry lay there for quite some time.

"Shall I turn on the speaker now?" I asked.

"What speaker?" asked Alan who had just walked in.

"The MRI makes a lot of noise when it's running," I told him.

"I know that, Jay," he said with none of the affront that would have been there before.

"Well, since it's not actually running, I rigged up a speaker with a tone generator to deliver a one hundred, fifty hertz tone at a little more than eighty decibels to add a little background music."

Dan couldn't help laughing again. "That volume at that frequency ought to make ol' Jerry feel like he's riding beneath a freight train. Yeah, hit it!"

I nodded to Trevor, who picked up the walky-talky and issued the instruction, and soon we could hear a deep rumble issue from our monitor.

"Trevor, you really outdid yourself with these pictures," I told him. "Look, you can even see the mole on his nose vibrate."

"Thanks. Sometimes I just amaze myself," he said, deadpan.

After a while and quite a bit of shaking, we had the speaker turned off and Tom came back into the room with the technician in the space-suit who pulled a visibly trembling Louis out of the tube.

"I'm afraid you're going to need emergency surgery, Mr. Louis," Tom said gravely.

"Look, get a hold of my doctor, Burkhalter; he's in the book." Jerry's voice had risen in register with his growing panic, and with the shaking almost sounded like he was singing with tremolo.

"There's no time, Mr. Louis," Tom told him. "We must act immediately."

The team had moved back in, and they quickly had Jerry back on the gurney. Off they went out the door again, and Trevor moved on to the next monitor.

Our OR was more forbidding than most as we watched through the monitor, its antiseptic atmosphere apparent even through the

348 JOHN ALVAH BARNES JR AND NAOMI LYNN BARNES

video system. I was very used to the ORs, having done hundreds of equipment inspections in them, but this OR was different. There were even more machines than usual.

They were everywhere. There was the usual five-foot tall, three-foot wide anesthesia machine to the head and slightly to the right of the operating table, on top of which sat a pulse oximeter. Next to these was a stand with a four-channel ECG machine. On the other side of the table was a capnometer, which measured CO_2 level, and beside that was a large oscilloscope on a cart which had no purpose in the OR, but we'd had it in the shop storeroom and thought it looked cool with the other stuff. We'd rigged it up with a heartbeat simulator, and the little dot jumped across the screen with a simulated heartbeat.

To the foot of the table was a five-foot tall cabinet with an arthroscopic video system in it, its monitor glowing brightly. Next to that was a fetal heart monitor that Dan had insisted on adding to the mix saying, "The asshole won't know what it is, and I think it's kind of ironic."

Next there was an electrosurgical unit turned on and all warmed up with its indicator lights a dim amber. And, last but certainly not least, was a defibrillator on a crash cart.

We were counting on Jerry being so freaked out at this point he wouldn't realize there was nothing wrong with him, not physically anyway. Apparently, he hadn't realized that Tom was an ER doctor, not a surgeon, and Debbie, Gracie and the others would not normally be assisting in the OR. At this point Jerry was likely experiencing heart palpitations, and with so many people feeding his fear, it hopefully wouldn't occur to him that it was all a put-on.

The team wheeled Jerry into the OR looking terrified and got him transferred onto the OR table and affixed an oxygen mask to his face. Max, our friendly anesthesiologist injected something into Jerry's IV and in no time, he was unconscious again.

"I hope you all know what you're doing," Max said. He'd been apprehensive about putting a healthy man under anesthesia, but after it had been explained to him what Jerry had been doing, he'd agreed to help. He stood behind Jerry's head and monitored his instruments.

"How long will he be out?" Tom asked Max.

"Just a few minutes. What I gave him won't last long," Max said.

Tom looked around the room. "Are we ready? Does everyone know their part?" There were nods all around. "Okay, it's show time. Let's give him a few minutes to come around enough to know what's going on."

Max removed the oxygen mask, and slowly Jerry began to show signs of life. His eyelids flickered and he coughed a couple of times.

Tom and company were busy making it seem like post-op, while Max spoke to Jerry and patted the sides of his face trying to force a response.

"Come on, Mr. Louis, we're all done. It's time to wake up."

Jerry tried to speak, and promptly threw up into an emesis basin that Gracie had placed next to his mouth. After a while his eyes stopped rolling around, and he seemed to be reasonably aware of what was going on around him. That's when Gracie and Tom made their move. Gracie was busy with the pretext of doing something or other when she looked up at the monitor.

"V-tach! Dr. Nellum, we've got a problem!"

Jerry's eyes went wide with fear and we could see that he indeed understood what was going on, or at least what was supposed to be going on.

Tom never missed a beat. "Damn! Bring that defib over here, stat!"

The crash cart was wheeled into position where Jerry could plainly see it looming next to him. Now his eyes were as big as saucers, with a wild animal look to them.

Tom pulled the paddles from their holders and rubbed them together dramatically after Gracie had applied some contact gel. She hit the charge button and the machine whined as it came up to power.

Jerry jumped off the table placing his hands defensively in front of him.

"No, No, No! That machine was rigged by Dorfly! It will kill me; you're not using it on me!"

"No, Mr. Louis," Tom reassured him. "This defib's fine."

"No, it's not! I know Dorfly did something to it! He's getting even with me for making him sabotage the other ones! It's revenge I tell you!"

"Did you get it?" Dan asked with concern.

"Yes, Dan, we got it," I answered as I patted the VCR.

"Good man!" He clapped me on the back.

There was dead silence in the OR as we watched on the monitor. Jerry stood there in his hospital gown with his bare feet on the cold tile floor and his bare ass hanging out. He had a very curious look on his face as the realization hit him that there was nothing wrong with him. Our medical team said nothing, they just shut down the equipment and quietly left the room turning out the lights behind them. Jerry was still standing there a long time after they had left.

At the direction of Jason Cantrelli, we went to the district attorney and gave her the story. She seemed to be quite interested. We took her everything we had, as Dan decided that she could deem what was usable and what was not. It didn't take her long to have Louis and Madas arrested and indicted and begin an investigation that took several months, as the pair languished behind bars.

As Jerry promised the books were a mess, at least the official set. After issuing subpoenas to search his home and office, a second set had been found in which things were quite in order. They laid out in great detail what had been going on. As we already knew, with Madas' help, Louis had been slashing budgets and rerouting money into several slush funds he had set up. The two of them had been able to squirrel away more than six million dollars, and they hadn't even completed their plans.

Just as Dan predicted, as it became known what had been going on during Harry Diamond's watch, the hospital board of directors had told him, in no uncertain terms to, 'hit the bricks', as Dan was so fond of saying. Harry had quietly left town and no one seemed to know where he had gone.

The board had decided the dissolution of the biomedical and maintenance departments should not occur at this time, and the contract with Medi-Max was null and void since Louis had not been authorized to enter into it. We all retained our jobs, which was very nice since we'd been contemplating having to look for new ones.

The trial lasted a little more than a week. Most of that was consumed in laying out the case for the prosecution. As for the defense, there wasn't much of one. All of the money in the slush funds was frozen, and Jerry's wife had filed for divorce and her attorney had come down hard. Louis and Madas were stuck with a public defender that looked like he'd graduated from law school the day before. His closing argument sounded like something I might have heard in Latin class in high school. I guess I don't know my habeus from my corpus.

As it turned out the former duo were invited to spend the next several decades as guests of the state. I didn't think they'd get a cell together as that might have inspired the other inmates to beat them to death, so I guessed they'd be spending the time apart. That didn't mean they'd be lonely.

Dennis had spent a lot of time with Dan and his family. It had taken a while, but with their support he'd gone from shying away from things to acting more like his old self. He was back at his janitorial job, telling his jokes and making people smile. The other thing that had taken time was getting Dan to agree to letting the techs occasionally ask Dennis for help when troubleshooting a difficult machine. After all that had happened, Dan was very reluctant, but in time it gradually became commonplace to sometimes see Dennis working at the bench, singing quietly to himself. He always seemed happy to be working no matter the job.

Debbie and I had dinner with the Harris' occasionally. She and Joyce had become close friends and often met for lunch at the Holiday Inn for old time's sake, though minus the wigs. I must admit though, I found Debbie in the short blonde one to look quite hot. Of course, that's true no matter what she is or isn't wearing.

Trevor had finally found a girlfriend. Her name was Tracy and, surprisingly enough, she was neither tall, leggy, nor blonde. She was about five-foot two and brunette with short hair, and she was cute as hell. She worked as a pharmacist's assistant in the hospital pharmacy. Trevor had been[1] inspecting a machine on the floor, and Tracy had been delivering meds to the nurses. He had turned to retrieve something from his cart and had collided with Tracy who was walking behind him. Somehow, they had both wound up on the floor, where true love evidently blossomed. They'd been together ever since.

Speaking of true love, Debbie and I are getting married in a couple of months. I don't know if you've ever proposed in a balloon, but I highly recommend it. The view was breathtaking, both the scenery and my bride to be. We declined Orville's offer to let us go for the mile-high club, since privacy was hard to come by in the basket, not to mention the logistics involved.

Orville was pretty much the same old Orville, though now he'd been promoted to Director of Building Services, or the maintenance department as everyone called it. I knew he wouldn't let the title go to his head, though he did announce that due to his recent ascension to a position of authority he should be able to officiate at our wedding. We're thinking about it.

We both decided we don't want a big wedding, just a casual event with a few friends to share the moment. We don't know whether to have it in a church or outside yet, but I know that Debbie will tell me when we've decided.

John Alvah Barnes, Jr. is a singer-songwriter who has performed as a solo singer-

guitarist, front man for various rock bands, and lead singer for smaller groups. He is a

certified Biomedical Electronic Technician and experienced in emergency medicine,

working as a first responder (EMT). After becoming disabled, he spent several years as a

docent at the Smithsonian National Air and Space Museum. His first three novels are

based on his later careers.

Naomi Lynn Barnes was an educator for over 40 years. In addition to teaching, she

managed education programs for medical education agencies, including the Philadelphia

Network of Cardinal Health, and medical societies including The American College of

Physicians. She has also been a consultant in continuing education and personnel management for various businesses and organizations.

Keep reading for an excerpt from the next Jay Barlow novel,

ESBENSHADE

The ambulance was on a dirt road I recognized. Sam and I had gotten a call for a hunter who had a heart attack in the woods up in the mountains off Route 9 the previous fall. It had taken a while to find him, and we had been all over this area several times.

Rory continued to hold his gun on us while the guard opened the rear ambulance doors. "We found this sitting in the woods. Amazing what some people will throw away. Please, hop in and take a seat. We won't be a minute," Rory said.

The women helped me hobble over, up onto the bumper and into the ambulance, and then they and Jim joined me. At least the interior lights were on.

Before he closed the doors, Rory leaned his head in. "It was naughty of you to borrow this without asking. I'm going to have a hell of a time explaining its loss to the brass."

"I'm sure you'll invent a good story," I said with contempt.

"I do hope you enjoy the ride," he said and then was gone.

I knew what he intended to do, and I knew we had to act fast. "Quick, strap yourselves in. We don't have much time."

Debbie looked at me questioningly. "Jay...?"

"Do it Deb!" I said more forcefully than I meant to. "Sam, help her." Sam seemed to understand what I had realized and helped her strap into the captain's chair that was just behind the driver's compartment at the head of the stretcher.

On the passenger side was a long bench seat where Jim and Sam sat. On the driver's side were a counter and cabinets to the front, a small 'CPR seat' where I sat, and more cabinets to the rear.

"Come on, Jim. Lie down here," I said indicating the stretcher.

Sam stopped me. "You're not staying there with that leg, Partner; you should be on the stretcher."

"Jim should be on the stretcher, Sam." Jim was sitting to Sam's left, and he didn't look good. His eyes and lips were badly swollen, and his skin was chalky white. He hadn't said anything for some time.

"You're not staying in the CPR seat," she said with determination.

Her reasoning was clear to me. We both knew the facts, and had both known people involved in wrecks. Ambulances did not fare well in accidents. The safest place to be was on the stretcher. It was bolted to the floor and faced backwards. If you had to pick a place to survive, that was it. Unfortunately, there was only one stretcher and four of us. I wasn't about to go on the stretcher when the others couldn't.

I looked at Sam with determination. "Jim goes on the stretcher."

There was no time for argument. Jim made no protest as Sam helped him lie down, and the two of us secured the straps over his lower body. Debbie secured the chest straps from her seat at his head. As soon as I had finished with Jim, I opened a locker, grabbed a backboard strap, and tossed it to Debbie, telling her to wrap it around the seat and her upper body. We were in the process of strapping ourselves to the bench seat when I heard the driver's door open and the idler engage.

Sam and I really needed to move fast now. There were four seatbelts attached to the bench seat, and Sam and I each lay on half of the seat with our legs touching, the inside ones dangling over the side. My injured leg felt like it was on fire, but I had no time to think about it. We felt the ambulance jump forward as it was put into gear, and we were moving.

We each used the belts in a crisscross fashion across our chests, and then there was nothing to do but try to hold on and pray. The ambulance began to buck and sway as it left the road, and the engine screamed as the tires lost contact with the ground, and the front end pitched down on a sharp angle.

The fact the lights were on made the whole thing more surreal, as the ambulance hit something hard and lurched violently and all the cabinets popped open at once. We were assaulted by a barrage of bandages, suction catheters, latex gloves, and oxygen masks. I hoped the spare oxygen cylinders were firmly secured in their cradles, though I didn't figure we had that much of a chance anyway.

We felt the rig begin to heel over and then it rolled. My chest was being crushed against the seatbelts, and then the pressure subsided as I crashed back down onto the bench seat. I caught a glimpse of Debbie being thrown back and forth like a rag doll, and I felt sick and helpless to do anything. I couldn't see anything out of the windows, but I could tell by the way the objects around us flew first to the ceiling and then to the floor that the ambulance was rolling over and over.

We felt a tremendous impact as a tree limb came crashing through the side window adjacent to where Debbie was sitting. My heart nearly stopped before *it* stopped inches from her head, broke off and began flying around with everything else, including glass from the window. The portable suction unit was wrenched from its bracket on the wall and hit me in the forehead, causing me to see stars. I thought I was going blind for a second, but then I realized the lights were flickering on and off, giving the whole horrid scene a strobe effect. I was watching our demise in slow motion.

The pitching, rolling, and banging seemed to go on forever like some amusement park ride from hell. I felt my head snap violently back and forth and then smash back onto the bench seat repeatedly. I was sure the box would break open like an eggshell at any second and we would all be strewn across the mountainside. One of the small oxygen cylinders came loose, and I managed to catch it as it whizzed past my head. I held it tightly against my chest; if the cylinder were to burst, the oxygen, under tremendous pressure, would either explode or cause the cylinder to become a deadly missile.

We felt another hard impact and then a shudder, and the lights winked off finally as the ambulance came to rest on its side. Sam and I were on the down side, and Jim and Debbie were suspended over us. I lay there for a moment taking inventory, amazed I was still alive, and then I called out to the others, hoping to God they were too.

"Debbie, are you okay?" I was terrified at the thought of not receiving an answer.

"Yes, Jay, I think so." A wave of relief swept over me at the sound of my wife's voice.

"Sam?"

"Yeah, I just need to get these damned belts off!" I could feel her struggling with her restraints.

"Jim?" No answer. "Jim?"

I heard a cough, and I could see Jim in the moonlight filtering through the rear windows, shaking his head as if to clear it. "Yeah, Jay. I'm still with you. Some ride, huh?"

"We've got to get out of here, guys. There's still a chance of fire."

I got my belts off and then started helping Jim unstrap carefully so he didn't fall. It wasn't easy being hampered by the pain in my leg. Sam helped Debbie undo her restraints and climb down. Because of the way the ambulance was positioned, we had to get what was now the upper of the two rear doors open before we could swing the lower one open. The ambulance box had warped considerably in the tumble down the mountain, and the doors were both wedged. It was no easy task getting them to swing free. Sam and Debbie crawled over to help, and with a lot of grunting and straining, we finally managed to push them open.

When we got out, the moon was still out from behind the clouds and we could see what was left of the ambulance. It was a mangled mess. The ambulance box was dented and bowed in a thousand places, and part of the front end had been sheared away. I was amazed we had survived.

As I surveyed the damage, I was struck with a thought. "You all realize that Rory and his thugs will soon come to see if they did the job. When they find no bodies in the ambulance, they'll come looking for us, and in our present condition they'll find us."

Debbie was standing a few feet away holding her left arm and grimacing painfully. "Do you have any ideas?" she asked through clenched teeth.

"Yeah," I said, an idea dawning on me. "The ambulance has to burn." I looked around at my companions. We had been through so much, things had gotten so absurd, no one even batted an eyelash.

"You got a match?" Sam asked me.

I rooted in my pocket and produced my cigarette lighter. "This should do it," I said, giving my wife a small ironic smile which, amazingly enough under the circumstances, she returned.

I started to crawl back into the ambulance, but Sam stopped me with a hand on my shoulder. "The way you're moving with that leg, they'll be here before you get out. I'll go," she said, and she crawled through the back doors, emerging a few seconds later with several rolls of gauze. "I opened the oxygen regulators; they're on full. Give me your lighter."

"No, Sam. I don't know how quickly this thing is going to go up and you're pregnant. I'll do it."

"Don't be stupid, Jay. How are you going to move with that leg?"

"I'll manage. Now, you and the others get well clear."

"Jay!" Debbie started but I cut her off.

"Go on, Deb. It's my idea and my lighter, and we don't have time to argue."

I could see the fear in her eyes, but she and the others moved a good distance away and laid on the ground. I knew I wouldn't be able to move fast enough to get to them, but there was a gully to my right about ten feet away, and I was pretty sure I could make that. I left the gauze rolled up in the packaging and the paper lit quickly. I took a deep breath and started diving for the gully even as I threw the burning gauze through the open doors.

more at: alvaharts.com

Also by John Alvah Barnes Jr

Jay Barlow Collection
Kirkwood
Kirkwood
Esbenshade
Esbenshade
Rollover
Rollover

Standalone
Roadwork
Roadwork

Also by Naomi Lynn Barnes

Jay Barlow Collection
Kirkwood
Kirkwood
Esbenshade
Esbenshade

Standalone
Roadwork
Roadwork